EVEN THE APE-MAN HIMSELF HAS HIS PRICE. . .

Thirty thousand or more years ago, some Old Stone Age peoples discovered something that gave them an extremely extended youth. It also made them immune to any disease or breakdown of the cells. Of course they could fall down and break their necks or slit their throats or get clubbed to death. But if chance worked well for them, they could live for what must have seemed forever . . . a man who took the elixir at the age of twenty-five would only look fifty at the end of fifteen thousand years.

I don't know the history of what happened between 25,000 B.C. and 1913 when the agent of the Nine first introduced himself. By then, the Nine consisted of Anana, a thirty-millennia old Caucasian woman, XauXaz, Ing Iwaldi, a dwarf, a Hebrew born about 3 B.C., an ancient proto-Bantu, two proto-Mongolians, and an Amerindian.

We "candidates," I estimate, numbered about five hundred. We were those who might be chosen to replace one of the Nine if she or he died.

ETERNAL YOUTH

LORD OF THE TREES
AND
THE MAD GOBLIN

PHILIP JOSE FARMER

SF
ace books
A Division of Charter Communications Inc.
A GROSSET & DUNLAP COMPANY
51 Madison Avenue
New York, New York 10010

LORD OF THE TREES
Copyright © 1970 by Philip José Farmer

THE MAD GOBLIN
Copyright © 1970 by Philip José Farmer

An ACE Book

This Ace printing: May 1980

4 6 8 0 9 7 5 3
Manufactured in the United States of America

The Nine must have marked me off as dead beyond doubt.

I don't know whether or not the pilot of the fighter jet saw me fall into the ocean. If he did, he probably did not fly down for a closer look. He would have assumed that, if the explosion of my amphibian did not kill me, the fall surely would. After hurtling twelve hundred feet, I should have been smashed flat against the surface of the Atlantic off the coast of the West African nation of Gabon. The waters would be as hard as Sheffield steel when my body struck.

If the pilot had known that men had survived falls from airplanes at even greater heights, he might have swooped low over the surface just to make certain that I was not alive. In 1942, a Russian fell twenty-two thousand feet without a parachute into a snow-covered ravine and lived. And other men have fallen two thousand feet or higher into water or snow and lived. These were freak occurrences, of course.

The pilot would have reported that the twin-engine propellered amphibian I was flying to the *Parc National du Petit Loango* had gone up in a ball of flame at the first pass. The .50 caliber machine guns or rockets or whatever he had used had hit the fuel tanks and burning bits of wreckage had scattered everywhere. Among the bits was my body.

I recovered consciousness a few seconds later. Blue was screaming around me. My half-naked body was as cold as if the wind were ripping through my intestines. The explosion had ripped off most of my clothing or else they had been torn off when I went through the nose of the craft. I was falling toward the bright sea, though, at first I sometimes thought I was falling toward the sky. I whirled over and over, seeing the rapidly dwindling silvery jet speeding inland and the widely dispersed and flaming pieces describing smoky arcs.

I also saw the white rim of surf and flashing white beaches and, beyond, the green of the bush jungle.

There was no time or desire to think ironic thoughts then, of course. But if there had been, I would have thought how ironic it was that I was going to die only a few miles from my birthplace. If I had thought I was going to die, that is. I was still living, and until the final moment itself that is what I will always tell myself. *I live.*

I must have fallen about two hundred feet when I succeeded in spreading out my legs and arms. I have done much sky diving for fun and for survival value. It was this that enabled me to flatten out and gain a stable attitude. I was slowing down my rate of descent somewhat by presenting as wide an area as possible to the air, acting as my own parachute. And then I slipped into the vertical position during the last fifty feet, and I entered the water like a knife with my hands forming the knife's tip.

I struck exactly right. Even so, the impact knocked me out. I awoke coughing saltwater out of my nose and mouth. But I was on the surface, and if I had any broken bones or torn muscles, I did not feel them.

There was no sign of the killer plane or of my craft. The sky had swallowed one and the sea the other.

The shore was about a mile away. Between it and me were the fins of at least two sharks.

There wasn't much use trying to swim around the sharks. They would hear and smell me even if I made a wide detour. So I swam toward them, though not before I had assured myself that I had a knife. Most of my clothing had been ripped off, but my belt with its sheathed knife was still attached to me. This was an American knife with a five-inch blade, excellent for throwing. I left it in the sheath until I saw one of the fins swerve and drive toward me. Then I drew it out and placed it between my teeth.

The other fin continued to move southward.

The shark may have just happened to turn toward me in the beginning, but an increase of speed showed that it had detected me. The fin

stayed on the surface, however, and turned to
my right to circle me. I swam on, casting glances
behind me. It was a great white shark, a species
noted for attacking men. This one was wary; it
circled me three times before deciding to rush
me. I turned when it was about twenty feet from
me. The surface water just ahead of it boiled,
and it turned on its side just before trying to
seize my leg. Or perhaps it only intended to
make a dry run to get a closer look at what might
be a dangerous prey.

I pulled my legs up and stabbed at it with
both hands holding the hilt of the knife. The skin
of the shark is as tough as cured hippo hide and
covered with little jags—placoid scales—that
can tear the skin off a man if he so much as rubs
lightly against it. My only experience in fighting
sharks was during World War II when my boat
was sunk in the waters of the East Indian Ocean.
The encounter with a freshwater shark in an
African lake is fictional, the result of the sometimes overromantic imagination of my biographer. Fortunately, my arms were out of the
water and so unimpeded by the fluid. I heaved
myself up to my waist and drove down with the
knife and rammed it at least three inches into the
corpse-colored eye. Blood spurted, and the shark
raced away so swiftly that it almost tore the knife
loose from my hands.

Its tail did curve out enough to scrape across
my belly, and my blood was mingling with its
blood.

I expected the shark to come back. Even if my
knife had pierced that tiny brain, it would be far

from dead, and the odor of blood would drive it mad.

It came back as swiftly as a torpedo and as deadly. I dived this time and was enclosed in a distorted world the visible radius of which was a few feet. Out of the distortion something fast as death almost hit me, and went by, and I shoved the knife up into the belly. But the tip only penetrated about an inch, and this time the knife was pulled from my grip. I had to dive for it at once; without it I was helpless. I caught it just before it sank out of reach of eye and hand, and I swam to the surface. I looked both ways and saw a shadow speeding toward me. Then another shadow caught up with it, and blood boiled out in a cloud that hid both sharks. I swam away with as little splash as possible, hoping that other sharks would not be drawn in by the blood and the thrash of the battle.

Before I had gone a half-mile, I saw three fins slicing the water to my left, but they were intent on following their noses to where the blood was flowing, where, as the Yanks say, the action was.

It was a few minutes to twelve P.M. when my plane blew up. About sixteen minutes later, according to my wristwatch, I reached the shore and staggered across the beach to the shade and a hiding place in a bush. The fall, the fight with the shark, and the swimming for a mile at near-top speed, had taken some energy from me. I walked past thousands of sea gulls and pelicans and storks, which moved away from me without too much alarm. These would be the great-great-great-grandchildren of the birds that I had

known when I was young. The almost completely landlocked lagoon on the beach was no longer
there. It had been filled in and covered over
years ago by the deposit of sand and dirt from
the little river nearby and by the action of the
Benguela Current. The original shore, where I
had roamed as a boy, was almost two miles inland.

The jungle looked unchanged. No humans
had settled down here. Gabon is still one of the
least populated countries of Africa.

Inland were the low hills where a broad
tongue of the tall closed-canopy equatorial forest
had been home for me and The Folk and the
myriad animals and insects I knew so well. Most
of the jungle in what is now the National Park of
the Little Loango is really bush. The rain forest
grows only on the highlands many miles inland
except for the freakish outthrust of high hill
which distinguishes this coastal area.

After resting an hour, I got up and walked inland. I was headed toward the place where the
log house of my human parents had once been,
where I was born, where the Nine first interfered
with my life and started me on that unique road,
the highlights of which my biographer has presented in highly romanticized forms.

The jungle here looks like what the civilized
person thinks of as jungle, when he thinks of it at
all. His idea, of course, is mostly based on those
very unrealistic and very bad movies made about
me.

Knife in hand, I walked quietly through bush.
Even if it wasn't the true jungle of my inland

home, I still felt about ten times as happy and at ease as I do in London or even in the comparatively unpopulated, plenty-of-elbow-room environs of my Cumberland estate. The trees and bushes here were noisy with much monkey life, too many insects, and an abundance of snakes, water shrews, mongooses, and small wild cats or longnecked servals. I saw a scale-armored anteating pangolin scuttling ahead of me and glimpsed a tiny furry creature which might or might not have been a so-called "bushbaby." The bird life made the trees colorful and the air raucous. The salt air blowing in from the sea and the sight of the familiar plants made me tingle all over.

As I neared the site of the buildings my father had built eighty-two years ago, I saw that the mangrove swamp to the north had spread out. Its edge was only a quarter of a mile to my left.

I cast around and within a few minutes found the slight mounds which marked the place where I had been born. Once there had been a one-room house of logs and, next to it, a log building just as large, a storehouse. My biographer neglected to mention the storeroom, because he ignored details if they did not contribute to the swift development of the story. But, since he did state that an enormous amount of supplies was landed with my parents, it must have been obvious to the reader that the one-room house could not have held more than a fraction of the materials.

Both buildings had fallen into a heap of dead wood and had been covered up by sand and dirt blown by the sea winds and by mud pouring down from the low ridge inland of the buildings. The ridge was no longer there; it had eroded years ago. A bush fire had taken away all the vegetation on it and then the rains had cut it down before new vegetation could grow.

On one side, six feet under the surface, would be four graves, but in this water-soaked, insect-infested soil the decayed bones had been eaten long ago.

I had known what to expect. The last time I'd been here, in 1947, the ravages of fifty-nine years had almost completed the destruction. It was only sentiment that had brought me back here. I may be infrahuman in many of my attitudes, but I am still human enough to feel some sentiment toward my birthplace.

I had intended to stand there for a few minutes and think about my dead parents and the other two buried beside them. But mostly about what I had done inside the cabin with the books and the tools I had found in 1898, when I did not know what a book or a tool or a chronological date was, let alone the words for them in English or in any human tongue. And I especially wanted to recreate the day when I had first seen the long ash-blonde hair of Clio Jeanne de Carriol.

There were others with her, of course, and they were the first white-skinned males I had ever seen, outside of the illustrated books I had found in the storehouse. But Clio was a woman, and I was twenty, so my eyes were mainly for her. I did not know nor would have cared that she was the daughter of a retired college teacher. Nor that he had named his daughter Clio after the Muse of History. Nor that they were descended from Huguenots who had fled France after the Revocation of the Edict of Nantes and established plantations and horse farms in Georgia, Virginia, and Maryland. All I knew about the world outside a fifty-mile square area was what I had tried to understand in those books, and most of that I just could not grasp.

I suppose I was lost in thought for a little more than a minute. Then I turned a little to the east, because I'd heard a very faint and unidentifiable noise, and I saw a flash up in a tree about fifty yards away.

I dived into a bush and rolled into a slight depression. The report of the rifle and the bullet striking about ten feet from me came a second later. Three heavy machine guns and a number of automatic rifles raked through the bush. Somebody twenty yards to the north shouted, and a grenade blew up the earth exactly over the site of the storehouse.

I had to get out, and swiftly, but I could not move without being cut down, the fire was so heavy.

Leave it to the Nine to do a thorough job.

They had found out that I was flying a plane from Port-Gentil, ostensibly to Setté Cama. They—their agents, rather—had figured that I might be stopping off at the Parc National du Petit Loango for a sentimental pilgrimage. Actually, my main purpose was to leave the plane there and set off on foot across the continent to

the mountains in Uganda. It would take me a
long time to make the approach to the secret
caves of the Nine, but it was better to travel
through the jungle across the central part of
Africa than to fly anywhere near it. In the jungle,
I am silent and unseen, and even the Nine can-
not distract me except by accident.

But the Nine had sent that outlaw fighter jet
to shoot me out of the sky. And, as a backup for
Death, they had arranged an ambush at my
birthplace. When the jet pilot had reported in, as
he surely must have, that I had gone down with
my plane, the Nine had not pulled off their ambushers at once. I suppose they may have had
orders to wait there a week. The Nine always
were enthusiastic for overkill and overcaution,
especially when one of their own—a traitor—
was to be taken care of.

Even so, they must have been surprised, they
must not have really expected me to come along
so soon after being burned to death or smashed
flat against the ocean and then eaten by sharks.
But they had maintained a very good silence.
The wind was blowing from the sea, so I had not
heard or smelled them. I think I caught them by
surprise; they may not have been sure that I was
the one for whom they were waiting.

The grenade was close enough to half-deafen
me but I was not confused or immobilized. I
rolled away and then crawled toward the men
shooting at me. Or shooting where they thought
I should be. Gouts of dirt fell over my naked
back and on my head. Bushes bent, and leaves
fell on me. Another grenade exploded near the

first. Bullets screamed off, and pieces of bark fell before me. But I did not believe they could see me. I would have been stitched with lead in a few seconds.

One thing, some of them must have seen that I was only armed with a knife, and that would make them brave.

Suddenly, there was silence except for a man shouting in English. He was telling them to form a ring, to advance slowly to contract the ring, and to fire downward if they saw me. They must not fire into each other. They must shoot at my legs, bring me down, and then finish me off.

If I'd been in his place, I would have done the same. It was an admirable plan and seemed to have a one hundred percent chance of success. I was as disgusted as I had time for. I should have approached more cautiously and scouted the area. I had made the same mistake they did, in essence, except that they were better equipped to rectify theirs.

I kept on going. I did not know how many men they had. I had determined that ten weapons had been firing. But others might be withholding their fire. It would take them some time to form a ring, since they had all been on one side of me. In this thick bush, they would have to proceed slowly and keep locating each other by calling out.

Men circled around swiftly and noisily. I could smell them; there were ten men on that side. So that meant there had to be as many or more ahead of me. Some had been holding back their fire.

I looked upward. I was close to the tree from which the flash had come as a sniper shifted his rifle. He was still about twenty feet up on a branch and waiting for me to make a break for it. I scrutinized the other trees around me for more snipers, but he seemed to be the only one.

I sprang out from under the broad leaves of the elephant's-ear and threw my knife upward. It was a maneuver that had to be done without hesitation and which involved much danger, since it meant I would be revealed, if only for a moment.

It was, however, unexpected. And the only one who saw me before I ducked back under the plant was the sniper. His surprise did not last long. He saw me and the knife about the same time, and then the knife caught him in the throat. The rifle fell out of his hands and onto the top of a bush. He sagged forward but was held from falling by the rope around his waist, tied to the trunk. The knife had made a chunking and the rifle a thrashing as it slid through the branches of the bush. But the shouts of the men had covered it up.

The rifle was a Belgian FN light automatic rifle using the 7.62-mm cartridge. It could be set for semiautomatic or automatic fire, and its magazine when full contained twenty rounds. I set it for automatic fire, since I was likely to be needing a hose-like action in thick foliage. It was regrettable that I did not have the knife, but, for the moment, I would have to do without it. I did not want to climb up to the body and so expose myself to fire from below. At any moment one of

them might see the corpse and know that I was
on the loose with the firearm.

The voices of the men to the east came closer.
The ones behind me and on my sides were not
closing in so swiftly. One, or more, had
grenades, and I especially had to watch out for
them.

My heart was pumping hard, and I was
quivering with the ecstasy of the hunt. Whether
I am the hunter or the hunted, I feel the same.
There is a delicious sense of peril; the most pre-
cious thing is at stake. You, a living being, may
be dead very shortly. And since my life could last
forever, or, over thirty thousand years anyway, I
have much more than most people to lose. But I
didn't think of that. I am as willing to risk it now
as I will be thirty millennia from now, if I live
that long.

When the nearest man was within ten feet, he
had a man on his right about twenty feet away
and a man on his left about thirty. He had
turned his head to say something to the man behind him. The butt of my rifle drove through the
branches of a bush into his throat. He fell backward and then I was on him and had squeezed
his neck with my hands. I took his knife and a
full magazine, which I carried clamped under
my left arm. But another man about twenty feet
behind him had noticed that his predecessor had
disappeared.

He spoke in English with an Italian accent.
"Hey, Brodie, where are you? You all right?"

I answered back in an imitation of Brodie's
voice. "I fell down in this damned bush!"

The man advanced cautiously, then stopped and said, "Stand up so I can see you!"

I put on Brodie's green digger's hat—it was several sizes too small—and rose far enough so he could see the hat and the upper part of my face. He said something and came toward me, and I threw Brodie's knife into his solar plexus.

At the same, there was a yell from behind me. The dead sniper had been discovered.

The leader, bawling out in a Scots English, told everyone to stand still. They were not to start firing in a panic, or they would be killing each other. And they were to call out, in order, identifying themselves.

I waited, and when the time came, I called out with Brodie's voice and then the voice of the Italian. I did not know his name, and the leader could have tripped me up there. But he gave each man's name himself before requiring an answer.

I counted thirty-two men. Some of them were, like the Italian, backing up the enclosers in case I should break loose.

By then I had gotten close enough to the man on my left to cut his jugular vein from behind with the edge of the knife.

It seemed to me that I had an aisle of escape. I could get away and be miles inland, and once I was in the rain forest of the higher lands, I could not be caught.

But I have pride. I wanted to teach the Nine another lesson and also cut down the numbers opposing me. Also, it seemed to me their base must be nearby and that they must have a powerful shortwave transceiver there.

Still, there are times to be discreet, and this
was one. I went on into the jungle. I had gotten
about fifty yards when I heard muffled shouts.
They had discovered the bodies, and they would
be scared now. No doubt many, if not all of
them, knew who I was. They would have known
my abilities in the jungle by report and now they
knew by experience. Moreover, adding to the
desperation at having me loose would be the desperation at having to report failure to the Nine.
They might as well be dead if I escaped.

I tried to figure where the radio would most
likely be stationed. At one time, I could have told
you, with my eyes shut, exactly where every tree
and bush and open area were. But the place had
changed too much; I might as well be in
completely new territory. Finally, I took to the
trees.

I carried the FN strapped over my shoulder,
and in the foliage at the top I removed it. I could
see ten of the thirty-one; the others were hidden in the bush. Nine were congregated around
a tall thin man with a thick black moustache.
His hands flew and his mouth worked as he gave
orders.

I had seen him before, and now that I recre-
ated his voice in my mind, I remembered it, too.
I had heard it in the caves where the Nine hold
their annual ceremonies, where the members of
their ancient organization come for the grisly
rites they must endure in order to get the elixir of
youth. He had not had a moustache then and he
had not been wearing clothes and it had been ten
years ago, so I did not immediately recognize
him.

His name was James Murtagh, a name not too different from his real name or that of his notorious father. He was born in 1881 in Meiringen, Switzerland, but was raised from the age of eight in Wales. Like his father, he was an extremely talented mathematician, if not a genius, and he had taught higher mathematics at Oxford and the University of Talinn. He looked as if he were about forty, so I suppose that it was in 1921 that he was invited by the Nine to join them.

Murtagh had not said a word about himself to me or to anyone that I knew. But the Countess Clara Aekjaer, the beautiful Danish Valkyrie who was my companion during the ceremonies over the years, knew much about him. She told me everything she knew. Perhaps she had been told to do so by the Nine, who were grooming me, without my knowing it, to become one of them if one died.

I could have gotten him with a single shot from my FN, but he might be a link to the next one higher up in the chain. So I set the rifle for automatic and sprayed about twelve rounds into the group. Five fell; the others dived into the bush. I dropped the rifle and slid down the tree before they could get reorganized and blast me from the treetops. I went through the bush southward. It did not seem likely that the base for the group would be in the mangrove swamp to the north.

By then the men were firing at the tree I had left. I continued to travel south while the sound of the weapons grew fainter. Then I heard a voice ahead and, a few minutes later, I peered through a bush at a large clearing. It may have been small a few days before, but axes and powersaws had cut trees and bushes down, and a jeep with a winch had dragged off the fallen plants. There were two large helicopters, Bristol 192's, at one end and six tents near my end. Inside the largest tent was radio equipment on a table; three men were by the equipment. An antenna reached high above the tent.

I scouted around the entire perimeter of the camp and found no hidden guards. I also was alert for booby traps and mines. Murtagh impressed me as the type of man who would think of such devices and smile while he was setting them. I appreciate that, since I also smile when engaged in similar activities.

There was a good chance that Murtagh would send men packing back to the camp. He would figure that I would know a camp had to be close and would go looking for it. He had not set guards around it because he had not really expected that I would survive the attack by the jet. I had to work fast.

Even though much of the vegetation had been dragged away, there were still clumps of uprooted bushes and the stumps of trees in the clearing. I ran bent over across the clearing, approaching the big tent from its closed rear. There I listened to the operator relay orders from his superior officer. Someone in the group that had tried to ambush me had reported via wireless that I had escaped. So the big shortwave set was transmitting a request for two jets and two more helicopters. These would carry napalm bombs and would bring in more men and dogs.

The code name used for me was Tree Lord, which I thought both appropriate and amusing.

I was puzzled about where the jets and copters could be based. It did not seem likely that they would be at Port-Gentil. This was approximately one hundred and twenty-six miles to the northeast. The men in the tent talked as if they expected the craft in about ten minutes. Somewhere, probably in a man-made clearing in the interior, was a base. Had it been set up some time ago just for me? Or was it a multipurpose base? It seemed more probably that it was multipurpose. Otherwise, why had not all its personnel and machines been sent down here to terminate me?

I went around the side of the tent to the opening. Two shots sent the two officers spinning backward and onto the ground. The operator had a .45 automatic in a holster. But he made no motion toward it. He placed his palms flat against the table and stared at me with his mouth open. His huge round eyes, pale skin, shock of wheat-colored hair, sharp beaky nose, and the earphones made him look like a very frightened owl.

"Tell them to cancel the operation," I said. "Tell them I've been killed."

He hesitated, and I stepped closer to him. The muzzle of the rifle was only a few inches from his temple. He gulped and obeyed me.

After he had finished, he stared at me as if he

expected me to blow his head off. He had a right
to expect it, and I had a right to do it, though I
have never bothered about rights as defined by
human beings unless they happened to coincide
with my beliefs. He was a member of an organization devoted to killing me; he knew it and
had taken part in it; he deserved to die.

My own philosophy is simple and practical
and not at all based on the idea that life is sa-
cred. If a man is out to kill you, you kill him first.
This has nothing to do with the rules of warfare
as conducted by nations. When I was a member
of the British forces in World War II, I observed
the Geneva rules. That is, I did except in two
cases, where I had orders from the Nine, and
their orders superseded anybody's. In return for
giving me a very extended youth, they demanded
a high price sometimes. But I had had no
qualms about killing the men the Nine wanted
out of the way, especially since they were the enemy. If I were to tell you that several of them
were the highest and most famous of our enemy,
you might find it difficult to believe. Especially
since the world believes that they committed suicide to keep from falling into the hands of the
Russians.

"Do what I say, and quickly, and I'll spare
you," I said. "And if you know anything about
me, you know I don't go back on my word."

He gulped and nodded. "Can you get
Dakar?" I said.

He could do so, and he did at once, asking for
Brass Bwana. He was operating illegally, of
course, and what the authorities at Dakar

thought, I did not know or care. The station was at the time out in the desert about thirty miles from Dakar, had been operating on a mobile basis for twenty-six years, and so far the police had not been able to come near it. I had used it when I worked for the Nine but had never told anyone else in the organization about it. Its operators were criminals, loyal to me, because I had rewarded them well. Now they were in contact with the organization that Doc Caliban had used when he was a disciple of the Nine. This station was somewhere in the Vosges and tied in with another in the Black Forest area of Germany.

I would have preferred to talk directly, but I could not do that and be free to look and listen for Murtagh and his men. The first thing I did was to tell the Dakar people that the code name for me was changed and that I would use the next name on the list the next time I contacted them. I also explained, briefly, that I had been forced to contact them through an enemy. I asked for Doc Caliban, using his code name of Brass Bwana, of course. A minute passed, and then Dakar relayed the message that Caliban could not answer himself. But my message would be passed on to him. However, he had left a message for me.

"The goblin has gone mad, and he is our enemy and the enemy of our enemies his former friends. The goblin is holed up, but we are digging him out."

I thanked Dakar and signed off.

"Do you know German?" I asked the operator.

He said he didn't, but he might have been lying. Not that it mattered. He was not likely to know that the goblin had to be Iwaldi, the old dwarf of the Nine. When I say old, I mean very ancient. He was at least ten thousand years old and possibly thirty thousand. If I understood Caliban's phrasing correctly, Iwaldi had gone insane and turned against the others of the Nine, too. Doc Caliban knew where he was and was going after him. Iwaldi was in the castle of Gramzdorf in the Black Forest. Though Caliban and I had been able to find out very little about any of the Nine's secret hideouts, we had discovered that Iwaldi lived at least part of the year in the castle near the village of Gramzdorf. Caliban had gone there with two of his men, recent recruits who were sons of the men who had been his aids in the old days. The fathers were dead now, but the sons had taken their places beside Doc.

I opened the case of the equipment and smashed the tubes with a hammer and ripped the wires out. Then I cut a slit through the back of the tent and ordered Smith, the operator, to step out ahead of me. We went swiftly to another tent which contained a number of firearms and belts on which to carry grenades. I put about seven grenades in hooks on a belt which I had secured across my chest. I tied Smith's hands behind him and secured him to a bush. It took me a minute to toss a grenade into each of the interiors of the two copters from a distance of two hundred feet. They exploded and burned furiously; they were indeed beautiful, though a little awing. I have never gotten over some feeling of awe for the larger machines that mankind makes. I suppose it's the residue of the first impact of civilization on me. When I blew those two fine but deadly machines, I was asserting the defiance of the savage against the complex and bewildering works of the technological man.

"Where is the base camp?" I asked Smith. "Don't stall. I haven't the time to play around."

"It's about thirty miles northeast of here," he said.

There wasn't time to find out if he was lying or not. I went into the bush by the edge of the camp.

The burning gasoline roared so that I could not hear Murtagh and his men, and the smoke was so intense that I could not have smelled them even if they had been upwind. But I could see quite well, and I smiled as I saw the scared or grim faces peeking from around bushes. They were not about to venture into the camp, since I might be waiting to ambush the ambushers.

Murtagh, of course, would wait until the two copters appeared and then bring them down for protection. But he did not do so. At least, not where I had thought he would. Instead, the men walked away. I had gone around them to come up behind them but by the time I got near the north end of camp, I found them gone. They were easy to track, which I did on a parallel path. It was well that I did, since the canny Murtagh had placed four men at two places to catch me if I came loping along after them. Each couple was back to back to make sure that I did not sneak up on them. I still could have wiped them out with short bursts from my conceal- ment, but I did not see any reason to notify Murtagh that I was on to them. I passed them by and presently was alongside the double file of men heading for the beach. Murtagh was in the lead, and four men who kept watching over their shoulders were the rear guard.

Murtagh was about six feet five and had very rounded shoulders and a forehead that bulged out like the prow of a ship. He removed his hat once to wipe a completely bald pate. The hair that rimmed the back of his head was gray. His eyes were set deeply under a bulging supraorbital ridge. His jaws were so outthrust he might have been an aboriginal Australian. His long neck was bent forward so that he always seemed to be sniffing for something, like a snake. The snakishness was emphasized by the steady movement of his face from side to side.

Behind him was a man carrying a flame- thrower and about six men behind him was an- other man with a flamethrower.

I went ahead to a point equidistant from both men and then I fired six bursts. The first shat- tered the equipment on the back of the first man, but the liquid did not catch fire. The men be- tween the first target and the second went down, and then the flamethrower on the second man exploded in a globe of fire that enveloped two men behind him.

I was away, rolling down a slight slope and then crawling into its bottom and along it until I reached a shallow ravine. The vegetation and the dirt above me whipped and flew as if a meteor stream had struck it. The firepower poured out in my direction was impressive and must have terrified the birds and the monkeys. But I was not hit.

I made a mistake by not killing Murtagh then. I should not have spared him because of wanting to take him prisoner for questioning later. But I did not regret not having killed him. Though I admit quite readily that I've made a mistake or erred, I never regret. What has been always will be and what is is. And what will be is unknown until the proper time.

Five minutes later, two huge helicopters settled down on the beach. The armed men in them got out and took their stations with the others along the edge of the beach and the jungle. Murtagh got new radio equipment from the helicopters, and the men of the Nine were ready to go into business.

My business was to get out as fast as I could, but I did not do so. I had been running so hard and so long from the Nine that I could not resist the temptation to give them even more punishment. I did, however, retreat to the north and into the swamp. I climbed to the top of a mangrove where I could get a good view. It was well that I did. While the men on the ground stayed on the beach, the two helicopters flew inward and dropped six napalm bombs. Two jets came in and shot six explosive rockets at random within a quarter-mile square area. Then they dropped napalm bombs and returned to strafe the jungle near the burning areas. After their

ammunition was exhausted, they flew off, presumably to reload for another trip.

If I had been hanging around close to the men
on the beach, I would have been burned to an
ash. Still, they had no means of knowing that I
was there, and it seemed a very inefficient and
expensive method of trying to kill me. Not that
the Nine care for expense or for inefficiency if the
goal is attained.

With ten baying bloodhounds and six German
shepherds, the men on the ground split into two
groups. Each went around the burning area. I
did not know what garment of mine the dogs
could have sniffed at, but I was sure that the
Nine had located something in my castle at
Grandrith. They weren't likely to pick up any
odor from me near the napalmed area, since the
smoke would deaden the nerves in their noses.
But if they did pick up something near the edge
of the swamp, the men would suppose that I was
in there, and the mangroves would get a shower
of the terrible jellied gasoline. The copters were
overhead now, one over each group, waiting for
orders.

I climbed down and waded through the
brownish, vegetation-sticky waters between the
massive buttress-rooted mangroves. After a mile
of this, during which I saw several mambas and
a large river otter, I went south and came out on
dry ground. Comparatively dry, that is. Though
this was not the rainy season, it was still raining
every day, and the soil around here seldom became dry. My footprints would have been evident if I had not been at such pains to walk only

on fallen vegetation. Even so, I was leaving a trail which the dogs could pick up easily enough.

As I headed east toward the highlands and the rain forest, I heard the distant whirring of an approaching chopper. It came through the smoke in the distance and then was suddenly headed toward me. It had come at a bad time for me. I was in a natural clearing caused by erosion of the thin soil from a sloping sandstone mass.

The swamp was a quarter-mile to my left. The edge of the clearing on my right was about fifty yards. Ahead was thick bush with about a mile to go before I reached the foot of the cliff which reared up to about five hundred feet. This was the first of the heights which, a few miles inland, became a series of plateaus about five hundred to eighteen hundred feet high and which was covered with the closed-canopy rain forest. This was the tongue of the highlands which extended from the interior and was a freakish formation for this part of the land. Along the coast here, the land was generally flat for about eight to ten miles from the sea to the highlands.

I ran on ahead, glanced back once, and saw two dark objects streaking toward me. I threw myself on the ground, forgetting that I had to be careful not to dislodge the grenades attached to my belt by their pins. The explosions half-deafened me, and dirt showered me. But the rockets had overshot me by forty yards and blown up in a shallow depression. I was up and into the bush ahead and then into the smoke created by the explosions before the wind had a chance to clear it. The next two explosions came behind me. Apparently the rocket man in the chopper had compensated immediately for the overshooting, and if I had stayed in the same place, I would probably have been blown to bits.

As it was, the impact knocked me forward; I felt as if a log had been slapped across my back by a giant. But the impact was softened by the trees and bushes between me and the rockets, and I was up and going again. The smoke from the second volley was carried eastward by the wind and so veiled me from the chopper for a minute.

The huge helicopter came charging through the smoke, its pilot apparently assuming that I was either dead or incapacitated by the explosions. Perhaps, he did not release the napalm bombs because he had orders to take me alive if he could do so. Or perhaps he just wanted to make sure he could plant his bombs exactly on the spot where my body or its remnants were and so ensure obliteration of me.

Whatever his reasons, he brought the chopper down to fifty feet above the ground and at a speed of about fifty miles an hour. I was completely at his mercy or seemed to be, because he was suddenly about ten feet to the north of me. The gunners on the right side saw me a few seconds after I saw them, and the snouts of their .50 caliber machine guns began flaming.

They were not, as usual, accurate but they did not need to be, because they were bringing their fire around like water from a hose, and the intersection would be my body.

I did not try to run away, because they had

spotted me, and I could not get away when they were that close. I stood up, while the gouts of dirt and pieces of bush torn by the bullets swung toward me. I yanked a grenade from the belt, leaving the pin attached to the belt, and I threw the grenade.

They would have expected me to fire back with my rifle, but this they had never expected. The grenade flew exactly as I had aimed it, went through the open port before the gunner on my right just as the bullets were on the point of intersecting, the scissors of lead about to close on my body.

But the gunner, or someone in the chopper, had been alert and cool enough to catch the grenade and start to throw it out the port. He was not, however, quite swift enough, and the grenade exploded in his hand. The covering of flesh was enough to soften its effect. He was killed and I suppose everybody else in the chopper was, too. But the fuel did not catch fire, not immediately, anyway. The chopped tilted and slid at a forty-five degree angle away from me and into a tree trunk about ten feet above the ground. By then I was running, and when I saw a gully, I dived into it. I was flying through the air when the fuel and napalm did go off, and I felt the heat pass over the gully. My bare back was almost seared.

My face was turned away, and I was breathing shallowly, because I did not want to sear my lungs. Then I was up and out, because if the first blast had not gotten me, I had a chance to get away.

The heat felt as if it were scorching the hairs off my legs and the back of my head, and smoke curled around me. But the explosion had taken place about a hundred and fifty yards away, and the heavy bush helped screen me. The napalm bombs were not large ones.

The other copter had hung back for some reason or other. Perhaps it was attached to the men with the dogs and was to play a part if the dogs treed me. But when the first chopper exploded, the second came up swiftly enough. It, however, stayed about three hundred feet up as its crew observed the wreck. They had no idea whether the copter had crashed accidentally or whether I had brought it down with my firearm.

I remained under the thick elephant's-ear plant. An observer in the air can see much more than one on the ground in these conditions. Heavy as the bush was, it still had open spaces across which I had to cross, however briefly, and once I was seen I had little chance to get away.

The chopper did not hover long over the wreck. It began to swing in a wide circle around, apparently hoping to flush me out or catch sight of me. Then it went back west, and I left my hiding place and traveled swiftly eastward. Just before I reached the bottom of the first cliff, I had to conceal myself again. The chopper was returning. It went by about a hundred feet above me and two hundred yards to the north. It contained a number of men and dogs.

I could not see it, but I guessed that it had settled down on the edge of the cliff and that dogs and men were getting out of it. Their plans now were to push me east with one party and hope to catch me with the one now ahead. Then I was able to see the faces of some men as they watched from the lip of the cliff. The copter took off again and began circling around. Occasionally, the machine guns in it spat fire. I could not hear the guns above the roar of the copter, but some of the bullets struck close enough for me to hear their impact against the trees. They were probing in the hope they could scare me out.

If I stayed where I was, the dogs of the party behind me might pick up my scent. Their baying and barking was getting closer. It was difficult to determine in that muffling foliage, but it seemed that they were headed straight toward me.

I was beginning to feel that I had gone through enough for one day. To survive a twelve hundred foot fall into the ocean and a shark attack should be enough excitement for a month, anyway, not to mention blowing up two helicopters on the ground and lobbing a grenade into the port of another in the air. And getting through the firepower of thirty-five men and a rocket-carrying, napalm-bomb-dropping aircraft. I had had enough for some time; surely my luck must be running out. My anger was getting dangerous, dangerous for me, that is. I could not afford to lose control. But I was feeling a tiredness very new to me. Those who have read the volumes by my biographer, or volume IX of my own memoirs, know that my energy is great. It can be called animal-like. But I had gone through an experience only two months ago which might be called unmanning. Afterward, I had had to go into hiding from the Nine with my wife and Doc Caliban and his cousin, Trish Wilde. I had been without adequate sleep for a week. I wanted to get back to the rain forest of my childhood and youth, to see the dark ceiling close over me, to hear the silence and feel the coolness of the green womb.

I crouched under the bush and tried to suppress my trembling. I bit my lips and clutched the rifle as if I could squeeze in the stock with my fingers. I wanted to leap up and run toward the enemy with my gun blazing and, when that was empty, throw my grenades, and when those were gone, close in on them with the knife.

The images were vivid and satisfying, but they were deadly. I enjoyed them, then laughed to myself, and some of the shaking went away. I had to get out from the closing jaws by going north to the mangrove swamp or south through more bush. Men were already descending from the cliff on both sides and five dogs were with each column. Their ascent was slow and dangerous, but they were determined to extend the jaws of the trap. Other men stayed on top of the cliff to observe. And the dogs were getting closer now; I could hear them plainly because the chopper had traveled to my south. And then it rose and two objects fell from it, and the jungle to my right was a hemisphere of flame and a spire of inky smoke.

The chopper swung back and over me, past me, stopped high above the edge of the swamp, and two more bombs fell. The mangroves for a stretch of a hundred yards were burning fiercely.

Their plan was a good one. Of course, they did not know I was surrounded, but they were acting as if I were. And, as sometimes happens, the *as-if* hypothesis was going to bear a theory and then a fact. Unless I managed, like many a hard fact, to slip through the net of hypothesis.

There was only one thing to do. I crawled toward the left and into the smoke edge of the smoke cloud. Though I was as close to the ground as I could get, I could not stay there long without coughing. Nor could I depend on the smoke to conceal me because of the vagaries of the wind. My purpose was to get where the dogs coming down from the cliff could not smell me or to get as close as possible to that area. Also, when I left that area, I would be reeking of smoke, which I hoped would cover up my body odor.

A man was saying something to a bloodhound, and then they were past me. I came up behind him, crouching, and broke his neck by twisting his head. Before he had fallen to the ground, I had also broken the neck of the dog. All this took place within twelve feet of the closest man and dog, but the roaring of the flames and the smoke swirling through the thick bush hid the noise and the sight of the dead. It took me a minute to get the dead man's clothes off and onto me. They fitted fairly well, since he was almost my height, six feet three inches, and he had a large frame.

The green digger's hat and the green shirt enabled me to get close to another man who did not have a dog, and he went down with a knife in his neck before he realized that I was the hunted. The next two victims were another man and a dog. I almost got caught, because a man was about ten paces behind them, but the bush concealed us long enough for me to be ready by the time he stumbled across the bodies.

They should have stayed back and let the helicopter saturate the area with napalm. They would have gotten me. But as long as they made the mistake of trying to roust me out with men and dogs in a bush in which I had lived a good part of my eighty-one years, they were bound to suffer. I then walked up the cliff, limping as if I'd hurt myself. I looked up twice and saw several men looking at me, and one was shouting at me, if his wide open and writhing mouth meant anything. I continued to limp and several times sat down as if I'd been badly hurt.

Halfway up the cliff, I saw two men coming down toward me. Apparently they were sent by their officer to find out if I had been wounded by their quarry. I sat down with my back to the descending men. The copter was circling tightly about two hundred yards away almost on a level with me. I could see some men and dogs two hundred feet below as they passed from bush to bush, but most of the enemy were concealed. Two men were coming toward me, and three men were on top of the cliff. I had to act swiftly.

My try at passing myself off as one of them failed. A man called down to me, "Cramer?" evidently thinking I must be the man whose clothes I'd taken. One look at my face would tell him his mistake.

I got up onto my legs as if it was painful to do so, with my face still turned away. The rifle was hanging from a strap over my shoulder, and my hands were empty, so that that must have lowered their guard, if indeed it was up at all.

"What the hell, Cramer," the man said in English with a Hungarian accent. "You know better than to leave your station! Did that wild man get you or did you just fall down, trip over your own feet, you clumsy lout!"

"Neither!" I said, and whirled around, the knife coming out of its sheath and through the air and into the Hungarian's solar plexus. The other man froze just long enough for me to pull the automatic from its open holster and shoot him in the chest.

Then I continued to fire up at the three faces hanging over the cliff's edge, three white faces with black O's of mouths. The Luger was a .45, the range was two hundred feet and at a difficult angle and at small targets, so I missed. I had expected this, but the faces did disappear, and I threw the automatic down, withdrew the knife and stuck it in its sheath, and ran up the steep and treacherous path—fit only for goat or baboons—removing my rifle as I did. A glance at the copter showed that, so far, the men in it had not noticed me. They were intent on something below them.

That would not last long. The men on top of the cliff had to have a transceiver of some sort, and they would notify the copter immediately.

By then, the top of the cliff was about one hundred and sixty feet away. I stopped, yanked out another grenade, and cast it. The grenade had to travel about fifty-five feet beyond the range most men can throw a standard hand grenade. It sailed just over the lip of the cliff as the three stuck their heads over to fire at me. The explosion threw rocks and dirt over me, but I saw one body sailing out of the smoke to crash against a projection, roll over and fall the rest of the way. I had to presume that the other three were out of the combat; if I was wrong, I would be dead. The copter had started to whirl around just before I threw the grenade. The pilot must have received the message from the man on the top of the cliff. I was ready for this, I'd yanked out another grenade, and I threw it.

It was probably the best throw of my life, as far as both distance and accuracy went. The grenade weighed about one and three-quarter pounds and the copter was about two hundred feet away when I threw the grenade. It had started to move before then and was coming swiftly. It was approaching nose first, so that its machine gunners could not aim at me. Its rockets had been launched during that first attack, otherwise it could have fired at point-blank range and disintegrated me and a good part of the face of the cliff.

But the pilot must have been jarred by the unexpected blast of the grenade, and he did not react to my pointing my rifle at him because I did not point it. Otherwise, I suppose he would have swung around so that the gunners on one side or the other could let loose.

By the time he decided to do that, the grenade

was well launched, and just as he pivoted his craft around and stopped it, the grenade struck the vanes. The vanes and the body of the machine disappeared in a cloud of smoke, pieces of machinery came flying out, the machine dropped almost straight down and crashed. A second later, it was burning furiously, and it may have fallen on a number of men and the exploding fuel may have splashed on some. The men on the ground were shaken up; the fire directed at me as I raced on up the path was ragged and misdirected.

And then I was on top of the cliff, ready to fire at any survivors of the grenade I'd tossed up there. But there were none.

One of the corpses had six grenades attached to hooks on a belt. I tossed these, one at a time, into the bush below the cliff and had the satisfaction of knowing that I got at least two men and a dog. Then I picked up a rifle and left running because I did not want to be there if more copters were called in or if jets were used. As it was, I had just entered a thick bush on top of the next higher plateau when two jets screamed overhead about five hundred feet.

I kept on going and did not stop until I had reached the green cliff of seemingly impenetrable jungle that marks the border of the rain forest. I wormed my way through it and then it was as if I had stepped into a quiet twilit cathedral grown by God. I was home.

And now is as good a place as any to recapitulate the events leading up to those in this volume.

My name is known wherever books and movies are known, and that covers at least three-fourths of the habitable world. Even those who have never read the books or seen the movies know, in a general sense, what my name stands for. (When I say my name I mean the one that my biographer gave me to conceal my real identity.)

My biographer has stretched the truth, added things which never existed, and ignored others that did exist. But, in the main, the first two volumes of my life were based on reality, and the later ones at least springboarded from an actual event. My biographer did give a fairly accurate picture of my personality. Perhaps I should say he reported my basic attitudes, with much verisimilitude, though he softened some of these because he wanted reader identification with me. And he did not go into any depth about the infrahumanity of my thinking. (Although here I may not be fair with him. The creatures who raised me, The Folk, were subhuman, but they did have a language, and I wonder if anybody who uses a language can escape being classified as entirely human. I suppose the dolphins could, since they live in water and lack hands. But The Folk were anthropoids, probably a giant variety of the ancient hominids, Zinjanthropus or Paranthropus. And while their language reflected a very peculiar way of looking at the universe—to English speakers—it was no more peculiar than Shawnee would be to an Englishman. And in many ways their *Weltanschauung* was remarkably close to that of Sunset Strip inhabitants.)

In 1948, I decided to write my memoirs. I could not publish them because I was then serving the Nine, and they wanted no slightest word of their existence printed. Or even spoken of among the noncognoscenti. I could not have published the memoirs if I had omitted any reference to them. Certain obvious phenomena, such as looking as if I were only thirty when I had to be sixty, and the source of my enormous wealth (on a small fraction of which I paid income tax), could not be overlooked by the public or the authorities. Moreover, aside from all this, my statement that I was not a figment of a fiction writer's feverish brain would have resulted in enormous publicity and invasion of my privacy. Not to mention the possibility that I might have been certified.

Nevertheless, I started to write the memoirs. Some day they might be publishable. Also, I liked the idea of remembrance of things past. (Yes, I have read Proust and in French, my favorite human language.) I have an almost photographic memory but it sometimes results in pictures which startle the humans who lived through the same events. Volume I begins with the first day I can remember, when I was suckling and looking up into those beautiful rusty-brown eyes, into the eyes of the only being who loved me for eighteen years. Volume I ends at the age of ten, or what I calculate as the age of ten, the night I first used a knife. Volumes I through VIII covered seventy-eight years. Some of the manuscripts were slim, some were over a million words long. They corrected a number of distortions or omissions of events and told the true names behind the names my biographer used. They included many items of information which I suppose would repulse the readers of my "biography." I have never had any hesitation about eating human meat when the occasion demanded, contrary to what my biographer stated. Nor have I been rigorously Victorian in some aspects of my life, to say the least. And I suppose, in fact, I know, that many would condemn me for serving the Nine. They would equate this with Faustus' selling of his soul.

It is easy enough to scorn. Let the scorner be offered thirty thousand years or more of youth and then we shall hear what they have to say.

My wife and I took the oath under conditions that would make a Mau-Mau initiation look like a Sunday-School Bible presentation. And I suppose we weren't honest or ethical even then, because we had unstated reservations. But we would remain with the Nine, and take their immortality, as long as we were not asked to do anything we just could not do and still respect ourselves. Fortunately, neither of us was asked, though I must admit that I am capable of much that would revolt most of the so-called civilized peoples. But then I have never really considered myself as part of humanity. This attitude can be for bad or good, depending on the circumstances.

Nevertheless, immortality brings a high price. It is true that you pay for everything valuable you get in this world. Nothing is really free. And so, for years, both Clio and myself felt a little less

than "clean." That is the only word I can think
of that is anywhere appropriate. Thirty thousand or more years ago, some Old Stone Age
peoples discovered something that gave them an
extremely extended youth. It also made them
immune to any disease or to breakdown of the
cells. Of course, they could fall down and break
their necks or slit their throats or get clubbed to
death. But if chance worked well for them, they
could live for what must have seemed forever.
They did age, but so slowly that a man who took
the elixir at the age of twenty-five would only
look fifty at the end of fifteen thousand years.

I don't know the history of what happened between 25,000 B.C. and 1913 when the agent of the
Nine first introduced himself. By then, the Nine
consisted of Anana, a thirty-millennia old
Caucasian woman, XauXaz, Ing, Iwaldi, a
dwarf, a Hebrew born about 3 B.C., an ancient
proto-Bantu, two proto-Mongolians, and an
Amerindian. They lived most of the year in various parts of the world, but once a year they held
a ceremony which must have originated in the
early part of the Paleolithic. This involved the
giving up of flesh on the part of the servants of
the Nine—a painful procedure—and the drinking of the elixir. The ceremonies were always
held in a complex of caves in the remote mountains near Uganda.

Over a period of several months, the "candidates" drank the rejuvenation liquid. No
samples were ever given out; the candidates entered the caverns naked and left naked. It meant
a hideous death to be discovered trying to smug-
gle the stuff out.

We "candidates," I estimate, numbered about five hundred. We were the elite of the organization that, literally, ruled the world in secret. How many were enlisted in the lower echelons, I couldn't even begin to guess. The lower echelon, the "servants of the Nine," probably numbered half a million. None of these even know of the elixir or had ever seen the Nine.

We candidates were those who might be chosen to replace one of the Nine if he or she died.

Volume IX of my memoirs opens with Clio in our estate at Grandrith, which includes a manor, a castle, a forest, and the village of Cloamby. (James Cloamby, Viscount Grandrith, is my true name and title.) I was in our house on the plantation in western Kenya. I was blasted out of my bed by a shell from a Kenyan Army artillery unit because old Jomo Kenyatta had given the order to wipe me off the face of the Earth. I had refused to become a Kenyan citizen or to leave Kenya, and he had put up with this for several years. Then he had decided to kill me (or perhaps somebody else in the Kenyan administration had). I survived and I escaped with the army on my tail. Not only that, an Albanian by the name of Enver Noli was after me with a band of heavily armed Arab bandits. He was hoping that I would lead him to the site of my gold mine in Uganda. I did, though the gold had long been gone. In the meantime, some mysterious enemy had let loose a lion on me. I found out that he was Doc Caliban, accompanied by two aged men, the last survivors of the band that had once helped him in his fight against evil.

Doc Caliban was as strange a phenomenon as I. You might say I was the Feral Man, the Man of the Jungle, whereas Doctor Caliban was the Civilized Man, the Man of the Metropolis. He had been trained since an early age to develop to the fullest potentiality his physical and mental powers, which must have been considerable. In fact, they were probably, next to mine, the greatest. And no wonder, when you consider that our grandfather had been an Early Stone Age Man, XauXaz, the ancient who was second only to Anana in age and power at the round oaken table of the Nine. That was why my bones and Caliban's were so much thicker than modern man's, thus affording a broader base for the attachment of massive muscles.

But we did not know, at the time, that Xau-Xaz was our ancestor.

Caliban was out to kill me because he thought I had killed his beautiful cousin, Patricia, when she was on a scientific expedition in East Africa.

Both of us were suffering the peculiar and un-predictable side effects of the immortality elixir. Ours occurred about the same time with the result that we each had very strange, and similar, psychoneuroses. Those who are curious may read Volume IX of my memoirs.

Our first face-to-face encounter came on the natural bridge that leads to the caverns of the Nine. But the Nine stopped us from fighting. XauXaz had died, and we two had been picked out of the five hundred candidates to vie for his place. After the ceremony, we would be set free and one should kill the other.

It was then that Anana told us that we were half-brothers. Our father had also been a candidate, and the elixir had had an unfortunate side effect on him. Lord Grandrith had gone mad. He had, in fact, become that savage maniac known in history as Jack the Ripper.

But he had recovered and he had emigrated to the States, where he took the name of Caliban. The side effects had passed, but they left a consciousness of what he had done and a revulsion against himself. He swore to raise his son to fight evil. I think that he meant eventually to reveal his past to his American son and to turn him against the Nine. He did most of this in secret, and thus, though his child could have established athletic records that would still not be beaten (if I had also abstained), he never entered sports in high school or college.

He did become the greatest surgeon in the world and he also was clearly the greatest in many fields; archeology, chemistry, and a number of other sciences and professions. But he avoided publicity as much as possible. However, a writer found out something about him and used him and his band of aids as the basis for a semifictional series in a pulp magazine. Caliban's "biographies" deviated even more from reality than mine, yet many of the adventures did contain a kernel of truth.

I left the caves and went to a tree house I'd built in the rain forest wherein Clio and I had vacationed. I discovered a madman aping me. He it was who had abducted Trish Wilde, Doc Caliban's cousin. I rescued her, and we went on to England, where I knew that Enver Noli and Doc Caliban were going. Both were intent on getting hold of Clio and using her against me.

By then I was beginning to wonder if the whole situation had not been brought about by the Nine. They could have given both of us something to bring on the "side effects." They could have set up the abduction and supposed death of Trish to cause Caliban to want revenge. And I was sure that the mysterious death of our father was caused by the Nine. They must have discovered that he intended to turn against them and killed him. But his American son, Doc Caliban, did not know anything at all about the Nine and never suspected, until then, that the Nine were responsible. When they offered him immortality, he accepted it, just as I had. Just as, I am convinced, any human would.

At the estate, Caliban and I had killed off Noli's group and then we fought, though I tried to talk him out of it. We tore each other up like two leopard males at mating time, and we both almost died. But one of the properties of the elixir is the regeneration of organs, and we grew our lost ones back.

We also had recovered from the madness brought on by the side effect. We found out we had been duped, and we swore to fight against the Nine. We knew what little chance we had of ever winning. But I killed the men sent to summon us to a meeting of the Nine in London, and we fled.

All this is told in Volume IX of my memoirs. Since then, Clio and I had been separated from Doc Caliban and his cousin. We had been around the world twice. During the first trip, I had dropped off the manuscript of Volume IX in a Los Angeles post office for your editor to publish. I had met him in Kansas City at the home of a common friend.

We went from Los Angeles to New York. Clio and I made an unchartered flight across the Atlantic in one of Doc Caliban's planes, which we got from a hangar near the tip of Long Island. We flew the jet all the way about twenty feet above the waves. We landed on an unattended strip in Devonshire on land owned by me, and we motored to London. I got in touch with Doc Caliban via the shortwave in our hideout in the apartment in Marylebone Borough. Doc reported that he now had two "sidekicks," sons of two of his former associates. The three men were on the trail of Iwaldi in Germany. He wanted me to come to Germany to join in the hunt, but I told him of my plans to scout out the caves of the Nine. I did not intend to attack anybody there, unless the chance of risk was slight enough to warrant it. I just wanted to map the area in my mind for the day when Doc and I would invade it.

I doubted very much that any of the Nine would be in the caves, since this was not the time for the ceremonies. But I did not know that. I suspected that there would be a formidable army of guards and that the entrances would be mined and booby-trapped. I did not know this, of course, but it seemed unlikely that the caves would be left unguarded. Though they were in a

remote and arid mountain range, and the caves
could be reached only with difficulty, there were
bound to be gold or oil prospectors around there.
The Nine had deliberately created a superstitious dread of the area among the natives just
outside the mountains. And the Nine doubtless
controlled in secret many of those high in the
administration of Uganda and Kenya. These
would take steps to declare the area officially off
limits if the Nine had to kill so many that people
got curious.

My plan was to approach the mountains from
the west coast of Africa, on foot and alone. If I
sailed or flew into the east coast, I might be
spotted, and the skein of the Nine would be flung
everywhere to catch me. Besides, too many people in Kenya and Uganda knew me. But if I
landed quietly on the coast of Gabon and traveled as I like best to travel, alone and lightly
armed, I could traverse the rain forests which
stretch across much of central Africa. I would
avoid all humanity, and I would come like a
shadow out of the west. Nobody would expect
me. And I should be comparatively free to investigate. It was the western end of the caves that
I knew nothing about. All candidates had always
been required to follow a strictly limited route
from the east, and exploration of the area had
been forbidden with a very painful existence and
eventually death promised for those who broke
the law.

Doc Caliban did not argue with me. He is very
self-sufficient. Also, though I could be wrong, I
think he preferred not to work with me. He was
probably right, since we both are so strongly in-

dividualistic. It is not that we can't take orders, because he served with distinction as a commissioned officer in the U.S. Army in 1918. And I was a major and then a colonel in the RAF in World War II. And both of us were under the strictest sort of discipline from ourselves and others when we went through medical school.

But we each have our own way of doing things, and there was in both of us a residue of doubt about who was the strongest. This seems childish, and perhaps is, but after you have *known* for many years that you are the most athletic man alive, the swiftest, the strongest, and then you run across somebody who seems to be fully as strong, then you doubt. Doc and I had fought at Grandrith Castle, and you may read the results of that fight in Volume IX of my memoirs. But when two are so evenly matched, and one wins, the loser is entitled to wonder if the outcome would be different the next time. I'm sure that Doc thought about this at times, chided himself for his juvenility, and then could not keep from speculating again.

So it was best that we tackle the Nine separately, for the time being, anyway.

Clio objected to being left behind, but I did not want to be burdened when I traveled through the rain forest. Tough and strong as this delicate and beautiful little blonde is, she was not born in Africa nor raised ferally. The only human being whom I would have considered taking with me, because he could keep up with me under the primitive conditions, would be Doc Caliban.

So I kissed her goodbye and left London,

which I hate because of the crowds and the noise and odors, and flew illegally to various ports. But I made a stop near Port-Gentil to check on some of my operatives, and it must have been there that the agents of the Nine detected me.

I had escaped where I had no right to by the usual mechanism and rules of probability of the universe. But, as I have said, I am convinced that I do have something about me that twists and distorts the odds against coincidence and good luck. It's what I call the "human magnetic moment," and it is what very few people possess. I am one, and Doc Caliban, from what he had told me, must be another. Of course, one day, the inevitable must happen. A bullet will plow into my brain or I'll fall off a tree or down the stairs or an automobile going through a stop sign will crush me or a faulty gas heater will asphyxiate me or . . . I remember a line from Merrill Moore's poen, "Warning To One": *Death is the strongest of all living things*.

It will come to me as to every man. But until the moment, I will live as if *I* were the strongest of all living things.

I was home again, and I breathed relief, though I knew it might not last long. For the first time in a long time, I could genuinely *breathe*. The air inside the closed-canopy tall equatorial forest is like that nowhere else. It sighs with the greenness of totally alive beings, animals or plants. Contrary to what most people think, this type of rain forest is not hot, even if it is in the equator. It may be staggeringly blistering just above the top of the forest. But below, where the ground is at the bottom of a deep well, roofed over by a tangle of layers and layers of branches and vines and lianas and leaves, it is cool. And the temperature does not vary much. Moreover, the area between the broad and tall trees is often park-like. It is free of that thick mass that can be penetrated only with difficulty by man and that people associate with the word *jungle* because of Hollywood's projections of what it thinks a jungle looks like.

In fact, if Murtagh's forces had caught me on the ground here, they could have blown me apart a dozen times before I fell. The area is too open for the sort of warfare through which I had just gone. Of course, if I had had a chance to get up a tree and into the various levels of the tanglery overhead, I might have gotten away. Here, despite my two hundred and fifty pounds, I could travel from tree to tree for long distances. It wouldn't be by swinging from lianas. That is another Hollywood idea and utterly unrealistic. (Though I have done it several times under extreme emergency conditions.) On foot, and traveling not too swiftly, I have often gone for miles in this area without once setting foot on the ground. And when I was much younger and lighter, I could do it much more swiftly.

Now I stayed on the ground because I wanted to make speed. I trotted along until I found a small pool and drank from it. Then, feeling hungry, I hunted, and I finally saw a small half-grown tusker. I ran after him, and he took off speedily, but I am faster and have more endurance, and eventually he stopped, breathing hoarsely, facing me, his little eyes savage and desperate, saliva dripping from his tusks. I did not use my rifle because of the noise. I sprang in, he tried to wheel to one side, and my knife cut open his jugular. I drank the blood while it was still pumping out and then I butchered the beast. I ate him raw and then proceeded on my way with about half of him—the best half— wrapped up in his hide. There had to be water near, since the bushpig seldom strays too far from water. Then I remembered the small stream about a mile to the north and made for it. I drank and then ate some more of the pig. I was lucky in running across this creature, since they usually lie up in dense reed beds or tall grass by day and come out at night to feed. And they usually run in groups of twenty or so.

I have heard people who did not know that they were talking to me, scoff at my ability to survive in this area. They say that if I had eaten all that raw meat, I would have been infested with worms and other internal parasites.

They overlook that there are any number of natives who eat raw meat from which some get infested and some do not. However, it is my opinion that I never got sick because, one, I lived in a healthy area, the closed-canopy forest, and, two, far more significant, I probably had something in me which killed off all bacteria, viri, and parasites. I am convinced the Nine were dictating the course of my life before birth. I believe that I was injected with something which made me immune, just as I believe that the Nine deliberately set things up so that I was raised as a feral human by The Folk. (The factors which made me conclude this are detailed in Volume II of my memoirs, unpublished as yet.) Thus, my unique way of life was not entirely "natural," any more than Doc Caliban's was natural. This had made me wonder how many other men, known or unknown to history, have been "modified" by the Nine. How many geniuses owe their shaping to the grim ancients who pull the strings from their secret mansions?

I was walking along, noting that it was now twilight at ground level, which meant that the sun must be sinking close to the horizon. It was still comparatively quiet here, though some males of a troop of sooty mangabeys were occasionally giving their loud chattering cry. These were large long-tailed monkeys with gray fur especially long on the sides of the head and with pink faces speckled with gray-brown freckles. They make good eating, as I well know.

I was thinking about going up and making a nest in the middle level when I heard the baying of dogs behind me.

Doctor Murtagh had not given up. I don't know who he had managed to catch up, since I had traveled faster than ordinary men with dogs could, unless he called in more copters.

I dropped the hog, ran to the stream, which was a quarter of a mile away, and washed myself in it. Then I climbed a one hundred and fifty foot high tree to the middle level. From there, I made my way across the tanglery to the source of the baying. I knew that they would find where I had gone up, and they would likely fire into the closed-canopy around there. They would be shooting for some distance eastward from where I had ascended on the theory that I was fleeing via the middle level. They would never, I hoped, believe that I had the guts to cross above them and travel behind them.

In about fifteen minutes, I stopped my cautiously slow travel. I hugged a branch which was almost entirely enclosed in lianas and vines and broad leaves. Down on the ground, it was so dark that the men were using flashlights and lamps. Where I was, the sunlight was still filtering down. By looking up, they could have seen me outlined against the lighter sky if it had not been for the dense green around me. My cloak of invisibility. Of course, I could not move now unless I did so very slowly, because my weight would bend the bridge of vegetation between the trees and the noise could be heard by the dogs or even by the less keen ears of the men. However, I could move while they were on the march as long as I trailed them by several hundred yards. They kept on my scent until the dogs broke into an eager baying and barking when they came onto the place where I had killed the bushpig. The dogs went swiftly after that, with the men stabbing their beams on every side. They would have liked to have camped for the night, I'm sure. They were in my territory, and they must have been spooked because of the day's events. But they drove on with Doctor Murtagh at their head and did not stop until they came to the tree up which I had climbed. A moment later, the gunfire that was aimed at the canopy aroused the monkeys and birds for miles around. The screeching continued long after Murtagh had given the cease-fire order.

If I had been hiding overhead anywhere within a hundred-yard square area, I would have been shot a dozen times. As it was, a number of bursts came my way, and I was two hundred yards back and behind a thick trunk. Then they probed the area with flashlights, hoping to find my corpse hanging from a tangle or fallen onto the ground.

Murtagh said nothing when his men reported no success. But his bearing, outlined in the flashlight, was a curse. He gave an order (which I could not hear at that distance, of course) and they pitched camp.

It did not take long. Every man except Murtagh carried a pack on his back. These consisted mainly of ammunition, food, water, medicine, and collapsible furniture and tents.

The tents were Doc Caliban's invention and known only to the servants of the Nine. The tents and the furniture could be likened only to that pocket-sized collapsible sailing ship of Norse mythology, Skidbladnir. A man would remove a neatly folded bundle of cloth about the size of a big handkerchief and snap it like a whip. Yards of green material unfolded, shot out like a flag in a breeze. The stuff was as thin and as light as spider webs, but it kept out light and cold, and it was as tough as an inch-thick sheet of aluminum. The framework of the supports for the tent slid out of a cylinder about two feet long and three inches thick and was set up within six-

ty seconds. Then the material of the tent was
arranged over it and tied down at the ends to
stakes driven into the thin forest soil. There
wasn't much dead wood available for fires, but
they did not care. They carried small metal boxes which unfolded and projected six large round
rings at the ends of thin metal stalks. These
burned a gas derived from a compressed liquid
and furnished a fire for cooking or heating.
Caliban had invented both the tents and the
burners in 1937, but only the Nine had benefited
from it then. Many of the things he invented in
the 30's are still ahead of their time.

The lamps were set up to bathe the camp with
additional illumination. Wires were strung and
little buttons were stuck here and there outside
and above the camp. The buttons would set off
alarms in the camp through the wireless. They
were set to react to any mass larger than a
monkey which would get near the magnetic field
they were radiating.

The tents were arranged in a circle with
Murtagh's in the center. There were about fifty
men and thirty dogs—enough evidence that copters had brought in additional forces. Double
guards were stationed every forty feet outside the
perimeter of the line formed by the tents. The
area outside was bathed in a bright light, and
the guards were relieved every hour. Of course, I
could have dropped onto Murtagh's tent, but I
didn't relish the idea of falling a hundred feet
even after having survived a twelve hundred foot
fall that morning. Also, what was the use of killing Murtagh if I got shot to pieces?

For the same reason, I did not shoot him at a distance with my rifle. I had been extremely fortunate to have survived the concentrated fire in the bush. Here, where I had to travel slowly in the canopy, they could have overhauled me and gotten below me unless I was very lucky again. I did not want to stretch my good fortune too far.

I did want to hear what they were saying. Slowly, I crawled through the canopy. This was necessary not only to prevent noise but to test the stuff holding me up. It is not always anchored securely. I have fallen several times when I was a youth living in this area, twice saving myself by hanging onto a liana that did not break and once managing to grab the end of a branch as I fell toward the ground a hundred feet below. I have seen three of The Folk who were not so fortunate when they went through the green trapdoor; they broke most of their bones.

Every now and then the bright beam of a small searchlight fingered the tanglery where I was. The beam was being moved at random; it pierced the forest at ground level, lighting up the huge trunks of the trees, making them look like crudely carved pillars of a deep mine worked by gnomes. And then it would leap up onto the dark ceiling overhead, sometimes catching red in the eyes of the owls and bushbabies and servals.

The men not on guard were eating the food they had cooked in their cans over the gas fires. Murtagh sat on a folding chair by a folding table just inside his tent with several of his officers. When I was directly overhead, I could hear a few words, but most of the conversation in the leader's tent was lost. It would have been convenient if the tent had been under a tree with limbs sticking out only about twenty-five feet above.

Nevertheless, I lay flat on a net of lianas and leaves supported by a thin branch and stared down through the net at camp. Some of the men had loud voices, and I hoped to learn from them. Two, a French Canadian and a mulatto Congolese, spoke in French, presumably on the theory that Murtagh couldn't understand them. Perhaps he didn't, but I think that an educated and cosmopolitan man such as Murtagh would have been very fluent in this tongue. Perhaps they were depending on him not to comprehend their two types of French. They may have been correct in their assumptions. The Canadian's French was only half-understood by me, and I doubt that a man skilled in Parisian French would understand the Congolese's patois. The two had to repeat much to make their own words clear.

The Congolese said, "If it is true that this white devil's plane was blown up, and he fell a thousand feet without a parachute, and swam ashore and then he got through us and killed half of us . . . then what are we doing here?"

"We are here because Murtagh said so, and because he is paying us very well," the Canadian said. "That *white* devil as you call him, is insane. He would have to be to take the chances he did. As for his falling that far from a plane, I do not believe that. And . . ."

"But I heard the report over the radio. I was

standing behind Murtagh when the pilot reported. He said the plane exploded, and he saw Grandrith's body falling. He watched it until it disappeared, and there was no parachute.''

"I read once about a man who fell two thousand feet into a snowbank and lived," the Canadian said. "It was a true story. It had to be, it was in the French edition of *The Reader's Digest*. It happened during World War II. And I heard about a man who fell a thousand feet into the sea and lived. So, why shouldn't this man live if others can?''

"And how do you explain that he also survived us?" the Congolese said. "Does a man have that much luck, to live through a fall like that and through our firepower and then burn four helicopters and kill fifteen men on the ground? Some with a knife while many others were only ten feet away? And kill dogs, too?''

While they were talking, moonlight fell on me. I was in the lower level of canopy, and above me was an opening in the upper level. I was not, of course, visible to those below me.

I listened carefully. The two discussed Murtagh and their officers and what they would do with their money when they returned to civilization. Then they said a few words about the base, which was apparently to the northeast somewhere, not too far away. The radio operator, Smith, had not lied.

I should have left then. The base was my next goal; I wanted to investigate that and perhaps harass its occupants. I could at least prowl around and pick up information by eavesdrop-

ping. Or perhaps abduct someone who might
have valuable information which he would give,
willingly or not.

But I stayed, hoping I would find out more.
And then I heard a thrashing in the leaves behind me and turned swiftly, my knife ready. My
rifle and belt with the grenades attached was
stretched across a web of lianas. I saw a blurry
form in the moonlight—a little guenon monkey,
I think it was—and then a larger winged form
after it. An eagle-owl had spiraled down through
the opening in the upper canopy and spotted a
tiny monkey and the monkey had seen it coming.
It flashed across a liana and then was on me. I
batted at it, struck it to one side, it gave a cry
and clutched a twig and then was off, somewhere. I don't know where or care. The owl had
been following it so closely that it did not see me
until it was on me and then it screeched and its
claws raked my chest.

I remember hearing shouting from below. A
bright beam spun its cone around and then cen-
tered on me. This happened just as I fell with the
owl. My perch had been precarious, and it did
not take much to topple me, especially since
I was so occupied with trying to tear the
bird's claws loose from its painful clutch on my
chest.

As I have said, there is something about me,
my "magnetic moment," which has tended to
cause coincidences which would be incredible in
fiction to occur around me. It has given me very
good luck many times.

But we have to pay with good for bad; for every action there is an opposite and equal reaction.

Bad fortune came. I fell a hundred feet, and this time, if my brain had not been frozen by the horror of it, I would have thought that I had come to the end of a long and unusually interesting trail. I could not expect to survive two long falls in the same day, even if this was much shorter than the first.

Rifles shot at me even as I fell. The owl screamed and tore itself loose and then it exploded in feathers. A bullet or two had hit it.

The bright lights and the dark green-black top of the tent expanded before me, whirled to one side, came back, shot away, the wind whistled through my ears, the rifles barked, and I kept my mouth closed, determined even then not to give them the pleasure of hearing me scream.

Then I was unconscious.

When I opened my eyes, I saw that it was still night. I was surprised, not because it was night but because I had expected to be dead.

By then the tent on which I had fallen had been set up again. I had hit it on my back with my legs and arms extended sidewise. The top had caved in but not lightly. I had hit the ground, but the impact had been considerably softened by the tent. Not enough so that my muscles did not ache but not enough to break any bones.

I was lying on my side inside a ring formed by six guards with rifles pointing at me. My hands were handcuffed behind me, and my legs just above the ankles had irons locked around them.

The irons were connected by a thick chain of duraluminum or similar alloy. Moreover, something had been secured around my waist—it felt like another duraluminum chain—and a plastic disc about six inches in diameter and an inch thick was held against my belly by the belt. My belt with its knife had been removed, of course.

Murtagh stood near me but just outside the nearest guard. He bent over to look at me more closely. His eyes were as empty of light as a dead man's. His jaws protruded apishly, and his head moved from side to side, repulsively and, I am sure, compulsively.

"Lord Grandrith," he said. "The only and only. *Pelus blancus simiarum.* The demon of the jungle. Last of the wild men. Lord of the trees. Pristine spirit of darkest Africa. Member of the House of Lords and one of the wealthiest men in the world."

His voice was high and harsh. There was nothing about the man to like. He even had a bad odor, though I doubt if the others could have smelled it.

"Traitor, also!" he said. "And a corpse soon! Right now, if I had my say about it! You're far too dangerous to let live for a second!"

There did not seem to be anything to say in reply, so I glared at him.

"Before long you'll wish that I had had my way," he said. "Old Mubaniga wants you taken to the base, so taken you will be. And when the Nine get their hands on you, you know what to expect."

It was cool in the night on the soft dank ground of the rain forest, but I was sweating. I was not afraid, but I do have a vivid imagination and I could visualize some of the things that would be done to me.

Murtagh said, "The mathematical probabilities for your having survived just the explosion of the plane, let alone the fall into the sea, are so small that . . . well, and then . . . Do you know, you are the only man ever to have reduced me to stuttering. Congratulations for that. Though there will be nothing else from now on to congratulate you for."

He looked hard at me, turned, and went into the tent. A man pulled the flap of the tent down. I rolled over without objection from the guards and looked around. Beyond my six guards were four more, stationed as backups. There did not seem to be anything I could do. I did not even test the handcuffs, since I was sure that even I could not break the metal of the links. And if I could, then what?

I closed my eyes and in a short time was asleep. This ability to relax is beast-like, and, as my biographer pointed out innumerable times, I am half-beast.

A hand shook me awake. I should have heard the man approach and smelled him, but I was utterly exhausted. I had had a hard day.

The man was Murtagh. He had come out of his tent a few minutes after I was asleep. I wondered if keeping me awake was going to be the first part of the torture. But he only smiled, managing to look even more reptilian, and he said, "Aren't you curious about the disc attached to your belly?"

I did not reply. He sneered and said, "It's an

explosive which contains a radio receiver. If you should by any chance get loose, you would not get far."

He took a small metal case and said, "If I snap the pseudo-lighter, the transmitter in the case will send out a frequency which will be detected by the receiver in the explosive. And your belly, and the rest of you, will be blown to little pieces. There will not be enough for the small birds to eat. And even if you should, somehow, get the handcuffs off, and then, somehow, detach the belt, you could not removed the disc without tearing off the skin of your belly. It is bonded with epoxy glue to your skin."

It seemed to me that the range of the transmitter would be limited. But I said nothing.

Murtagh hesitated and then said, grinning, "Oh, yes. I almost forgot. I was one of the ten candidates chosen to replace you and Caliban. If I capture or kill you, I was to be one of two. The other, I suppose, will be the man who gets Caliban. And that may be I, since I will be allowed to go after him once I've turned you over to the proper authority. In which case, I am bound to sit with the Nine."

I remained silent. He bared his lips, showing thick yellow teeth, and made a sucking noise as if he were going to spit on me. But he turned again, and the flap over the tent fell down. Within a few seconds, I was once more asleep.

At six in the morning, I was awakened. I had been half-awake for some time during the night because it had rained. The canopy kept much of the rain from falling directly onto me, but drops and occasional trickles startled me from a deep sleep. However, I am accustomed to this; even a more extreme change of temperature and humidity would not have made me suffer much. The guards around me complained about having to stand outside, but they did so in low voices that showed they did not wish Murtagh to hear.

A few minutes after the whistle sounded to wake the camp, Murtagh appeared from the tent. He stared at me a minute as if to satisfy himself that I was still there or to gloat over his reward for catching me. Then he went back in, and I heard the whir of the electric razor. Breakfast was cooked in cans over the heater, and the cuffs were taken off my wrists so I could feed myself. Six men still guarded me. After eating, I rose and stretched and bent this way and that to get the kink and the pain out of my muscles. I was still sore from the fall, and being forced to sleep in the cramped chained-up position had not relieved me.

I submitted to having my hands cuffed behind me again, since there was nothing else I could do. My leg irons were taken off, and I was allowed to pace back and forth. During this time, the tents were quickly taken down and folded up into handkerchief size again, the support frames were collapsed, along with the furniture, and formed into small cylinders and stuck into the packs. The cans were pressed flat under the heavy boots of the men and then piled into a heap with other debris and garbage. A man sprinkled a fluid from a container onto the pile, smoke curled up from the pile material; the whole took on a gray cast, changed to ashes, and collapsed. The ashes were blown about, and we marched away with no sign of a large camp having been there. The footprints and the holes left by the stakes had been pressed down by men wearing broad discs on their boots.

The march was led by Murtagh, who frequently consulted his compass and also a small device which he held to his ear. These were guiding him through the rain forest, and it was fortunate that he had them. It is easy for anybody except a native to get lost in the forest. By native, I do not mean the average African native. He shuns these places; he hates to venture into the arched columnar world. The pygmies and the anthropoids and The Folk and the beasts of the quiet green mansions know their way around. And I know.

I did not understand why Murtagh did not lead us back the way he had come, since it was only about six miles to the edge of the forest. But he seemed to know what he was doing. And, after a half a day's journey, we broke out of the forest into a clearing. This was a recent, man-made well into which helicopters could drop. A few minutes later, a Sikorsky S-62 appeared and settled down. My leg irons were replaced, and I was forced to hop to the craft and climb awkwardly in. Murtagh and twelve of his officers got in, and we took off. Apparently the copter would return to pick up the others in several trips. It was some satisfaction to me that I had destroyed so many of their copters that they were reduced to one.

This was not true. After a twenty-minute trip,
as registered by Murtagh's wristwatch, we came
over another clearing. This was also man-made
but much larger. There were about forty large
tents arranged in concentric circles and, to one
side, a space for copters. Two small craft
squatted there. There was no sign of jets or of a
landing strip for them.

Murtagh had sat ahead of me. He did not
speak a single word during the flight. Once, he
looked back at me and smiled. He seemed self-
congratulatory, as a "great white hunter" would
who was returning with the head of the largest
elephant ever shot. The others did not speak
either. I would have thought they would be
much more jubilant, and then it occurred to me
that they might be dreading reprimand or punishment of some kind. After all, they had not
been so efficient; they had allowed one man to
decimate them. And I had been caught, not
through their cunning, but by sheer accident.

Why did Murtagh, their leader, the man responsible, not share their feelings?

Perhaps he did not care if he was repri-
manded, since he had achieved his mission. And
that, really, was all the Nine required of their
servants.

After I had clambered out, my leg irons were
removed. Murtagh removed the transmitter-ac-
tivator from his pocket, showed it to me as he
smiled slightly, and then gestured at my guards
to conduct me ahead of him. We went through
three circles of tents and stopped before the tent
which was the center of the circles. This was also

the largest, being thirty feet high. There were four guards in front and two at each corner outside the tent. When we went inside, I saw two at each interior corner.

A wall of cloth made two rooms. Murtagh reported to the officer at the table before the wall and presented a small plastic card. I'm sure that the officer knew Murtagh quite well, but he still went through the established procedures. He inserted the card into a small metal box with a screen above it. I could not see what the screen showed, but its presentation satisfied the officer. He picked up a wireless phone and said that he would send in Doctor Murtagh and the prisoner. He listened for a moment and then put up the phone.

"Give me the activator," the officer said, pointing at the device.

Murtagh did not say anything or move at all for a few seconds except for the sidewise oscillation of his head. He opened his mouth as if to protest but checked himself. The officer took the activator and went through the flap over the entrance in the wall. When he returned, he no longer had the device.

Evidently whoever was to receive us wanted to make sure that he controlled any detonation of the explosives in the disc glued to my belly. I admired his caution. If I had been he, I would have made certain that such an ambitious man as Murtagh did not get a chance to blow up the prisoner along with his superior and claim it was an accident or had to be done to keep me from escaping.

There was really little chance that Murtagh would do that, since he had half-won his seat at the table of the Nine. But the person within had survived so many millennia by not taking unnecessary chances.

This was Mubaniga.

He sat in a high-backed folding chair at a large folding desk. Leopard skins cushioned his thin wrinkled flesh and frail millennia-old bones. His kinky hair was white, and his face and hands were valleys and ridges of grayish-black skin. The sunken eyes were black with red streaks mixed with yellow. His teeth were very thick and widely spaced. He wore a white jumpsuit with a black scarf around his age-corroded neck.

This was Mubaniga, one of the Nine. I had seen him at least once a year for fifty-seven years. Each time except one he had always been remote, and the meeting had been brief enough though painful for me. This was during the annual ceremony when a piece of flesh was extracted from the candidates and the elixir was given in return. But when I was the Speaker for the Nine, a sort of major-domo for several months, I came into more intimate contact with the Nine. Mubaniga had never talked to me except to give me orders now and then. But I had stood by and listened while the Nine talked among themselves. And often he talked to himself in a language which had to be the ancestor of all the Bantu and semi-Bantu languages spoken in Africa today.

I have the most intimate practical knowledge of African languages of any man, white or black,

and also have a Ph. D. in African Linguistics
from the University of Berlin. My doctoral thesis
(unpublished so far) was in fact derived from
what I learned indirectly from Mubaniga. I got
so I could understand some small part of what
he muttered to himself, and I established a
linguistic connection between proto-Bantu and
the language of a small inland New Guinea tribe
I had come across during World War II. My
thesis was that the Negroids had originated in
southeastern Asia, possibly in some parts of
southeastern India, and had spread out in two
directions. One branch had migrated to Africa
and evolved into the Negro types we know now;
the other had migrated to New Guinea and Mel-
anesia and evolved into the types now existing.
Those who had stayed in the land of origin had
been absorbed into the Caucasoid and Mongol-
oid population.

Mubaniga, of course, had been born long after
the migrations had taken place, even if he was
twenty to twenty-five thousand years old. But he
remembered the legends and the myths and the
folk tales about those migrations in the days
when there was a land bridge between south
Arabia and Africa.

The Negroes had been diverted southward by
the whites who lived in North Africa and had
killed or absorbed the ancestors of the Hotentots
and Bushmen.

My thesis was almost rejected. I knew it was
based on valid evidence, but I could not produce
Mubaniga as my witness. But the German doc-
tors finally agreed that I did have some slight

linguistic evidence, enough to call it brilliant but not really conclusive.

So now ancient Mubaniga sat before me and looked at me with eyes as fiery cold as a leopard's. He could speak a wretched English but addressed me in Swahili, which he spoke a little better. My own Swahili is perfect.

"At last," he said, "you have come to the end of the long road. Long for you, I suppose, but it seems a short one to me."

He could say that without contradiction.

I shrugged and said, "Once you're dead, what's the difference whether you have lived thirty thousand years or were born dead? To you, there is no difference. And if I have come to the end of my road, yours is not too far off."

Mubaniga cackled. He held up the activator and said, "Since the end is so close for me, I might as well press this. It will remove you and me and everybody in this tent and quite a few people outside."

Murtagh must have understood Swahili, because he drew in air with a hiss and paled.

The ancient put down the activator, though he kept his hand on it. He said, "You would have made a fine man to sit at the table. You are as cunning as the hare and as strong as the leopard, and you have a hyena's ability to survive. You might have sat at the table for thirty thousand years, as Anana has. But no, you had to throw away all that just because you could not stomach some deeds which have no significance for immortals. Don't you know that these people you pity will all be dead within a few years? Nothing you can do to them can really hurt them or deserves your pity. The only important thing is that you will live almost forever. What happens to the others does not matter."

"I understand the philosophy," I said. "But Caliban and I have self-respect, and we were choking on what you were shoving down our throats."

He shrugged and said, "Other candidates have felt the same way, and they died because they tried to fight us."

He spoke in Swahili to Murtagh. "You won't have to use the drugs to find out where Caliban is. Our agents have seen him in Gramzdorf, West Germany. But it is evident that both of them have an organization they're using against us. You will extract all the information from Grandrith about this. And then you will go to Germany to take charge of the hunt there, unless Caliban is caught before you are through with Grandrith, of course."

"Thank you very much, sir," Murtagh said. The only visible effect the news had was to slightly increase the sidewise oscillations of his head.

Mubaniga smiled and said, "You may thank me within the next hour, if you can."

Murtagh's oscillations stopped for a minute. I thought that his skin became even paler. I did not know what Mubaniga meant, but I soon found out. Contrary to what I'd expected, I was not at once conducted to a tent where the drugs would be injected. Instead, I was fed at noon, and then was conducted to one side of the clearing. A chair was brought outside for Mubaniga. He still held the activator. About forty feet before us were twenty-five eight-foot high posts. I was led toward the posts but was stopped by my guards ten feet from them.

Then Murtagh and twenty-four men, all stripped to the waist, were led out under guard. Smith, the radio operator whose life I'd spared, was among them. They faced the posts while their hands were tied above them to the tops. A man whose name I later found out was Greenrigg approached them with a long whip. He was six feet six and weighed probably three hundred. He had a paunch of no great size and a sheathing of fat, but if he had dieted he still would have weighed two hundred and seventy.

He raised the whip at a signal from Mubaniga. The first lash was on Murtagh's back and brought blood from a deep gash. Greenrigg then went on to the next man and down the line. He returned to Murtagh for the second round. Ten lashes were delivered to all except Smith. By then, some men were screaming and some were groaning and some had fainted. Murtagh stood upright and silent, and when he was untied he walked slowly and dignifiedly to the medical tent to have his wounds treated and bandaged. The others, however, were not permitted to leave immediately. They had to watch Greenrigg whip Smith until he died. No one told me why he was treated so, but I knew enough of the Nine to guess why. He had allowed himself to be taken prisoner by an enemy of the Nine, and they did not know what,

if anything, he had told me. They could have
found out by using the drugs they planned for
me. But this would have taken time. Besides it
was a good object lesson to the others to kill him
so painfully.

Murtagh had not been relieved of his position,
since he had attained the Nine's goal. But he had
not conducted the operation to the complete satisfaction of the Nine and so must pay. Undoubtedly, if he did not do any better with Caliban, he
might lose his candidate's position or even his
life.

One of the men who had not been whipped
because he had not been a member of the original force made a mistake. He taunted Murtagh
with his inefficiency. Murtagh pulled out his automatic and put a .45 into his heart. Mubaniga
said nothing about this. Murtagh was within his
rights. He had paid for his mistakes and, since
he had not been demoted, he was to be treated
with the respect due an officer of the Nine.

I was immediately chained down by the legs
to an eyebolt in the floor of one of the small helicopters. Murtagh and two others accompanied
me. We lifted up while Mubaniga stood by the
door of the big copter and watched us. The last
I saw of him was a small black-faced white-
suited figure. I wondered if I would ever see him
again, and hoped that if I did I would be holding
his neck between my hands. Even in that situation, I was still an optimist. I was not yet dead.

We flew about five hundred feet above the solid green roof for two hundred miles and then
landed by the side of a strip cut out of the forest.

We were transferred to a two-jet British plane which held six passengers. I was again chained by my leg irons to an eyebolt in the floor, but my hands were cuffed before me. Murtagh, I noticed, had the activator back. It must have been handed to him just before he stepped into the copter. He was not likely to use it on the plane, but I was even less likely to have a chance to force him to use it.

We ate. Night came. I slept. A man called my name, and I awoke just before the jet began to let down for a landing. This strip had also been cut out of rain forest. It originally had been a fairly level land at the bottom of a valley. From the high mountains around us, the valley might still be far above sea level. The jet had to come in between two mountains forming a narrow pass and the strip itself was almost to the sides of the precipitous walls. There was barely room for the jet to taxi around so it could take off.

The strip was brilliantly lit, however, and a number of men, mostly blacks, received us. We got into a jeep and drove on a narrow road by the side of the strip out of the valley and to the right around the mountain. This took us up along the mountain. The driver, a Zanzibarian wearing a fez, sped like a maniac along the dangerous road with the right wheels often a few inches from a sheer drop-off. Finally Murtagh, whose back had been making him wince, told the driver to slow down. Murtagh was not suffering as much as he would if he had not been a servant of the Nine. The ointment was swiftly healing the lash wounds and deadened most of

the pain. It was another product of Caliban's
genius and would have been a boon to the world
if it could have gotten it. But this, like so many
of Caliban's inventions, was restricted for use
among those who served the Nine. I suppose that
the ancients of the oaken table liked to keep such
things for themselves. Also, if Caliban had been
allowed to reveal a small fraction of his inventions, he would have been the most famous man
in the world. The Nine did not want him publi-
cized. In fact, Caliban's original career as a
brain surgeon at a prominent New York hospital
had been cut short by the Nine. He had attracted too much attention with his great skill
and the new techniques and tools he introduced.

The jeep went along so slowly then that we
could talk easily. Murtagh said, "You answered
every question and we have already radioed the
information. Your men will be scooped up.
Caliban will soon be caught."

"You mean that you drugged me on the
plane?"

The reflection of the headlights from the
grayish mountain walls on our left lit up his features. He smiled and said, "Yes. The drug was
in your food. Even so, you were a reluctant sub-
ject. I had to use all my knowledge to dredge up
the information. But you talked. And the men
you've been using will be taken."

"They had no idea they were fighting the
Nine," I said. "In fact, as far as I know, they
have never heard of the Nine."

He shrugged. "It doesn't matter. They were
helping you against us."

The men had known they could be in great danger if they helped me. They had been well paid, and they were expecting to die if things did not go well. But I still felt that, in some obscure sense, I had betrayed them. Rationally, I knew that I could not have helped talking. Knowing that did not erase a sense of guilt.

His statement that Caliban would soon be caught could not be based on anything I had told him. Caliban has his own organization, and while there was verbal contact between his men and mine, there was no way for Murtagh to find a path leading from my men to Caliban's.

Then I suppressed a groan. Murtagh must have seen some tremor and guessed the thought that made me sick.

"Oh, yes, you told us where your wife was."

He waited. Seeing that I would not reply, he added, "If it's any consolation to you, we'll be bringing her to you. We wouldn't want to separate a man and his wife."

There was always the chance that Clio might get away, but I told only myself that. He was not going to get any satisfaction out of my responses if I could help it.

But I was so furious—though more at myself than at him—that I might have seized him and jumped over the side of the trail and down the mountain, if I had been able. But my hands had been cuffed behind me and my legs were chained to an eyebolt on the jeep floor. And Murtagh and another man held pistols on me.

Murtagh said, "There is no doubt about the great capabilities of yourself and Caliban. Of course, you should have been candidates. But the fact that XauXaz was your grandfather must have been the main reason why you two were picked to fight for his seat."

He could not have known that unless he had questioned me while I was drugged. He was playing a dangerous game, since the Nine did not like inquiries into their personal business. But then any man who qualified as candidate for a seat at the table did not lack guts.

That he felt it necessary to reassure himself that nepotism was the chief basis for the choice of Caliban and me revealed much about his own self-doubts, however. That he could not resist telling me that he knew that XauXaz was our grandfather added more light to his character.

The sky began to pale above the jagged peaks on our right. The road led downward, and by the time we'd reached the bottom of the mountain, dawn had filled the valley. The road went through a semi-desert area. There was so little evidence of rainfall that I wondered if we were near the back parts of the mountains which hid the caverns of the Nine. There is rain forest on all sides of this range, but a freakish climatic condition carries rains over or around the mountains here.

Presently we were stopped by a gate in a wall which blocked the narrow valley. Above the mortared stone ramparts were sentinel towers, and three machine guns and a Bofors rapid-fire cannon stuck out from embrasures. The man on the driver's left got out and stuck a card through a slit in the wall. After a minute, the gates swung open. The jeep drove through; the metal gates, which were twelve feet high, swung shut. The road wound through a camp of the exceedingly light tents. I counted thirty men there and twenty at the wall. Then we were past the tents and going down. The mountains on both sides pressed in.

I had wondered why a copter had not lifted us over or around the mountain. But if this was indeed the rear entrance to the caves, then copters or any aircraft might be forbidden. That did not seem likely. Murtagh, at that moment, answered a call on the radio and at the same time answered my question. Some observers ahead, who were hidden from us, were asking for identification again. The security measures here were very strict indeed, and this was one more piece of evidence that the caves were nearby. Murtagh identified himself and the party and then said something about when copters would arrive. It was evident from the conversation that followed that they were in short supply. I did not know why, but I surmised that important missions (among which may have been my capture) had taken them from this area.

We passed under a projection of gray, red-speckled granite. Holes had been cut in the face and in the bottom of the rock, and from these the white and black faces of guards looked. When I was past the projection, I looked back and upward. About a hundred feet above the outthrust was a dark opening containing armed men. That could be the rear entrance to the caves. The surface of the mountainside was so smooth that I

suspected it was man-made. And from the opening to as high as I could see, the mountain
leaned outward.

A helicopter could not have gotten close
enough to the entrance to deliver passengers.
Some sort of crane would have to drop a lift to
hoist people up. If there was an elevator shaft
within the mountain, its entrance at the base of
the mountain was well-hidden.

The jeep drove on around the shoulder of the
mountain. After two miles on a rough dirt road,
the jeep stopped. Here the mountains were even
closer. The sun would not be seen most of the
day, and at this time a pale twilight filled the
bottom of the valley with a seemingly liquid
light.

The jeep stopped. The men got out. The
chains through the eyebolt were unlocked, and I
was told to get out. We marched down the road,
which was too narrow now for even a jeep to
traverse. After two minutes, we were challenged
again. The post here consisted of four men. A
few feet beyond them, the path stopped. Beyond
was a sheer dropoff of two hundred feet.

A thousand feet to the north, the two mountains merged.

Murtagh shoved his gun into my back and
forced me to the edge. I looked down. The floor
of the canyon was mostly bare rock with a few
plants growing alongside a stream about six feet
wide. The source of the stream was a small lake
at the extreme end, and this derived from a
spring, I supposed. The water ran down the
middle of the canyon floor and then disappeared

in the base of the cliff on which I stood. The only signs of habitation were three small huts built of stone halfway along the eastern wall.

A motor roared to my right. I turned to see a truck backing out of a cave. Its bed held a crane and a large drum of cable. At the end of the cable was a sling of leather. Evidently, I was supposed to sit in it so I could be lowered to the bottom of the canyon.

Murtagh, his face moving slightly from side to side, his thin lips pulled back to show long yellow teeth, watched while my cuffs were removed. I flexed my arms and did some knee bends. Then, at a gesture from him, I got into the sling. I could do nothing with all those guns aimed at me. The truck backed up until its wheels were close to the edge of the precipice, and I hung in the air past the edge. The motor and the cable drum worked, and I was lowered swiftly to the bottom. While I went down, I noted that the sides of the canyon inclined outward and were very smooth. If there had been any roughnesses which could be used for handholds, or any projections, they had been removed.

I got out of the sling, and it rose up quickly. Faces sticking out over the edge were small white or black pie plates. This hole was to be my prison until the day of judgment. Evidently they were not worried that I would try to kill myself. They knew me well enough.

I smelled the water and tasted it. It seemed to be excellent drinking water. I started walking along the stream. When I came to a point opposite the stone huts, I stopped. I smelled a human female and that of another creature which I could not identify for a moment. Then the hackles on my neck rose, or felt as if they did, and I growled automatically. A male of The Folk was inside the hut.

A woman stuck her head out of the hut and seeing me, called, "James!" She stepped out then, but I knew who she was as soon as I heard her voice. She was the six-foot one-inch high titian-haired beauty, the Danish Countess Clara Aekjaer. The last time I had seen her was at the annual ceremony eight months ago. She was dressed exactly as she had been then. She had no makeup, but she really did not need any.

She walked toward me with all the "vibrations made free" that Eve must have had for Adam. She was smiling as if she thought I had come to deliver her from this place.

I could not pay much attention to her just then because I was concentrating on the occupant of the other hut. He had stuck his head out, confirming what my sense of smell had informed me.

I did not know him, which was not surprising, since The Folk of the mountains in eastern Africa have always been very few and very shy. In fact, I had thought they were now extinct, with the possible exception of one female. Eight months ago, I had been forced to kill a male, $st\text{-}tb^h$ or Leopard-Breaker, as the name translates somewhat freely. He was the last male of his species, I had thought, and since his child was dying, his female would die without issue. But here was a big and apparently healthy male.

He came out into the twilight which filled the box canyon and stood before the entrance of the stone hut for a moment. He was about six feet three and probably carried three hundred and eighty pounds on that massive skeleton. Long russet hairs covered a dark brown skin. Actually, he had fewer hairs than a human, just as a chimpanzee has fewer, but their length made him seem hairier. His body was humanoid except for the relatively shorter legs and longer arms. His feet were not those of ape's but more like the feet of Neanderthal Man. He had the rounded buttocks and pelvic structure which would cause an anthropologist to unhesitatingly classify him as hominid. He never walked on fours, like a gorilla, as my biographer described the walking posture of The Folk. But my biographer did not know all the facts when he wrote the first two volumes of my life and so drew more on his imagination than on anything. Later, though he discovered his error, he clung to it to maintain consistency.

The neck was thick and powerful. The face was, at first glance, gorilloid, and I suppose a layman would continue to think of it as so after a long familiarity with it. Though I can't imagine any human except myself wanting to maintain close contact with it unless there were bars between him and the male. The immense ridges of bone above the eyes, the flat, wide-nostriled nose, the protruding jaws, the undeveloped chin, the thin black lips, and the long yellow canines, plus the low forehead and the roach of hair on top of his head would have frightened, or at least made uneasy, most humans. He looked much like the reconstructions of Paranthropus, the big vegetarian hominid that lived a million years ago in East Africa. He was basically vegetarian, too, but his teeth were more like those of the gorilla, who is not a meat eater. But The Folk eat meat whenever they can get it. He's an anomaly because his teeth are more apish than human, yet his brain is larger than a gorilla's. And he has a language. He is the living basis of African folk tales, a giant variety of the little hairy men the East African natives call *agogwe*.

He rolled toward me, swaying from side to side, his arms hanging loose but the huge black-brown hands working. His paunch stuck out before him, and the massive chest rose and fell swiftly.

I spoke to him in the whispering speech of The Folk. He stopped and blinked, then continued. I spoke again. He stopped again, and he said, "What language is that?"

I was astonished. No wonder. He spoke English. The pronunciation was not accurate, but the structure of his mouth would prevent the exact reproduction of a number of English phones. And he often did not voice his vowels of *u* in *untamed* or *o* in *son* or the second *a* in *galaxy*. But he spoke as fluently as if English were his native tongue, which it was. He had never heard the speech of The Folk before.

His bearing was not aggressive. I had just assumed it was, since all male of The Folk, on meeting strangers, act belligerently whether they feel so or not. He was merely approaching me to talk to me and was prepared to speak English or Swahili.

What he could not explain, Clara could. Twenty years ago, an agent of the Nine had brought him in when he was a few days old. The mother had died of some disease. Under direct orders of the Nine, Dick, as he was called, had been raised with the children of two Kenyans who were agents for the Nine. He had lived a good part of his twenty years on the edge of the rain forest of the mountains along the east Congo border. When he was twelve, he had been sent to this area.

For what purpose?

"Ah, James," Clara said, putting her long-fingered hand on my arm, "I suspect the Nine thought they would have some use for him eventually. And the eventual has come. I think they mean to put you two together in an arena of some sort, where you will be torn to pieces, if things work out as they expect."

"Is that true?" I said to Dick.

"I don't know," he said. "A man kept calling me names and throwing stones at me when he thought I wasn't looking. And he put stuff in my food to make me sick. I didn't see him do it, but I knew he did it. He hated me for some reason, though I had never done anything to him. I complained to my superior, and he told the man to lay off me. But this man, Scannon, he kept on bugging me. So, one day, when I crawled into bed and found a poisonous snake there, with no way for it to get there unless someone put it in my bed, I got very angry. I hit Scannon. I didn't mean to kill him, but I broke his jaw and his neck. And they put me down here, even though I told them it wasn't my fault."

It was strange to hear one of The Folk speaking English. Actually, though he was born of them, he could not be considered one of The Folk in any except a genetic sense.

Clara said, "I don't think he was put down here because he killed Scannon. That was just an excuse."

"And what do you think?"

"I think he's our jailor. Yours, rather, since they wouldn't really expect me to be able to escape from this place. And I think that it would be just like the Nine to pit Dick against you for their own amusement."

She could be right. On the other hand, he could be telling the truth, and *she* could have been set here to keep an eye on me. Or not so much to watch me as to pump me for information that Murtagh and the drug hadn't been able to get. The drug works well, but the one being questioned gives very restricted answers. And if the questioner doesn't ask the proper question, and word them just right, he isn't going to get much. Perhaps the Nine, knowing my fondness for Clara, hoped she would get me to talking.

I didn't ask her why she was imprisoned, expecting that she would volunteer soon enough. And so she did, though with a tone of exasperation at my seeming lack of curiosity.

She had been sent on a mission for the Nine to Rio de Janeiro. But she had delayed leaving London immediately because she was in love with an Englishman. So she had been drugged and put into a plane and shipped here. She supposed she would be an object lesson for the servants of the Nine in some hideous fashion. She did not seem to be frightened at the prospect, but Clara was a very courageous woman. Or perhaps she just did not care. She was a wild woman, one who lived intensely for every moment and was reckless of consequences. But she was intelligent and she must know what could be in store for her. Also, she could be a plant, as I said.

"You knew what would happen if you did not follow orders at once," I said. "You really have no one but yourself to blame."

"But I was passionately in love!" she cried.

I smiled. Clara was always in love, although she seldom stayed in that state long with one man.

At noon, the food was lowered to us in a net tied to the cable. We were given no utensils to use, on the theory that they might be adapted to make tools or weapons, I suppose. The food was good, though cooked too much for my taste. Dick was given meat along with the bamboo shoots, nuts, berries, and bananas. During the meal, I asked him if he wished to join me in an attempt to escape. It did not hurt to ask him, I thought, since even if he had been placed there to watch me, I would be expected to try escaping. And if he relayed the information to my captors, he would have to be quick and sly about it to get by me.

The same reasoning applied to Clara.

"Yes," Dick said, peering out from under the massive frontal bones. "I want to escape. These are bad men. But where do we go? Even if we can get away, which we can't."

That was difficult to answer. He certainly couldn't settle down with any group of natives I knew. They would kill him or sell him to scientists. He could not go into the wilds, because he did not know how to survive there. He would have been as lost and helpless as a European astray in the rain forest.

"Well," I said, "if those canines were removed, and you were shaved all over and put into a suit of clothes, you might be able to pass for an unusually ugly specimen of humanity—no offense intended. You could make a fortune as a wrestler or boxer. I could introduce you to an honest manager, relatively honest, anyway. But you wouldn't be happy there, and sooner or later some zoologist would look closely at you, and the game would be up. Besides, city life would sicken you, you couldn't stand the gas fumes, the factory stinks, the noise, the crowds, but . . ."

I shouldn't have told him all that. I needed him, and it wouldn't help any to discourage him with the truth. If he had been a human being, I would have lied to him. But he was one of The Folk, and even though I have loved only two members of that genus, tolerated some others, and hated most, I could not lie to this simple trusting soul. That is, if he was as open and simple as he seemed to be. I had to remind myself that he could be a cunning agent for the Nine.

"There was a time when you could have lived with me on my plantation in Kenya," I said. "But I lost that, and I can't ever return to Kenya, not unless I'm disguised. But I'll think of something. The important thing is to get out of here. As soon as possible."

"If anyone could do it, you could," Clara said. "Or maybe Caliban. But nobody can. You'd have to be a bird to get out of here."

At dusk our supper was lowered. We went into a stone hut to eat and talk. There was no furniture there except for a pail to throw our garbage into. Our only bedding was a pile of old blankets, but these sufficed to keep us warm, with the help of each other's body heat. Back of the hut was a latrine ditch. As soon as night fell, and it fell early here, while the sky, three thousand feet above, was still a dark blue, we left the hut. The south end was lit by powerful beams, and a searchlight probed the valley. But we walked to the far north end, ignoring the light when it followed us. I plunged into the pool, sixty feet long and thirty wide, at the base of the northern wall. The water was icy, but I waded waist-deep until I got near to the wall, where I had to dive down. There were several openings in the rock through which water bubbled. But all were too small for me to get into.

After thoroughly exploring the bottom, I got out. I ran all the way to the other end to dry myself and warm up. Dick and Clara followed me at a brisk walk.

I was visible to the men above in the lights glaring down. They could see what I was doing,

and if they wished to stop me, they had the
means. But I think they were just laughing at
me. I went into the tiny pool there and dived
down to the bottom. This was about thirty feet
deep, and the water flowed through an opening
about six feet across. But a thick metal screen
had been affixed to the rock with many metal
spikes. I tugged at the screen about a dozen
times, coming up for air each time. By the time
I gave up, I was half-frozen, and it took me a
long time to stop shivering. Somebody at the top
of the cliff hooted at me for my efforts.

However, I did not feel that I had been foolish
or wasted my time. That they had felt it necessary to screen the hole indicated that the hole
might be an escape route.

After I had gotten warm under the blankets
between Clara and Dick, I crawled out. Dick
wanted to sleep; despite being raised by humans, he was one of The Folk in being unable to
look far into the future. I told him he might lose
more sleep before we got out of this, and if we
didn't, he'd have as long to sleep as anybody
ever wished for. Grumbling, he followed me out.
We sneaked past the probing searchlight to the
detritus of flint I had seen at the northeast corner. Apparently, it had fallen there when a projection was blown off about fifty feet up.

Since there was no light, I could not work the
flint. But when dawn came, I went to the door of
the hut with a blanket over my shoulders. By the
dim light there, I hammered and chipped away
until I had several handaxes, long stabbing
knives, scrapers, and choppers. I had learned the

techniques from a French anthropologist who was once a guest at Grandrith Manor.

"What do you plan to do with your Early Paleolithic weapons, my cave man?" Clara said.

"I don't know yet," I said. That was true, but if I had a plan, I would not have told her until just before I initiated it.

"Well, at least you're keeping out of mischief."

The day passed just like it had before, except that Dick and I dived down to the bottom of the outlet pool and strove to pull the screen loose. When we came up for air, we could look up and see the faces of our guards there. They did not fire down to drive us away. It may be they felt there was no slightest chance of our loosening the screen. And if we wanted to exercise and to provide them with some slight amusement in a deadly dull job, so be it.

We gave up after a dozen dives. If our combined strength could not pull a corner of the screen loose with our bare hands, then tools were needed. I spent the rest of the day traveling around the base of the canyon and examining the walls. The northeast corner formed an almost square junction. By putting my back against one wall and pushing with my feet against the other, at a difficult angle, I might be able to inch my way up for the first hundred feet. After that the walls leaned slightly outward until, near the top, they were at an angle of about eighty-two degrees from the horizontal. The corner still maintained its squareness, but I would have to exert a tremendous pressure to keep from falling. I was not sure at all that I could do it.

As far as I could tell, there were no guards on that side.

Two hours before dusk, two men holding rapid-fire rifles were lowered. They stood guard while their officer, a Lal Singh, rode down. Then two other riflemen rode down. Then a man with scuba gear.

We three prisoners were allowed to stand within forty feet and watch them. The scubamen came up with a satisfactory report. Then our huts were examined. They did not find the flint weapons because I had hidden them beneath the surface of the north pool. The scubamen did not look into that pool. Evidently they knew that I could do nothing there.

After making searches at random in other parts of the canyon, they left. Just before he was hauled away, I asked Singh what had happened to Murtagh. He did not reply. I surmised that Murtagh had been sent to Germany after Caliban. Probably nothing would be done with me until he was killed or captured. But I could not bank on that. If Clio was caught and brought here, the Nine might think there were enough victims for a Roman holiday.

As soon as it was dark, I sneaked out and cut down some of the hardwood bushes. I trimmed them off and sharpened their points. I still did not know what to do with them, but if a situation arose where they would be handy, they would be waiting and ready. And they could be used as pitons, if I found a big enough crack.

I wanted to tell Clara and Dick what I

planned. If their stories were true, then they should be with me. I did not think that Clara, strong though she was, could manage that climb. Dick was powerful enough, stronger than me, but he was also much heavier. And I just could not chance that they were spies. That the men had come down to search the area did not mean that either of my fellow prisoners had informed on me, of course. Almost everything I had done had been visible. And if my flint tools had been discovered, I might have suspected that I had been betrayed. No, they would say nothing about the flint.

An hour after nightfall, I slipped out from the blankets. Clara and Dick both stirred, and Dick said something, in Swahili, in his sleep. I stood there for a while, made sure they were deeply asleep, or else pretending to be, and left with my sticks. I waited a while by a bush to see if anybody would follow me. No one did. The beams probed around at random. I avoided them, went to the north pool, and recovered my flint weapons.

Before starting the climb, I had to get rid of the plastic bomb stuck to my belly with epoxy glue. I began chipping away at it with a flint dagger. The disc had a two-inch diameter and was two-tenths of an inch thick. The plastic was very hard and not easy to get at because of its snug position between my belly and the metal belt, which was two inches broad. I had to bring the flint down with considerable force to chip away the plastic. For all I knew, the concussion would set it off, though it did not seem likely that an unstable explosive would be used.

As I found out, the plastic was a rather thin shell around a tiny radio receiver and the tiny chemical detonating cylinder attached to the receiver. The problem became ticklish when I got to the detonator—not literally, of course. It was probable that a hard blow could set that off. So I pried away around it. The darkness and the angle at which I had to look at it made the task more difficult.

But, eventually, I pried both receiver and detonator loose and dropped them into the pool.

A shell of plastic was still adhering to my belly. It would have to stay there until I was able to find a chemical to cancel the bondage of the glue. And the belt was too tight for me to wriggle out of.

I had torn a strip of blanket off earlier that day. I tied this around my waist and shoved two daggers and six short sticks into a fold of the cloth. Since I would be bent forward with my back against the one wall and my legs drawn up with my feet against the other, I would keep the stone and wood from falling out.

The stone only got warmed up in winter time when the sun was directly overhead, and it lost its heat quickly. The skin of my back felt cold, at first. Later, as friction between skin and rock increased, the skin got too warm. And, of course, my back started to bleed. I left a trail of blood on the cliffwall as if I were some slug dying of hemorrhage.

To ease the rubbing away and cutting of the skin, I went slowly. But I got to the final fifty feet within an estimated twenty minutes. By then the strain was beginning to affect me. The pressure I had to maintain was draining my strength, and I was losing more blood than I had expected. Or at least it felt as if I were. The juncture of the two walls did not afford a perfect corner of a square. The walls were at oblique angles which varied, and this meant that often one leg had to be stretched out much further than the other. The unequal pressure sometimes brought me close to an uncontrollable shaking of my left leg.

Meantime, the beams continued to probe through the canyon, and several times they passed directly over me. When the cone got close, I stopped moving. The light, weak at this distance, did not reveal me to the men on the cliff, if they were watching. They must have been convinced that no one could escape. For all I know, the searchlight was operated by a machine, and they only occasionally looked down from their card games or whatever occupied them.

I began the ascent on the part that projected outward. From that time on, I was like a fly on a ceiling. I had to be even more of a living wedge, one which proceeded by minute movements. The sliding of feet and the inching along of my back succeeded each other very slowly and very painfully. Now I bled more profusely, and my back became more slippery. The closer I got to the top, the more the cliff leaned outward. The only compensation for this was that the juncture of the two walls became more of an acute angle and thus gave me a better hold. I had planned on

that, of course. If the corner had not become
more narrow, I don't think I would have tried
the climb. But the lesser space squeezed me
down as if I were an embryo trying to give birth
to myself.

I scraped across several narrow cracks in the
rock but did not try to drive in any sticks as
pitons. I did not need them, but when I got to
the lip of the cliff, I might.

It seemed hours, but it must have been only
fifteen minutes that it took me to get up the last
fifty feet. Then I was hanging over the ground,
wedged in tightly, with the edge of the cliff just
above me. And here, where I was closest to safe-
ty, I was in the most danger. To reach up and
over to clamp a hand down on the edge meant
that I had to lose my grip on the corner. I could
not leap out, because that would take me away
from the edge. The only thing I could do was to
reach up, place my hand on the lip, which was
solid rock, let loose and hang by one hand, then
reach up with the other, and pull myself up and
over.

First, I had to get my daggers and sticks onto
the edge, if I could. Otherwise, when I straightened out, they would fall out of the fold. This
required a slow withdrawal of them, one by one,
from the fold, and a quick throw with a looping
motion. The two flint knives clinked on the edge.
Two sticks also got onto the top, but four
bounced off and fell. They seemed to be striking
something.

Then, without hesitation, I reached up, bent
my hand so it was at right angles to my arm,

spread the fingers out on the rough granitic stone, and let my body sag. I could not kick myself away because my grip was too precarious. Everything had to be done quickly, yet not violently. I swung out, and my weight started to pull my hand loose, since it had nothing to hold onto but was depending on pressure alone. And even though the rock was rough, it was not knobby. The surface friction was not much.

Despite my agonized efforts with my one hand, the hand slid away, tearing off skin against the rock. I reached up with the other hand, and got its palm flat against the rock, too. For a moment I hung there, and then I lifted myself up with a slow straining that made the muscles of my back, too long tense, crack as if they were splitting wood. When my chin was above the ledge, I used it to hold me up too. In fact, my chin supported the full weight of my body for about twenty seconds while I slid my arms forward until they were fully extended and flat against the surface.

Then, scraping the skin of my chest, I inched upward and over, my fingers digging into the rock, pulling me along like the legs of Lilliputian horses. Once my chest was fully over, I kicked with my legs, and gave a final convulsive effort that pulled me up and over the edge. To crawl all the rest of the way was easy, but it seemed to take a long time.

For some time, I lay there gasping for air. The cold air made me shiver, because I was covered with sweat and with blood on my back, my hands, my chin, and my chest.

When my breathing became regular, I sat up. Just ahead of me was a six-foot high rise of rock, a tiny cliff. It was against this that the four spinning sticks had struck and bounced back and fallen over the edge. The two knives had fallen close to the edge, and I had been forced to slide over them when I pulled myself over. They had ground into my chest, but they had not cut me.

I got up, stuck the one knife and the sticks into the cloth belt, held one knife in my hand, and started to work my way along the thin ridge of the canyon top. Close at hand were the higher walls of the mountains, and I could have tried to climb them to get away. If my suspicions that this area was the back end to the caves were correct, I could go over the mountains eastward and eventually get to the front entrance. Or I could take off to the west and be out of the dry desert area and into rain-forest covered mountains where the Nine would have no chance of tracking me down.

But my original intention had been to locate and spy on the back entrance to the caves. Having familiarized myself with it, I was to meet Caliban in Europe, or wherever we could, and then we would plan our campaign. Our idea was to attack the caves during the annual ceremonies, when we knew that all of the Nine would be there. Just how our small force was to make an effective attack was something we had not yet worked out.

I had given myself about a month and a half to traverse the central part of Africa on foot, from the coast of Gabon to these mountains. Due to my enemies' participation, I had arrived six weeks sooner than planned.

The moon sailed directly over the gap between the two mountains. I slid along like a ghost from shadow to shadow, hugging the base of the mountain with the top of the box canyon a few inches to my right. I also kept watching for mines or booby-traps, but if there were any along here, I was lucky and missed them.

It took me about an hour to get to the south end of the canyon. There were times when the ledge narrowed to nothing and I had to feel along with my face pressed against the rock, my toes groping for projections, my fingers hanging onto knobs and in fissures. Then the ledge came back to existence again, and I moved swiftly.

The battery of lights along the south end was directed downward, but there was enough reflection to reveal me when I got close to the end. I went swiftly, hoping that none of the guards would see me during my brief passage.

There were four. One was sitting on a chair by the big probing searchlight, which was, as I had suspected, randomly directed by a machine. He was bundled up and drinking coffee from a thermos. Two men were in the cab of the truck. Its motor was running, so that the heater could be operated, I presumed. The fourth man was inside a tent with all flaps closed. His head and shoulders were behind a small plastic window in the side. He seemed to be at a desk, reading something.

I took the man in the chair on the edge of the cliff first. It was easy, since the truck was facing away from him, and the two men in the cab were looking away. If one had looked into a rear view mirror, he might have seen me, but that was a chance I had to take.

I did not use my flint knife. I came from behind, gripped the man's head, and twisted. The crack of the snapping spine was sharp, but no one seemed to have heard it. I relieved the man of his knife and his belt, which held ammunition and a holster with a .38 automatic. There was also a Bren machine gun by the chair.

The knife had good balance. I pulled aside the flap of the tent; the man looked around to see who it was; then he jumped up, whirling. I threw the knife, and it went deep into this throat, shutting off his cry.

The tent held a desk and a shelf full of paperbacks, a coffee-making machine, and a shortwave radio. There were also automatic rifles and boxes of ammunition, magazines, a medicine chest, tins of food, biscuits, and a small gas stove of the Caliban type.

I munched on several biscuits and drank a cup of hot coffee, which I love. Then I went out to the truck.

I was the last thing the two men expected. They must have been tough to have been selected to work for the Nine. But one man stuttered, he was so flabbergasted. The other's voice shook. Both rallied quickly enough. By the time they had gotten out of the cab, one following the other out of the left side, their hands clasped on the backs of their necks, they were tense and wary-eyed. I made them lean forward with their hands against the side of the truck, their legs and arms stiff, and then I used my knife on one. The one who had stuttered I spared.

Under my directions, he backed the truck up and then showed me how to operate the cable, and then I cuffed his hands before him. I made him sit in the cradle at the end of the cable, and then told him what he must do if he wanted to live. I had to get into the truck then, and he could have tried to swing back onto the ground and run for a rifle. But he preferred not to try for a hero's grave, and he sat still while he was lowered into the canyon. I had to get out of the truck twice to check on how far down he was. Then he trotted away toward the stone huts. After a while, the huge dark figure of Dick and the blanket-wrapped figure of Clara appeared. Getting them back up took some time but eventually it was done. The man stayed in the stone hut; I assume to make sure that I did not try to shoot him.

Clara got into the clothes of a man I'd killed. They fitted fairly well, although the boots were too large. Dick put on a coat which restricted his movements but did warm him up. They drank coffee and spooned out hot thick soup while we talked in the tent. I watched them closely, because I still did not trust them. It would have been more realistic, from my viewpoint, to leave them in the canyon, since they could be very dangerous. But, like most human beings, I am not always realistic. I value friendship and love, and I have more concern for individual human beings than my biographer indicated. However, he was basing his evaluations on my early attitudes, when I had not yet adjusted to human society and still thought of myself as one of The Folk. I can be, from a civilized point of view, horrible, but that is only when I am dealing with my enemies.

Clara put one of Caliban's quick-healing and very soothing ointments on my torn and abraded skin, and then I fitted myself out in clothes as well as I could. Clara and Dick found my story of how I had escaped almost unbelievable, but that I had rescued them and therefore had gotten out of the canyon was undeniable.

We loaded the jeep with food and ammunition. Our plan for getting away was sketchy. We would just have to drive up to the main camp and improvise from then on. If I had been alone I would have tried to find out how to get into the caves themselves, but my immediate duty was to get Dick and Clara into the rain forest. From then on, as far as I was concerned, they would be on their own, and I could return to this area.

I kept the pistol and the Bren handy at all times, and my knife was loose in its sheath. My main concern was treachery on Dick's part. Clara could be dangerous enough, but Dick, combining the enormous strength and quickness of a gorilloid hominid with all the human skills of karate and boxing and knowledge of firearms, could be the most deadly antagonist I had ever faced. So far, he had acted as if he were just what he said he was. But I wasn't going to turn my back on him.

Dick was quite capable of driving a jeep. In

fact, I doubt that he could not handle anything mechanical that a human could handle. My conversations with him had been necessarily limited to practical matters, so I did not know how capable he was of really abstract thought. His brain was small, but the size of the brain is not an index of intelligence. Nor did it matter that he might not be able to appreciate the subtleties of Plato or Spinoza, Shakespeare or Joyce. How many humans can?

Clara sat in the front seat beside Dick. I was in the back seat. She drove at about twenty mph with the headlights on. We passed the cliff with the carved entrance a hundred feet up. The men stationed at the foot of the cliff did not come out to challenge us, nor was there any reason except excessive caution to make them do so. The road we were on was about sixty yards from the cliff base.

After a quarter of a mile, passing between cliffs so close we could almost reach out and touch them, we came into the open area of the main camp. There were lights at regular intervals around its perimeters; these came from lamps hung from poles. The tents all had closed flaps except one at the south end of the camp. There were four guards there, two on each side of the road, and an officer sitting at a desk within the tent.

Clara slowed down. We would stop—if we were challenged. If we were not, we would proceed at the same slow pace as long as nobody objected. The only illumination at this point came from the large lamps strung along a wire

between two posts. They were quite bright, however, and it would be easy for the guards to see
that Clara was a woman and that Dick was the
man-ape.

I was hoping that the guards would be frozen
by surprise for a least a few seconds. And so they
were. Dick and Clara did not shout out a warning. But then they knew that I could easily blow
both their heads off if they did.

A guard stepped in front of us, calling to us to
halt, and then his eyes widened. Clara opened
up with her automatic rifle on her right, as I had
directed. I fired with my Bren to my left. Clara
got the guard before us and the one on the right.
I spun the two other guards around and brought
up the fire, hose fashion, across the ground and
then up. The officer had jumped up and started
to run out through the front of the tent. My
bullets caught him in the legs and then the
belly.

Nobody at this point was going to stop us, but
I wished it had been worked out otherwise. Now
the men at the wall that ran from cliffside to cliffside would be alerted. And they could swivel
their machine guns and Bofors rapidfire cannon
around to face us and undoubtedly were doing
so even now.

And the firing had also alerted the main camp
behind us.

I should have sneaked around behind the tent
and tried to get the drop on the guards while the
jeep, with Clara and Dick, approached them.
But I could not do that because I would have put
myself in front of the jeep and the fire of Clara
and Dick. I might have tried to keep the guards

between me and the jeep, but if either Clara or Dick were loyal to the Nine, he or she would have been capable of killing his own men in order to get me.

Clara and Dick got out of the jeep and preceded me into the tent. There were loaded automatic rifles, and bazooka tubes with racks of rockets in the rear, and light machine guns on tripods, and hand grenades in the rear. I told Dick and Clara to slip the straps of their rifles over their shoulders so they could take a bazooka and several rockets. I could keep their hands occupied with the tube and the missiles. Dick took the tube. He said he did not know how to operate bazookas, but Clara said she knew all about them.

I attached about ten grenades to hooks on my belt so that all I had to do was to jerk them off to arm them. I yanked the phone wires loose from the short pole behind the tent. We got back into the jeep with me in the back seat again and drove until we were about an eighth of a mile from the wall. We stopped at the bottom of a dip which completely hid us, and Dick and Clara got out ahead of me. Both were sweating heavily with tension, and there was an additional element in Dick's sweat. I could not identify it then, but if I ever smell it again in one of The Folk, I'll know the odor of treachery.

The two searchlights on top of the wall ahead of us were swinging back and forth. No doubt the officer there had phoned into the camp, but they could not tell him anything as yet. When they got to the guard tent, they would know, and they would then switch to wireless.

Dick got down on one knee with the level of the road even with his chest. Clara loaded a rocket in. I fired a burst at both searchlights, and they went out. I shouted, Clara activated the rocket, and, its tail flaming, it arced down the road. It struck dead center and blew the gate apart. Clara immediately loaded and shot another one, this time at the fire-spitting muzzle of the Bofors. Its explosive shells danced across the earth but not directly at us. The rocket struck the wall below the gun emplacement, but it must have killed the crew.

The cannon started shooting again about thirty seconds later. Clara and Dick ducked down to load a third time. I stood up, firing at the dark area immediately around the Bofors until its shells were exploding fifty yards from me, and then I dived for cover.

We were lucky. One shell blew up near the edge of the dip and deafened us and covered us with a spray of dirt and a cloud of smoke. The shell just after it hit the edge behind us at such an angle that it struck a little distance beyond the edge. This explosion showered us, too, and increased our deafness, and, for a moment, numbed us. But I got to my knees, with my Bren pointed at Dick and Clara, and gestured. Even though it was dark, there was enough light from the lamps still operating along the wall for them to make out what I was doing. They got up and loaded and fired, just as the Bofors stopped. There was a heavy fire from two machine guns on one side and one from another—apparently the bazooka had taken out two machine guns, too—and about six automatic rifles.

They were firing blindly, fortunately, and when our fourth and last rocket struck, their fire was momentarily stopped. Clara was a superb bazookist. She placed that rocket just below the Bofors, and it disappeared in a cloud of smoke. We jumped back into the jeep then and roared up out of the dip, headed straight for the shattered gate. Clara fired with her rifle at the machine gun on her side, and I sprayed the left side of the wall. Then I dropped my weapon and threw two grenades in quick succession at the right and the left.

Bullets stitched across the top of the jeep, piercing the hood at an angle from left to right and shattering the glass of the windshield at the extreme upper righthand side, just missing Clara. It seemed impossible to get through that hellish rain. But the grenades disconcerted them and may have killed or wounded some. Clara's cool firing, I am convinced, stopped several riflemen. Then we were through the gate, the jeep crashing into a piece still standing, and sending us off to one side of the road.

That was a touchy time, because now Clara would be entitled to turn around and fire past me. And she only had to move her rifle a little to cut me in two. But I crouched down so that she had to fire over my head and I could keep watch on her rifle out of the corner of my eye.

It was not as bad as it could have been. By the time the machine gunners could swing around, we were two hundred yards away. Two riflemen sent a stream after us; the tracer bullets spun along the ground as the streams swerved toward us. But our fire stopped them for a moment, and by then we were around a corner of the mountain.

After our first turn onto a higher level of the road, I told Dick to stop the jeep. We listened. Behind us was a roaring as of a dozen vehicles on the road, perhaps a half-mile away. Clara slipped forward and peered over the edge of the road.

"I can see their lights," she said. "There are exactly ten vehicles. Two trucks, the rest are jeeps."

"You two go ahead," I said.

They protested, but I said that I was running this ship. I jumped behind a big boulder on the lefthand side of the road, facing downward, so I could get out of line of the fire of Clara and Dick if they tried anything. But Dick drove off with Clara looking backward.

I ran across the road and down the side, slipping and sliding. I got behind a bush about twelve feet up above the road. And I waited. Presently, the first jeep skidded around the corner of the road, and I jerked a grenade loose and lobbed it into the floor of the jeep. I had one each inside the next two jeeps before the first went off. The resultant explosions were quite satisfactory. I did not remain to assess the damage until I had gotten to the edge of the road above. By then the mountainside was bright with burning gasoline from the three vehicles. When I looked over, I saw that the road was blocked for some time. The lead vehicle was on its side, the one behind it was catty-cornered across the road, and the third was rammed nose first into it. If the truck behind them had tried to push them off the road, its crew would have been burned to a crisp. I wished they would try it.

However, the men, under the shouted orders of the officers, were climbing up the sides of the mountain to get to my level of the road. I lobbed four of my five remaining grenades down the slope. That apparently killed or wounded many, because the fire from the survivors was feeble. It was strong enough to kill me if I remained, however, so I retreated up the side to the next level. But I was cautious about doing so, since the light from the burning wrecks was enough to illumine me as a dark figure to anybody above.

I still had one grenade, a .38 automatic with a full clip, a knife, and the Bren. The latter probably had very few rounds left. I had just gone behind a large boulder when I heard a muffled sound from above. It could have been Clara. I crouched for a moment and then there was a bellow of outrage and the clatter of a metallic object striking a rock and then slipping and sliding down the slope against other rocks. It sounded to me as if a rifle had been thrown down the mountain, and as if Dick was mad about this.

There were several interpretations I could put on these sounds. But whoever was in trouble would be needing my help. I went on up, though taking advantage of every bit of cover.

As I got closer, I could hear the shuffle of big feet in the earth of the road, pantings, and a woman muttering something. There was a slight swishing, which I interpreted, correctly, as a knife slashing air.

I stuck my head over the edge of the road. In the faint light cast by the fires far below, Dick was an enormous bulk advancing on Clara. He had his hands out ahead of him to grab her, but she was backing away with her knife slicing at him. The jeep, its headlights out, was a few yards up the road.

I stepped out, the Bren pointed at them, and said, "What's going on?"

They stopped. Dick backed away from her.

They both started talking at the same time. I said, "Ladies first. I mean you, Clara."

As usual, my attempt at humor was ignored or misunderstood. Maybe I should reserve them for situations less tense, but I have always thought that tense situations are those that most need humorous relief.

"This traitor, this thing, was going to shoot you!" she said in French. "I hit him over the head and threw the rifle away. He had no other weapon and I only had a knife handy. I couldn't get to my rifle, which is empty anyway, I think. I was trying to keep him away with my knife when you got here."

"That's a lie!" Dick said. "She was the one going to shoot you, when I grabbed the rifle and threw it away."

Dick had spoken in English.

I said, "Since when did you learn French, Dick?"

He stuttered then, and I said, "Why did you

feel it necessary to lie to me about that?"

"I didn't lie!" he bellowed. "I can understand some French, even if I can't speak it! I didn't tell you I couldn't understand it!"

If he was innocent, then the omission was trivial, but if he were a loyal agent to the Nine, then this omission was one of a chain of very important facts.

Whatever the truth, I knew now that my caution had not been wasted. One of them was a spy, my enemy. And I could not abandon them to go on my own way because I owed one a debt of gratitude. And the other a debt of revenge. I don't walk away from those who would kill me.

Clara was reluctant, and she reproached me for lacking faith in her. But that was only to relieve her emotions. If she had been in my place she would have done the same, and she knew it. She dropped the knife and backed away so I could pick it up. I had her frisk Dick, and then he frisked her while I watched both. Neither found anything. I put her rifle in the back seat. They got into the front seat with Dick driving again. We went along the road at about fifteen miles, the maximum speed without lights on this narrow winding road.

We had gone about two miles when I saw lights ahead and below. Two vehicles were approaching us from about a mile and a half away. They had to be from the jet strip on the other side of the mountain. I stopped the jeep and watched the lights climb and wind, and then, suddenly, they went out. I returned to the jeep, warily, of course, and said, "Either they've stopped to ambush us or they figure they're getting so close they should turn off the lights. We'll proceed for a mile and then . . ."

We stopped every hundred yards to listen. Sound carried for miles along that high slope. We could hear shouts from far below us and the motors of the two vehicles approaching us below.

The third time we stopped, we failed to detect the jeeps. After a minute, I concluded they had heard us, and they had stopped to wait. I told Dick to shut the motor off. The slope of the road was steep enough so we could roll on down without pushing. In fact, it was necessary to apply the brake frequently to keep from picking up speed. We went for another half-mile, and then I had the jeep stopped. Our ambushers could hear the brakes from a distance.

I said, "I'm going up the side of the mountain and get above them, Clara. I'll leave your knife here, just in case you are telling the truth. I'm taking your rifle with me, though. You two stay here until I get back. That's an order."

"But he'll kill me!" Clara said.

"She'll knife me!" Dick said.

"I think both of you can take good care of yourselves," I said. "Just stay away from each other."

I went up the slope and left Clara's rifle behind a rock after determining that it had four rounds left in the magazine. It took me about fifteen minutes to work my way up the slope and then down, across the road at a point where Clara and Dick couldn't see me, work down the slope a distance, then along it, and then back up.

I came out about thirty feet behind the jeeps we had heard. There were eight men crouching behind them. That left four men at the airstrip, if I had seen all of them when I left the jet.

"They must have seen us," an officer said. "We'll have to send out scouts."

He delegated three men to go ahead. They should fire at the first suspicious sign. If they ran into an ambush, they should take to the side of the roads.

The three left. I slipped along the slope, crouching, and then stuck my head over the edge. All five were standing together by the hood of the lead jeep. This made things very easy. My only regret was that I had not been in a position to catch all eight. But my grenade went off with a roar two seconds after it landed with a plop in their midst. They froze; they may not even have known what it was, but one of them suspected. He shouted, "Grenade!" and leaped away, but the explosion lifted him and sent him over the edge of the road to my right. He kept on sliding for a long time.

The blast had killed the others, too, and lifted the jeep up and slightly askew in relation to its former position. It had not caught fire but its two right tires and the metal from much of the right side were ripped apart.

The three came running back when they heard the explosion. By then I was up on the slope and I emptied my Bren in a burst that got all three even though they were strung out.

I went down the slope, picked up the rifles and automatics and knives and tossed them into the back seat of the undamaged jeep. I bent over just then fortunately for me. There was a metal box on the floor in the rear which I hoped contained grenades. Four shots sounded in rapid succession from the slope above me and bullets went through the metal of the door and over my head. I dropped flat onto the ground and the last two bullets would have pierced metal and me if I had remained in a crouch.

Then there was a whish of air and a thump as the empty rifle was thrown. It landed behind me in the dirt.

I doubted that Clara had the strength to throw the weapon that far. I doubted that any man except for Caliban and myself, could have cast it that far.

I felt cold then. What had happened to Clara?

"Come on down, you shambling mockery of a man! You ugly stinking ape!" I shouted. "Come on down! I won't shoot you! Use the knife you took from Clara, and I'll use my knife! I want the satisfaction of cutting your big belly open, you missing link! You treacherous beast! Lickling of the Nine!"

There was no answer. He was not going to give his location away. And well for him that he did not, because I had opened the door, removed an automatic rifle and then I let loose at the mountainside. I emptied that magazine and a second and a third, sixty rounds in all.

The echoes died away, the bullets quit ricocheting. There was silence except for a far-off harsh scream of some bird awakened by men's nocturnal activities.

At that moment, I heard the jet. It was high up and, until that moment, had been flying without lights. But they suddenly winked on, flashed, and then swung around. From around the corner of the mountain the light came. The big lamps along the strip had been turned on to guide the jet into the narrow valley.

I jumped into the jeep, turned on the motor, and roared away with a screeching of tires. I headed back up the road because I had to find out what had happened to Clara. I doubted that I had hit Dick. He would have hidden behind one of the many large boulders strewn over the slope. But he was armed with only a knife as far as I knew.

I even turned on the lights so I could go faster. I had gone not more than forty feet when a piece of the night detached itself and leaped from a great rock and landed in the back seat.

He came down in the back instead of on me because I had pressed the accelerator the second I saw him out of the corner of my eye. And I had estimated instantaneously that he would land just behind me. Which is why I rolled out from under the wheel and out of the jeep and onto the ground, leaving the vehicle to conduct itself wherever natural forces led it. If I had stayed there I would not have been able to turn around swiftly enough to defend myself, especially with the wheel cramping me. And he would have struck as soon as his feet hit the back seat.

He bellowed when he realized that I had slipped away. I was only half-aware of it because my head had struck a rock, and I was seeing sprays of light in the night.

If he had bounded out as soon as he had jumped in, he might have had me. But he crouched for a moment while the jeep turned toward the edge of the road. Only when it started to go over did he jump. He landed and rolled like a huge ball, and the vehicle, out of sight, crashed and clanged down the slope and then burst into flames. The glare from below illuminated his silhouette, great and broad, long-armed and crest-headed. It also outlined the knife in his hand.

I sat up and groped for the butt of the .38 automatic that should have been sticking out of the holster at my belt. It was not there. I could not think why and then, as my head cleared, I remembered that I had placed it on the seat by me so I could grab it. The only weapon I had was a knife. That would have been enough at one time. I have killed males of The Folk with just a knife. But they were jungle-reared, ignorant of the use of such weapons, ignorant also of such refinements of fighting as judo and karate.

I got to my feet, unstrapped my belt and held the end in my left hand and the knife in my right. Crouching, Dick advanced on me. His knife gleamed dully, reflecting the brightness from below.

In the distance were shouts and, very faintly, the thud of running feet. The men from below were catching up.

From behind me, from around the corner of the mountain, came the thunder of jets as the plane lowered for the final approach.

My head was fully clear now. I stepped toward him and lashed out with the buckle end of the belt. He had not seen what I had behind my back, and so he was surprised. He leaped back, but the buckle hit the end of the knife. He did not lose the knife, but he was not as confident as he had been.

Then I lashed again, and he caught the buckle in his free hand. He was fast, faster than any man I'd ever fought and, of course, stronger than any man whatsoever, including myself. The belt was jerked out of my hand so violently it burned the skin. And it almost carried me into range of his knife.

He came in with a thrust for my belly, which he did not finish. My knife parried his blade and then I stepped back and threw it. It was all-or-none in this case. If he blocked it, he had me.

The knife sank into his paunch.

His own knife dropped. He staggered back, clutching at the hilt. Then he fell on his back, and air rattled in his throat.

Rifles exploded down the road. Bullets whizzed by me. Others raced along the dirt, just missing me. I had no time to pull my knife from Dick. I should have taken the time, have risked the bullets. If I had pulled that knife out . . . but I didn't, and what is done is done.

To have gone down the slope was to put myself in the twilight illumination from the burning jeep. I leaped across the road and was up the slope and crawling among the rocks. The men probed the slope with heavy firepower. However, they had seen me only at a distance and unclearly, and they had no idea where I was on the mountainside. They concentrated most of their fire on the area behind me, since they assumed that I would be traveling away from them. Then they quit, probably because they were running short of ammunition.

I went back down the road on a course about fifty yards parallel with it. There were no men where I wanted to cut down the slope to the lower level where I had left Clara, so I went swiftly there. The jeep was still standing where I'd left it. I did not understand why the pursuers had not used it. By it stood a single man with a rifle. On the road at his feet was a form. It was too dim there to see well, but I smelled her. She was still alive.

It was easy to come up behind the guard and break his neck. Once more, I was armed with rifle, pistol, and a knife.

Clara was bound hand and foot and gagged with strips torn from her shirt. Dick had taken her alive and tied her up so that she could pay properly for her defection. I untied and ungagged her.

"Can you climb up the hill?" I said.

She cleared her throat and said, "Yes. How in the world did you get away from them? And Dick?"

"He's dead. What's the matter with the jeep?"

"I don't know. The bullets must have damaged it somewhere. When the men came, they tried to start it, but the motor wouldn't even turn over."

I could not have used it anyway. I picked up a
bag of canned food and two containers of water.
I gave her a rifle and two magazines from the
jeep's floor.

We started up over the mountain. A few
minutes later, the sky grayed. We increased our
pace. Within an hour, we were still going strong,
though she was panting. Far below us, two jeeps
carrying armed men stopped by the men who
had been pursuing us. The jeeps evidently came
from the airstrip on the other side of the mountain. They were too far away for me to identify
the newcomers. So far, the jet had not taken off.

Crouching behind a rock, I watched the long
conference. Occasionally, an officer turned his
binoculars up the slope and swept the terrain.
None stopped with me in their line of sight.
Then the jeeps started toward the valley. If any
of the Nine were in the jeeps, the men in charge
at the camp would be lucky to get off alive. The
Nine would never forgive them.

There was no more smoke from any of the
burning vehicles. The roads were clear now, and
jeeps full of armed men were coming up the
roads. I counted eight. These were almost
bumper to bumper as they raced along the dry
earth, throwing up large clouds of dust. Then
they pulled over to the extreme edge, the wheels
on the rim of the dropoff, to let the jeeps from the
airstrip by. As soon as these had passed, the
jeeps resumed their dangerous speed. I had assumed that the men in them were out to hunt
me down, but the vehicles continued on around
the mountain. Perhaps they were going to come

up from the other side to cut me off.

They did not have enough men for that to adequately cover the area. If they had had a copter, they might have done it.

When we got to the top of the mountain, I saw what they were doing. The jeeps, so far away they were almost invisible, were parked near the two-motored passenger jet. Evidently the newcomers intended to leave soon, and they wanted to make sure I did not attack them at the plane or try to steal it.

We went on down the mountain and by late afternoon were near the bottom. The sun flashed frequently off the binoculars directed toward our slope. But if they saw us, they made no move. And I did not believe they would not come after us if they did see us.

Clara said, "Why are we heading straight toward them?"

"They don't expect us to do so," I said. "At least, I don't think they will. I'll admit I've been very aggressive, but that was because I was trying to escape. I want to get as close as possible because I suspect that one or more of the Nine came in on that plane. And it's obvious the plane is waiting to take them away again. Also, if we get a chance to steal the plane, we will."

Clara kissed me and said, "You're wonderful! A real Tarzan! A beautiful *Starkathr!* My lovable black-haired, gray-eyed *Uebermensch!* Samson and Hercules and Odysseus rolled into one! Nobody but you could have gotten out of that canyon, and anybody else would have left us there! And then to get away and kill so many of them!

And then to attack them when we could get away!"

"I *have* been pushing my luck these last few days," I said.

For some reason, she thought that was funny. She choked trying to repress her laughter.

Halfway down, we were forced to dive for the shelter of a large boulder. Mortar shells began exploding below us. We clung to the rock, our faces pressed into the hard ground, while at least thirty-five shells roared along the face of the mountain. The closest, however, was about forty yards below us. That was close enough, but, except for shaken nerves and insulted eardrums, we were not hurt.

After waiting for five minutes after the last of the shells, I looked out over the boulder. The tiny figures were engaged in doing something, but they were not attending the mortars, which glittered in the sun just before the shadows of the western mountain fell on them. Nor was there any movement toward us. I decided that they had lobbed the shells just to scare us out if we were anywhere in the neighborhood.

We stayed behind the boulder for another fifteen minutes and then started our descent again. By the time we were three-quarters of the way down, the shadows from the other mountain had fallen on us. We kept going in the twilight. When we were about a quarter-mile from the jet strip, we stopped to eat cold food from our cans.

Just before we finished the meal, a helicopter chuttered around the side of the mountain to the west. The lights along the strip flashed on, but

the machine continued on over us and disappeared. There was no longer a lack of choppers.
This one was going to pick up the newcomers
and bring them to the jet, I was sure of that.
That would avoid bringing them on the road in
jeeps and so open to ambush from me.

Moreover, when daylight came, the chopper
would undoubtedly be out looking for us. And
other choppers might be on the way to aid in the
hunt.

When night was fully alive, I left Clara behind
a boulder near the foot of the mountain. The
lights were on along the strip and around the
four tents. I couldn't see them, but I had no
doubt that mass-detection buttons were strung
around the perimeters of the camp and the jet.
Four men had just finished erecting a metal
structure about thirty feet high on the tip of
which was an antenna array. A minute later, the
array began rotating. I stayed behind a bush. It
looked as if it was a personnel detector, either
radar or a heat-sensitive device. It must have
been brought in by the jet. When detectors exist
which can distinguish between the gait of a man
or a woman at a range of twelve miles, the
skulker at night has to be exceedingly careful
and crafty. Clara and I had been lucky coming
down the mountainside. If the detector had been
installed then, we would not have been able to
get away from the helicopter.

I watched for a while and determined that
there were thirty-six men in all. Half were stationed as guards outside the camp and around
the plane. The rest were cooking or lying down

on sleeping bags on the ground or were doing something in the tents. I could smell their tension, and the infrequent but sharp laughter verified my nose.

There were two 60-mm mortars with piles of about sixty shells apiece. There were six .50 caliber machine guns along the perimeter of a circle described around the jet and the camp. Every man carried an automatic rifle. The jeeps were parked inside along the perimeter so that the men could fire from behind them.

The logical place for the choppers to land would be close to the jet so that the passengers could be transferred with the least exposure.

I crawled back to Clara, taking a long time because I had to keep behind boulders or in depressions as much as possible and when I could not I moved only when the antenna was turned away from me.

"The chopper will be coming back on one of two routes," I said. "Either all the way around the mountain, along the shoulder. Or directly over it, the shorter route. They know we have an M-15, so they will be flying high, either way. But maybe they won't be too high. They must figure that we won't be dumb enough to hang around here once our escape route was open. Especially since the chopper came. But they also must figure that they can't rely on me not to be dumb. Their experience must have convinced them that I don't always run."

She chuckled and kissed my cheek and said, "I think they don't know what to think."

I told her what I wanted her to do, if she

wished to cooperate. If she didn't, she must leave. I did not want her around unless I knew exactly where she was and what she was supposed to do. She agreed, without hesitation, to obey me.

Even so, she was reluctant to part with me. She kissed me again, and she said she hoped she'd see me again. But she was happy, even if somewhat scared. She was out of what had seemed a hopeless situation, and she might yet get out of this one.

It would take most of the night for her to get stationed, since she had to go back over the mountain and then around to a place along the shoulder. I crawled back down to a position about a quarter-mile from the camp. If the chopper did come directly over the mountain, it would start lowering close enough for me to get it in my range. Of course, I would have to get the hell out immediately, because the combined firepower would be directed at me.

The chance of getting the chopper was about a hundred to one, and the chance of getting away alive was about a thousand to one.

If the enemy had been anybody but one of the Nine, I would not have risked it. But I hated them so that I was willing to take the risk. Clara was out of range of fire from the camp, so that if she got the copter, she could get away.

The night fell to pieces, and the sun came up again. I had suspected that the chopper would carry the newcomers by day. It would be easier to spot us then, and it was also safer for the jet to take off. About a half hour after dawn, I heard

the chutter of the machine. It was much lower
than I had expected, about five hundred feet up.
But it did not fly directly in a straight line. It
zigzagged, and at first I thought it was taking
evasive action. Then it came to me that this
might be a dry run. It was not carrying VIP's; it
held armed men. They were trying to fool us into
exposing our positions by firing at them. Then,
after dealing with us, they would go back for
their passengers.

Trust the Nine to be supercautious!

I got under the overhang of the huge boulder
and lay still. The machine passed almost directly
overhead. It went as far as the camp and then it
returned, but further to the north. It disappeared over the mountain. I suspected that it
would come back again, this time around the
shoulder, near where Clara was. I hoped she
would not fire, that she would figure out that this
was a dry run.

There was nothing to do except wait. The
bulk of the mountain deadened any sound on the
other side. I could not get up and climb to the
top, because of the personnel radar. Therefore,
wait it would be. My patience is great; I learned
it in a hard school when I was young, hunting for
meat. But this was the most painful watch I had
ever put in.

An hour passed. Then the chopper came over
the top, and this time it was even lower. Obviously, it was making another sweep, daring us
to shoot. If we were lucky enough to bring it
down, the Nine would have lost another helicopter and some servants, but they could then

use the jeep to get to the jet. Or they could wait until another helicopter arrived. After ten thousand or so years, they had developed the ability to take the greatest of pains and to use as much time as needed.

I was certain that one of the Nine had to be involved. This much trouble would not have been taken for anyone lesser, not even for an important candidate for the empty seat.

It was not enough for the machine to be taken over this mountain. It went over the camp to the mountain on the opposite side and cruised up and down and back and forth for an hour. It seemed to be about only two hundred feet above the surface.

Then it rose straight up and flew back over my mountain maintaining several thousand feet height above ground level.

By then I decided that I had been wasting my time. I had taken a long shot and should have known better.

I waited. And I waited. The sun sank behind the western range. The camp showed no unusual activity. Several jeeps, which had left at noon, returned before dusk. These carried only the men who had left earlier and two bazookas and bazooka rockets.

I crawled to the top of the mountain and descended much more swiftly on the other side. I knew where Clara was and so called out softly to her and then waited for the counter-word. The wind was carrying the scent to me, and so I knew that she was alone.

"I don't know what he's doing," I said. She

understood by *he* that I meant one or more of the
Nine. "I'm sure he's inside the caves and probably sending out all sorts of messages. There must
be a powerful shortwave set in there. I don't
know when he's coming out, but you can be sure
that we'll never get close enough to get the chopper that carries him unless we want to commit
suicide."

"Perhaps it's too big a job for just us two," she
said hopefully. "We can run away and fight
again another day."

"We'll try one more day," I said. "If nothing
happens we leave tomorrow night."

Part of that night we spent working our way
down the mountain to the end of the valley into
which the jet had flown. We approached the end
of the strip by a shallow ravine. This lay about a
hundred yards beyond the rammed earth of the
end of the strip. Behind us was rough land with
sparse bush for two hundred yards, and then a
mountain began to curve gently up. The jet had
to swing down over its two thousand foot height
and come down close to the surface if it was to
settle its wheels at this end. The strip was long
enough to take the two-jet type but not a four-
jet.

The personnel radar on top of the tower at the
north end of the strip was undoubtedly able to
detect us. And at this distance we would not
have been able to see it if the lights had not been
turned on. We crawled along out of the ravine
until we were past the foot of the mountain on
our right and out of the radar's line of sight.

I told Clara what I intended to do. She said

that it sounded forlorn and, indeed, suicidal. I agreed and said I would try it, anyway.

The rest of the night we slept peacefully, except once, when I awoke and thought I had heard a leopard. But the scream was so far off, and I got in on the very end of it, so I could not be sure. If there were leopards here, they would not be man-eaters. I went back to sleep.

At dawn we ate the last of our food and drank the last of our water. An hour later, I heard the chopper. It rose high over the mountain and came down vertically exactly over the camp. The figures that got out of the machine were tiny, of course, because we were so far away. We were behind a rock at an angle to the camp, looking past the shoulder of the mountain west of the camp. But one of the figures was so bulky and long-armed and crest-skulled, it had to be Dick. I had not killed him after all. The knife must not have gone in as deeply as I had thought. And he may have been pretending to be dead so that I would approach to pull the knife out, and he could take me by surprise. He might well have done so, if those riflemen had not run me away. He was walking without any help, so he must have been quickly patched up. Caliban's medical inventions had long been of great service to the organization of the Nine.

The second figure that magnetized my attention was that of a broad-framed, black-skinned, white-haired man. His walk, distinctive even at that distance, identified him as Mubaniga.

The third figure was a tall skinny bald-headed man who could be none other than Doctor Murtagh.

For some reason, he had been called back from his journey to Germany.

Mubaniga got into the jet with a number of armed men. Dick and Murtagh remained on the ground. I knew then they had been left behind to hunt for us. Murtagh had been recalled to complete a job that he had erred in marking off. He undoubtedly would have liked to tell Mubaniga that I should have been executed the moment I was captured, but he would not have dared.

Two jeeps rode out along each side of the jet. At the end of the strip, they stopped, and the five occupants of each got out. They advanced with rifles ready and investigated the terrain for several hundred yards in each direction. Two men took stations on the edge of the ravine and faced outward. The others formed two lines near the end of the strip.

The jet took a long time warming up. I ducked down into the ravine at a point where it curved and so kept me from being seen by the two guards. My moves were dictated then solely by my hearing. I crouched there with the rifle in hand, the .45 in its holster, and the knife in its sheath.

Clara Aekjaer was in a hole beneath the overhang of a boulder set on the hillside but out of line of the personnel radar. She had her orders to come out when she saw me running.

The twin jets roared, but the pilot was still testing them. Then I heard something unexpected. The copter was swinging across the strip. I do not know why I had overlooked it in my plans. I suppose because I had regarded it solely as a carrier in the last stage of getting the jet away with its important passenger. But it was coming down the strip now and would then go up and down the gently sloping mountain to make doubly sure that no one was hidden there.

I shoved myself against the bank and tried to look like a rock. My skin was smeared with dirt, and my clothes were covered with clay, so I probably did look like a rock. And there was a projection above me to throw me into the shade.

The copter flew over about a hundred yards ahead of me. I dared to turn my head slowly to look over the opposite side of the ravine. The big chopper was zigzagging at only fifty feet above the ground. Its sides bristled with machine guns and rifles. It proceeded for about half a mile and then, its occupants believing that anybody beyond that could not harm the jet because it would be too high then, returned. It was on its way to land when the change in the noise of the jet showed that the plane was taking off.

That was my starting gun.

I ran down the rocky bed of the ravine, but I was still crouched over. Clara should have started to crawl out of the hole the moment she saw me go. She would get out just far enough to shoot down the nearest guard. He, fortunately, had not resisted the temptation to turn and look at the jet for just a moment. Perhaps he wanted to reassure himself that he was not in its direct path. I had not been counting on him to do that, but it helped. It gave me a few more seconds to get down the ravine before I had to slow down and start shooting at the guard at the far end.

The copter was still coming down and its

vanes, plus the roar of the jets, helped drown out Clara's fire.

The guard nearest me turned his head, saw me, froze, and then he crumpled to one side, dropped his rifle, and slid out over the ravine. He fell in front of me. I leaped over him, swinging my rifle up to point at the other guard, who had just become aware that his comrade had fallen. But he fell, too, hit by Clara's fire.

Halfway between the two corpses, I stopped. I listened and then, visualizing just how far down the strip the jet was, I bent down, gathered my leg muscles, and leaped to the top of the ravine, six feet up, and over it. My rifle was spitting as I came up and I caught every man on the right end of the strip. The burst stitched them together in death.

That they were facing outward and away from me helped the surprise.

The man at the nearest end of the line on my left side had seen the first guard fall. He had started to fire without warning the man on his right. This man, however, had heard the gun shooting even above the noises of the two craft. He had started shooting in Clara's direction, and then the others heard and began firing.

Clara's fire and mine were like two hoses started at each end, and they met in the middle.

The pilot of the jet must have seen what was happening. It was too late for him to stop. He could do nothing except try to get past us.

I crouched, Clara continued to fire at the oncoming plane. It lifted, perhaps prematurely in an effort to escape our bullets. I don't know. But

I raised up and threw the rifle so that it spun once and then the barrel went straight into the plane's port jet.

I had not time to throw myself down. The wing shot a few inches above my head, and I was deafened by the roar.

Theoretically, the jet could fly with one engine dead. But things happened too fast. The rifle had wrecked the engine, the pilot had lifted the plane a trifle too early, and, for all I know, Clara's bullets had hit someone or something vital.

The jet plowed into the side of the mountain behind us and blew up. Pieces of metal spun through the air and fell around us. Fire shot up, and black smoke poured out a hundred feet high.

The people at the other end of the strip were paralyzed. I had banked on this. I leaned down, took Clara's hand and pulled her up onto the ground so swiftly that she cried out with pain. We ran to the nearest jeep. Clara got into the driver's seat and started the motor. By then the people in the copter had recovered some of their senses. It started to lift off, turned, and a machine gun and a rifle in its starboard bay began to shoot fire. And the men on the ground were piling into the jeeps there. In the first jeep were Dick and Murtagh.

If they had had any time to reflect, they would have fled without paying any attention to us. They had allowed one of the Nine to be killed, and their own lives were forfeit. Murtagh's candidacy was automatically canceled, and he was as much the quarry of the Nine as I.

But they reacted with their reflexes only. They were still carrying out the Nine's orders, and they intended to kill the man who had thwarted them so much.

Clara wheeled the jeep around with tires screeching and headed toward the copter. He spun the copter around and started away, then stopped it and started back toward us. The fire from the gunners dug up the dirt on all sides of us and a few bullets pierced the hood. But Clara drove the jeep as if it were a bull with a nest of hornets hung under its tail. It swerved this way and that so violently that I had to jam my feet against the back of the seat in front of me and my back against the seat behind me. I fired as steadily as I could, and then the chopper veered away on its side and crashed in the path of the oncoming jeeps. It blew up, spraying flaming gasoline everywhere. Clara jammed on the brakes just in time to keep us from slamming into the inferno. She backed up quickly enough while our faces seared, turned around, and raced off.

The other jeeps backed up and went around the flames, and then the chopper exploded again. Presumably, it was the overheated ammunition. Fire like surf shot out and covered some of the jeeps. Men jumped out of the nearest vehicle while it was still going and rolled screaming on the ground.

Murtagh's jeep was partly splashed, but he and Dick got away. I shot at them but did not think I hit them.

Those behind, however, were occupied by determined men. They came around the flames and pursued us as if they had learned nothing from the past few minutes, not to mention the previous three days. And perhaps they were right in refusing to learn, since my good fortune could not last forever.

Clara took the jeep along the edge of the ravine, cut across its end, and we were loose on very rough country. We bounced high and hard, so violently that all I could do was hang on. But those behind us could not shoot either. Our course was strictly dictated by the terrain, which was as wrinkled as the face of a centenarian. The jeep cut back and forth, leaped out from the edge of ridges and slammed into the ground with bone-cracking and muscle-snapping force. Once she tried to stop the vehicle in time to keep it from going over another ravine, which was too broad for us to traverse. The jeep skidded toward the edge, stopped, teetered, and then went over on its side. Clara leaped out one way and I the other. I jumped up at once and looked down, expecting to see her crushed underneath the vehicle. But she was on its other side, flat against the earth. The jeep lay on its side.

I jumped down, picked her up, said, "Are you all right?"

She was white-faced, but she nodded. I handed her a rifle and said, "Keep them off while I fix this!"

"How can you fix that?" she said, but she moved on down the ravine and stood on top of a rock so she could fire over the edge.

I crouched down, got a good grip on the jeep,

and slowly straightened up. The jeep, groaning, came up, I almost slipped, but not quite, and the jeep was upright.

Clara started shooting then. I ran up to her, tapped her shoulder, she turned, started, and then grinned. Some of the color was returning. The racket of gunfire and the gouting of earth along the edge of the ravine was still going on when we drove off along the bed of the cut. We did not go swiftly or too far. About three hundred yards down, we were stopped by a dropoff of about twenty feet. She drove the vehicle over, abandoning it just before it reached the lip of the little cliff. I had hoped that the jeep might survive the fall. But it dived into the dirt nose first, and the sturdy radiator, which had suffered so much, finally broke. Water pooled out from it.

Even so, we had a good headstart on the others. They were very cautious about approaching long after our fire had ceased. The steep ridge which had caused Clara to skid the jeep prevented their vehicles from going any further unless they went far to the north. They did follow us on foot, however, because I saw them coming out of the ravine when we were about five hundred feet up a mountain. This was partially covered with bush and trees. The rain forest would start just on the other side of this mountain, and the only one who could track us then would be Dick.

If he had been raised by The Folk, he would have been somebody to fear. His nose was keener than mine, but he had been raised by humans who lived on the edge of the rain forest but seldom went into it. He would be lost. And he could not travel as swiftly as Clara and I. He had too much weight to carry, and his legs were too short.

I kept on going with Clara panting heavily and having to stop now and then. The gap remained between us and the pursuers. But when, at evening, we plunged through the dense rim-growth into the cool and dark mansions of the rain forest, I stopped.

After getting Clara up into a tree, I returned to the tanglery by the border between bush and forest. From a branch a hundred and fifty feet high, I watched the tiny figures toil up the hill. They were lost from time to time in the bush, and then, as dusk fell, they became invisible.

I had discarded one rifle when it ran out of ammunition. The other was with Clara, and it held only six rounds. I carried the .45 automatic and my knife. I was tired. I would have liked to hole up for the night. Clara and I had satisfied our thirst at a pothole and filled our canteens. She had eaten nothing since breakfast, and I had had only a small golden mouse I caught by the tail while I was on my way out.

But I had a job to finish.

I climbed down and went through the bush, though very cautiously. Dick's keen ears and nose made him worth all the others put together in the jungle, and I did not want to stumble over him lying in ambush.

About a hundred yards away, I heard a very strange noise.

They were all chanting my name.

"Lord Grandrith! Lord Grandrith!"

If it was a trick, and I did not know what else it could be, it was unique. It also whetted my curiosity to the point where I could not have stayed away.

At the last, I climbed a tree and peered down through the branches of two trees ahead of me at the camp.

They were cooking over Caliban's lightweight stoves. Eight of the ten were shouting out my name together. Dick squatted by the stove, his voice booming above the others. Murtagh stood in the center of the small open area with his hands held out.

I called out from behind the trunk during a pause in their chanting. "What do you want?"

Murtagh shouted back, "We want to parley with you."

"Why?"

"I think you know why. We failed, and so the Nine will kill us. We would like to team up with you. Some of us now believe that you and Caliban might actually have a chance against the Nine. And we have talents that you can use, since you can use every bit of help you can get, despite your fantastic success so far!"

"Throw your weapons into the bush! All of them! Knives and derringers, too, if you have them!"

They were reluctant to do so but only because they felt naked without them. And they could not be sure that I would not then mow them down.

When the last weapons, which did include two

derringers, were tossed over a bush, I dropped from branch to branch, fell twelve feet to the ground, and then walked into the clearing. My pistol and knife were in their sheaths.

Murtagh was smiling now. I did not like him trying to be friendly any more than I had when he was trying to kill me. But alliances in wartime are not based on likes or dislikes. When he started to speak, I held up my hand.

"If you are to join me," I said, "you must make it worth my while to accept you. I need much information. What do you know about my wife? And what is the situation in regard to Caliban?"

"I am a candidate," he said, "but that does not mean I am fully in the confidence of the Nine. You know that. I have heard nothing at all about your wife. I do not even know the name of the man who is in charge of the business of getting her. As for Caliban, well, I was ordered to Germany to track him down after I had put you away in the canyon. I was told that he had been seen in the vicinity of Gramzdorf, a village and a castle in the Black Forest. I was told that he had been trying to kill Iwaldi. I was also told that we were to kill Iwaldi, if we got a chance, and . . ."

The world was certainly turning topsy-turvy. Here I was discussing an alliance with men who had been trying their best to kill me. And here I was being told that the Nine were trying to kill one of their own—old Iwaldi, the wrinkled dwarf whose white beard fell to his waist.

Joining forces with hated enemies was, of course, nothing new for mankind. Or even for me. I killed a number of Germans in East Africa during World War I, not for patriotism but for personal revenge. Then I found out that the atrocities that had set me on the blood trail were the work of a small band of criminals in the East African German forces. They would have been shot by their commander if he had known what they had done. Later, I became very good friends with Colonel Paul von Lettow-Vorbeck, who kept two hundred thousand British troops at bay with just eleven thousand men, most of them black Africans. Of course, anyone reading the volume of my biography dealing with this phase of my life would get the mistaken notion that it was the Germans whose hordes would have overwhelmed the British if it had not been for me. But my biographer was always more interested in dramatic values than in facts, and he was full of the intense anti-German feeling of that time. The truth is that von Lettow-Vorbeck was a greater guerrilla leader than Lawrence of Arabia, but he did not get any publicity. Besides, he was on the defeated side.

I doubted that there was anything admirable about the reptilian Murtagh to make me respect him as I had von Lettow-Vorbeck. But he was highly intelligent and ruthless, and he could be used, even if never fully trusted.

He said, "I was on my way to Germany when I got a message saying that I should go to Paris instead. Caliban had disappeared there. And then I got another message telling me to return. You had escaped. I couldn't believe it, but I had to. I met Mubaniga at a strip in the Congo, and we came here. He put me in charge of killing you, and then he took off, as you know. He did not say where he was going. But I got hold of a message which indicated that he would be going to Salisbury, England. Why, I don't know."

I smiled. If he was able to read an intercepted message, which he had no business doing, he had learned how to translate the language the Nine used among themselves. I have no idea what this language is or how ancient. But I got hold of a number of papers while I was the Speaker for the Nine during an annual ceremony, and I learned how to interpret that language, too. I surmised that Murtagh, when he was the Speaker, had done the same. He was a brave man or a foolhardy one to take that chance.

The language itself, as a side comment, seems to be distantly related to Basque. It is my guess that it was the original tongue of Anana, the terrible old woman who is chieftainess of the Nine. It is probably one of a superfamily that extended around the Mediterranean and possibly over much of Europe, before the Indo-Hittite speakers came out of the forests of what is today middle Germany.

"Where is this strip in the Congo?" I said. "Does it have a shortwave set that can reach Europe? Can we get there swiftly on foot? Or do we have to steal a copter or plane?"

He reached slowly into his jacket and pulled out a map. He unfolded it on the ground in the beam of a flashlight.

"It's there, in the Ituri forest," he said.

The map was French, and his finger hovered

above a cross made of red ink in an area marked *Pygmées*.

It was about eighty miles from where we were. I could make it on foot in twenty-four hours if I knew exactly where it was. But if I let the others accompany me, I would take anywhere from six to eight days. I needed them. At least, I needed Murtagh, and I did not want to abandon Clara. Once we got to civilization, she could do what she wanted to do. But I had to get her out of the wilderness because I owed it to her.

"Are any more planes coming in to the strip back there?" I said, indicating the area outside the caves.

"Several choppers, at least," Murtagh said. "They should be there now or coming in very soon. Oh, you have cost the Nine dearly!"

"Not as dearly as I plan," I said. "Wait here. I'll be back within twenty minutes."

I returned with Clara Aekjaer. While we ate, we went over my campaign. Murtagh tried to overrule me several times; he could not give up the idea that he was the leader. But I put him in his place without humiliating him, and after a while he saw that he could not push me around in any way. On the other hand, I did accept several suggestions of his for improving our plans.

Late at night, we all bedded down. I could have retired into the forest with Clara to make sure we weren't jumped on while we slept. But it was a case of full acceptance of partnership or none at all. I was ready to dissolve the alliance the moment I saw signs of treachery. Until then,

I could not treat them as leopards ready to turn on me.

Even so, I had trouble getting to sleep. Perhaps it was Dick that kept my brain occupied. I did not know what to do with him. We could not take him to England with us. Even if we had shaved and clothed him and pulled his long canines, he still would have attracted attention we could not tolerate for one minute. I could have left him in the forest, but, as I said, he had been raised as a human, not as one of The Folk, and he would starve or go crazy from loneliness.

If I had had time, I could have gone into the wilderness with him, taught him how to hunt, how to build a nest against the rain and the cold. And the female I had seen last year might still be roaming the mountains in Uganda. We could find her and Dick could take her as his mate. And they could have young, and The Folk might not die out.

But that was a fantasy. Dick's tastes in food were set. He could not adapt to a diet of juicy white grubs, rodents, birds' eggs, raw birds, wild nuts and berries, and an occasional piece of meat, not always fresh by any means. In the wet and often chilly rain forest of the mountains, he would probably suffer from colds and he would likely die of pneumonia. He could migrate to the rain forest of the Gabon lowlands, but I doubted that he would get the female to go there with him, even if he could find and successfully woo her.

Besides, as I had found out when in the box canyon, Dick desired human females because he had been raised as a human. He probably would have thought the female of The Folk to be as ugly as a human thinks a gorilla is.

I told myself that I had no cause to worry about him. Though he had tried to kill me while pretending to be my friend, that was only something anybody would do to gain an advantage in war, and I did not hold it against him.

Then I fell into a fit of nostalgia. Suddenly, I wanted to shuck off this kind of life. I was tired, sick even, of killing and of being on the run or the attack. I wanted to get away from all these humans, and the subhuman, and travel deep into the forest. I wanted to go naked and hunt the pig and the antelope with only a knife. I wanted to sleep in a cozy nest in the trees, hear only the muted noise of the animals of the closed-canopy forest, be in the shadow and the silence. I did not want to see another human being for . . . for a long long time. I wanted to be free with an obligation only to myself. I could commune with the beasts, with Nature, as Whitman expresses it in several of his poems. I hated civilization, especially the big cities, especially London with its wet chilly air and coughs and sneezes and running noses, its blare and screech and roar, its citizens bumping into each other, the grit and rasp of hatred and madness fouling its air along with the physical poisons.

If it had not been for my wife, and for Caliban, I would have risen then and walked into the forest and left them to work out their own problems. As long as the Nine left me alone, I would not have bothered them, would not even have thought of them.

But Clio might be in danger. And Caliban,

once my most dangerous enemy, was now my best friend.

I sighed deeply, turned over, and managed to fold in the night over my brain.

In the morning, Dick asked me if he could go with us to London. I told him why that was impossible. He finally admitted that all the logic was on my side. But he asked what he could do then. I replied that he should return to his foster parents, who lived in a hut near the edge of the rain forest. The time would come when Caliban and I would be ready to attack the Nine in the caves. Then we would need him, since he was a truly formidable antagonist. He grimaced and touched the bandage just above his navel. The next time someone came at him with a knife, and he himself had only a knife, he would throw it. He was not going to get tricked again.

My knife had not gone deeply because he had grabbed it even as it struck. He had cut his hands, too, but the pseudo-skin which Caliban had devised for wounds had been applied to the cuts. The knife wound had had to be glued after repairs were made, again with the use of one of Caliban's medical inventions. Dick could not exert himself fully yet without fear of tearing the wound open. The ride on the jeep when I was being chased had caused him considerable pain. But he would be completely healed within a week unless something broke open the wound.

Dick nodded when I said that they also served who waited. But he scowled, and that was a fearsome sight. The bulging bones above the sunken russet eyes, the blue-black skin, the protruding jaws with the long sharp yellow canines, all these looked fierce enough when he was smiling. On the way back to the jet strip, he was silent, except when addressed, and then he was curt and surly.

The first thing Murtagh did when we reached the jeeps was to report over the radio to the camp. The operator at the receiving end could not conceal his astonishment. He had supposed, along with everybody else, that Murtagh had either been killed when he took off after me or else had kept on going to put as much distance between himself and the Nine as he could.

"I have taken Lord Grandrith prisoner, and I am bringing him in," Murtagh said to the officer who had been summoned. "I also have the countess, Clara Aekjaer, prisoner."

The officer, a man named ibn Khalim, was flabbergasted. Part of his reaction was because I had been taken alive. But the other part, which he would not admit if he had been asked, was amazement that Murtagh thought he would be forgiven now that he had me in custody. That he should have allowed Mubaniga, one of the Nine, to be killed was unforgivable. But if Murtagh was stupid enough to come back, so much the better.

Ibn Khalim quit talking for a moment, apparently to consult a higher authority. Then he ordered Murtagh to come in immediately. Clara and I were to be brought in alive. This was the personal order of Anana herself, relayed by radio from somewhere in Europe.

The ancient woman must have splendid things in mind for me. She might even be planning to save me for the annual ceremonies, when

I could be tortured as an object lesson for the candidates. I could imagine her anger. And I smiled, though smiling at the thought of her is like being amused by the thought of Death Herself. If things worked out as I planned, she was going to be even angrier.

The journey back was much slower and more confortable than that out. I sat in the front seat of the land jeep with two rifles at my head and my legs and arms seemingly tied together. Clara sat in the front seat of the second jeep, also seemingly bound. About a half-mile from the strip, a chopper met us. It flew about fifty feet above us all the way to the strip.

The mass of armed men I had expected to be waiting for us at the strip was not there. There were twenty men altogether, and six of these were stationed at the strip at all times. The others had come up by jeep from the big camp around the mountain. This small a number could mean that Murtagh and his men were to be treated as conquering heroes, so they would be put off their guard. Once Clara and I were turned over to the soldiers, Murtagh and his men would be separated. And then, dispersed, each would be arrested.

This would be a much less bloody way than attacking them while they were armed and organized. The Nine had lost so heavily that they were taking the subtle way.

This was more than I expected, especially since we had no plans for going deeper than the strip. We were prepared to open fire on whatever number of men was lined up to receive us. If we jumped the gun, we might be able to bull our way through. Now the task was so much easier.

The chopper settled down just as we drove up. An officer strode forward to greet Murtagh, who got out of the jeep and shot the officer through the chest.

We lost two dead and one wounded. But most of the others were cut down before they could bring their rifles into action.

I flew one chopper and Murtagh the other. We took off as soon as our men had climbed in and we had determined that we had enough fuel. We kept close to the tops of the forest once we got past the mountains, and we came into the strip in the middle of the Ituri forest with our wheels almost touching the treetops. There was one four-motored jet and two choppers near the small camp. The fighting was brief and bloody, and the four survivors ran into the jungle rather than surrender. We let them go.

While Murtagh was warming up the jet, and his men were placing dynamite to blow up the camp and the choppers, I sent a message to my men in Dakar. I did not expect to receive any acknowledgment, since Murtagh told me he assumed that my men had been located and killed. But they were a mobile unit—how mobile I won't reveal because I will be using them again. And they answered.

It was true that I had revealed the code to Murtagh under the influence of his drug. But, as I said, a questioner isn't going to get everything he should know unless he asks the right questions. Murtagh did not ask me if there was more than one code. He got the code for the particular day he questioned me. The Nine had transmitted a message on the following day, and so they had used the wrong code. My men had answered, given misleading information, and then had moved on.

Today was Wednesday, and so I transmitted the proper code for that day. I outlined what had happened, told them what I needed and how soon I'd be there. And then I asked if they had heard anything about my wife or from Caliban.

They knew nothing of Clio. But they had a reply to my first message sent some days ago.

It was from Doc Caliban. He was leaving for the county of Wiltshire in southern England. His ultimate destination was Stonehenge, the ancient ruins about seven and a half miles north of Salisbury. I was to get there as quickly as possible unless I considered events in Africa to have taken a very important turn. He was hot on the track of Iwaldi, and the business at hand might mean the end of the world—in a sense.

The message had been sent the day before.

If that proud and almost neurotically self-sufficient man was asking me for help, he must be in very hot waters indeed.

I sent him a message which I did not think he would get until it was too late, if he ever received it. Then I ran out of the station and signaled the others to get into the plane. Dick stopped me. He bellowed at me against the roar of the jets.

"Can't you take me with you? I could be of great help. Do you know anybody who has my strength?"

I shook my head and shouted back, "I'm sorry, I really am! But you can be of far more value to us if you stay here! When the time comes to go into the caves, we'll need you very much! And we just can't take you with us! You'd attract attention, which is the last thing we can stand! You might cause us to be killed by your very presence!"

"Then go to hell!" he bellowed, his throat sac swelling, and by that I knew he was almost insanely furious.

Logic told me to shoot him then and there, because there was no telling what he might do to hurt us. We could not afford to take the least chance. But I did not follow logic, of course, since I just could not kill him without adequate provocation. I even yelled at him to get into the jungle before the explosions.

Then I got into the plane, and the port was closed, we took off, and, as we swung back around, I pressed the button that transmitted a frequency to sets below. The two choppers and the tents blew up in a great cloud.

When the Nine heard of this, they would be doubly enraged, if that was possible. Never had they been so threatened, so outraged, so thumb-at-nosed-at, if I may use such a phrase. (It parallels the structure of Folk speech.) I hoped that old Anana's veins would swell up and up and she would die of a stroke.

But I knew that it was the end of the affair that mattered and that I might be dead, or wish I were dead, in a day or two. Or even sooner.

Within fourteen hours, we were getting off a

small boat on a beach near Bournemouth, a city of Hampshire County. We walked up a steep flight of wooden steps to the top of a cliff. Four automobiles awaited us. It was four o'clock in the morning, and fog pressed heavily around us. Though the driver of my car could not see where he was going, he seemed to be trusting to instinct. He drove at what was a suicidal clip in the blindness, forty miles per hour, through the streets of Bournemouth. But a radar scope on the dashboard showed ghostly images of cars and people and street lamps and signposts, though we could not read the signs, of course.

Our trip had been smooth and speedy all the way. At Dakar, rather, at a strip in the desert many miles outside Dakar, the metal belt was cut off me and the shell of plastic explosive and the epoxy glue was removed. We were given new clothes and forged papers before transferring to a plane which took us around Spain to a small airport off the coast of southwestern France. From there we took an amphibian which set us down next to a small motor yacht twenty miles off the coast, just outside the fog. If you have enough money and have spent some years in building up your own organization, just in case you have a falling out with the Nine, you find that you can get much done quickly and quietly. As long as I could keep feeding my men money, and I had enough gold stashed away in Africa and elsewhere to do so, I had more than just myself to rely on in this battle. And, of course, Doc Caliban had his own organization, just as he had his own supply of gold.

It pays to be rich, as Clio often told me.

It was still dark and foggy when we were dropped off before a small hotel outside the city of Salisbury off Highway A338. Clara sat up in bed for a long time smoking until I asked her to quit or else go into the next room. I smoked heavily when I was first introduced to civilization, but that dissipation did not last long. It left too foul a taste and reduced my wind and was a nuisance altogether. Now I could not endure to have smoke anywhere near in an enclosed bedroom.

The maid woke me with a tap on the door at six. Clara was asleep but awoke shortly after I had shaved. She said, "I was trying to think last night why the Nine should be here. I know that they are supposed to have tracked Iwaldi here. But why here? Then I remembered some years ago when I ran into a man I'd only seen twice before, both times at the caves. I was in London then, visiting friends. William Griffin, a son of Lord Braybroke, I believe, told me of overhearing a conversation between a Speaker and his woman. We candidates are great gossips, you know, trying to find out all we can about the Nine. The Speaker had overheard Shaumbim telling Tilatoc that the world had changed so much that it would be impossible to hold funeral rites at some of the places most closely associated with the Nine. Anana's birthplace, for instance, was now covered by a great office building in Spain."

Shaumbim was one of the two Mongolian members of the Nine. Tilatoc was the ancient

Central American Indian.

"XauXaz was the one who died. Do you know anything about him at all? Could he have been associated with Stonehenge?"

"I've heard XauXaz speaking in an ancient tongue, some sort of proto-Germanic," I said. "And he spoke to me in English several times when I was Speaker, but only to give orders. Just before Caliban and I were sent from the caves with orders to fight each other to the death, Anana told me a few things about Caliban and myself. We're half-brothers, and our grandfather was XauXaz. He may also have been our great-great-grandfather. God knows how many times he was our ancestor. He used Grandrith Castle as a breeding farm in some kind of experiment. I suspect that his brothers, Ebn XauXaz and Thrithjaz, who are also dead, may have bred the Grandrith family, maybe a long time before the Grandriths came to England, when they were Norsemen. And maybe a long time before then, maybe they started when our ancestors were just forming their Germanic speech. I don't know, I'm guessing. I also suspect that old Ing, he whom the original Old English speakers worshiped as a living god, and he from whose name England was derived, may have taken a part in the breeding of the Grandrith line. Just as I suspect that my being raised by subhumans may have been an experiment of the Nine.

"But I'm digressing. I don't know what XauXaz had to do with Stonehenge. He was at least eighteen thousand five hundred years old when Stonehenge was built and maybe three times as old. He has been associated with the Germanic people from the beginning. And I doubt very much that the builders of Stonehenge, the 'Wessex' peoples, who probably descended from the Bronze Beaker peoples, were Germanic. The proto-Germanic language wouldn't even have existed then.

"But maybe he was associated with the Stonehenge people, maybe he was their living god. Maybe he supervised the building of Stonehenge. And then the Wessex people declined or he left them and went to the land between the Oder and the Elbe rivers. It is possible."

We might never know. But the Nine were here for what must be a very good reason for them.

Murtagh entered with a noticeable increase in the frequency of oscillations of face. His skin was pale, and his mouth was as thin as the edge of a fingernail.

"Are you exceptionally nervous?" I said.

"Exceptionally so," he replied. "But I always am when on the brink of an important action. You will find that my nerve won't desert me. I can be relied upon."

I told him what Clara and I had been discussing and asked him if he had any information.

"The Nine, as you well know, are sticklers for tradition," he said. "I suppose when you've lived as long as they have, you will be, too. Though the way you live I doubt you'll reach even a hundred. No offense!" he added sharply. Apparently, though he had thrown in with me, he still resented me.

"I rather believe that the ceremony will be the burial of XauXaz, if he is associated with this place. Not a genuine burial, because even the Nine don't have enough influence to bury him in the center of Stonehenge and keep all questions suppressed. But the funeral could be held there, and he could be buried nearby in some private land."

It seemed like a sound theory. I started to comment on it when the phone rang. I was closest, so I answered. A strange voice, deep as a hog grunting at the bottom of a well, spoke.

"J.C.? D.C. here!"

It was the proper challenge, and I gave the proper response. "Seedy? Seejay here!"

"Speaking for D.C.," the deep voice said. "Van Veelar. My friends call me Pauncho. Trish said to say hello. O.K.?"

By that he must have meant that the naming of Trish was an additional reassurance that he was sent by Caliban. Patricia Wilde was Doc's beautiful cousin, whom I was supposed to have killed but who was very much alive, as both Doc and I discovered.

"Meet you at the corner of Barnard and Gigant Streets," he said. "Be smoking a big cigar. You know what *G. beringei* looks like?"

That had to mean gorilla beringei, the mountain gorilla. I said, "Very well."

"That's me. A dead ringer for old beringei. You can't mistake me. Smoking a cigar in a big black Rolls. Always travel in style. See you. Hurry. This line may be tapped. Oh, and don't forget! Anybody with metal fillings in their teeth is out. Or with metal plates in their heads. Or anywhere in their bodies. Right? You got the message? Right!"

There was a click. I passed the word out, and in five minutes we had paid our bill and were driving away. The fog was as thick as ever. The sun was an exceedingly pale halo just above the housetops. The radio said that the fog had been in the area for two days and showed no signs of leaving. It was a freak phenomenon, extending inland for forty miles north of the coast.

I had been to Salisbury twenty years before, but I have a good memory for topography and direction. And we had a city map. So we found the corner of Barnard and Gigant and located the Silver Cloud in an illegal parking area. I approached the car from the sidewalk side while Clara and Murtagh came on him from the street side.

His window was open, and the collar of his thick black coat was up and his bowler hat was tipped forward. The cigar reeked in the heavy wet air. I bent down to look at him through the window. His profile was much like that of a male of The Folk.

Clara said something to him, and he motioned to me to come into the car. Clara and Murtagh went onto the sidewalk side and leaned in to hear through the window on that side, which he had opened. He turned on the ceiling lights. His eyebrows were the thickest I'd ever seen. His nose was a smudge; his upper lip was proportionately as long as an orangutan's; his jaws protruded; his teeth were thick but widely spaced.

The eyes under those heavy supraorbital ridges were small and gray-blue. Despite his intense ugliness, he radiated likableness.

"Doc told me all about you," he said. "I don't know anything about our gang, but he said that you were the boss at your end of things, so I'm your obedient servant. I think we'd better get going, 'cause time is of the essence. You got pocket communicators so you can tell 'em back here to stick close to us. Easy to get lost in this soup."

I showed him the cigarette-lighter shaped transceivers which had a range of a half-mile. He was familiar with them, since Caliban had invented them. We got into the cars, I gave orders, and the four cars started up close on Pauncho's rear bumper. He had exceptionally long arms, and the body under the coat was keg-shaped. He talked out of the side of his mouth while the cigar bobbed up and down.

"I ain't got time to tell you everything that happened in Germany. Suffice it that we've tracked Iwaldi to this area. He's here because he knew the Nine would be holding XauXaz's funeral. They're on to his being here. They are also on to us being here, but all they know, so far, is that we are in the area, too. They've been looking for us; we've had some narrow escapes here. But that's all polluted water under the bridge. Listen, watch the road signs, will you? We got to take A-three-six-o northwest out of town. I made a dry run last night, but in this fog . . . whoops! Watch it, you crazy fool!"

A dark form swerved away from us, its horn blaring.

"Listen, the radio last night interviewed some crackpot that claimed this fog was caused by witches. Said there was a coven lived near Stonehenge. I ain't so sure he was too far off the beam. Doc says old Anana has some strange powers that reach way back into the Old Stone Age. But I'm getting off the track. Here's the shape-up. Doc and Trish—what a dish!—and Barney, my dumb-dumb buddy, are near Stonehenge, by the long barrows at the crossing of A-three-six-o and A-three-o-three. Doc says if they're gone when we get there, we should proceed on to Stonehenge. The ceremony'll take place sometime today. The Nine won't be bothered by tourists on account of the fog or the local police. They've pulled strings to assure that. Doc thinks the police have been told that the British secret service wants the area kept clear while they run down enemy agents there. It's easy when you figure that some of the biggest big shots on Downing Street are servants of the Nine."

Pauncho added that Iwaldi was in the neighborhood, though Doc and his aids had not actually seen him. The battle would be three-way with my forces and Doc's definitely in the minority. But our strategy was to hit and run. If we could get just one of the Nine, we would feel happy.

Pauncho van Veelar told us to open the small chests on the floors. We did so and brought out chain mail shirts and loinguards and close-fitting helmets. All were of irradiated plastic.

"Put them on now," he said. "Once we get there, you won't have much time to change.

Those shirts, by the way, resist a direct impact to a considerable degree. But if a man is strong enough—I am—he can tear the links apart."

We started to undress in the cramped quarters. I said, "Doc's message was rather curt. It said not to bring anyone with metal fillings in their teeth or with metal anywhere in their bodies. Now that I see this plastic armor, I'm beginning to get a vague idea of what was behind that cryptic order. Would you mind explaining so our mental fog isn't as thick as that out there?"

"Yeah, sure," he grunted. "Sorry. One thing at a time, I always say. You see, one of Doc's inventions is an inductive-field generator. It sends out a fan-shaped beam with an extreme range of half a mile. It's atomic-powered and eats up a lot of power but an amplifier enables it to radiate almost as much as it takes in. It heats up all metals within its field. Teeth fillings, rings, various articles such as watches, guns, knives, you name it. Copper telephone wires and aluminum high-tension power lines melt, and the towers get too hot to take hold of. The gas in a car's tank will explode from the heat of the metal.

"But we got weapons that we can use in a field in our trunks. Clubs—baseball bats—and plastic knives okay for stabbing but lousy for cutting. And small fiberglass crossbows with gut strings and wooden bolts with plastic points. And plastic grenades with compressed gas and detonators in them. Gunpowder, TNT, cordite, all types of explosives, become very unstable so you can't use them in plastic firearms or bombs.

Even the gas in Doc's grenades is a special type of gas."

"So it's back to the primitive?" I said. "I like that."

It was ironic that the servants of the Nine and I had fought each other in the primeval forests of remotest Africa with helicopters, napalm bombs, automatic rifles, personnel detectors, and every up-to-date weapon available. Yet here in one of the most technologically advanced and most populated nations of the world, we were to engage in battle with clubs and knives and tiny bows. And with this heavy fog, we were liable to end up using only the clubs and knives and, indubitably, our hands and feet.

"Except for the materials, the weapons'll be primitive," Pauncho said. "And the inductor prevents the use of personnel radar or other detectors in this fog, too! The Nine'll have their own inductor going, you can bet on that, and the same kind of weapons we'll have, all of which Doc invented. And maybe Iwaldi'll have his inductor on, if he really shows. Of course, he won't unless he's crazy, but he's crazy, no doubt of that. The Nine'll have an army of thugs, and they'll be using them as a big net to catch Iwaldi, not to mention us, if they win the battle, that is.

"Oh, by the way, we'll have to hoof it a mile or so. We can't take the cars inside the inductor area. But Doc says that the Nine'll have cars, enough to carry them inside the area. They got three. Steam driven and plastic. Doc made them for the old geezers for just such a setup as this. Antipoetic justice, ain't it? We ride shank's

mare, and they ride in style in cars Doc's genuis
built for them!"

We got onto A360, and Pauncho pushed the
car at eighty all the way. He talked without
letup. Ordinarily, such chatter would have
rasped my nerves, but he provided much information which I desired. He told me that he
was the son of "Jocko" Simmons and that
Barney Banks, his *dumb-bumb buddy*, was the son
of "Porky" Rivers. These were the old men who
had accompanied Doc Caliban on their last adventure at the age of eighty. I have described
them and their heroic deaths in Volume IX of
my memoirs. They were the last survivors of a
group of five who had dedicated their lives to
helping Caliban in his battle against evildoers.
(Never mind that Caliban was also working for
the Nine because they offered him immortality.
Caliban was given a free hand to battle crime as
long as he did not interfere with the Nine. I do
not condemn him for that; I succumbed to the
temptation of immortality, too.)

Pauncho and Barney were born in 1932, shortly after their mothers divorced their fathers.
Rivers and Simmons spent too much time with
their leader and their wives, fed up, cut loose.

"I remember my father, the old ape, visiting
me now and then," Pauncho said. "My mother
remarried about two years after the divorce, and
her husband adopted me. He was a great guy.
But I was torn. I liked my father at the same
time I hated him because he had, in a sense,
deserted me. Now I can appreciate why he decided in favor of adventure. But I loathed

chemistry even though my father was one of the world's greatest chemists. Maybe because of that."

Pauncho remembered visits from his "Uncle Doc" and visits to his wonderland laboratory in the eyrie of the Empire State Building. Pauncho and Barney had grown up together, since they lived three houses apart. They were in the same outfit in the Marines during the Korean War. They were visiting Doc after the deaths of their fathers, when he invited them to join him. Both had apparently inherited a love for adventure and combat from their fathers, and when they found out that Doc's own researches were close to the point where he would be able to reproduce the immortality elixir, they accepted his offer.

At the rate Pauncho was going, we would have reached the junction of the two highways in ten minutes. But we had to stop to avoid running into a pile-up of three cars. He slowed down to forty after that. Then, after a glance at the milometer, he crept along until the junction suddenly moved out from the fog. He turned right and drove for a few feet and then parked the car on the side of the road. The other cars followed. Two of the drivers got out swearing about the crazy fool Yank.

I could see no more than a few feet, but I knew that the country for miles around was as flat as Illinois farmland. A303 ran like a cannon barrel slightly northwest for about a mile and a quarter before crossing an untarred road. To get to Stonehenge, you turned left onto the untarred road and went about an eighth of a mile before

passing Stonehenge, which was behind a fence in
a field. At the junction of A344 and the small
road, you turned left and then almost immediately were at the entrance to the "venerable
and stupendous work on Salisbury Plain, vul-
garly ascribed to Merlin, the Prophet," as described by John Wood, architect of Bath, in
1747.

If the air had been clear, we would have been
able to see the white chalk wherever the soil had
been cut away.

Pauncho got out of the car and removed his
heavy overcoat. Since I was only a foot from him,
I was able to see how he got his nickname. His
belly stuck out as round as a gorilla's after a
heavy meal of bamboo shoots. But it gave the
impression of being as hard as a gorilla's chest.
His arms were freakishly long, and his legs were
very short. Even so, he stood six feet high, unlike
his father, who had been not quite five feet high.
Pauncho looked as if he weighed three hundred
and twenty pounds or so.

He opened the trunk of his car and passed out
the weapons to us. I took a baseball bat, a plastic
seven-inch long stiletto, which I put in a sheath
at my belt, a short quiver of bolts, also hung
from my belt, and a crossbow. This was small
and held with one hand, like a pistol, when fired.
The bowstring was pulled back by hand, requiring a strong man to pull it all the way back. A
catch secured the string, both of which were released when the trigger just ahead of the pistollike butt was pulled.

"If the string is set at the extreme of the three

positions and shot within a range of three feet,"
Pauncho said, "the bow will send a bolt through
the armor we're wearing. Not very far, probably
not more'n a half-inch into your flesh. But that'll
smart, and if the bolt hits unprotected flesh, it'll
go almost all the way through you."

The grenades looked like tennis balls. From
the top of each protruded a half-inch long pin.

"Twist the pin to the left as far as it'll go. Pull
the pin and then throw." Pauncho said. "Don't
dillydally. Six seconds later, the mingling of two
gases produces an explosion equivalent to one
and a quarter pound of TNT. The plastic shell is
almost atomized, so these depend on concussion
for main effect."

Two steps behind him, I followed Pauncho
into the field. We sprang over a fence, the wire of
which was warming up under the inductor's
field, and walked a few steps. He stopped. The
mound of the barrow had loomed out of the fog.
Pauncho called softly, "Hey, Doc! It's me,
Pauncho!"

There was no answer. The others, fanning out
around the barrow, called quietly. I went up and
over the mound and then along its other side.
There was no one there. By bending down with
my eyes close to the grass, I could see footprints
in the wet earth.

We returned to the cars. Pauncho swore and
blew on his enormous hands. "It's cold! That
fog goes right through my bones!"

He called out, "Hey, Countess! You any good
at warming up a man?"

Clara laughed softly and said, "You could

chase me, my pithecanthropoid friend. That would warm you up! But save your strength!"

"We'll talk this over a martini sometime," he rumbled.

"I'll meet you after the fight," she said.

"Wait'll I tell that would-be-swinger, Barney, about this," Pauncho said, and he chuckled like a troll under a bridge.

I said, "Silence!"

Shouts were drifting through the gray wetness. Muffled cracks, as of bats striking bats or armor or, perhaps, bone, disturbed the cloud.

I called them in around me and told them what we should do for the moment. We started out just as a few more cracking noises came and then a scream which was cut off as if a knife had plunged into the throat. A grenade boomed three seconds later. Then silence returned.

If there were many people at Stonehenge, they were not conducting a full-scale battle. The sounds gave us the impression of blundering around, of probing activity by men who were not sure even after they had closed with another whether he was enemy or friend.

"We'll walk along the road until we're just opposite the first of the tumuli."

"What the hell's a tumuli?" someone muttered.

"A tumulus is an artificial mound, a round barrow," I said. "A grave for the ancients. This area is filled with them. We'll scout around there, take it easy, because Iwaldi or the Nine may have stationed people there. Keep close together. We don't want to get separated in this fog. Yes, I know bunching makes us better targets, but that can't be helped.

"And don't fire at the first person you see. He may be one of Doc's people. Now you've gotten the descriptions of Doc and Banks and his cousin. If you can identify them, sing out and identify yourself. Pongo is the code word."

"Identify them? In this fog soup?" a man muttered.

"Do your best," I said. "Outside of Caliban's group, everybody is our enemy."

I did not really expect Murtagh's men to refrain from shooting until they were one hundred percent certain. They were all very tough and self-centered characters, and they were not about to wait until hit before they opened up. But at least they knew what their allies were supposed to look like.

We walked on the edge of the road with me in the lead. I held the butt of the crossbow in my right hand and the bat in my left.

The sounds had ceased but as soon as we reached the burial barrow three explosions deafened us. All of us dived for the wet ground, even though there was no indication that the grenades were being thrown our way. Then I rose, and, crouching, ran to the ditch around the outer wall of the barrow and dived into it. I fell on top of a man squatting on his heels. He grunted, I grunted, and I broke his jaw with a backhanded blow from the butt end of my bat.

Somebody nearby in the fog said, "What the hell is that? You all right, Meeters?"

The man I'd knocked out was not named

Meeters, because he answered on my left about ten feet away.

At that moment Clara and Pauncho appeared in the fog, so I jumped up, yelling, and started swinging with the bat. I kept hold of the crossbow, which was loaded, until I was facing two at one time. One I shot through the mouth with the bolt and the other I knocked down with a blow that broke my bat, his bat, and his skull under his helmet.

I think I cleared the ditch on my side. But there were men on the other side of the barrow. Instead of charging around the ditch or coming over the top of the barrow, they took off. Somewhere in the fog some of them got down on the ground and began firing bolts back. All these did was to bury themselves in the dirt of the mound. But we scrambled into the ditch as if they could hit us. And of couse they might flank us.

While I checked for dead or wounded among us, and found that only two of us were out of the fight, Murtagh and Pauncho examined the enemy. All ten were dead or unconscious. But there was no way of determining if they were Iwaldi's or the Nine's. They were dressed in civilian clothes with a bright yellow band pinned across their chests. All had plastic chain mail shirts under cloth shirts, plastic loinguards, and helmets shaped exactly like ours.

Gbampwe, a black from Central Africa who said he was a champion spear thrower, and I cast grenades into the fog. I threw mine with a force which should have taken them about four hundred feet. They opened up the fog with a red roar. I couldn't tell if I hit anything because the only reply was a volley of bolts, some of which hit the soft earth of the barrow above us.

Somebody far away called. I could not make out the words, which were either garbled by the atmospheric conditions or were purposely distorted.

I bellowed, "Pongo! Pongo! Pongo!"

"Pongo your . . . !" somebody yelled, his last words lost in an uproar of shouts and screams and cracking bats.

Pauncho growled, "The farmers around here must be screaming their heads off for the police. And I'll bet they can hear those grenades clear on the other side of Amesbury. It's only two miles away."

It must have been a strain on the local police to give excuses for the explosions and for the loss of power. They must have wondered themselves just what the secret service was doing out around Stonehenge. But they would, of course, obey their orders. I took it for granted that the same orders had gone to the armed service posts in this area, of which there were many.

I threw another grenade. It went off almost exactly between the locations of the two previous blasts. Bolts whistled nearby after the explosion, but none struck us. It seemed reasonable that I might have killed the men we'd run out of the ditch, and that these missiles came from another group. On the other hand, they might be holding their fire, hoping we would think just that.

To our right, approximately at Stonehenge, another flurry of cracking noises came muffled through the fog.

I gave the order to get out of the ditch and to advance across the field. We would go parallel with the road on a course which would bring us near the so-called "slaughter stone." This lies outside the circle of the trilithons and sarsens and near the heel stone, which is named thus for no verifiable reason.

Suddenly, there was not a sound except for the rustle of our feet moving through the wet winter weeds and a slight sucking as feet were pulled up from mud. We were formed in three lines. I was in the lead with Clara, Pauncho, and Murtagh behind me at the limits of my sight. If I had stepped up my pace a trifle, I would have been all alone, as far as my ability to see was concerned. About halfway to the slaughter stone, or at a point which I believed to be halfway, I threw up my hand. The three behind me also signaled, and then the whole body was at rest. There was no more sound than if we had been at the bottom of a deep cave.

The only thing you could hear was the hum of nervous tension.

Out there were many men moving slowly, their eyes straining against the gray cloud, their breaths controlled, their feet descending and ascending slowly to avoid the suck of mud and brush of wet grass. Their ears were turning this way and that to catch a betraying sound.

My hearing and sense of smell are far keener than most humans, for reasons which I have explained in Volume II of my memoirs. But there was not a breath of wind, and the heavy droplet-ridden cloud seemed to be killing both sound and odor. I had a mental picture of enemy all around us, men who, if they knew where we were, could have cut us down with their crossbows or overwhelmed us with numbers alone. The blindness was to our advantage because of our very small force.

I gestured for us to advance. And then I heard a poofing sound, which I interpreted immediately, and correctly, as it turned out. I turned and gave the signal to hit the earth and then did so.

No sooner had I hugged the earth than an intensely bright light shot through the cloud above us. Somebody had sent up a flare. It had to be entirely nonmetallic, of course.

It did not turn night into day, but it did outline a mass of figures beyond the depression in which was the slaughter stone. And it showed me some vague figures gathered around the somewhat tilted sixteen-foot high heel stone to my right near the road.

There were six or more ahead and about eight to the right. None of them made the signal agreed upon if visibility should be restored.

But they had seen us stretched out on the ground. They had also seen each other.

We fired crossbow bolts back at both groups as they fired at us and at each other.

That seemed to be a signal for bedlam. Beyond, in the gray mists around the circle of Stonehenge, grenades opened the fog with flames. Men behind me screamed, and men ahead of me screamed.

And then there was silence again except for the groans of the wounded. These were shut up as quickly as we could with our hands over their mouths and then with morphine. I suppose the other groups had done the same, because I could not hear any wounded from any quarter.

Silence again.

If those two groups had not moved ... I lobbed two grenades in quick order at where I thought they should be. The blasts came one after the other. There were screams and moans after the reverberations had died away. Then answering blasts, the flashes of which I could not see. The wounded quit making noises. By then I was up, crouching, and had told my men to follow me to the left, across the field. I was afraid that those not hit would retaliate with grenades. And while I doubted that anyone of them could throw a grenade as far as I had, we would still be within stunning range. Or one of them might run forward and toss the grenade.

It was a mistake on my part. A dark body suddenly appeared ahead of me, a crossbow string twanged, others near it let loose, and about six of my men, as I was to find out, were killed. I went down but not because I was shot. I fell forward, shooting my crossbow as I went. After I had hit the earth, I reloaded my weapon. The men ahead were silenced, and when I crawled forward, cautiously, I found three corpses and one wounded, unconscious. He had a bright yellow strip, splashed with blood, across his chest. I put him out of his misery with my stiletto.

Our outburst triggered off another in the vicinity of the ruins. Bolts whistled overhead. I think they were strays, but even so, one caught one of my men in the neck.

I crawled on and came across the first of many bodies within a narrow area. I counted twenty-five.

"Listen!" I said to Pauncho. "I don't know what is going on. But I doubt that any of the Nine would expose themselves as we have. They value their wrinkled hides far too much. But they must have come here because they would want to bring Iwaldi out in the open. And they *will* take chances. So they have to be here. I wonder if they could have exposed themselves long enough to bring Iwaldi's men out and then cut and run for it? Or they could be holed up in their cars."

But, cautious as they were, they were not cowards. And they were completists. They would want to make sure that Iwaldi had been killed. And if they knew that there were other forces operating in the grayness, they would be certain that these would be Doc or I or both. They would not rest until our heads had been brought before them.

I said, "I'm going to go back to the road and scout along it. You come along as far as the fence. Stay there for twenty minutes. If I'm not back by then, it's up to you what you do."

"Doc probably needs our help!" Pauncho said. "There are a hell of a lot of men out there!"

As if to prove his statement, the fog was shattered with three grenade explosions somewhere to our left. And then we heard the whoosh of several bolts very near us. Somebody was shooting at random.

Clara wormed to me and said, "I want to go

with you, James! I proved I can fight along with you!"

"All right," I said. "Let's make for the fence."

"Doc said I was to be under your orders while I was with you," Pauncho said. "But he told me I could rejoin him as soon as I got the chance. Well, now I got the chance. And that dumb-dumb Barney, he'd fall down and break his leg if I wasn't there to hold him up. And Doc may need me. No telling what's going on out there."

"You do whatever you think best," I said. I appreciated his loyalty and his concern for his comrades, and he had carried out his mission: to get us to the battlefield.

"Yeah, I'd like to stick with you, but I got a hunch they really need me," Pauncho said. "So long. Good luck."

He crawled away. I led the others to the road and ended up by the heel stone. This tilted to the south as if it were an ancient tombstone and the earth around it had yielded up its dead. Ten corpses lay around it. I looked them over and determined that about five had been killed by a blast, presumably from the grenade I had thrown. These men had yellow bands across their chests.

Murtagh said, "I would prefer that we all go together. If we don't, we're likely to end up shooting each other in this damned fog!"

At that moment, the firing stopped again for a few seconds, a pistol fired, there was some shouting, and then silence.

I said, "Clara and I'll go down the road. If you hear firing down there, stay here. I'll give you

the code word when I come back. Pauncho
knows where you are, so if he finds Doc he may
bring them here."

Clara and I started to go down the dirt along
the right side of the road. We had gone only a
few feet when I heard the tires of a car accelerat-
ing swiftly, near the vicinity of the crossroads.
There was no sound of a motor, so I knew it was
a steam-driven car. And immediately after,
grenades broke loose across the road from us. I
don't know that they were throwing them directly at us on purpose, because they could not have
seen across the road. But Murtagh and his men
lobbed their grenades back across the road, and
then suddenly figures loomed out of the fog. The
roar of the car increased, and then I felt a hard
blow against my chest. I looked down, dimly saw
a grenade at my feet, leaned down and threw it
back. It went off in the air and the grayness became black.

When I recovered consciousness, I was lying
on my side on the cold wet earth. My ears rang,
and my head felt as if it had swelled to pumpkin
size. I put my hand on my head and felt a stick-
iness. I tasted my fingers. It was blood running
out from a small cut on my throbbing head.

The noise level around me must have been
high, because surely there were men screaming
and groaning. Two bodies lay within touching
distance, and when I got to my hands and knees
and began crawling around, feeling for a club or
a crossbow, I came across three more corpses. I
found a crossbow and a quiver containing six
bolts on a still body. I got to my feet and stag-

gered across the road, stumbled over another
body, fell down into a small depression, crawled
out, and stopped. Something large and black
and metallic-feeling was blocking my way.

I pulled myself up onto it, and then my senses,
slowly clearing, told me it was the plastic steam
car. It was lying on its side; the doors on the
upper side were open. I looked into it and saw
one body huddled down against the lower side in
the back. I looked up across the car and saw a
few flashes, like fireflies on a broad meadow.
They were from grenade explosions, but I could
not hear a thing.

Prowling around the car in the milky fog, I
found a man in a chauffeur's uniform face-down
on the road. He had been hit on the head with a
bat and then stabbed in the throat.

I went back to the car. I hated to be trapped
inside it, but I had to find out who that was in
the rear seat. I climbed up and into the well with
less than my usual suppleness and strength. The
explosion had taken much out of me. By the
corpse, I lit a match and shone it on the face for
a moment.

He was one of the Mongolian members of the
Nine, withered old Jiizfan. Those eyes, which
had been young when there was still a land
bridge between England and the continent, were
closed. There was no sign of a wound except a
dark mark on his forehead.

I put my ear against his chest and heard nothing. Then I placed a thumb on his skinny wrist
and detected a very light pulse.

I raised my head and looked into the ragged
pits of his eyes.

His hand moved. I caught it and squeezed. The bones ground together, and he screamed out.

It was a pitiful cry, but he had been responsible for the deaths of thousands, perhaps millions, during his multi-millennia-long life. God alone knew how many he had tortured. And he would have had me killed instantly if it was in his power.

I turned on the flashlight for just a moment, shining it on my face so he could see who it was. Then I cast the beam in his face. His eyes were wide open, his mouth was sagging.

Before I could reach up and twist his neck, his hand fell back and he slumped down. I felt his pulse. His heart had given out on seeing me.

However, a man who has lived that long, especially for so long in the Orient, may conceivably be able to stop his own heart for a while through mental means. When I climbed out, I carried his head by the long white hair. I wasn't sure what I was going to do with it. Toss it among his men if I could find them, I suppose. But I laid it down by the car while I investigated, and I never did pick it up again.

From the wounds on the bodies around the car, and the bashed-in rear, and the skid marks, I reconstructed the accident. Just as the men had charged across the road, to attack us or to run away from attackers, the lead car had plowed in among them. It had knocked several high into the air but its wheels had struck several bodies on the road, and it had turned over. It must have been going about sixty miles an hour when it hit. The car behind it had run over some bodies and rammed the rear of the first car just as it turned over on its side. Then the second car had backed up and taken off.

The occupants of the wrecked car, except for Jiizfan, had managed to crawl out, assisted by the chauffeur. (I suddenly remembered seeing him at one of the annual ceremonies.) He had been shot down, perhaps by his own people in the fog. The others, whom I presumed were of the Nine, had gotten away. Whether they had gotten into the second car or were walking along the road through the fog was something I could only determine if I went after them.

I did not know how long I had been unconscious. I did not know whether or not Clara or Doc were within a few feet and shouting out the codeword.

I circled around and around and found all of my party dead except for Clara, Murtagh, and Szeleszny. The attack that had gotten me must have gotten them, too. One of the corpses was carrying a quiver with several bolts. I fitted one to my bow, picked up a bat, checked that I still had my knife and two grenades. The fog, which had started to turn whitish, was much darker. Apparently, above the fog, other clouds had moved in.

I went down the route I had started before being so violently interrupted. My head still felt as if somebody were pumping a very painful gas into it. My ears had not stopped ringing.

The fog became less dark again as I came to the junction of the two roads. I turned around in the slowly whitening mists to the left and cut across the road. Moving along the road on my right, I came to the entrance to the ruins. By then the ringing in my ears was not so loud, and my head did not feel quite so much like a balloon. But it still hurt.

Out of the thick milkiness, dark figures appeared, one by one. They were corpses on the white chalky path before me. Between the entrance at the northeast corner of the field and the flat stone at the perimeter of the ruins, just beyond the end of the path, I counted thirty-three bodies. I did not stop to investigate all of them, but many that I did had caved-in skulls, broken necks, or shattered jaws. Those with no marks of violence except swollen heads, bulging eyes, and bloody issues from nose, eye, and ear were the victims of grenades.

I stood for a while by the flat stone and tried to listen. I also sniffed the air, but could smell nothing but a wet wooliness. Then I advanced slowly to the left until two flat stones bulked out of the mist. These were broken stones lying on their sides. If I remembered correctly, just beyond the farthest was the first of the upright monoliths of the "gigantick pile." A few steps showed me that my memory had not failed me. The blackish-gray tablet seemed to drift out of the fog as if it were the mast of a stone ship.

Three bodies lay between its foot and the flat stone by it.

I determined, while I stood there, straining my senses to detect living bodies in the cloud, to go to the right, toward the center of the inner circle of trilithons and monolith. There the fu-

neral ceremony for XauXaz would have been
held, if the Nine had been allowed to hold it.
And there his body might still be, if the Nine had
been routed.

Then, to my right, a body did emerge from the
milkiness. It put one foot before the other while
it leaned forward, straining to see. It held something in front of it which, a second later, I saw
was her crossbow.

We moved closer. Her bow was up, and her
finger was ready to squeeze the trigger, and then
she recognized me.

I did not speak because I did not want anyone
else to hear us. And I could not hear Clara. I
would have to read her lips, which would not be
easy in the syrupiness.

Something came down out of the cloud. It
seemed to have dropped from an airplane, but it
must have been crouched on top of the monolith
to my left, about fourteen feet high. It landed
hard and rolled and disappeared and then was
up on its feet and bounding toward Clara. She
had jumped back, almost disappearing from my
sight, and then she came forward again but with
her right side turned to me. She loosed the arrow
at the monstrous figure, which had been swallowed by the fog again but which she must have
seen because she was closer.

Then the hulking shape leaped out of the fog
as if vomited by it, grabbed her arm, went on,
turning her upsidedown and then over. I ran up
to her. I was too late. Her right arm had been
twisted and torn off, along with the jacket and
the chain mail shirt, by the enormous strength of

that brute. The dark blood gushed out over the white chalk. She was dead.

My beautiful and brave and loving Clara was dead.

Her sudden death and its manner froze me. But I was additionally horrified because of the unexpectedness of the creature's appearance. I had thought that Dick was in Central Africa, waiting for me to return.

I did not know how he had gotten here, but the Nine had to have something to do with it. He had gotten into contact with them, and they had decided to use him against me instead of killing him. They needed somebody who was stronger than I and knew all the techniques of hand and foot fighting. And who, in an arena where gunpowder and metal were forbidden, would be like a lion loose. A lion with the mind of a man.

And while I stood over her and was as motionless and as dumb as those ancient piles around me, the huge shape dived out of the fog.

I went down. But, before he touched me, I came out of the horror as if I had been slid down a greased chute. I went onto my back and my feet kicked up. The bat and the crossbow were flung to one side. His hands were over my face—they would have taken my face off if they could have gotten a grip—and he went on over me and into the fog, propelled by the impact of my feet on the underside of his great paunch.

I grabbed the bat—the crossbow was lost in the mists—and I got on my feet and was ready when he came out of the wooliness again. But this time he was feet first, his body almost par-

allel with the ground, and those short but
gorilla-powerful legs bent. They straightened
out, and if they had hit my chest would have
broken the bones. They did hit the club with
enough force to knock it from my hands.

I rolled back and away into the fog and came
down hard because I had not been fully prepared for that type of attack and I had slipped in
Clara's blood.

He came down on Clara's body, then disappeared.

I was up and heading toward where I hoped
the nearest monolith would be. I wanted to get
my back to it, get my feet against it, and then
launch myself at him, if he showed again. There
was the chance that we would blunder by each
other, perhaps not see each other again in this
place. But his hearing was, as far as I knew, un-
affected, and mine was still absent. That gave
him an advantage. I wanted to stay in one spot,
where he could not approach me from the rear,
and wait for him. Even my breathing would have
to be silent; I controlled the urge to suck in deep
breaths.

At the foot of the rough pillar, blackish in the
fog, the toe of my shoe nudged something. I knelt
down and felt it. It was Clara's arm, thrown
aside by the anthropoid.

I picked it up by the wrist with my right hand
and drew my stiletto with my left hand. I waited.
I could see about a foot before me. I wondered if
there were sounds of a frantic battle going on
around me. Perhaps Doc Caliban or his men or
Trish Wilde or Murtagh were crying for aid only
a few feet from me.

Suddenly, I smelled him. He had to be very close for me to detect him in the thick-droppled cloud. And he would, of course, smell me.

I swung the arm as hard as I could before me, and it slapped his dark shoving-forward face just as it came like a black ghost out of the mists. But a powerful blow from him struck my wrist and knocked the stiletto into the mists.

The force of the blow from Clara's arm squeezed more blood out of it over his face. It blinded him, disconcerted him, and so the club he swung in his left hand missed me and broke against the stone where I had been. And I came up with my left fist with all my force into his belly, exactly against the wound I had given him on that mountain road in Africa.

He bent forward, clutching at his belly, and I slammed my right fist behind his left ear. He sagged forward and went down on his knees, and I hit the back side of that huge massively muscled neck with the edge of my palm.

If he had been a man, he would have died. But he was only half-stunned, and he came up and around with his right hand in a karate chop—though I think it was purely a reflex—and my left arm felt as if it, too, had been torn off.

The agony would come later. At that moment, the arm was thick as mine. I also hurt my knee so much that I could only hobble for a long time after that. But it was worth it.

He fell face-down, and I thought he surely must be dead. But he rolled over while I stared at him and I bit my lips to keep from groaning with the agony of my knee and my left arm. I stared while he got to a sitting position. I started forward, determined to kick him with my left foot, though I did not know how I could stand on my right while I was doing it. He looked at me moving through the fog at him and then he fell back and stared upward. Suspecting a trick, I circled him, with difficulty since I could not move without great pain. I approached him from behind. He did not move. Then I knelt down, again with difficulty, and closed my one good hand around his throat. I began to squeeze. His eyes opened. His tongue came out. He rolled his head slightly, but his arms did not move. And then that enormous chest quit rising and falling.

It could as easily have been me on the ground and probably would have been if he had not skidded in Clara's blood.

I released my hold on his throat and turned away. At that moment, announced by a grenade exploding in the distance, as if some dramatist in the sky had arranged matters, the first breeze cooled my face. The wind increased as I walked toward the inner circle of the ruins, and within a few strides I could see se

There were bodies everywhere, clubs, bows, arrows, and plastic knives. Murtagh was not among them.

In the center, lying on his back, his arms crossed, was XauXaz.

His catafalque was of ornately carved oak with affixed golden images. His enormous white beard covered his chest and his stomach. The old wide-brimmed floppy hat lay above his head; his right eye was covered with a black patch held on by a thin black band. A huge black raven sat on each shoulder.

As I approached, they flew away, crying harshly.

Beyond, over the body, the mists were thinning.

There were more corpses past the trilithons.

I stood by the body of my grandfather, of the man who may have fathered many times in the Grandrith line, the millennia-old man who had once been worshiped as a god, as Wothenjaz by the first Germanic speakers, then as Wothen and Othinn and Wodan. The Mad One. He had many names, but in the caves of the Nine, he was called XauXaz, which meant, in proto-Germanic, High. And his brothers were Ebn XauXaz, or Just-As-High, and Thrithjaz, or Third. All dead now.

Soon the mists would be blown away. And the rude and massive and brooding stones would be revealed on this level land. And there would be visible this ancient, very ancient oaken catafalque and the body of the man who looked as if he were a hundred years old but had actually been born sometime between 10,000 B.C. and 20,000 B.C. And there would be the body of a creature that science had thought had perished a million and a half years ago. And there would be the other bodies, and the primitive weapons by which they had perished, the clubs and the bows and arrows with plastic tips and the plastic daggers.

Unless the Nine arranged to keep the area shut long enough to have the bodies hauled away, and all speculation hushed up, the story of the battle at Stonehenge would go around the world. And the mystery would be pondered on for years. Perhaps for as long as men were on this planet.

But I knew the Nine, and I knew that those who had gotten away, old Anana and Ing and the others, would arrange to cover up everything.

In fact, if I did not get out at once, I might be caught in the net they had undoubtedly spread to drag in all who would try to leave this area.

I hobbled past the great stones and out across the field. I thought I had seen, for a brief moment when the mists had parted, a number of bicycles on the edge of the field. These would be plastic, of course, and might have been brought here by Caliban. If I could pedal one of these, though handicapped by a useless left arm and a knee which it was agony to bend, then I could get to a car. I might have to steal one, but I knew how to do this, even though born and bred in the jungle.

It was then the fog split, and I saw the giant figure of a man with a peculiar bronzish hair and skin. By his side was a tall woman with the same coloring and a man with grotesquely broad shoulders and long arms, Pauncho. There were four men and a woman I did not recognize.

Bodies lay near them.

I hurried toward him, then had to slow down because of the pain.

Doc had stopped and was waiting for me. Then, seeing I was in such trouble, he ran toward me.

I smiled for the first time in a long time. We had gotten through, and we would get away. I would find out what had happened to Clio. And then we would go to the mountains which conceal the caves of the Nine and there do what had to be done.

THE MAD GOBLIN

*A Note From
Philip José Farmer:*

Although the editors of Ace Books insist upon pub-
lishing this work as a novel under my by-line, it is
really the work of James Caliban, M.D. Doc Caliban
wrote this story in the third person singular, though
it is autobiographical. He feels that this approach enables him to be more objective. My opinion is that
the use of the first person singular would make him
feel very uncomfortable. Doc Caliban does not like to
get personal; at least, he doesn't like to do so with
most people. Even the largest mountain throws a
shadow.

Three figures moved in and out of the shadows of clouds and trees. The moon was riding high over the alpine mountain of Gramz in the Black Forest of southern Germany, only a few miles from the Swiss border. Long black clouds raced under it like lean wolves lashed by moonlight beams. Their shadow selves loped over the precipitous western side of Gramz Berg, bounding over the squat and massive stone pile of the castle on top of the mountain, writhing down the jagged slope toward the narrow sheen of the Toll River two thousand feet below.

The three figures were men toiling up the rock-strewn, pine-dotted slant. One was six feet seven inches high. He had the body of a Hercules. His bare head glinted dark-bronzish in the moonlight. If there had been more light, his eyes would have been a very light gray-green with many flecks of bright yellow.

The second man was about six feet tall but

seemed much shorter because of the enormous breadth of shoulders and trunk. His arms were disproportionately long and his legs almost freakishly short. The forehead was low and backward slanting. The ridges of bone above his eyes were massive. His nose was a flat wide-nostriled blob, and his chin receded. His ears stuck out like the wings of an owl. His hair was the color of a rusty nail.

The last in line was also six feet tall, but he had the body of a greyhound. His face was that of a handsome fox. His hair was as black and as straight as an Apache's.

The lead man climbed swiftly, though he was burdened with an enormous backpack. The second man, huffing and puffing, called out. He sounded like the grunting of a bear at the end of a long hollow log.

"Have a heart, Doc! You're killing me!"

The third man said, "Yeah, Doc, maybe you ought to put him on your back, too! Carry old softy Pauncho van Veelar like the baby he is! Forget your pacifier, Pauncho? I brought one along just in case!"

The gorilla-bodied man turned and said, "Barney Banks! You gotta lotta guts! If it wasn't for you hanging onto my coattails, if I didn't have to drag you along, too, I wouldn't be near so tired! Besides, you ain't got the weight I got to carry, you scarecrow!"

"We'll rest," the big man said. His voice was deep and resonant, as if his throat contained many small bronze gongs. He sat down on a boulder and waited patiently. Though he could have kept on going without rest at twice the speed all the way to the top, he did not mind stopping. Nor did he mind the bickering of Pauncho van Veelar and Barney Banks. It reminded him of the old days, when their fathers, who looked and sounded so much like them, had carried on a similar running verbal battle.

While the two murmured blistering insults, he looked up the silver-and-black-brindled mountainside. A cloud whipped past the moon, and its lights shone again on the black many-turreted *schloss* still six hundred feet above. The lower wall looked as smooth as the palm of his hand from this distance. But, having gone near it in a helicopter in the daytime, he knew that there were projections and fissures on it. He had studied the photographs and planned the exact course he would take and alternate routes if circumstances barred him from the first.

Doc Caliban reached into a pocket of the vest under his thick jacket and pulled out two pills. He gave one to Barney Albany Banks and one to William Grier van Veelar. They popped them into their mouths and, a few seconds later, felt invigorated.

Doc Caliban began climbing again. The moon raced the clouds and lost but still gained distance across the starry arc. The last six hundred feet were the toughest. Here the mountain became solid perpendicular rock. The three put big flexible plastic discs on their hands and applied these to the rock. The degree of suction was controlled by the degree of pressure on the handles inside the discs.

They reached the junction of rock and the
base of the castle. Here they clung to their discs.
Their progress was slower from this point on.
The alternation of exposed moon and concealing
clouds flickered light over them. They seemed
like lumps of stone, so minute was their ascent.
But as time went by they gained their goal: a
narrow opening about sixty feet from the base.

A minute before Doc Caliban pulled himself
level with the bottom of the embrasure, a light
shone in it.

Doc hung by one disc while he squeezed the
other down into a small cylindrical form and
stuck it in a pocket in his vest. He then took out
a small handweapon from a pocket in his jacket.
This was of .15 caliber and shot explosive bullets
with a velocity of 4,000 feet a second. The accuracy was, of course, limited, but by holding on
the trigger, the entire clip of fifty bullets would
be emptied within six seconds. The butt contained a compressed liquid which became a gas
ignited by a spurt of another gas into the firing
chamber.

Doc Caliban held the gas repeater ready if
someone should look out the window. But no
sound was heard or object seen from the embrasure. The light, however, remained.

After a few seconds, Doc replaced the gun and
took out the disc for his right hand and began his
turtlelike climbing. When his chin was above the
ledge of the opening, he stopped. The light
showed him a narrow landing of stone within
stone walls. Opposite was a narrow door of black
wood with a tracery of red-painted iron. The embrasure had one vertical bar set in it and a win-

dow of glass which would have to be swung inward to be opened.

Hanging by his left disc, Doc Caliban withdrew two long wires about a twelfth of an inch in diameter. He tied one end around the lower part of the iron bar. Then he released the pressure of the disc. He pulled himself upward with one hand by the bar, reached up, and with one hand tied the end of the other wire around the upper part of the bar. After this, he lowered himself until he was below the embrasure, put a disc on his right hand so he could hang on the wall, and pressed a small button in a tiny device in a pocket in his vest.

Fire spurted from the wires around the bar. Doc went back up the embrasure, pulled the bar out and then laid it on the embrasure with its end sticking out. Inside the narrow opening, crouched with his back against one wall and his face almost touching the other, he tested the window with one hand. It did not seem likely that an alarm would be installed on this window, where only eagles could be expected to land. But there was only one way of finding out. He cut the glass with a diamond after applying a suction disc to it. When he had lowered it to the inner wall of the landing, he climbed through. A few minutes later, Pauncho's broad shoulders and big hard stomach came through. He groaned as his shoulders caught on the edges, and Barney, below him, said, "What's the matter, fatty?"

Barney could not see Pauncho, of course, but he guessed what was happening.

As Barney's head came above the ledge of the embrasure he found himself looking into the savagely grinning chimpanzee face of Pauncho.

"Who's a fatty, Bones?" he said.

"Quit clowning around!" Barney said. "I'm tired of hanging around here like a bat! I know you like it, since you're half-batty. But I don't! Let me in!"

Pauncho put a huge hand, the back of which was covered with thick dark-red hairs, against Barney's face. "One shove, and you can solo without wings."

Doc Caliban said, "We haven't time for that." Pauncho backed away, and Barney climbed in. Doc Caliban pulled up the latch of the door, but the door would not swing out. He then started down the steps, the little gas-operated gun in his big hand. Behind him on the stairway, which was too narrow for two men abreast, were Pauncho and Barney. Each held a gun like Doc's.

They went down three complete windings of the corkscrew staircase before coming onto a broader landing. Doc tried the wooden door here, and it opened noiselessly, its hinges having been recently oiled. The room beyond was huge, reached by a short flight of steps leading downward. At one end was a big canopied bed. The walls were naked granite blocks except where covered by huge tapestries. There were a few pieces of massive oak furniture. Heads glared down from the walls: elks, elephant, rhinoceros, African buffalo and American bison, wolf, lion, tiger, leopard, jaguar, kodiak bear. They were fine specimens but nothing extraordinary. They could be found in the game room of any man with money and time and the need to slaughter.

But on a table in a corner, near the huge fireplace on the western wall, was a mounted animal that he had never seen outside some drawings based on speculation and a photograph that could be faked.

"*Tatzelwurm,*" he said.

It was a lizardlike reptile with a long slim snakelike body about five and a half feet long. The skin was brownish on top and somewhat lighter on the bottom. Its four legs were very short. The heavy and blunt-snouted head merged into the thick body with no bridge of a neck. The eyes were large and round and a light green.

"What's a *Tatzelwurm?*" Pauncho said. He stood beside the specimen, and the two, except for Pauncho's clothes, would have made a prehistoric tableau. He could have been a Neanderthal and the lizard a leftover from even earlier days.

"It's a reptile that's been reported as living in the Alps," Doc said. "There have been too many witnesses with similar descriptions over too long a period of time for any doubt, about its existence. It could be a form of giant salamander or skink. But the longest ever seen was about three feet long. This is a monster. I wonder where Iwaldi got this? And I wonder how many years ago?"

There was enough dust on the furniture and specimens to indicate that this room was not much used. Nor was there anything of value for the business at hand.

Caliban, however, went over the room as swiftly as he could, looking for hidden entrances to tunnels and electronic detection devices. A few minutes later, he led Pauncho and Barney out of the room and down the winding staircase. On the next landing, they found a hallway running to the north and walked down it. There were three doors along the hall and one at the end. Caliban looked into the first three and found them empty rooms with piles of boxes and furniture. The door at the end revealed another huge bedroom. This was furnished with expensive tapestries and a bed and table like the one above, but it lacked the mounted heads. The fireplace was glowing with coals, and the bed was in disorder and still bore the impression of a body.

A closet door was behind a tall wooden screen on which was painted a medieval battle scene. The clothes hanging in the closet were those of a woman, but the variety was amazing.

"She sure must go to a lot of costume balls," Pauncho said. "Or else she's a collector of historical clothes."

The closet was big enough to have made a satisfactory bedroom in most houses. By walking down the various racks, the three walked through history, starting approximately at the middle of the seventeenth century. Most of the clothing was preserved in airtight plastic bags filled with gas, probably helium.

This was interesting and somewhat puzzling, but they were not inside the castle for a Cook's tour. Caliban said, "Go!", being one who hates to waste words, and they left the closet and started toward the door to the hallway.

There was a slight chuffling sound behind them. It was heard only by Doc Caliban, whose ears had been sensitized by a chemical he had invented. He whirled, and the others began to turn as soon as he started to move. A section of the stone wall had slid smoothly aside and out of the blackness leaped huge gray forms. They were Canadian timber wolves, and they uttered no sound except for the click of nails on the stone floor. On top of each of their heads was a hemisphere of some gray material about the size of a ping-pong ball cut in half.

Ten bounded out of the hole, their jaws open and slavering, the white teeth ready to clamp down, driven by jaws powerful enough to take off a man's arm with one bite.

The first wolf, arcing toward Barney, who had been at the end of the line, suddenly found the giant with the dark red hair and the peculiar gray-green-and-yellow eyes at the end of its leap. A hand with muscles like pythons seized the wolf by the throat and Caliban whirled. The wolf shot out of the suddenly opened hand and went past Barney and Pauncho, its tail flicking Barney's face. It crashed into the door and fell in a limp heap.

Caliban kept on whirling, and the edge of his palm struck the second wolf in its midleap and broke its neck with a sound as of an axe chopping a tree.

Pauncho knew the necessity of silence, but he found it almost impossible to throttle himself when he was in a fight to the death. His first cry was like a bull fiddle being strummed way down in a mountain hollow, and the strummings came faster and faster but somewhat higher as the struggle continued. His enormous fists smashed into the tender noses of the beasts or on top of their heads, crushing the delicate hemispheres and stunning the brains beneath. Twice he shot animals with the gun in his left hand. Twice he went down, bowled backward by a body the jaws of which closed on his jacketed plastic chain-mailed arm.

Barney had shifted his gun to his left hand too, and a six-inch knife had suddenly appeared in his right. Like a ballet dancer, he whirled among the wolves, bending, bounding, thrusting. Then he went down with the impact of a huge male on his shoulders, and two others jumped in to savage him.

Pauncho, roaring, kicked one of the wolves so hard in the rear that he raised it off the floor and sent it rolling over the tangle of Barney and wolves. The wolf did not get up again. Then Pauncho seized a tail and dragged the wolf, its legs pumping frantically to keep its grip on the floor, away from Barney. The wolf turned to bite Pauncho, but Pauncho fell on it with his hands around its throat. Another wolf leaped on his back only to be lifted up and smashed against the wall by Doc Caliban.

Barney yelled when the teeth of a wolf exerted very painful pressure on his calf. They would have cut through his muscles if it had not been for the plastic chain-mailed longjohns he was wearing. Barney shot the wolf, rolled away, put up his arm to ward off another wolf, and blew its eye and a good part of its brains out.

Caliban had grabbed two wolves by the throats as they leaped together at him and banged their heads together again and again. A third fastened its teeth around his leg, tearing the cloth of his pants. The pressure of the jaws hurt Doc's leg, but he made no sound. His face expressionless, he dropped the two unconscious wolves and seized the third beast by the ears. He jerked upward so violently he tore the animal's ears off, and it let loose of him and fled back to the hole. But before it reached it, it stopped, stood trembling for a moment, then wheeled and charged Doc again.

Caliban was amazed at its behavior. Its actions could only be accounted for by some influence from the hemisphere on top of its head.

He charged the wolf and as it rose upward toward his throat he bent over beneath it and then came up with his fist into the beast's belly. It kept on going, but its hind quarters flew up with the impact of the blow and it turned over and landed on its back. It did not get up.

Suddenly, the fight was over. There was silence except for the heavy breathing of Pauncho and Barney. Not once had the wolves uttered even a growl.

Doc Caliban smelled the sting of explosives and the rich undercurrent of blood. There had been a time when he had savored those odors, even though he had not liked killing. Only once in his life, when he had gone mad from the side effects of the immortality elixir, had he enjoyed killing. Now he could not tolerate the odors associated with death once the immediate need for

being in their neighborhood was over. He said,
"Let's go!" and they picked up their guns. The
section of wall had slid back into place. It was
obvious that whoever was controlling it was not
going to open it again unless to release another
form of death. It was possible that the opening
was done automatically, and that they could find
the controls to reopen it. But he wanted to get
away from here in case the action was not automatic. Besides, alarms would be ringing somewhere in the castle.

Doc wrenched off several hemispheres from
the dead animals' heads, and they went down
the corkscrew staircase again and came to another landing. For the first time they heard the
muffled sounds of helicopters and of rapid fire
rifles. Then there was a rumble—a bomb going
off?—and, very faintly, screams.

Pauncho laughed one of his surprisingly shrill
laughs—he had two different laughs—and said,
"Iwaldi's giving two parties, and he didn't want
either one, heh, Doc?"

Doc said, "It does sound as if he's being attacked on the front. We'll take advantage of
whatever happens."

They walked swiftly down the spiral, their
handguns ready. They went down four levels
and still had not seen any other life. But the battle noises were louder and they were coming
from the front of the castle. Through an open
window they heard the *chuff-chuff* of a number of
copters. There were several more booms.
Grenades, probably.

The backside of the castle was on the edge of

the 2,600 foot and almost perpendicular mountainside. The front of the castle was on a much less steep slope. A road ran from the drawbridge down the mountain, snaking back and forth between and through heavy woods. It eventually led to the village of Gramzdorf, where six hundred citizens supported themselves by working for several ski resorts in the winter and farming in the summertime. The ski runs were on the Heuschrecke mountain across the valley from the Gramz.

Wherever the choppers had come from, they had not come from Gramzdorf. Nor could Doc imagine who was attacking Iwaldi.

They went down another level and came out into a huge luxuriously furnished hall. It would have done credit to the magnificent palace of the mad King Ludwig of Bavaria. Iwaldi had been collecting artifacts for many hundreds of years, perhaps thousands of years, though this castle was not built until 1241, if the records were to be believed. But Doc had reason to think that there had been an older structure on which the *schloss* had been erected, and this may have gone back to Roman days. And he also believed that beneath that ancient building, inside the granite of the mountain itself, were extensive halls and shafts, many levels, most of them hacked out of the stone in an unimaginably distant age.

The staircase continued to wind on down, but Doc decided to go toward the source of the noise. He removed from the pack on his back six objects which looked like tennis balls with pins stuck in each. Two he put in his pocket and he

gave two each to the others. They went on brisk-
ly through hall after hall and room after room,
all with furnishings and *objets d'art* that would
have astonished scholars in many fields.

Then he stepped behind a massive marble
pillar covered with golden filigree. The deaf-
ening reports of rapid-fire rifles and pistols were
coming from the next room. A man ran into the
room and fell on his face. Blood spread out from
beneath him.

Another man ran into the room, holding an
FN automatic rifle. He stopped, looked around,
and gestured to someone out of sight in the other
room.

Doc whispered, "They're retreating, clearing
the way for Iwaldi."

Doc could not believe that he would have
Iwaldi in his sight so quickly. It had only been
four days since an agent had reported seeing
Iwaldi in Paris. It had been only three days since
Doc had received a report that Iwaldi had flown,
via chopper from Freiburg, to the castle of
Gramz. Of course, organizing the search for
Iwaldi and conducting it had taken five months
of hard work. But the lair of Iwaldi had finally
been located, and here the millennia-old man
had been cornered. But Iwaldi had not survived
this long by being careless or minus a sixth
sense. It seemed to Caliban that things just
could not be quite right if he got that ancient
dwarf so quickly.

Part of this feeling came from the awe he could
not help feeling for one of the Nine. It was they
who had given him the elixir which enabled him,

at the age of sixty-six, to be, physiologically, only twenty-five. It was they who had controlled the world for unknown thousands of years. If they did not actually rule it—and they might, for all he knew—they exercised a power that exceeded that of all the combined nations of the world. Doc Caliban, who had turned against them in disgust, could not tell the world the truth. He would not live for more than a day if he came out in the open to proclaim the truth. And, moreover, the world would not believe him. They would think he was insane.

Old Anana, thirty thousand years old at least, was the woman who headed the Nine, and it was she whom he would have liked to have had within the sights of his gun. With her dead, the others would not be quite as awesome and dreadful. But they were dreadful enough, and Iwaldi had killed thousands who had thought to kill him.

Three more men with rifles came in. Doc took one of the tennis-ball like objects from his pocket, waited while he peeked around the massive column, then saw the white hair and long whiskers of the squat dwarf. He got a flash of a face as wrinkled as the neck of a vulture turkey, and the long arms and short thick bowed legs. The dwarf was dressed in a peculiar suit that seemed to be made of badgerskin. Perhaps, he wore this for some ritual reason. Or perhaps he was, being so old, hard put to keep warm.

Doc stepped halfway around the column, twisted and then pulled out the three-tenths-of-an-inch pin that extended from the north pole of

the little globe, and tossed it. The riflemen began
firing almost immediately, but he had whipped
back behind the column. Bullets screamed off
the marble; chips flew. The three men clung to
the side of the column. Then there was a roar
half-deafening them as the two gases in the
plastic ball mixed. Doc leaped out at once, his
gun ready. There was very little smoke from this
type of grenade. The riflemen were all lying on
their backs or sides, spread out in a sort of petal
arrangement.

Iwaldi was nowhere in sight.

Doc at once pulled the pin from his other
grenade and tossed it exactly through the middle
of the wide and tall arch. It bounced on through,
being as resilient as a tennis ball, and six seconds
later, it exploded. But Iwaldi and his men were
not in sight nor was there any sound of firing
from them. Nor was the other party firing.

Doc ran to the archway and looked around its
side. The room was a huge one, about one hundred feet by sixty. At the other end, the main
entrance, a few heads were beginning to stick out
from the side. A number of bodies lay here and
there and chairs and massive tables with marble
tops had been turned over to provide protection.
But Iwaldi and his men were gone.

The men by the main entrance began to fire at
him. He slipped back through the archway and
gestured to Pauncho and Barney to follow him.
Waiting for a pause in the firing, he leaped
across so swiftly he must have seemed a blur to
the invaders. They fired again but too late. And
the other two, bending over, ran past the space

where they would be exposed to the firing when there was another pause.

Someone shouted then. Many boots slapped on the marble floor. Pauncho spun and pulled a pin and bounced a grenade off the side of the archway and into the next room. Before the first had exploded, he had sent a second after it. All three were racing toward the exit at the far end of the room when the blasts came, one, two.

And then three, four.

The last two went off near or under an enormous table of mahogany and marble, twenty yards behind them. It broke in two and soared out of the smoke. The concussion pushed them on through the doorway out of the room and knocked them down.

They scrambled to their feet. Pauncho roared, "Our grenades and theirs passed each other!"

Doc gestured at Barney, who slipped out his two grenades and threw them, one after the other, at the far archway. One hit the edge and bounced back into the room. The other caromed off at the proper angle. The three stepped around the corner to be out of the direct influence of the explosion.

Two roars succeeded their two as someone tossed in grenades from the other side.

Doc signaled that they should keep on going. They passed through several large rooms and then Doc stopped. He had detected a slight crinkling of a large tapestry hanging on the wall to the right. Lifting the tapestry up, he looked behind it. The wall was of solid stone blocks bound in mortar. Or they seemed to be. But he had seen the stone-block wall in the bedroom upstairs slide away, and the tapestry might have been caught slightly, or bent, when a section behind it closed.

He quickly examined the area behind the tapestry and pressed here and there but nothing happened. Either the opening device was too well hidden, or certain spots had to be pressed in a certain sequence. Or possibly the activator for the opening mechanism was on the other side, and this opening was to be used as an exit only.

He went out from under the tapestry and started away when Barney's sharp metallic voice said, "Doc!"

Doc wheeled and saw that the tapestry was sagging in the middle. Understanding at once what was happening, he jerked his thumb at a group of large chairs against the opposite wall, and they quickly hid behind one of them. Doc passed out two more grenades to each of them but cautioned them in a whisper to use them only if they could not use their guns. Then he extended a slender flexible telescoping device under the chair and looked through it. By turning it on his end he could rotate the other end within 180 degrees and sweep the room. The end was uptilted, thus giving him a worm's eye view.

A red-headed man stuck his head out first. He was followed by six men, and then, through the doorway through which Doc and his friends had passed, twenty others came. Doc knew then how Iwaldi had disappeared so swiftly. He had taken a secret entrance in the wall of the outer room and gone through the tunnel to this room. The invaders had seen him and followed. Doc was glad that Iwaldi had not then cut back and taken Doc's party by surprise on the flank. But Iwaldi had not wanted to delay for anything. He had wanted to get away as fast as possible.

The invaders carried FN rifles and .45 automatic pistols, and four had hand grenades attached by the pins to their belts. There was even a bazooka team, one man with the tube and one carrying three rockets in a case on his back.

Doc made signs to Barney and Pauncho. They should let the invaders go on by. It was true that three grenades, thrown at once, could catch the whole party together and so dispose of them. But, though he had been compelled to fight them for the sake of survival, he did not know that they were basically hostile to him. Moreover, it would be best to use them to hound Iwaldi.

The party passed through the archway but left one man behind as a rearguard. Doc took out from a little box in his pack a ping-pong-sized, transparent ball and threw it when the man was looking the other way. The man spun on hearing the material break on the stone, looked around, then collapsed. Doc and his men had not even bothered to hold their breaths, since they were outside the influence of the vaporized curare. Doc sped to the man and applied the end of an air-operated syringe to his neck. He struck a sharp blow on the man's chest, and the man began to breathe again. But he was now unconscious and would remain so for half an hour.

Doc told Barney to return to the outer room

and find where the secret entrance was. Pauncho appropriated all the man's weapons. Doc searched him for documents or other identification and found nothing. He was not even carrying a wallet.

The tapestry bulged, and Barney called out, "I've found it!"

"Who couldn't?" Pauncho said. "They left the door open, right?"

"I could tell you where to put the door, but I'm a gentleman," Barney said, coming out from behind the tapestry. "I'll define the term *gentleman* for you when we're not so busy."

"Would you mind spelling it for me?" Pauncho said. He grinned at Barney. He looked like a chimpanzee who'd just seen a fresh banana. "Hey, Doc, this Yale graduate's a real sooper-dooper speller. Did you know we were in Korea six months before he found out you don't spell it C-H-O-R-E-A? Haw, haw! Of course, he wasn't too far wrong. Korea was a disease, as far as us marines were concerned."

"That's a disgusting lie!" Barney said. "As far as that goes, you thought Korea was in the South Pacific, and you're a Berkeley graduate!"

Doc said, "Stick something in that door under the tapestry. Not something big enough to make it stick out noticeably. We might want to use it for a getaway."

Barney looked disgusted, but he was angry at himself for not having thought of the idea. And he did not like Pauncho's grin. He knew his squat buddy was telling him, silently, that he was a dummy.

Doc was thinking how much the two resem-
bled their fathers. Yet neither had gone to his
father's college or taken up their professions.
Perhaps this was because they resented or even
hated their fathers at the same time that they
loved them. Both Porky Rivers and Jocko Simmons had been divorced by their wives because
they spent too much time away from home on
their adventures with Doc Caliban. Both women
had remarried, and their husbands had adopted
their stepsons. But the real fathers still had visiting privileges, and they came about four or five
times a year to take the boys on trips. Doc had
met them and even entertained them in his
apartment high up in the Empire State Building
or on his Lake George estate. The boys had
grown up imitating their real fathers because
they were mysterious adventurers who roamed
the world and did all sorts of fabulous and dangerous deeds. They were the sons of men who
had married late in life, and so they had fan-
tasied that they would replace their fathers when
these grew too old for the man-killing exploits
demanded of them by close relationship with
Caliban. The old men had finally retired. But
then they had come out of retirement for one last
great adventure in Africa, when Doc Caliban
was on the trail of the man he believed had killed
his beloved cousin, Viscount Grandrith, a man
whom most of the world believed to be a purely
fictional character and whom the world knew
largely by a name that had originated in a non-
human language.

Grandrith had not killed Trish Wilde. He had

not even known of her existence when she was
reported murdered by him. But Grandrith was
mad at that time, insane in a peculiar way from
the side effects of the elixir of immortality given
to him by the Nine in return for certain services.
Caliban was also insane because of the elixir's
side effects. But he and Lord Grandrith discovered that they were half-brothers; and then
Porky Rivers and Jocko Simmons died in their
last battle at Castle Grandrith.

Pauncho van Veelar and Barney Banks had
had a big shock when they saw Doc Caliban in
1968 after five years' absence. Of course, they
had always remarked on how young their "Uncle Doc" looked. But seeing him again had
brought up some very disturbing questions. How
could a man born in 1901 still look thirty years
old or younger? He should show *some* signs of
aging! And so Doc Caliban, who desperately
missed his old sidekicks, no matter how self-sufficient he seemed to others, took their sons into
his confidence. They would have joined him just
to be able to get into the most exciting life on
Earth and to follow in the footsteps of their
beloved-hated fathers. But the chance of becoming immortal would have been more than
enough inducement.

Barney had picked up two rifles and extra
magazines of 20 rounds each. Doc said,
"Thanks," and inspected his rifle for working order. Pauncho finished taping the mouth, wrists,
and ankles of the sleeping guard. Doc said, "If
my suspicions are correct, Iwaldi will be making
for his underground labyrinth. He'll probably

leave the way open so his enemies will follow him down. They'll find out why he's so hospitable."

They had just entered the next room when they heard and felt the explosion. The floor quivered, and air moved against their faces. Two rooms on, they came to an entrance made by a section of wall sliding back. Faint streamers of smoke and an odor of dynamite were being breathed from the dark mouth. Doc removed from his vest pocket a cap with a small tube atop it and put it on his head. Then he unfolded dark goggles from the same pocket and put them on. The others also put on caps and goggles, and then they went into the tunnel. This was unlit, but it did not impede them. The device atop the cap projected a "dark light" and their special goggles enabled them to see whatever the light hit. They had contact lenses which would do the same work, but these required time and effort to get in and out, and they preferred the goggles in this situation because they could be ripped off if the situation demanded.

The tunnel curved away from the entrance and then straightened out. The smoke got thicker. They inserted nose plugs to filter it. Thirty feet past the bend, they came to the entrance of a vertical shaft. Doc went down the steel ladder first, his backpack rubbing against the stone wall of the shaft behind him. He counted forty rungs about a foot apart before he stepped onto the bottom of the shaft. A horizontal shaft joined it, leading in an easterly direction. It was designed for dwarfs or designed to make men of normal stature uncomfortable. All three had to duckwalk for thirty yards before they came to a place where they could straighten up. This was a forty-foot square room, carved out of granite, furnished only with corpses.

These were near the opposite doorway. Apparently they had touched off some kind of trap loaded with explosives. Doc counted the bodies. Eight. That left eighteen. The bazooka team was not among them. He would have to be cautious about going too fast, since the survivors would be proceeding slowly now. However, the explosives in that confined area must have deafened and injured others, and the effective number of fighters in their party should be cut down. Also, it was possible that they would get cold feet, for which he could not blame them, and would return. To run head-on into them in these cramped tunnels could be fatal to his small party. But there was nothing to do but push on.

They walked bent-kneed through a thirty-five foot tunnel which ended when it joined another tunnel at right angles to it. Doc squirted some vapor for several yards down both directions. Suddenly, glowing footprints—glowing only because the goggles revealed them—sprang out. But the prints were in both directions, and Doc did not have any way of separating the Iwaldi party's prints from those of the invaders. It was true that Iwaldi was not over four feet five inches high, but his feet were disproportionately large. Nor was there any way of determining the weight of the person who had left prints. The vapor settled on the floor and was illuminated only where there was a difference in elevation of

the material of the floor itself. Even a difference
of two microns briefly illuminated the powder.
There was enough dust on the floor for the boots
to make some impressions.

The prints indicated that their makers had
been going and coming on both sides of the tunnel at right angles to the one from which they
had just emerged.

Doc cast up and down the tunnel for thirty
yards. There were many more prints to the right,
and then he found a stain of blood on the side of
the wall to the right. He turned and beckoned to
the two men, who could see him plainly in the
radiation cast by their projectors.

"It's possible that they split up and some went
the other way," he said.

Twenty yards further, the tunnel made a turn
to the left. After another twenty yards, they
found the tunnel almost completely blocked. A
section of solid stone, three feet high and twenty
long, had thrust itself out of the wall on the right
and crushed a number of men against the left
wall. Doc removed his pack and shoved it ahead
of him while he crawled between the top of the
block and the ceiling of the tunnel. He counted
eight heads, most of which were above the stone,
the bodies being squeezed into forms three inches wide. That left ten ahead, if the party had
not split up.

"If I was them, and I'm glad I'm not,"
Pauncho said, "I woulda taken off by now."

"Maybe you shouldn't try to get through
there," Barney said in a mock solicitous voice.
"With that belly, you'll get stuck, and I won't be

able to get by you. You stay here and guard my rear."

Pauncho chuckled, and the echoes came back from ahead. Doc said, *"Sh!"*, but Pauncho whispered, "Any time I get a chance—"

He stopped when Doc repeated his warning. Then he heard the noises, too.

Pauncho did have some trouble getting his huge belly through, and he was huffing and swearing when he fell off the other end of the block. By then the yelling and screaming of men and the weird shrill cries had increased. They duckwalked swiftly, Pauncho groaning softly and swearing that he would quit drinking beer if he ever got a chance to drink beer again. The tunnel bent at ninety degrees to the right, continued for ten yards, bent ninety degrees to the left, continued for twenty yards, and then they were at the arched entrance to a room so large it could almost be called a cavern.

It was lit only by the flashlights of the men inside but Doc's blacklight enabled him to see everything clearly. He removed the goggles for a moment so he could get an idea of how the situation looked to the men. The beams shot here and there and then dived for the floor, lay there shining, and were picked up again, though not always by the one who had dropped them. Some of the beams briefly illuminated large birds: white snow owls, golden eagles, bald eagles, African vultures. They swooped through the beams, their eyes flashing redly, their wings beating loudly, their talons outspread. Some closed in on the holders of the flashlights as if they were riding the beam down to their target. The butts of rifles flashed; one struck an eagle on the wing, and the great bird fell out of sight.

No rifles were being fired. Apparently the men were afraid of ricochets. They were using the weapons as clubs. But the birds did not seem discommoded by either the darkness or the lights shining in their eyes. They attacked from all angles, and men went down screaming under their beaks and talons.

Doc replaced his goggles.

The birds uttered no cries whatsoever. They were as silent as the wolves that had attacked Caliban's group in the bedroom. It was this that caused Caliban to look for the tiny hemispheres attached to the tops of the birds' heads.

Doc motioned to his colleagues to retreat with him. They duckwalked back to the end of the block and waited. Barney whispered, "What's going on, Doc?"

"Keep your rifles ready. We can shoot if we're attacked in here. As to the strange behavior of the animals and birds, I'll explain when I'm certain of its cause."

The screams went on for about ten minutes and then died out. The only sound was Pauncho's heavy breathing and the ripping of flesh as the birds tore at the corpses. Doc, not wanting to make any noise at all, put his hand on each man's arms and transmitted in Morse with the pressure of his fingers.

"The hemispheres may be electronic devices to control the animals by remote control. It's possible that the operator thinks his enemies are all dead and has shut down control. In which case, we might be able to stroll on by the birds without their attacking us. I say we should try it."

Barney and Pauncho simultaneously squeezed back, "You're the boss, Doc. You give the word."

He transmitted, "Ordinarily I would. But this is a very bad situation, and I would not blame you one bit if you decided to retreat now so we could fight later—in a situation more advantageous to us."

"If we go back, will you go back with us?" Barney transmitted.

Doc hesitated and then said, "No."

"Then we'll go on with you. Don't you like us, Doc, you want us to miss out on this? We have to earn our immortality."

Doc smiled slightly, and it was a measure of how deeply he was affected that he allowed his self-control to lapse even this much. Or perhaps it was a measure of his progress in getting rid of the too-rigid self-control of his past. He was trying to act more humanly, or more openly, since being too self-controlled was as human as not being self-controlled enough.

"O.K.," he squeezed back. "You cover me from the entrance. If they attack, I'll drop on my back and shoot upward, and you fire over my head."

He waddled into the room, straightened up, and walked toward the nearest body and the golden eagle feeding on it. The eagle looked fiercely at him and turned on top of the corpse, flapping its wings. Its beak opened as if it were uttering a silent cry. But it did not fly away. Nor did it attack. And the other birds continued to eat after glaring at him and assuring themselves that he was not belligerent.

Doc turned to signal to the two. Barney shouted, "Look out, Doc!"

He wheeled, bringing up his rifle, having heard the flap of wings at the same time that Barney yelled. The vulture flew at him with beak and claws outspread, and behind him was the thunder of two dozen pairs of wings. All headed toward him.

He fell on his back, firing as he did. The vulture flew bloodily apart and spun to one side under the impact of the bullets. Blood and feathers and flesh spattered Doc. He continued to fire at the great birds, and then the explosions of his colleagues' FN's were added to his. Bullets ricocheted off the walls and the ceiling, wheeing by him, and his face stung from chips of stone. But the birds blew apart from the many high-velocity bullets striking them. And when Doc and the two men had emptied their magazines, they dropped the rifles and began firing with the .15-caliber explosive bullets from their gasguns. Able to see in the blacklight, they had no trouble aiming, and within sixty seconds all twenty-four birds were heaps of feathers.

Doc jumped up and ran toward the entrance of the tunnel as they quit firing and dived into its shelter.

Pauncho said, "What's up, Doc?" but Caliban did not reply.

He waited for some sign of action, knowing
that the renewal of attack by the birds probably
meant that the operator had happened to look
into the room and see him. Or perhaps it meant
that the operator had seen him from the first but
had not stimulated the birds until he thought
Doc was off his guard. It also meant that the
operator could have a form of blacklight, since
Doc had stayed out of range of the beams of the
flashlights still operating.

Nowhere was there any evidence of TV camer-
as or one-way windows, but it would be easy to
simulate rock.

There was a groaning behind them and a
trembling of the floor. They turned to see the
huge stone block withdrawing into the wall. The
heads of the collapsing bodies struck the stone
with a plop.

Doc nodded, and they got up and walked
across the room, pausing only by the bodies to
shove an extra magazine into their capacious
jacket pockets. The exit was another archway at
the far wall. They looked down its round length.
Doc wondered why the tunnel was round instead
of square, as all the others had been. It went for
at least forty yards before making a turn. The
roundness might preclude any section of the wall
sliding out to crush them. At least, the interior
was smooth, seemingly carved out of the granite.
But material in paste form, looking like stone,
could have been spread over to cover up the lines
of demarcation of a separate piece. He whispered to them, and they walked to the tunnel
and entered, crouching. They held their rifles

across their bellies so that the muzzle and stock extended past their sides.

They had gone ten yards when the wall to their right crumbled and flew outward, propelled by a block of stone. The mass squealed as it slid across the floor—but not loudly, indicating that the bottom was lubricated—and then the three were knocked sidewise. But the block stopped short with a crash; their rifles acted as rigid bars to hold the block back. And it was evident that there would be no more pressure put on them. The rifles had bent just a trifle but showed no signs of increasing buckling.

Doc crawled over his rifle and scooted on out past the block. He felt naked without the rifle to keep off the block, even though he knew that the three already wedged in were doing their work. Pauncho and Barney came after him with Pauncho snorting indignantly because Barney was making cracks about hippos in subways. But when they were out of danger, they sat down and wiped the sweat off.

Barney said, "Do you think—?" He stopped. Of course, Doc Caliban had no way of knowing whether or not there would be more such traps ahead. And they now had no rifles. They could go back and pick some more up. But, if they were being observed, the block could be withdrawn as soon as they went past the wedged rifles. And it could then be slammed in again with an excellent chance of catching them.

Barney and Pauncho had both thought of this, because Pauncho said, "I'll stay there holding on to a rifle and make sure that if the stone's moved, I'll be there to catch it again."

"Three rifles were strong enough to withstand it," Doc said. "I don't know that just one would do it."

"They're close enough I could reach out and grab two," Pauncho said. "And Barney could hold the other."

Doc looked at the block. This one was so much closer to the ceiling that crawling on its top was ruled out. It was as long as the other, and it had slid out when the three were halfway along its length.

"No," Doc said. "It could be withdrawn and slid out before we could reach the rifles. There's nothing to do except go ahead."

Barney and Pauncho looked dismal. Doc Caliban kept his face expressionless. It hurt him to see them express any kind of faint-heartedness or lack of faith in him. Yet his reaction was illogical whereas theirs was founded on a realistic attitude. They certainly were not cowards or easily downcast. His little experience with them had convinced him of that. Moreover, they had fought together in the worst of the Korean fighting, had escaped together from a Chinese prisoner-of-war camp, and both had won many medals for valor (though none for good conduct). After the war they had returned to school to get their higher degrees. And they had formed a business which had taken them into South America, where they had been captured by bandits and had again escaped. They did not lack courage or resourcefulness.

His own reaction was a hangover from the

past, when he had gotten from their fathers a never-diminished gusto and optimism. They had never faltered. Or they had seemed not to falter. Perhaps they were more self-controlled and would have been ashamed to let him see their dismay. Their sons were more open, less vulnerable to shame. Moreover, if he, who prided himself on his logical behavior, was not doubtful about pushing on, then he must be missing something in his own character.

Doc Caliban thought, Well, not really. It's just that I know that I have more capabilities than they do.

Now was no time for soul-searching. He could do that when he retired to that hidden stronghold which had once been in the far north but which he had relocated at the bottom of a lake. Lately, when he had retreated, he had ceased to work on scientific devices and had taken to pursuing Oriental philosophies and their techniques.

He shook his head. Pauncho said, "What's the matter, Doc?"

Doc put his hands on their wrists and squeezed a message. Then he said, loudly, "We'll go ahead, take what comes, play it by ear!"

He turned and Pauncho got on one side and Barney on the other as they started across the room, which was about twenty feet high, sixty long, and forty wide.

Doc took two steps, whirled, and flashed back into the tunnel, sped crouching down it, and dived for the nearest rifle between the wall and the stone. Having seized it, he turned over and slid under it, releasing it only when Barney grabbed it. The two had started immediately after him but they were a few seconds behind since he was so swift. To any watcher he must have seemed almost a blur.

Pauncho, who was three times as strong as Barney but not as quick on his feet, caught up with Barney and grabbed his rifle. In a short time, they each had hold of a gun.

They waited for a moment. That the block had not withdrawn and then slammed in when Doc made his dive seemed to indicate that it was not being remote controlled. A watcher should have been startled by Doc's sudden return and operated the controls in sheer reflex.

It was also possible that the renewed hostility of the birds had come from an automatic mechanism. Doc had triggered off an alarm, perhaps by cutting across a beam.

While Pauncho braced himself between two rifles, and Barney gripped one, Doc slid out and then duck-ran back to the room. He returned with three more rifles. The two took them while Doc gripped the two rifles jammed against the wall and then he dived out and away, just in case there was a remote controller. The stone block did not move.

This room was without furniture or decoration except for a black, red-headed eagle, twice as large as a man, painted on a wall, and a ceramic container which might have been used for bathing small humans. The archway led to another round tunnel, but this was large enough for even Doc Caliban to stand erect in. At irregular intervals along the tunnel, about three feet up, were painted the symbols—squares with looped corners—which the Finns called *hannunkaavuna* and the Swedes *St. Hans's arms*. Doc knew this symbol well. It was carved on the staff which the Speaker for the Nine carried during the annual ceremonies in the caves in the mountains in Central Africa. The upper half of the staff bore a carved *ankh,* the cross with a circle on top, a symbol as ancient as Egypt.

The *hannunkaavuna* made him think briefly of Grandrith. That tall man with the black hair, gray eyes, handsome near-aquiline face, and Apollo-like body with its Herculean strength— his half-brother—should be near the coast of Gabon now. He would land there and proceed on foot across Central Africa, sticking largely to the belt of the rain forest, where few humans would see him. And then he would come up onto the bank of the mountains which held the caves of the Nine, and he would do what he could there. If he was confined to scouting and spying, he would wait until his brother could join him in an attack on the Nine during the annual ceremonies. If he had a chance to kill one of the Nine, he would do so.

The memory of pain twinged him in the back of the neck and elsewhere. His fight with Grandrith had not been without loss and agony.

They got out of the tunnel without incident. Pauncho wiped sweat off his shelving brow and said, "Whoo!"

Barney said, "I kept expecting the side of the wall to jump out at us."

Doc looked around. This room had hexagonal corners and was painted with many scenes of long-bearded squat little men fighting crocodile-sized creatures looking exactly like the stuffed *Tatzelwurm*. The focus of the battle was a big pile of gold rocks. A twilight illumination came from naked plastic bulbs set in widely separated brackets on the walls. Wires ran from them to black boxes on the floor.

Pauncho said, "Listen, Doc, do you think that once there may have been big whatcha-maycallems, and these gave rise to the legends of the dragons?"

"Your guess is as good as mine," Caliban said, and he led them to the next archway. This was painted black, and the tunnel was black. They proceeded ten yards when they came to a hole in the center of the floor. Doc pointed his headlight down it, making sure that his rifle was still held at the proper angle across his belly. The shaft went straight down for about twenty feet and then became a hole in the ceiling of another tunnel. A section of wooden ladder lying flat on the floor was visible.

The atomizer revealed that someone had gone down the shaft by putting their back to one wall and their feet against the other. It also indicated footprints going on in this tunnel, but the light from the prints was not as bright as that on the walls of the shaft.

"It could be another trap," Doc squeezed on Barney's arm. Barney transmitted the same message to Pauncho.

"We're playing follow-the-leader," Barney

squeezed back. His thin foxily handsome face looked eager. Pauncho was grinning like an orangutan dreaming of durian fruit.

Iwaldi seemed to be going to the lower levels. At least, that would be the natural direction for him to go when his home was invaded. Perhaps he did not know that his traps had killed all of one party of invaders and that just three men were tracking him. Perhaps he did, and he was crouching in some room and watching them even now, waiting for the proper moment so he could press a button or pull a lever or just watch while an automatic trap was sprung.

Doc leaned over and dropped his rifle, butt first. It struck and toppled over. He waited. Nothing happened. There was nothing to do but go down the shaft then. Near its bottom he removed a suction disc from his pocket, stuck it against the shaft wall, and lowered himself by his left hand down from the shaft, his legs drawn up. He swung like a gibbon from a branch, turning to take in the round tunnel which ran for ten yards in either direction and then curved out of sight. The ceiling was eleven feet from the floor, and the greatest distance between the walls was twelve. There were eight bulbs on brackets along the walls.

"How is it, Doc?" whispered Pauncho.

Caliban looked up. The ugly but congenial face hung over him.

"Only one way to find out," he said. He released his grip on the handle of the disc, it fell, he grabbed it, and he dropped down to the floor. But his other hand had his gasgun out before his feet struck the stone.

Pauncho came down, grunting, and then Barney.

The moment Barney landed, the world seemed to tilt. Doc made a leap forward for the shaft with his left hand, which still held the disc, extended. And when the disc slapped onto the inner edge of the lip of the shaft, he squeezed down on the handle. The disc held, and he hung there, while the ladder, his rifle, and his two friends went down the slope of the tunnel, which had suddenly dropped and was rapidly becoming vertical.

Sick, he looked down past his feet while Pauncho and Barney, their fingers grabbing for a hold on the smooth stone—or what seemed like stones but could not be—hurtled downward. And then they were gone around the bend, shot out of the gigantic chuteychute. The rifle went with them, and the ladder, bending at a number of places like a wooden snake, shot out by their side.

Panicked though they must have been, neither had screamed or yelled. Pauncho had groaned, and Barney had hissed between clamped teeth, but that was all.

Doc hung there, rotating slowly by the turning of his wrist. He could swing himself up and get his feet against the wall of the shaft and so climb back up to its top. Or he could swing out and back until he had enough momentum and then release the disc and land on the edge of the newly formed vertical shaft and go on down this tunnel. Or he could then climb down the

chuteychute, using the discs and see what was
down there. It seemed certain that Iwaldi would
be waiting for him there, but he could not abandon his colleagues, not unless he knew for certain that he could help them by action
elsewhere.

Within a minute, he was going down the shaft
of the trap. When he came to the bend he proceeded more slowly. He lifted the goggles for a
moment and, seeing that there was light ahead,
left them up. He could see only a whitewashed
wall ahead, but when he got to the end of the
tube and looked down, he saw Pauncho and
Barney.

Below them was another shaft about twenty
feet wide and so deep he could not see the bottom. The shaft was in the center of a large room
which seemed to be the storehouse for hundreds
of wooden brightly painted statues. These
ranged from beautiful nudes and fully clothed
humans and dwarfish peoples to dragons to elk
to wolves to badgers to monsters of various sorts.
The light came from a dozen glass bulbs on top
of stone lamps.

Pauncho and Barney were at the bottom of a
net. This was composed of many thin and apparently sticky cords. Their weight had pulled
the net, which originally had been stretched
across the top of the shaft, to a baglike shape
with them at the bottom and about twenty feet
down the shaft. They were struggling and curs-
ing in low tones, but their efforts only entangled
them more thoroughly in the cords. Seeing Doc
Caliban, they stopped thrashing around.

"Get me out of here, Doc," Barney said. "This guy's so hairy, he's making me itch."

"Yeah, get me out of here," Pauncho said. "He's so bony he's cutting me."

Doc did not answer. He began to swing back and forth until he had enough momentum. He released the pressure on the disc handle as he started an outward swing, and he landed on the edge of the shaft. Neither of the two made a sound, though it might have been expected that Doc would teeter back and fall into the net with them. His toes only struck the lip of the shaft. But he snapped himself forward and then was solidly on the floor. He turned and began to pull on the net, hauling up the four hundred and seventy pounds of the two men and the hundred pounds of the net as if they were a minnow on a string.

The sticky cords clung to his hands, but he just walked backward, pulling the two over the edge with a bump and a scrape that brought groans from them. After they were on the floor, he managed to pull his hands loose and then he started the tedious and slow task of freeing them.

When they were out of the net, Pauncho and Barney were as dirty looking as coal miners at the end of a shift. The dark brown substance had smeared their clothes, faces, and hands.

"One thing I'll say," Barney muttered. "You look just as good dirty as you do clean. Maybe better because it's more natural."

Pauncho's thick teeth flashed in a grin. "As an authority on dirt, your opinion is to be valued. It takes one to know one, as they say."

"Takes one what to know what one?" Barney said.

"If you two will quit your clowning around now," Doc Caliban said, "we'll proceed. Though where I don't know."

From a pocket in his vest he took an object the size and shape of a large pocketwatch. Its face bore a number of dials and graduated markings and also a thin tube with a red column, like a thermometer. The others did not comment. They knew that this was a device with several functions. One of them was to detect objects of a certain shape and density. The device could be set to register when such and such an object was near its field of radiation. Doc now adjusted it by turning a small wheel on its back, and then he advanced down the room holding it out before him.

If there was anything immediately behind the walls or under the floors or above the ceiling, this detector would send a pulse of yellow light up and down the column on its face. The drawback of the detector was that it could not be used in the near vicinity of guns and knives or other considerable masses of metal. It registered the metal even if its radiating field was directed away from the metal. There was a certain amount of back radiation, an echo as it were, and this detected the metal. So Doc Caliban had to give his pistol and knife to Pauncho to carry while he preceded them by thirty feet.

He stopped at a wooden ladder sticking out of a shaft and the two halted with the same distance maintained between them and their lead-

er. He swept the detector around and then went
down the ladder. They followed a minute later.
The next level down was a long corridor hewn
out of solid granite. It ran for as far as they could
see in both directions, and it was well lit with
naked electric light bulbs on iron brackets about
five feet from the floor and spaced about forty
feet apart.

Doc sprayed some more of the atomized
differential-level substance around. It revealed
many footprints, but the freshest seemed to go
off to the right, so he elected to go that way.
They passed tools lying on the floor or propped
against the walls: picks with broken handles or
worn points, great sledges, bars with chiseled
edges, brooms. Some of them looked as if they
had been lying here a long time. Then they came
to a broad staircase cut out of the rock. It led
down for about sixty feet at a steep angle. They
went down it, still guided by the electric light
bulbs, and came to a room at least a hundred
feet square and forty high.

Doc stopped, and Pauncho and Barney, forgetting that they were not to get close, almost
bumped into him. The red column in the center
of the face changed to a bright yellow light which
pulsed.

Doc told them to move back, and the light
went back to its quiescent state. Barney whistled
softly and said, "Looks like they had a fight
sometime ago, doesn't it? A long time ago!"

The footprints were plain here. The dust was
so thick that it rose with every step. Pauncho
almost strangled trying to keep from sneezing

while Barney choked trying to keep from laughing at Pauncho's desperate grimaces.

There were about ten complete skeletons and parts of others scattered around the room. Rusty swords, knives, and double-headed axes lay under the dust, many still clutched by bony hands. Some of the skulls had been cracked or caved in; an axe was still wedged in the top of a skull.

Doc said, "Most of them were dwarfs. And an early type of Homo sapiens. Look at the thickness of those bones, the huge supraorbital ridges."

The fresh footprints led through one of six archways. Doc went through this cautiously, ready to jump back at the slightest sign of anything suspicious. The room beyond was immense and lit by bulbs in brackets secured to the granite walls. There were more skeletons and axes and swords. And in the center of the room, sitting on an oaken high-backed ornately carved chair on a granite slab, was a figure.

They approached slowly, though it was obviously a corpse.

It was a very old corpse, a mummy. Its white hair fell over its shoulders and its white beard covered its lap and its knees. The dark eyes stared at them.

It wore a cap like a dunce's crown and leather garments and leather boots with curled-up toes. The brown, wrinkled, and heavily veined hand held a golden scepter with six diamonds inset on the polygonal knob of gold at the end of the scepter.

On the slab and around the oaken throne were

many figurines of stone about a foot high. They represented a squat, hairy people: males and female adults and some children. They were dressed in clothes similar to that on the mummy. There were a few figurines of animals, mostly badgers, but two were of some sort of monster.

"What do you make of it, Doc?" Pauncho asked.

Pauncho did not expect an answer. But Doc said, "I am not sure. The mummy looks much like Iwaldi, as you know from my description and my sketch of him. And the figurines are modeled after his people. How this man came to his death, why he's been preserved, I don't know. But you must remember that Iwaldi's people are—were—some sort of dwarfish Caucasoids with a slight Mongolian mixture somewhere along the line. They're the little people who gave rise to the tales of gnomes, kabolds, and even trolls. I'm sure of that. They did a lot of mining and tunneling, and if my theory is correct, they survived in Germany and some parts of Scandinavia up to 1000 A.D. Then they were absorbed or just died out. Iwaldi kept on living. He would, of course, being one of the Nine. And he had this castle built over the ancient stronghold of his race during the medieval period. Though I think he also was the one who built the earlier fortress on which the castle was based.

"This man here may have been some king, perhaps a son of Iwaldi. If we get Iwaldi alive, maybe we can find out about all this. But I would prefer that we kill him. The moment we get the chance to. That old man is too wily, too dangerous, to let live for more than the time it takes to cut his throat."

He quit talking, and the oppressive silence returned. Pauncho shifted uneasily. The fierce-eyed and long-bearded figure seemed to have moved, though he knew it was an illusion. For the first time, he became aware of the millions of tons of stone over his head. The silence was as heavy as the stone. He was so awed by this that he whispered his feelings to Barney. Barney might have laughed at another time and place, but that he did not do so now showed that he felt much the same as Pauncho.

Doc gestured at them to follow him. He held the detector out ahead of him. Its light was flashing yellow, but the masses of iron weapons were responsible for that. He passed through a tall archway into another room which was filled with digging tools and swords and axes, all neatly stacked in piles along the wall. He chose to go down another broad staircase of stone steps. Footprints led away from it, but footprints also went down it and these seemed to be fresher. The stairs went on and on. Doc counted a hundred, then two hundred, then three hundred with no end in sight. The bottom was hidden somewhere in the shadows below. Along the wall there were bulbs which had been set much further apart.

Moreover, the walls began to move in closer, and the way slowly curved to the right. Then it straightened out for a hundred steps, after which it curved to the left.

"I wonder how far down these diggings go?"

Pauncho whispered to Barney. "If this Iwaldi geezer is 10,000 years old, he may have started digging back then. The whole mountain could be honeycombed."

Abruptly, the stairs ceased. Doc waved the detector back and forth before the huge oaken door before them. The column in its face was red.

"Hey, Doc!" Pauncho said. "Those hinges are gold!"

Doc signaled and Barney handed him the knife. Doc touched the golden latch on the door with the knife as if he expected an electrical spark to leap out. Nothing happened. He slipped on the goggles and examined the door and the latch under the "blacklight." Then he raised the goggles and said, "We'll have to take a chance. Stand way back, you two."

The door swung outward, revealing a cavernous room beyond. This was lit with the ubiquitous bulbs. It seemed to be a storehouse for many things: battle-axes, swords, cuirasses, and leggings, oaken and stone chests, many of them open and glinting with gold bars or gleaming with jewels. There were also statues, ranging from a foot high to life size, carved out of stone or formed from gold and silver. Some were of well-proportioned humans, some of the squat and muscular and thick-calved dwarfs, some of animals, of monsters.

The three walked slowly into the chamber, pausing to look at but not to touch the wealth strewn everywhere. Some of the chests contained coins and paper money of many nations.

Doc kept his attention on the fresh footprints

in the dust. These led straight across the immense room toward a set of three arches at the far end. But before they reached them, they halted. On their right, set into the wall, was a steel framework with steel bars. This was at the entrance to a small cell cut out of the stone.

Pauncho and Barney said, simultaneously, "Wow!"

Doc Caliban's face did not lose its expressionlessness. But a close observer might have noticed those peculiar yellow-flecked eyes narrow.

A young man and a young woman were staring at them from behind the bars.

It was the woman who had caused the two men to express delight, surprise, admiration, and desire.

"Your cousin has finally got some real competition," Pauncho said to Caliban.

The woman's hair was long and loose and of an unusually deep red. Her skin was very clear and white, and her eyes were large and violet. Her only makeup was a bright red lipstick. She wore heavy hiking clothes and boots, but they were tight enough to reveal a superb figure.

The man was wide-shouldered and muscular but very short. He had black hair and brown eyes and a handsome face.

The woman's voice was throaty and caressing even though she was evidently under heavy stress. She gripped the bars and said, "My God, where did you come from?" and then, "Please get us out of here!"

The young man had also grabbed hold of the bars, but he did not say anything.

Doc Caliban looked past them. The cell was furnished with a double bunkbed and some light blankets and pillows, a washbowl with a pitcher of water and a glass, an open toilet bowl, and a stone shelf on which were two trays with dishes on which were the remnants of food.

"Did Iwaldi take the key to this lock with him?" Doc said.

"Who?" the man said.

"The old dwarf," Doc Caliban replied.

"He went thataway," the woman said, pointing her finger at the far end. She smiled, but she was evidently trying to be brave. Her fingers were white where she was clutching the bars.

"How many men did he have with him?" Doc said.

"Ten," the man said. His speech was, like the woman's, Received Standard English—that of an educated Londoner's.

Pauncho and Barney were pulling rolls of thin wires from their vest pockets. Doc raised his hand as if to check them, then let it drop. The cell and its prisoners might be an elaborate booby trap of some sort, but the only way to find out was to try to free them. The two wrapped several turns of the wires around the more slender bars which held the lock to the door. They pressed the button on the battery in their pockets; flame spurted out from around the wires; the bars and the lock were removed with a yank. Pauncho pulled the barred door open and said, *"Exitez-vous, madame."*

She smiled ravishingly at him; Pauncho, ravished, smiled back.

The man introduced himself as Carlos Cobbs and the woman as Barbara Villiers, his fiancee. They both taught archeology at a university in London. They had been digging on the mountainslope three days ago when they were captured by the dwarf and his men.

Doc thought at first that they meant that Iwaldi's men had picked them up near the castle. But they said they had been digging in the woods near the bottom of the massive stone cap on which the castle rested. The earth had fallen in at the bottom of their trench, and they had gone in with it. Their shovels and picks had broken through the top of a tunnel. Exploring the tunnel, they found that it was part of an immense labyrinth of many levels.

They had pushed on, fascinated because they had come across stone figurines and the skeletons of men who were obviously early paleolithic. And then some men had captured them and brought them here, despite their protests. After a while, a strange long-bearded dwarf had appeared and questioned them. Barbara called him The Mountain King and said these were his halls.

"He wouldn't let us go," she said. "He—what'd you say his name was. Iwaldi?—said we were spies and that he'd kill us. But not before he found a use for us, since he didn't believe in wasting anything. He kept muttering something about the nine. Just the nine. Nine what?"

Doc did not reply. He entered the cell and prowled around with his detector in hand. Then he came out and said, "If I were you two, I

wouldn't report this to the local authorities. Or
any authorities. I'd just quietly get out of Germany and get back to London. I know you can't
forget this, but you should act as if you had."

"Really?" Carlos Cobbs said. "Why should
we?"

"You would probably die very soon after you
started to talk about this. There is another group
which is out after Iwaldi's hide—and mine—
which would shut you up the hard way. Hard for
you, easy for them."

"And who are you?" Barbara said.

"Your liberator," Doc said. He was thinking
that he should send a radio message to his cousin
in London to check on these two as soon as he
got back to the village. "Barbara Villiers?"
Barney said, smiling. "An old and . . . uh . . .
well-known name. You aren't related to the late
Duchess of Cleveland, Countess Castlemaine,
are you?"

The woman smiled back at him and became
twice as beautiful. "You mean the wicked woman who was born in 1641, the daughter of Viscount Grandison? The mistress of Charles II,
John Churchill, and William Wycherley, not to
mention others common and great?"

"Yes," Barney said.

She laughed and said, "Yes, I'm related to
her. But I don't have a title. I'm just a com-
moner."

"You're true royalty—esthetically speaking,"
Pauncho said.

Barney glared at him.

"Don't you wish you'd said that?" Pauncho

said, sneering at Barney.

"We're going after Iwaldi," Doc Caliban said. "That'll be very dangerous. Besides, I don't want to have to worry about you when the fireworks begin. I suggest that you go back the way we came."

"Won't that be dangerous, too?" Barbara said. She was looking him up and down and evidently liking what she saw. Doc felt uncomfortable and cursed himself for being weak enough to experience the feeling. He never got over it. He always attracted women, and he always felt uneasy at their admiration. What was worse, he now knew why he got uneasy, and he did not like that at all. After his final encounter with Lord Grandrith in that old castle in the Cumberland, when he had been invalided with a broken neck and was regrowing some rather roughly removed skin and flesh, he had done some deep self-probing.

"Either way is dangerous," he said. "But the trail blazed is always less dangerous than the trail to be blazed. Generally, anyway."

She looked at Carlos Cobbs. "I'd feel safer if we were with them even if we might run into that dirty old man and his gang."

Carlos Cobbs shrugged. He said, "Anything you say, my dear."

"We can't spare any guns," Doc said. "Pick up one of those swords or an axe and stay well behind us."

"Maybe one of us ought to stay close with the lady and see she doesn't come to any harm," Pauncho said. He grinned at the titian-haired

beauty and managed to look even more like a
baboon.

"If she stays with you she will come to harm,"
Barney said. "Just looking at you is enough to
bring anybody down with a fatal case of the ug-
lies."

Doc walked away with Barney and Pauncho a
few steps behind and the couple following them.
He halted before the archway, swept his detector
back and forth, and then started through. He felt
the floor dip and leaped high into the air like a
scalded cat. The detector flew out of his hand as
he grabbed for the rough stone along the edge of
the point of the archway. Even though his leap
took him above the heads of his two men, his
fingers could not find a purchase on the stone.
He fell back and into the hole below him and
after Barney and Pauncho. Their yells were coming up the shaft even as he hurtled through the
hole. He saw Cobbs and the woman staring
open-mouthed and pale at him, and then the
walls of the shaft were the only thing he could
see.

Far below came a splash, then another splash.
And then it was not so far below, and he plunged
into icy water.

He went down deep, but his fall had been perhaps fifty feet, enough to kill a man if he struck
the water at the wrong angle. His hard heavy
boots took the major part of the energy of the
impact. Even so, he was half-stunned. But he
had secured the cap with the blacklight device
onto his head by holding it with one hand, and
he switched that on. Then he slipped his goggles

down onto his eyes, sliding it over the skin to keep the water out, and held tightly with the other. As he rose toward the surface, he removed two plugs from a vest pocket and slipped these into his nose. He began breathing through them immediately. They strained oxygen from the water quite efficiently, and he breathed the carbon dioxide out through his mouth.

There was no light down here, and he would have been blind if it had not been for his black-light projector and goggles. Even so, the water seemed to have a suspension of plant growth or perhaps of dirt and he could not see far. But he did make out Pauncho's form and when he had swum near enough for Pauncho to see him, Pauncho gestured outward. Doc swam even closer and could then make out Barney's shadowy figure. In a moment, Barney had swum close.

Both had retained their caps with the projector and their goggles, and they had also inserted into their nostrils the filters. But the icy water was rapidly numbing them.

Doc reached into another pocket and removed an object the size and shape of a boy's marble. He popped it into his mouth, chewed on it, and then swallowed it. A minute later, he began to feel warm. The sense of disorientation that had started to slip through him disappeared. The pill not only provided a source of energy the output of which was proportionate to the demand for warmth, but it fought shock.

He reached the surface but could not stick his head into the air. The water at this point boiled into a ceiling of rock. He and his two colleagues could only stay under and let themselves be taken away by the powerful current. There was no use fighting against it. Even Doc Caliban's massive muscles, anchored to a skeleton almost twice as thick as a normal human being's, could not have made progress against that force.

For approximately five minutes, as registered by the hands of his wristwatch, they were swept between stone walls that came closer and closer. This narrowing of the channel also increased the power of the current. They sped by walls of granite worn smooth by other rocks tumbled along in the past by the river. They kept hold of each other's hand so they would not be separated, and they went around and around as if they were on a dancing streamer around a maypole. But then they began to get cold again, and they had to swallow another energon.

He had one pill left apiece. After the effect of that was gone, their chance for survival was small. Unless—At that moment he heard a roar, and suddenly the water was boiling. A sharp ridge of stone passed a few inches below his drawn-up legs, then he was sliding on an apron of slick rock and then he was half in the air, half in the water, falling and turning over and over. Paucho's hand was torn from his; a second later, he struck something. His ribs hurt so much that he could not repress a gasp, and water choked him.

When he awoke, he was lying on a muddy bank and was cold, cold, cold.

He sat up and began coughing. A shape ap-

peared out of the darkness. He got to his feet as
swiftly as he could but with agonizing slowness.
A voice rumbled, "It's me, Doc. Take it easy."

He felt his head. His projector was still here.
But his goggles were gone. Then his eyes became
more adjusted to the dark and he saw that he
was on a mud bank that sloped gently for several
yards and then rose at ninety degrees for about
forty feet. The sky was paler up there. The side
of a mountain hung over them on the opposite
side; the less precipitous slope was on the other
side.

"Where's Barney?" he said.

Pauncho grunted like a sick hog and said,
"He's trying to find a way out of here. You all
right, Doc?"

Caliban felt his side. "I think I cracked some
ribs. I won't know until I get back to Gramzdorf."

"I thought you were a goner. I saw you slam
into that boulder at the bottom of the falls."

Doc could hear the muted roar of the cataract
to his left. They must have gone quite a distance
downstream before making this bank.

He swallowed another energon. When he
started to feel warm again, he said, "Let's go
after Barney."

They walked into a side street of the little village of Gramzdorf just before dawn. They were
no longer cold and wet and dirty and hungry.
But they went silently and stealthily and studied
the outside of the inn, at which they were guests,
for a long time before entering.

Doc had resumed his disguise of Mr.

Sigurdsson, the old Norwegian tourist, and Barney was wearing a false red beard and red wig in his guise as a Mr. Benjamin. Pauncho wore contact lenses to change the color of his gray-blue eyes; he had a huge blue-black beard and his hat was jammed down to hide his enormous supraorbital ridges and his slanting forehead.

At this time of the year, when most of the snows were melted, there were few tourists. The locals, who stayed inside the village to work at the inns and the ski slides and associated businesses in winter, had retreated to their farmhouses. The clerk on duty in the lobby was asleep on his stool. The three walked past him and took the stairs to the third floor, the top floor. Doc inserted the slender tube of his see-around-a-corner and twisted it to inspect the front room from one wall to the next. Then he stuck another tube through the keyhole and pressed a bulb, pulled it out, and reinserted the *saac,* as he called it.

A little box attached to the opposite wall was flashing an orange light. That meant that it had photographed no one entering the room, and that, presumably, it was safe to enter.

Barney, who had been at the end of the hall and looking out of the window, signaled Doc. When Doc got there, he saw two figures coming down a side street: Carlos Cobbs and Barbara Villiers.

Doc Caliban was gone like a rabbit scared by a coyote. Though six feet seven and weighing more than three hundred, he moved as swiftly and as lightly as a tiger. He was down the hall, down the steps, and out onto the lobby just as the couple entered. His timing was precise. The two had no chance to get away if they had wanted to do so. Doc had considered not revealing himself so that he could watch the couple when they thought they were safe. But his own great size and difficulty of disguise for Pauncho van Veelar would also make it easy for the two to recognize them. Besides, he wanted information now, and he did not feel that the waiting game was the one to play at this time.

So he spoke to them in his own voice as they approached.

The jaws of both dropped, and their eyes were wide. But both recovered swiftly. Cobbs did not try to smile, but Barbara managed a brilliant and lovely smile. "I'm so glad!" she said, advancing with her arms open. "So glad! And so overwhelmed! I thought you were dead! You dropped into that awful hole and were gone! But the others? Are they . . . ?"

"All right," Doc said. "Would you mind coming to my room? There are some things we have to establish."

"Why not in the morning?" Cobbs said. "We're very tired. With good reason, as you know."

"I would think your curiosity would be too great for you to think of sleep," Doc Caliban replied. "You must have seen some things that you would have thought could not exist. And Iwaldi. Didn't—"

"Oh, yes, darling!" Barbara Villiers said,

placing a lovely white hand on Cobb's arm. "He's absolutely right! Besides, why is he disguised as an old man? I'm dying to find out! There must be some tremendous mystery here! I couldn't sleep thinking about that! I don't think I could sleep anyway, not with that mad goblin on the loose yet!"

Doc said, "The mad goblin. A good description indeed of Iwaldi. Will you go with me?" and he turned as if he fully expected that they could do nothing else.

They followed him up but stopped short when they saw Pauncho and Barney standing before the door. Cobbs said, "Who—?" and then, "Very good disguises those! But those long arms and that nose and mouth! No, I think I'd recognize him anywhere no matter what!"

Doc unlocked the door and let the others through and then locked the door and secured a little box against the upper part of the door with a disc. Barney had turned off the mechanism that was flashing a light and was removing the film.

Pauncho said, "What about a drink to warm us up and give us courage to face the morning sun? I thought I'd never see it again."

All took some brandy except for Doc, who never drank alcohol unless a disguise required it.

Pauncho lit up a long green Cuban cigar and said, "Doc, the floor is yours."

He added, "And the furniture, too, if you so desire."

Barney groaned. Cobbs and Villiers sat down before Doc could ask them to.

Doc said, "Did you two have any trouble getting out?"

"No," Cobbs replied. "We just walked out the front way. Everything was clear."

The titian-haired woman shuddered and said, "All those bodies . . ."

"You didn't tell the police here," Doc said. "Obviously you didn't have enough time; you got here so fast."

Cobbs said they had come straight down the mountain path to the inn. They did not know what was going on and they did not care to know. Their brief interviews with Iwaldi had scared them. The ancient dwarf—the "mad goblin"—had impressed them deeply. He seemed to be evil incarnate, and they were convinced that even if they had escaped him they would not be safe until they got to England.

"Just what were you digging for?" Doc said.

"Some years ago, when we were here on vacation, we heard about a shepherd who had discovered a stone with some strange markings on it. We investigated and found a rock with inscribed runic signs, made by some Germanic speaker by the name of, by a curious coincidence, Iwaldi. Probably the runes were incised between 600 A.D. and 800 A.D. We sniffed around that area and found a site of a small village. So, every now and then, we dig around here during our vacation. We're on sabbatical leave just now."

Doc made a mental note to check on their stories.

He could understand their fear. But what they had seen in the labyrinthal tunnels would estab-

lish them among the world's greatest
archeologists if they were to reveal their dis-
covery. All they had to do was to get the police
up there, and Iwaldi would have to run for cover.

On the other hand, they may have reasoned,
quite correctly, that Iwaldi had enormous influence and could abort any attempt by the police to get into his castle.

Doc asked a few more questions. Cobbs said
that the helicopters which had landed the invaders had left by the time they reached the
castle's front door. But he was convinced that
some of the invaders had gotten out alive. Apparently, the invaders must have split up, and
the second party had survived. He thought so
because he had seen the glow of cigarettes far
below them on the mountainside path. It was
true that the smokers could have been extremely
early hikers or maybe forest rangers, but he
doubted it.

"I'm asking you to stay here for a while. For
today, anyway," Doc said. "If any of those invaders are now in the village, you could identify
them for me."

"And what would you do to them?" Cobbs
asked.

Doc did not answer. He looked at the young
Englishman with all the intensity of his peculiar
brass-shot gray-green eyes. Cobbs returned his
stare with one just as unabashed though not as
intense. Doc had been a practitioner of hypnosis
for years and had been able to disturb many a
man to the point of hysteria just by looking at
him. But Cobbs was a tough and cool character.

Barbara Villiers, who looked devastatingly beautiful despite staying up all night, said, "I'll stay if you think it'll help you any."

"Babs!" Cobbs said reproachfully. "You might at least consider my feelings in this matter. After all, we are engaged! And we agreed that I am the head of the family!"

"There isn't any family yet!"

"Fabulous!" Pauncho said, grinning like a hungry monkey at her.

Cobbs sneered at Pauncho and said, "Discretion directs me to get out of here now! But I don't want you to think I'm a coward, and if my fiancee insists on behaving foolishly, then I'll stay too. But only long enough to look over the guests here and ascertain if we can identify any as the men we saw in the castle."

Barney had opened his mouth to say something, then he thought better of it. He looked as if he would explode if he did not get to ask Doc Caliban something at once.

Doc, guessing what he wanted to say, turned away from the couple and winked at Barney. Barney went into the bathroom. Doc said, "If you'll feel safer, you can sleep here in our beds. We'll make do on the sofa or the floor."

"I would prefer we do that," Cobbs said. "To return to our own rooms now would be stupid. Of course, we have to go there to pack, but we can do that later."

Doc suddenly spoke to the two in a somewhat musical speech, low-pitched and with many glottal stops and fricatives.

The two only looked startled. Doc spoke in

English. "Your profession hasn't taken you into the Central American jungles, then?"

"No," Cobbs said. "What was that for?"

Doc spoke to Pauncho, who listened intently and asked him to repeat several words. He and Barney had only recently learned the speech of the People of the Blue, a dialect of the "red-skinned Athenians of Central America," and they were a long way from being as fluent in it as their fathers had been. Pauncho nodded and left the room for the lobby downstairs.

Cobbs said, "Look here! I don't like this mysterious conversation. If you have anything to say, speak English, man! We're not under suspicion, you know!"

"You're not innocent until proved guilty," Doc said. "Not in this affair. Everybody is suspect. You are not being detained by force, however. I must insist that you understand that. You may leave at any time you wish."

Doc removed his jacket and his vest. Barbara Villiers stared and then said, "I thought you looked awfully fat in the body, yet your face wasn't fat at all. And your friends looked incongruously bulky, too. Good heavens! You must be carrying enough weight in those vests to sink a battleship!"

Doc did not reply.

Cobbs and Villiers went into the large bedroom where he sprawled out on Doc's bed and she on Barney's. Barney came out of the bathroom and spoke softly in the speech of the People of the Blue.

"I sent out a message to Grandrith. His wife

answered. She said he'd taken off for Africa a few hours before. She also said she might have to leave her rooms and go hide out in another place. She noticed a couple of suspicious characters hanging around in the street below. She said they might not be interested in her, but she's taking no chances."

"You told her about the events of the past few hours?"

"Everything. She said she'd pass it on to Grandrith when she got a chance. He's supposed to send her another message as soon as he's ready to leave the plane on the coast of Gabon." There, near the place where he had been born, Grandrith would proceed on foot through the belt of rain forest stretching over a good part of central Africa. He would live off the plants and the animals native to the land, killing them with arrows or his knife. He would avoid all human habitations; he would go like a shadow, like *the demon of the forest* as so many natives called him. Some used the name that an American writer had given him after accidentally finding out about him. On foot and almost naked, he would go faster than any human should through the silent closed-canopied, twilit rain forest where the only humans are the pygmies and where the pathetically few hairy and long-canined hominids, those beastmen of native legend, not long ago roamed.

Grandrith's wife, Clio, was staying in a slums district of London where she was operating a shortwave radio.

Caliban's cousin, Patricia Wilde, was also in

London. She was on the trail of old Anana, the
woman who headed the Nine. She believed that
Anana lived at least part of the year in a town
house in a wealthy residential district, and she
was investigating a number of houses there.
Caliban did not think she would have any luck,
but at least it would keep her busy, and she did
have a sharp nose for clues; she would have
made an excellent private eye.

The phone rang. Doc was across the room like
a bronze shark and had picked up the receiver
before the second ring. Pauncho, speaking mainly in the language of the Blue People, said, "I
checked out their registration here, Doc, after
greasing the desk clerk's palm. Cobbs and the
redhead have been registered here for a week.
But the clerk says they aren't around much. I
just saw two guys that looked pretty mean to me,
like they could take care of themselves and others, too, if they were paid enough. They've been
registered here for a week. They're Germans,
Heinrich Zelner and Wilhelm Gafustimm.
Zelner moves slow and careful, as if he's hurting.
They're in room 215. You want—?"

Caliban asked for a detailed description.
Zelner could have been one of the men he saw
when he had looked into the room where the invaders were. He may have been wounded during
the fighting.

"I'll be right down," he said. "Meet you outside their room."

He checked the pockets of his vest, which had
dried out very quickly after he'd come out of the
Toll River. He was short of anesthetic gas

bombs, so he went into the bathroom and pulled a section of the wall aside. The shortwave radio and their supplies were stored here. Pauncho had cut out a piece of the wall and made a receptacle in less than fifteen minutes after they had moved in. His work on concealing the new door had been so skillful it would be doubtful that anyone would ever know about it until the inn was torn down.

The grenades were actually little plastic balls which shattered easily on impact. Their surface held a little nipple which could be squeezed off and a slender tube could be inserted into the hole created. Doc also took several of the tubes. Cobbs and Villiers seemed to be sleeping. The woman was heart-achingly beautiful.

"You stay here and keep an eye on them," Caliban said to Barney.

"Why does that *Pan satyrus* always have all the fun?" Barney said, more to himself than to his chief. But this time he was surprised. Doc did answer.

"Pauncho'll be jealous because you'll be with the woman," he said. "He'd like the job of guarding her."

"Some guard! But what good is that going to do me with that Cobbs fish . . . ?"

He stopped talking. Caliban had gone as silently and as swiftly as a wind-blown cloud across the face of the moon.

On the floor below, Pauncho came down the hall with the rolling gait of a gorilla unaccustomed to walking only on its hind legs. He was grinning, and he held a stethoscope device in one huge hairy hand.

"I listened in on them," he said. "They didn't talk much but I heard enough. They were up at the castle. They're waiting for orders from someone."

"We'll find out," Caliban said. His voice was level, but inwardly he was disturbed. What group could be fighting the Nine? Or was it some group that knew nothing about the Nine but had it in for Iwaldi for some reason? They must really hate him to go in for such overkill tactics.

Doc decided not to transmit the gas via a tube through the keyhole. He knocked on the door and then Pauncho listened with the sound-amplifier applied to the door. He grinned and whispered, "They didn't say a word. But I'll bet one signaled the other to cover him while he answers."

A deep voice spoke in Austrian German. "Who is it?"

"Telegram, sir," Doc said in the local dialect and with an adolescent squeak.

"Slip it under the door."

"Sorry, sir, I can't. It has to be signed for."

There was a click, and the door swung open a few inches. An eye looked out. Doc seized the knob and jerked the door open with such force that the man was left staring at his hand. He had been holding onto it and had not expected that anybody short of a gorilla could have pulled the knob loose from his grip.

A second later what could have been the hypothetical gorilla charged into him, lifting him up and off his feet and doubling him over a hard shoulder. The man went *whoof!* Doc Caliban came in on Pauncho's tail, struck the man on the jaw as he went by, and then stopped. The other man, a tall skinny fellow with a shock of yellow hair, had stepped out from the bathroom. He held a .38 automatic in one hand.

Doc raised his hands. Pauncho dumped the unconscious man from his shoulder and also lifted his hands. A moment later, the skinny man looked surprised, and he started to open his mouth. Doc caught him as he sagged forward and eased him to the floor. By then, it was safe for him to begin breathing. He had broken two of the gas balls under his feet just as he stopped to raise his hands. It was an old trick that had been working for thirty-five years.

When Zelner and Gafustimm awoke, they were in chairs and their feet and hands were taped and their mouths were gagged. Doc was about to inject Zelner with fluid from a big hypodermic needle.

After he had shot both men in the arm, and they had gone back to sleep, he removed the gags. His questioning was swift and direct, because he did not know how much time he had. The inn was beginning to stir. Even though the ski season was long gone, there were a number of tourists who had come here to bathe in the mineral waters of Gramzdorf, which were reputed to have medicinal effects. It would be impossible to carry the two men up to Caliban's room without being observed now. And the two obviously expected visitors or a message that had to be answered soon.

The men replied to each question as all men

did under the influence of calibanite. But they
answered literally and only to the detail specifi-
cally required by the inquisitor. Both men told
similar stories. They had been hired six years
ago in Hamburg. They worked for an organization which they knew was larger than their immediate group. But that was all they knew of it.
They had never heard of the Nine nor seen anyone answering to the description of the Nine.
Their immediate superior on this job was a scar-
faced Prussian known to them as Ruthenius von
Zarndirl. He had led them into the castle last
night but had disappeared during the fighting.
When Zelner was wounded, Gafustimm had
been ordered to go with him to the upper levels
to route any stragglers while the others went off
in two groups after Iwaldi. Thye had found no
one, had returned to the ground floor, waited a
while, then come down to Gramzdorf. On the
way, they had run into van Zarndirl, who had
told them to wait at the inn for instructions.

Doc removed the tapes and ordered them to
go to bed. Like zombies, they shambled forward
and climbed into their beds. After receiving a
shot of a sleep-inducing drug, they began snoring
loudly. Doc and Pauncho left the room, and
Pauncho hung a DO NOT DISTURB sign on
the knob.

They went back up the steps and down the
hall to the door of their room. Pauncho rapped
out the recognition code on the door with his
knuckles. There was no answer.

Doc inserted the *saac* into the keyhole, twisted
it as he held one end to an eye, and then quickly
withdrew it.

"Barney's on the floor. Lots of blood." he said.

Pauncho grunted as if a big fist had slammed into his stomach. A second later, he was inside the room with Doc on his heels.

Doc Caliban said, "Some of the blood is his, but most of it is somebody else's."

The bronze-skinned giant removed a case which looked exactly like a cigarette lighter from a pocket of his vest. He pressed down on the lever, and a humming emanated from it. He passed the device back and forth over Barney's head at a distance of two inches. After a minute, Barney's eyelids fluttered and then his eyes opened. Pauncho had brought a glass of water. Doc popped a pill into Barney's mouth and Pauncho held his head up while Barney drank.

The most serious wound was from a knife that had penetrated a half inch into Barney's shoulder. Instead of sewing up the wound, Doc held the edges of the skin together and sprayed it from a can. The spray dried and solidified quickly, looking just like a piece of Barney's skin. The other two wounds were treated similarly, and then Barney was given another pill. His color returned, and after a while he said he was hungry.

Pauncho complained that his mother did not raise him to be a cook or a bellboy, either. Doc told him to go down to the inn's kitchen and supervise the preparation of breakfast, and never mind if the chef thought he was acting peculiarly.

By then Barney had told his story.

A few minutes after Doc had gone down to the second floor, someone knocked on the door.

Barney asked for identification. It identified its owner as Joachim Minter, chief of the local police.

"What do you want?" Barney said.

"We want to question Mr. Cobbs and Miss Villiers," Minter replied. "We have received some information about them from the Ministry." He did not say what minsitry.

"Open up, please!" the voice said sternly.

Barney did not know what to do. To gain time he said that he would wake up the Englishmen and ask them what they wanted to do.

He turned to walk into the bedroom, heard a click, turned again, saw the door open, and three men enter. All three were in police uniform. The chief, a tall man with a big nose and several knife scars along his cheek, said, "You will please stand aside, Mr. Banks."

Barney started to protest when one of the policemen struck him on the chin with his fist. But Barney rolled with the punch and countered with a fist in the solar plexus. Then he felt a shock in his shoulder and was dully aware that he had been stabbed.

Barney brought his own switchblade knife out and stabbed the man who had stabbed him. The two grappled. Barney was aware that the pseudochief had gone into the bedroom, but he was too busy to determine what happened after that. He cut up both men but one hit him on the temple with his fist, and that was the last he remembered until he saw Doc above him.

"You were lucky you didn't get your throat cut," Doc said. "I suppose they didn't want the hounds called out after them. A corpse might get the authorities aroused."

"Then Cobbs and Barbara are gone?"

"Gone," Doc said. "You feel up to any violent activity yet?"

"I'm shaky, but breakfast will fix that up," Barney said. "Why?"

"The men who took them away are doing one of three things. They're holding them someplace in this inn or maybe in the village. Or they're taking them up to the castle. Or they're taking them out of the village to some other place. But I doubt that they'll try to keep them prisoners in the village itself for very long. That'd be too difficult. But they would have to change clothes immediately, because the real police are too well known. So the pseudochief—sounds from your description like von Zarndirl—and his men may be inside the inn yet, changing clothes and arranging for a getaway.

"If von Zarndirl is working for Iwaldi, then the two'll be taken up to the castle. I don't know what value Cobbs and Villiers have for Iwaldi. The fact that he didn't kill them when he caught them in his castle and that he wants them alive now—if von Zarndirl is working for him—shows that they've been holding out on us."

"You should have used calibanite on Cobbs and Villiers," Barney said.

"If I get my hands on them again, I will."

The phone rang. Doc was across the room as if the ringing was a starter's pistol in the hundred yard dash. "Doc!" Pauncho's bottom-of-the-barrel voice said. "I just saw three men driv-

ing out of the courtyard with Cobbs and Barbara
in the back seat!''

"Be right down!" Doc Caliban said. "Meet us
at our car! Bring food; we'll eat on the run!''

Pauncho was standing by the car with a big
cardboard box balanced on one huge hand. Doc
lifted the hood of the Mercedes-Benz and looked
for bombs. Then he slid under and inspected the
bottom for explosives or signs of sabotage. Satisfied, he got out from under and into the driver's
seat. Barney got into the back seat and Pauncho
sat down beside Doc.

There was only one way out of Gramzdorf.
Doc drove as swiftly as he could through the narrow streets, which were occupied by enough locals that he had to take it easy. He used his horn
when they showed a reluctance to get out of the
way. But Gramzdorf was small, and within five
minutes they were on the asphalt road which
wound up the mountain for many miles and then
would begin a descent. Von Zarndirl's car was
not in sight yet, even though it had only about
five minutes' headstart. Doc was driving over the
narrow road as if he were on the Indianapolis
Speedway. Pauncho ate with a nonchalance that
irked Barney, who did not care at all for the
depths whizzing by a few inches from him.

"Karlskepf is twenty miles away," Doc said.
"They can take a private plane from there."

The sky was blue above them, and the spring
sun would be above the mountain across the valley to their right within an hour. But to the west
black clouds were advancing. Pauncho stopped
stuffing his mouth long enough to turn on the car

radio. A German announcer verified the threat of the clouds. A storm was blowing in from France.

Barney moved over to the left side where he did not have to see the abysses springing up at him every time they took a curve. He said, "Pass some of that wienerschnitzel or whatever it is back here."

"Very good stuff," Pauncho said. He lifted a bottle of dark beer from the box, tore off the cap with his thick teeth, and drank deeply. "Ah! Nectar!" he burped.

Barney said, "You're disgusting! What about it, Doc? You want Pauncho to feed you while you're driving?"

Doc shook his head. He did not want to be distracted by anything. Besides, he had just seen the car they were chasing, another Mercedes-Benz far ahead. It was on a higher level and just going around a corner of the mountain. It was moving suicidally fast, too.

The whole affair was puzzling. What group could be fighting the Nine? And why? Who were Cobbs and Villiers? Obviously, they were more than just archeologists on a sabbatical.

Doc drove as if the car had become, in a mystical manner, a living thing that was also part of him. Even Barney felt this emanation from Doc and relaxed, though he still did not move back to the right.

Then their auto screamed around a curve and there, some fifty yards ahead, blocking the road, was von Zarndirl's car.

"Hey, Doc!" Pauncho said. "I saw Barbara

going up the mountainside! Up in the woods there!''

Caliban could not spare even a glance to look where Pauncho's finger was pointing. He was using the brakes to halt the Mercedes-Benz before the ambushers could fire at close range. He succeeded in stopping the vehicle, though not without some fishtailing and then backed it up with a roar. The expected gunfire did not materialize.

"What's going on?" Barney said.

Doc gestured with a thumb behind him. He had been looking in the rearview mirror. Barney and Pauncho turned their heads and saw two men coming out of the brush behind them about fifty yards away. One held a rifle; the other was looking down into a metal box he held before him.

Doc started the car forward with a surge that burned rubber and threw the others back against their seats. Brakes and tires screaming, he stopped the car with its nose almost touching the side of von Zarndirl's car. He threw open his door and fell out, was on his feet, and racing around to the other side of the car blocking their path. Von Zarndirl could be in the bushes just above waiting to catch them when they retreated from his aides, but he had to take that chance. He opened the righthand door in the front and looked inside. The keys were still in the ignition lock.

Pauncho, looking in on the other side, said, "Hey, Doc! Why don't we just drive this—?"

A crack from up in the hills made him dive to the road. A bullet struck the pavement near him and screamed off. The report of the second shot came almost immediately after.

Doc leaped up, ran to the front of the car, lifted the hood, and then dived back to the pavement by the side of the car. The hood was perforated twice and the windshield once. But Doc was up and looking down over the side of the car at the motor. He rolled away as three more bullets went through the raised hood and through the windshield. Then, fluid bronze, he was back again, had reached in and yanked loose a wire and dived away again.

Pauncho and Barney were firing at the two men far down the road with their automatics. Seeing that the range was too far for accuracy and that the men were not even bothering to fire back, the two stopped shooting.

"What are you doing, Doc?" Pauncho called.

"I just disabled a bomb under the hood," Caliban said. "They expected us to drive their car out of the way; we'd have been blown to kingdom come!"

There was a trail up the mountainside. It was visible only in a few places, and in one of these Doc saw Villiers' red hair and Cobbs' black hair for a moment. His gaze kept going up the slope until it stopped on a whitish object. This could be the front of a house perhaps a thousand feet up.

Doc Caliban relayed this information to his men. "They didn't pick this spot for an ambush just by accident," he said. "They've got a place up there!"

If that was true, then the group von Zarndirl

represented had planned well ahead. The two men Caliban had questioned probably knew of this place. But they would have said nothing about it unless they had been asked about it. And since Doc did not know about it, he could not have asked about it. Doc swore to present future prisoners with some general questions which might turn up items like this.

"Look out!" Pauncho yelled.

Doc stuck his head up, risking another bullet from the sniper, to see what Pauncho was alarmed about. He did not hear the bullets, but he did hear the two reports coming from somewhere in that mass of evergreens above. And he saw the thirty or so ravens and hawks swooping down the mountainside toward them. They were so close together they almost formed a solid black ball, and they were only a few feet above the tips of the trees. They made no cries, and they bore little white objects on top of their heads.

All three men began firing, then stopped as a dip in the ground took the birds out of their view. The man with the rifle down the road began firing slowly, forcing Pauncho and Barney to get between the two cars and lie flat on the road. The sniper in the trees continued to shoot at Doc. And then the birds, wings beating, beaks open, were on them.

It was impossible to stay out of sight of the two riflemen and fight the birds at the same time. Barney and Pauncho tried; they rolled over on their backs and shot straight up into the feathery avalanche that hurtled on them. Doc hosed the eight ravens and three hawks that came at him with the .15 caliber bullets from his gasgun, and the lead birds exploded in blood, bone, and feathers. But five birds got to him, and he had to drop the gun and defend himself with his bare hands. All of them tried for his head, and in so doing they got in each other's way: wings beating against wings knocked them down, talons extended to sink into his flesh touched another bird and automatically sank and beaks snapping for eyes and nose closed on wings and legs and heads.

Ignoring the sniper because he had to, Doc reared up like a whale coming from the deeps, sending ravens and hawks flying off him. He whirled around and around, his hands chopping out, breaking wings, cracking necks, smashing thin skulls. But one hawk got through and its talons sank into his face. He fell forward and rolled over and over and then began to unhook the agonizing steel-sharp claws from his cheeks. Blood flowed down his face and over his chest as he cast the body of the hawk away from him. He had twisted its head off with one turn of the wrist.

Barney and Pauncho were killing the last of their attackers with their bare hands, too. Like Doc, they were bleeding profusely from deep gashes on their faces.

Doc had two of the plastic tennis-ball-sized gas grenades in a pocket of his coat. He removed them, twisted the pin of one to the left, and pulled it from the ball. Then he stood up, exposing himself to the fire of the sniper in the hills.

He threw the ball as hard as he could over the top of his car. It soared in a high arc as the rifleman down the road shot at it. And while he was doing that, Doc, .15 caliber gasgun in one hand and the second grenade in the other, was racing toward the rifleman.

To explode within effective range of its target, the grenades had to travel one hundred yards. The rifleman did not expect the ball to get anywhere near him. Not at first. But he was trying to explode the grenade in the air to make sure it didn't get close enough to make him even uncomfortable. And so Doc was speeding toward him while the magazine of the rifle was being emptied at the ball. When the rifleman realized this, he aimed at Doc. One round was left, and this missed Doc, who had bounded to one side.

Then the grenade blew up before it hit the ground sixty feet from the rifleman and the man with the box. Doc threw the second grenade then, as the rifleman dropped his FN and pulled out his automatic pistol. Doc continued to zigzag, firing with the gasgun. The second grenade struck the ground and bounced high and exploded a few feet above the heads of the two men.

Doc raced in while bullets from the sniper in the hills *whee*-ed by him or struck the road near him. Then he had picked up the FN, fitted it with a new magazine, stuck two more in his jacket pockets, put the metal box under his arm, and was running back to the car. Even with his heavy hiking shoes and clothes, burdened with a rifle and a metal control box, and on a tarred road, he was running swiftly enough to have breathed down the neck of an Olympic dasher.

When he reached the cars, Barney and Pauncho were in the one that had blocked them, and Barney had the motor going. Caliban dived into the back seat—Pauncho had left the door open—and the car backed up, stopped with a screech, and then screamed away down the road and around the curve of the hill while bullets struck the car or the road nearby.

About three hundred yards down the road, Barney pulled the car off onto the side of the road, where a stone fence had been erected to keep sightseers from falling off the edge. There was also a little stone restroom and two wooden picnic tables there. Doc gave quick first aid to everybody, himself last. They popped blood-building pills into their mouths and felt the pseudoskin he had sprayed over their wounds.

"Almost as good as new," Barney said, but he was exaggerating.

The blood-building pills, however, had to be taken with food to do much good. They ate the rest of the breakfast that Pauncho had brought along, even though their appetites were gone. The fight had shaken the two up, and Doc, though he looked calm enough, did not down his food with any pleasure. The pills would send their temperature up by a degree for half an hour and make them feel a little woozy. But their lost blood would have been replaced.

Caliban said, "Von Zarndirl will've arranged matters for us in Karlskopf. At least, I'm presuming he will have. Another ambush might not find us so lucky. Besides, I'm not going to bypass that house; it may contain the key to this puzzling affair."

Barney felt his shoulder and winced a little bit. Doc said, "You up to climbing that mountain and maybe mixing it up with those baboons?"

"You know I am, Doc," Barney said. He took the FN rifle held out by Caliban.

Doc Caliban untaped the six sticks of dynamite from the chassis next to the motor, saying, "We might use these."

"Hoist them on their own petard!" Pauncho rumbled. "I like that!"

They crossed the road and began climbing. The woods were heavy with firs and pines, but the underbrush had not begun to leaf out yet. Within an hour they were on top of the ridge on which the house rested. This was about half a mile to the south. From there on they proceeded even more cautiously because there was always the chance of mines or ambushers. Doc went on ahead to allow his puffing and panting compatriots to get their strength back. He saw the white house through the trees a hundred yards away from it. He also detected the gray slice of a partly hidden wire stretched across the path that wandered up from the road. He went around the tree to which one end of the wire was fixed and approached within twenty feet of the rear of the house. It was a one-story frame house with a big stone fireplace at the north end, the end near which he crouched. It was built in the form of an L and had about four narrow windows on each side. The blinds were pulled down almost to the bottom of the windows.

He returned to his men. "There's no sign of life," he said, "but you can bet they're all in there, waiting. Of course, they don't know we've come up here, but they can't afford to ignore the possibility."

Each of them had two of the bouncing gas grenades, the last of their supply. Doc said, "Let's go," and he seemed to the others to have dissolved into the forest. Pauncho said, "Don't foul things up in your usual slaphappy manner, Barney. Try to keep from falling over your own feet."

"You low-browed hairy monstrosity!" Barney said. "I hope you can keep from swinging from the trees; they must really be tempting you! Keep your mind on our business and don't shoot me by accident!"

Pauncho grinned and said, "It wouldn't be any accident."

They saluted each other with fingers to noses and, still grinning, slipped into the woods. Barney went east, below the house, and cut across the path. Though he was not the equal of Caliban in moving swiftly and quietly through a forest, he was superior to most men. His rapier form moved past naked-branched bushes and over twigs with not a sound. Pauncho, even though he went much more slowly, made more noise. He cut to the west on the back side of the ridge and far enough below the house to make sure he wasn't seen. Then he worked his way up to the south end.

There was a silence for a long time. Only the
faint cries of ravens and the *skreek* of a hawk disturbed the air. The sun reached the zenith and
began to slide down the blue steps. The storm
that had been in the west showed no signs of
coming closer; it seemed to have run into a wall.

Doc waited. He studied the windows for signs
of life, but the thick curtains and the lack of light
inside the house hid any faces looking from under the blinds. He was sure that armed men
waited there. They had probably called for help;
helicopters might appear at any time. The machines that had been used in the attack against
Iwaldi could not be too far away. He could not
wait until night or until they got so tense that
they sent men out to poke around.

Doc cupped his hands close to his mouth and
gave the cry of the lark native to these mountains. A few seconds later, the call was answered.
Perhaps the men inside the house were fooled,
but Doc knew that Barney was returning his signal.

He wormed between the little fir plank outhouse and a small log house from which came
the odor of birds of prey.

The piles of lumber and firewood there made
for good cover. That would have occurred to the
men in the house, too, and they would be keeping a bright eye on the piles.

A third cry of the lark came. This was even
less convincing than Barney's.

Doc wormed along the ground until he came
behind the outhouse, and he stood up. He could
see the limestone chimney on the north easily

enough. He stepped back, estimated the distance and the wind again, and tossed the gas grenade underhanded. It flew up in a high arc and came down almost in its target, the square hole on top of the chimney.

It struck the edge, however, bounced up and down onto the sloping roof, bounded along and leaped from the roof's edge and fell onto the ground just below a window. Doc had stepped behind the outhouse by then and put his fingers on his ears. The blast was still getting echoes from the mountain behind him and across the valley when he tossed his second grenade. This disappeared down the chimney and exploded before it reached the bottom. At least, it should have done so. He had sent it higher than the first so that the six-second interval between pulling the pin and the mingling of gases would result in a blast halfway down the stone shaft.

There was the chance that Cobbs and Villiers might get hurt, but they would certainly be hurt if their captors got clean away with them. They would have to take chances, too. They were adults who knew very well what the consequences of this game might be if they lost.

The echoes of the second explosion had just died when a third, Barney's, blew up just outside the front porch—if Barney had thrown accurately. Doc charged toward the house just as Pauncho's grenade, thrown from the south, blew up the side porch.

Doc was hoping that the rapid succession of blasts would stun the defenders and yet would not kill the prisoners. He ran with the bundle of dynamite sticks held by a cord in one hand. He threw it ahead of him so it landed on the roof, leaped up, grabbed the edge, and swung himself up with the agility of a leopard. An automatic rifle began firing immediately afterward, and the muzzle, stuck from the window, tried to follow him up. But it was too late.

Somebody began to shoot through the roof. The bullets did penetrate the three-ince thick planks, but he had moved on to a station just beside the chimney. When the firing ceased, he yelled down the shaft.

"Come on out with your hands behind your necks! Or I'll drop this dynamite down the chimney!"

"If you do, you'll kill Cobbs and the girl!" a man shouted.

Doc said, "So what?"

There was a pause. He resisted the temptation to put his head over the mouth of the chimney to hear what they were saying. Somebody might be down there waiting to shoot his face off.

"O.K.!" the same voice shouted. "We know when we're licked! We'll come out with our hands up!"

"Send the prisoners out first!"

There was another pause. Then the man said, "Here they come!"

A banging as of the front door being violently opened announced the exit of somebody. He could not see who it was, but Barney suddenly stuck his head out from behind a tree and signaled. Cobbs and Villiers were being released. A few seconds later, he saw them walking toward

Barney, who was waving an arm at them. They
looked disheveled, dusty, and a little bloody.
Their hands were tied behind them.

Two men came out of the back, three through
the front door, and two through the hole blown
in the south side of the house by Barney's
grenade. They came out shooting wildly. Cobbs
and Villiers threw themselves on the ground, but
von Zarndirl's men did not care to waste bullets
on them. They wanted to get Doc and his men
first.

Doc, knowing that some of them would turn
and shoot at him, tossed the bundle of dynamite
toward the rear door to panic them. Then he
leaped past the chimney and down to the
ground, landing on both feet but going forward
to the ground and rolling. His massive muscles
and thick bones enabled him to take the shock
without injury. He came up onto his feet, his
gasgun spewing at the men in the front, two of
whom had run to the north so they could get him
in their line of fire. His little bullets ran across
their chests, sending up gouts of flesh and blood.

Barney's FN had cut the third man almost in
half.

The men in the back had taken off when the
dynamite fell near them. They did not know that
it had no fuse. They kept on running and so were
caught in Pauncho's gasgun fire.

The two men who had gone out through the
hole in the south side had been wounded in the
legs by Pauncho's first few bullets. One got to his
elbows and started to shoot, and Pauncho had to
kill him. The other man put up his hands,

though he was unable to stand up when Pauncho ordered him to.

Barney had untied the hands of Cobbs and the redhead. She did not look so beautiful now what with the dust and the blood and the grayish skin. But, seeing Doc, she smiled, and at that moment, disheveled and shocked or not, she was beautiful.

Pauncho came around from the side of the house dragging a man along behind him, by the jacket collar. He dropped him before Doc, and said, "We're in luck! Von Zarndirl, if those scars mean anything!"

Caliban gathered together the metal box and the weapons, and Pauncho dragged von Zarndirl into the house. It was necessary to give him three of the blood-building pills. There was food in the house, and the German ate after the initial effects of the pills had energized and deshocked him. Doc put Barney on guard outside with orders to watch especially for helicopters. There was a transceiver by which they could have called for help. It had been on a table near the fireplace, and it and the operator lay in two heaps on the floor. Doc's grenade had blown out the upper part of the fireplace, and the stone fragments had shattered the radio and driven a sharp piece into the operator's neck.

The interior of the house was a mess. Shattered glass, ripped blinds, curtains, overturned tables, and pieces of stone and dust lay over the single big room.

Doc injected calibanite into the arm of von Zarndirl. Within fifteen minutes he had cleared up some of the mystery.

Von Zarndirl was working for an organization which had to be the Nine, though he did not know what its name was or even that it had a name.

Doc's face did not show it, but he was shocked. Even though he and Grandrith had turned against the Nine, he had never thought about others doing so. And Iwaldi himself was one of the Nine who sat at the table of power.

Von Zarndirl was too far down in the echelon of the Nine to be a "candidate." He did not know that Iwaldi was one of the millennia-old rulers of the organization for which he worked as cutthroat or whatever job was required of him. All he knew was that orders had come through to get the white-bearded old dwarf, Graf von Gramz. Von Zarndirl was lucky. He had led his group upstairs and lost some men to wolves and owls, and then he had gone down to the ground level to look for the other group. They had found a concealed entrance to the underground passages, but this was not the one which the first group had gone through. (Von Zarndirl did not know this, of course, but his description told Caliban that he had missed the obvious trail. How he had managed to do this, Caliban could not know. He supposed that the man had simply found an entrance before he had gotten to that left open by Caliban.)

Almost immediately, three-fourths of the group had been crushed against the wall by a sliding stone block. Van Zarndirl, in the lead, had escaped by an inch. The survivors, five men, had refused to go on. Von Zarndirl had returned to Gramzdorf (the choppers having departed long before by prearrangement), and he had reported via radio to a Herr Schmidt, whom he had never seen. His men had observed Caliban's group, but whoever it was that received the report did not recognize any of them. Or if he did, he did not tell von Zarndirl their identities. Schmidt ordered that Cobbs or Villiers be taken for questioning. The old Norwegian, Sigurdsson, and his two companions were to be kept under close observation. If a chance arose, they were to be taken alive. But if they looked as if they might get away, they were to be killed.

Doc Caliban was puzzled. Schmidt knew that the two Englishmen were somehow connected to the old Norwegian (Doc Caliban) and his cronies. But what of it? Unless Schmidt knew that Caliban was in Gramzdorf in disguise, he would have no reason to suspect Cobbs or Villiers. He did not know that they had been Iwaldi's prisoners or that Caliban had helped them escape. Although von Zarndirl's men had seen the two Englishmen go to Caliban's room, that would not mean anything.

And if any of the servants of the Nine had suspected that Sigurdsson was really Caliban, von Zarndirl would have been ordered to attack Caliban without thought of consequences. Cut him down in public, in front of the police station and a hundred witnesses if you have to! We'll get you off later, you can be assured of that. And you'll never have to work again or want for anything, short of a seat at the table of the Nine.

His disguise had not been penetrated. But he had been gone from the inn during the night of

the attack, and that may have been what
aroused suspicion.

He asked von Zarndirl if this were true. The
scar-faced German, sitting on a chair, staring
glassily straight ahead, replied in a hollow voice.
He did not know. One man had been left behind
to observe the village during the attack and to
warn the attackers if the villagers became aware
of what was going on at the *schloss*. He had reported the disappearance of the Norwegian and
his companions. Von Zarndirl had passed this
information on.

And Cobbs and Villiers had disappeared for
three days. Anything out of the ordinary, anything unexplained, was to be reported.

He continued to question von Zarndirl. Yes,
he supposed that the next time many more men
would be used. Yes, he did not think it likely that
Iwaldi would remain in the castle now, but such
decisions were not up to him. If they were to attack an empty castle, they would do so. Whatever his boss, Schmidt, ordered, they would do.

Doc took one of the plastic hemispheres from
a pocket and showed it to von Zarndirl. He
asked him a few questions and received answers
which confirmed his guesses.

The metal box and the plastic hemispheres
were developments of devices Caliban had been
working on when he had gone mad from the side
effects of the elixir. The hemisphere housed electronic microcircuits which were connected to the
brain of an animal through tiny holes drilled into
the skull. The electrodes were inserted into those
areas of the brain controlling specific behavior

and also were connected with the visual neural system. The hemisphere transmitted a line-of-sight beam of what the animal saw to the transceiver of the metal box. This had a screen which displayed a picture of everything that came within the animal's vision. This was fine in the case of sharp-eyed birds, but the images were often fuzzy in the case of dogs or other near-sighted animals.

An animal or a group of animals could be roughly controlled by moving dials on the face of the control box. An animal could be driven to attack by stimulating the part of the brain which controlled aggression. But if it saw two persons before it, and the operator wanted it to attack only one, the animal was likely to attack both anyway. A fast operator could alternate states of aggressiveness and of fear very swiftly in the animal and so crudely stimulate or inhibit its attacks when it was confronted by more than one person.

The screen of the control box was also capable of producing up to twenty different simultaneous views, and a skilled operator could control that many individually, though not to the degree wished. Or the operator could control the entire group as one.

Doc Caliban had been close to finishing his prototype just before he went insane. After he had turned against the Nine, their agents had taken over his laboratory in the Empire State Building and his research facilities in his estate near Lake George. They had studied all his notes and the plans for many devices which he had perfected but had not yet released for use by the Nine.

Doc Caliban had guessed all this when the wolves had attacked him in the bedroom of the castle. Iwaldi had—or once had—his own animals, and the others of the Nine had theirs. Doc wondered where the man who had directed the wolves first and then the birds in Iwaldi's castle had been stationed. Of course, though the transmission was only on a direct line-of-sight and very limited range basis, the beams could be detected by transceivers and transmitted by wire to remote control posts.

Doc Caliban asked von Zarndirl what frequency his group used when directing their animals. The German did not know. This did not disturb Caliban, because he would examine the control box himself.

Barney came into the door—after calling out that he was entering—and said, "A chopper's coming. There may be more than one. It's hard to tell. The storm must be coming closer, too."

Doc Caliban looked out the window. The grayish-black western skies had broken loose from whatever was restraining them. The ominous clouds were spreading eastward as if chased by furies.

He saw the flash of sunlight in the air above the distant peak just before the sun was veiled by the clouds. Then he saw three tiny objects.

He turned and said, "Let's get out of here. Pauncho, you take care of von Zarndirl."

Pauncho said, "What do you mean, take care of him, Doc? Bring him along or shoot him?"

"Bring him along. He's of no use to us anymore, but . . ."

This was a war in which no rules of humanity applied. Or had been applied. But Caliban was getting increasingly reluctant to kill his enemies in cold blood. It was one thing to kill during combat. But to shoot a helpless prisoner was another thing. Not that he had not done that nor that Barney and Pauncho had not. When Doc was only seventeen and a lieutenant in World War I, he had captured two German soldiers at the same time that he had been cut off by the advance of the enemy. It had been necessary for him to get back to his own lines and yet he could not do so with the burden of the two prisoners. He could turn them loose or tie them up and leave them. While he was trying to make up his mind, he was joined by a captain and two sergeants, also cut off.

The captain had said that he was sorry, but they could not take the prisoners back. It would be too risky; they would be lucky to rejoin their forces without the burden of the prisoners. And it would not do to release two men who would soon be shooting at them again. The captain ordered the prisoners shot.

Doc had told the captain that he should perform the execution himself. If he couldn't do it himself, he should not ask his men to do so. The captain became furious and threatened Caliban with a court martial when they returned. Caliban replied that he had not disobeyed an order. He had merely stated an opinion. Besides, he doubted that the generals would permit such a charge to be made. The last thing they wanted was the civilian populace to know that such deeds were not rare. It did not matter that the French, British, Italian, Turkish, and German armies were all doing this under similar circumstances or even when there was no good reason.

The captain ordered Lt. Caliban to shoot the prisoners.

Caliban had never forgotten the faces of the two Germans. One, a tall brown-haired man with a black stubble of beard, had not said a word. He had glared at Caliban and then spat at him.

The other, probably even younger than Caliban, was a slight tow-headed man with greenish eyes. He had tried to be brave but, as Caliban raised his pistol, he had fallen to his knees and begged for mercy. The .45 in his chest knocked him backward into the mud. The other German, screaming his hate, rushed Caliban with his bare hands. Caliban shot him in the forehead and stepped aside to let the body, carried by the charge, slide on its face down a slope and into a shellhole full of water.

"There," Caliban had said to Captain Wheeler. "I have done the job you weren't man enough to do."

Wheeler was white with rage, but he said nothing. They started to sneak through the German lines. Caliban halted suddenly, and, for one of three times only in his life—that he remembered—wept. He sobbed for ten minutes and then continued on his way. When he was close to the American lines, he was shot at. The bullets were close, but he got away and then came up on the would-be killer from behind. The man was Captain Wheeler.

Caliban took his automatic away from him. Wheeler said he would charge Caliban with trying to murder him. Caliban said he did not think so, since a dead man could not bring charges. He stuck Wheeler's face into the mud and held it there until Wheeler quit breathing.

That was when he first met Barney's and Pauncho's fathers. Rivers was a colonel then and Simmons was a major. (Both were to be promoted shortly after.) They had been captured by three soldiers but had escaped. They came up just in time to see Wheeler try to murder Caliban and his execution afterward. At first, they were hostile, even though they knew that Caliban had been provoked.

He explained exactly what had happened, expecting to be put under arrest. But these two were not the dyed-in-the-wool military type; they were highly unconventional, and both had gotten into trouble because of some of their antics and their outspokenness. They told him to forget it, that Wheeler had it coming. As for the shooting of the prisoners, that had been necessary and it was doubtful that the sergeants would report it. Or, if they did, that their report would get very far.

Rivers (Barney's father) got Caliban attached to his staff. He recognized even then the genius of this young giant. In the few months that Caliban remained in the infantry (his true age was discovered and he was discharged), Caliban

came to dominate the two older men. Or, perhaps, it would be better to say that he fascinated
them.

Caliban kept in touch with the two after the
war. He went to Harvard (Rivers' school) and
graduated in two years. He had never competed
in athletics because it would not be fair, and he
did not want the publicity to interfere with his
studies. Even though he was capable of getting
through medical school (Johns Hopkins) with
the highest grades in two years, he had to take
the normal amount of time. But he had plenty of
opportunity to study many other subjects than
those required, and his friendship with many
professors enabled him to use the laboratories.
In 1926, he completed his internship, but he had
the equivalent of several Ph.D's in widely separated fields. And he continued his studies in
them and took up new subjects even while he
was practicing brain surgery.

In 1927, the Nine made their first contact with
him. In 1928, he was formally invited to join,
and in 1929 he first attended the grisly and horri-
fying ceremonies in the caves of the Nine in east
central Africa. But he was now immortal, bar-
ring accident, suicide, or homicide. His life
would end by homicide if he did not obey the
Nine in everything they ordered—he was assured of that. In matters which did not concern
them, he could do exactly as he pleased. He
could carry on his battle against crime as he
wished, could perform brain operations on criminals to eliminate their compulsive antisocial attitudes. There were, he found out, times when he

had fought and eliminated certain great criminals who were servants of the Nine and, in two cases, candidates. But the Nine had not seen fit to interfere with him since he was not interfering with any of their projects at that time.

Caliban's father had trained him from infancy to be a superman dedicated to fighting evil. Of course, if his son had not had the potentiality, he could not have developed into a superman no matter how much training he had had. But Caliban's heritage would have made him the greatest athlete of the modern world—except for one—even if his childhood had been normal. His grandfather had been one of the Nine. XauXaz had been born about 10,000 years ago—or more. And XauXaz's father had been born about 40,000 B.C. (here Caliban was speculating), so that old XauXaz was actually one of those Old Stone Age men whose massive skeleton and muscles made them much stronger than the strongest of modern man. Moreover, there was some evidence that XauXaz and his two brothers had been contributing their genes for a long long time to the family which eventually became known as Grandrith.

Caliban's father, a candidate of the Nine, had gone mad from the side effects of the elixir in 1888. He had become that infamous murderer, Jack the Ripper, for a short period, and then, recovering his senses, had fled to the States. But not before fathering James Cloamby, the future Lord Grandrith, known also by The Folk as *tls* and in the human world by the anglicized name his "biographer" had given him.

Caliban's father had been so horrified by what he had done when insane that he had sworn to make amends. He had raised his second son as a deadly weapon of retribution against evil. And this extreme physical and mental and moral education had resulted in a superman.

But you get nothing without paying for it, Caliban thought.

The universe was a check and balance system from macrocosmos through microcosmos. Man, intermediate in size between the two, atom and the star, but the most complex of all objects, is no exception. James Caliban had paid. His high ideals and his high goals had resulted in too much self-control. Too much inhibition. And, admit it, a feeling of superiority, no matter how carefully he hid that feeling from others and, worse, from himself. That superiority—which did exist—had alienated him in many respects.

A stranger in a world he had never made; his father had made it.

And his father had intended to turn him against the Nine eventually, he was certain of that. His father must have blamed the Nine for that period of murderous insanity and for the price they sometimes exacted for their immortality. His father had prepared him not only to fight the obvious criminals of the world. He had secretly waited for the day when he would launch him against the Nine.

But the Nine had offered the elixir to the son before the father could reveal his plans. Caliban, who prided himself on his invulnerable morality, had said yes to evil when offered a chance to live for 30,000 years. His father had not known that, any more than Caliban had known that his father was also a candidate. Neither had ever attended the ceremonies at the same time, and neither had had reason to tell the other that he was a candidate.

And so the Nine had found out that his father was planning treason. Or his father had failed the Nine in some way. And they had killed him. Caliban had no proof of that, but he was sure that they had. The circumstances of his death were such that only the Nine would have been responsible.

Caliban had tracked down his father's murderers, but these had not known that they were working for the Nine. And the man who had transmitted the orders from the higher-ups had died without revealing that he was not the originator of the murder.

It was his father's death that had caused Caliban to devote himself wholly to the fight against evil—except where the Nine decreed otherwise. The lust for immortality had made him schizophrenic. He knew that now. He had known it then, but he had pushed that knowledge down into the mass of his unconscious.

He had gathered around him men who were highly knowledgable and multiskilled and who had a thirst for adventure. Rivers and Simmons and Williams and Shorthans and Kidfast. He had met the other three a few months before he was discharged. He had kept contact with them while at Harvard and Hopkins, met them now and then. His father became good friends with them, and they sorrowed almost as much as Doc when his father died. It was then that they had accepted his invitation to join him in his crusades, and the first thing they had done was to help him run down his father's murderers. And—

"Doc! Hey, Doc!" Pauncho growled. "What's the matter, Doc?"

Caliban shook his head and blinked. He said, "I was thinking. . . ."

"The choppers are coming fast," Barney said.

Caliban went out swiftly with the others behind him, Pauncho behind von Zarndirl, guiding the somnambulist with a word now and then. They went down the path for fifty yards and then cut into the woods, the cars their destination. Doc returned up the slope and climbed up a fir as agilely as a young gorilla.

One of the choppers settled down in the space north of the house, and men carrying rifles scrambled out. Another landed near it; more men got out. Then a man carrying a black box got out and turned some knobs. About twenty hawks flew out of a port of the second chopper. They spread out in all directions, two flying toward his area. He dropped from branch to branch swiftly and fell the last twenty feet to the ground.

The party was still making its way down the mountain toward the road. Doc Caliban caught up with them, appearing so suddenly that Cobbs and Villiers jumped.

"Give me the box," Doc said. Von Zarndirl handed it to him, and he quickly checked out the operations of the controls, all of which were marked with their functions. The power gauge indicated that the battery was almost discharged, and he had no other.

There was a flutter above a tree to their right. They moved backward to crowd behind a tree, but Doc did not think that the hawk would miss them. The dial had been set at a frequency which he supposed was the one being used when the original operator had dropped the box. He adjusted two dials beneath the four-inch square screen, and then pointed the red arrow marked on the center of the upper edge of the top of the box at the bird.

One of the disadvantages of this was that the beam between animal and box was tight. A fast-moving bird was hard to keep track of. This device, however, bore a dial which moved to indicate the direction in which the animal had moved when the beam lost contact with it. Also, it continued to move in the same general direction of the target if the operator pressed a button. This activated a broadcast pulse which triggered off a mechanism in the hemisphere, and the operator, by moving the box and noting the swing of the needle, could narrow down the area in which the target was. Then it was up to him to catch the tight beam again.

An operator needed lengthy training to be skilled. Doc Caliban, after a minute of experimenting, acted as if he had been through the required courses. But he had an advantage in that he had originated the theory of the TV-controlled animal.

The whiteness of the screen was suddenly a green and black picture—no color-blindness in a hawk—of branches and the ground seen between the branches sliding by swiftly. And then there was a bronzed face down by a tree. Other faces and parts of bodies. The hawk had spotted them and was coming toward them.

Doc looked up from the screen, saw the wide wings spread out stiffly as it sailed between two trees, and he said, "Get him, Barney!"

The FN banged three times. The hawk flew apart under the impact of at least two bullets.

Doc pulled out his handydandy, a combination knife, corkscrew, screwdriver, crescent wrench, and you-name-it. He quickly unscrewed the four screws holding the instrument panel to the box and ran his gaze over the circuits. It would have taken him much time to ascertain the function of each if he had not designed the prototype himself. He pried up four connections and exchanged them, and then said, "Down to the cars! I'll be behind you!"

The chutter of a helicopter became louder. They retreated under several bushes and stayed motionless while the craft circled around and around near them. Suddenly, a hawk flying at near top speed flew over them, turned, and shot back. But it had spied the dead hawk on the ground. It flew around and around until the chopper nudged it away and hovered over the spot.

"They know we're close!" Pauncho said.

Doc did not reply. He had moved the box around and now had zeroed in on the hawk. He pressed a button, and the hawk, zigzagging crazily, flew off. But it returned a moment later on a straight course.

"I set up the circuit to trigger its fear center," Doc said. "There isn't any button on this particular instrument panel for that, but the circuits can be arranged to stimulate fear if the button is pushed."

The hawk circled again, apparently again under control by the enemy. The copter moved toward them with rifle and heavy machine gun barrels sticking out of the ports. Doc pressed the button again, and the hawk wheeled swiftly and ran head-on into the nose of the craft. It bounced off and fell soddenly into a tree.

Doc spoke to Barney while still looking at the screen as he moved the box to try to pick up another bird. "Move slowly. Give me a grenade."

Barney extracted a pressed-down grenade from a big pocket in his vest. It expanded to its tennis ball size as he opened his fist to hand it over. Caliban slowly squatted down, laid the box on the ground, and took the grenade. He waited for the chopper to come close enough so that the men in it could discern them under the bushes. Pauncho and Barney had readied their FN's. Doc Caliban said, "Save your ammunition unless I miss. We'll need all we have if the other choppers come after us."

But the chopper swung away westward. They got away as fast as they could at an angle down the mountainside. The roar of a chopper was suddenly on them, and then, a moment later, a wind struck the forest. It was the storm.

Lightning veined the dark eye of the sky. Thunder cannonaded. The chopper dipped as the first fist of the wind struck it. It went on over the two cars parked on the other side of the road, swung out over the valley, rose straight up, and then beat a path against the increasing wind back up the mountain slope.

The air whistled through the limbs of the trees, which thrashed like the arms of men trying to keep warm. Pauncho yelled, "Good thing that storm hit when it did! They must have known we were here when they saw those cars! Anyway, they would've landed and checked out the registration and then they wouldn't have stopped till they found us!"

"Why always tell us the obvious?" Barney howled. He and Pauncho grinned at each other, happy because the storm had saved them.

Doc told the others they should wait until it got even darker or until rain came. Though the choppers were probably being tied down in the clearing by the house, men might have been sent up into a tree to survey the road. And if they saw the two cars driving away, they might send a chopper out after them, wind or no wind.

In ten minutes the rain came down half-frozen. The black asphalted road became grayish white with the first drops and then black as the drops melted. They left the woods and got into the cars. Doc ordered that they return to Gramzdorf, since that was the last thing that the enemy would expect them to do. Their rooms were still available, since they had not canceled them.

Doc drove his own car with Carlos Cobbs and Barbara Villiers as passengers. He was silent for half the journey back and then he said, "Are you up to going with us tonight?"

"Where are you going?" Cobbs said.

"I intend to get into Iwaldi's place again. I could find the place where you two fell in when you were digging, but it would be quicker if you pointed it out for me."

"I'll be glad to!" Cobbs said. He lit up an American cigarette. "I owe that insane goblin a debt. But I still don't know why you don't just call in the authorities."

"They would just come in and look around and then depart without doing a thing," Doc said. "Unless we had some evidence that they could not overlook. You can bet that Iwaldi has cleaned up the mess in the castle and buried the bodies some place. And you can bet that he would bring pressure to bear in the highest polit-ical circles to keep the police out. What must be done will be done by us."

"Or by this organization that von Zarndirl belongs to?"

"They may try again tonight, storm or no," Doc said.

The car rocked with the wind's buffets. The half-rain, half-snow splopped on the windshield and was carved away by the wipers. Doc was driving at about fifteen miles an hour because of the limited visibility and the wetness of the road.

"I don't want to be left behind just because I'm a woman," Barbara said.

"The invitation included you."

He turned on the headlights.

She patted Caliban's huge arm and said, "I like your trusting a frail vessel such as myself."

Doc flicked a sidewise look at her but he did not reply. She had not shown the slightest sign of fear or hysteria, and outside the house she had picked up an automatic rifle and checked it out as if she were a veteran soldier.

He drove for several miles more in silence, wondering why they did not ask more questions. He was taking a chance by bringing them along if they were agents for the Nine. They might get an opportunity to trip him up. But if he left them at the village, he would not be able to keep his eye on them.

The storm continued for hours after they got back to the inn in Gramzdorf. Cobbs and Villiers went to their rooms. Barney immediately set up the radio in the bathroom. The contact man in Paris reported that no word from Lady Grandrith had been received. But he did have a message from Lord Grandrith. It had been sent by an operator for the Nine while Grandrith held a gun to his head.

Grandrith's communications, as usual, were more than cut to the bone. They went all the way to the marrow. He had been met by a big party of men out to kill him, and he had eluded them so far. He would be going on, as planned, on foot. It was doubtful that Caliban would hear from him again for several months. Caliban wished that Grandrith had added more details. Then he smiled slightly. His half-brother was no

more taciturn than he was. Both talked as little
as possible. But his brother did so because he
had been raised in the jungle with sentients who
did not converse much after they became adults.
And he had spent much time with himself during the formative years. Grandrith's close-
mouthedness was "natural." Caliban's was the
result of his father's training and was
"artificial." And also "neurotic." There were
times when it was clearly to everyone's benefit to
talk much, and he found it difficult to do so then.
He did, however, talk vicariously through the
pseudohateful banter of Barney and Pauncho, as
he had done with their fathers. Though their insults sometimes irritated him, he needed the two
men.

Von Zarndirl, having received another injec-
tion, slept on Doc's bed. Pauncho brought up
more food from the kitchen after observing its
preparation. He grinned as he told about the
curious looks that the chefs gave him and how he
had pacified a waiter with a huge tip.

"They think we're crazy, and of course they're
talking about us. Half the village must know
we're acting very peculiarly."

"We'll move out at nine o'clock," Doc said.
"According to Cobbs, the cave-in is only two
miles from here, on the north side of the mountain and about 2,000 feet below the castle."

At nine o'clock the storm had been dead for an
hour. The wind was gentle but icy; the clouds
were ragged, passing below the moon slowly as if
they were battle-torn veterans on parade.

Von Zarndirl, taped and gagged, slept on the

floor of the bathroom. The others, bundled up in climbing clothes, carrying alpenstocks and various boxes, went out a side door of the inn. They tromped through the slushy streets to where they had left the cars. After examining them for booby traps, they opened the doors and got out their rifles. They put on the caps with the black-light projectors and their goggles and began tramping up the mountain, Cobbs leading. Water fell on them as they passed under the low branches of trees or by bushes. The earth was often slippery under them, but they dug in with their stocks and slogged on up.

Cobbs stopped for a moment and said, "It's about a quarter mile ahead."

"We'll go more cautiously now," Doc Caliban said. "Iwaldi is no dummy. He'll have back-tracked after he caught you and either shut up the entrance or stationed a guard there."

They started walking again. The moon came out. Doc, looking up, saw the first of the big winged shapes. The broad beam from the projector revealed *lammergeiers*, the eagles of the Alps. There seemed to be dozens, and all were heading toward them.

He said, "Look out above!" and shifted the metal box he had been carrying on a strap around his shoulder to a position on his chest. "Don't fire!" he said. He pressed a button on the top of the box and held it there.

None of the humans could hear the noise that was broadcast from the box, but the eagles turned and flapped away swiftly to escape the eardrum-paining frequencies.

Immediately after, Barney said, "Doc! Wolves!"

Doc looked up and saw the first of the big beasts bounding over a bush to their left. But it was not a wolf. It was a large blackish German shepherd dog. Behind him came three more and behind them six big Doberman pinschers. Their mouths were open, revealing their sharp teeth, but they uttered no sounds.

A few minutes later, they turned and bounded away as if they had seen a pack of tigers.

Doc and his party climbed on toward the excavation, taking advantage of every bit of cover. The eagles and the dogs would undoubtedly be back. The noise had momentarily overcome the stimulus of the microcurrent in the hostility area of their brain. But once they were out of the influence of the supersonic frequencies, they would return.

"How can they see us, Doc?" Pauncho said. "I mean, how can the operators of the control boxes see much through the eyes of the animals in this dark?"

"I doubt they're using TV tonight," he said. "It's too hard to keep the narrow beams locked in under these conditions. They probably are just transmitting the code that turns on the juice to the aggression areas of the brain and letting the animals attack whatever they come across."

"I hope so, Doc," Pauncho said. "If they can spot us through the eyes of the birds, we're going to have a hard time."

"Here they come again," Caliban said. He had turned the sound generator off so that the animals would not be affected until they got close.

The eagles, their only noise the flapping of their wings, and the dogs, their only noise the brushing aside of the wet rain-covered plants, came in swiftly. They had but one intention: to tear apart these strangers in the dark.

Then Doc pressed the button, and the dogs whirled so fast they slipped in the mud and fell on their sides or scrabbled desperately to keep from sliding on down the slope. The eagles veered away and were swallowed by the night.

A minute later, the birds and the dogs were charging in again.

Thirty seconds later, they were frenziedly trying to get away from the invisible agony.

"How long's this going on, Doc?"

"Until something—or somebody—breaks," Caliban said.

Pauncho knew it was useless to ask him to elaborate.

The next time, the birds came in first and the dogs did not appear until the birds had been turned away.

"They're catching on," Barney muttered.

"And probably moving in on us," Pauncho said.

"Isn't it really too risky to stay in this one spot?" Cobbs said. "I think we should be moving about a bit."

"That's up to you," Doc said. He pressed the button again as the first of the birds appeared. This time they kept on coming and had almost reached them, with Doc saying, "Hold your fire!'' when they broke and flew upward.

The dogs bounded down the slope again, just as the birds turned away. Doc said, "Hold your fire on these, too, unless you can stick your guns down their throats."

"The whites of their eyes, heh, only closer yet?" Pauncho said.

Some of the dogs slipped in the mud and slid into them. The others turned away just before the final leaps and went crashing into or over the bushes and down the hill.

Three dogs hurtled in, sidewise or fangs first, and Pauncho and Barney slammed one each over the head or the back and then kicked them on down the hill. Cobbs and Villiers hit a dog at the same time with the barrel of their rifles, breaking its ribs.

Doc said, "It ought to be over soon, one way or the other."

"What makes them voiceless?" Pauncho said. "I looked in the neck of a bird with its throat cut open back at the house on the mountain, and its vocal cords were all there."

"I saw you," Doc said. "But I supposed you'd guessed the answer. There are a number of electrodes at various areas of the brain. During the time that the animal is released for attack, its voice centers are inhibited."

"I wondered about that," Cobbs said. "But things have been happening so fast, I didn't have time to ask about it."

"I just supposed their vocal cords had been cut," Barbara said.

The others did not comment. Pauncho had

asked Doc about the lack of voice after the attack
by the wolves in the castle and Doc had given his
opinion. But after the attack of the birds at the
house on the mountain, he had told his colleagues not to mention anything about the characteristics of the animals. He had wanted to determine if the English couple would be curious
about the strange lack of cries from the animals.
If they did not comment, they might refrain because they knew the reason.

On the other hand, it was true that events had
come one after the other and might have distracted them. But Barbara seemed to be a very
stable and self-possessed person, and Cobbs,
though he showed some apprehension, was far
from hysterical.

The birds came first and the surviving dogs,
going much slower because they had to climb
uphill in muddy earth, attacked simultaneously.
This time the wings of the eagles beat so close
that the tips of some touched their faces. But the
birds swerved again and shot back overhead.
The dogs turned tail when they were still a few
feet from closing with the party.

"I'd think they'd go crazy," Barney said.
"They're being pulled apart by the opposing
drives."

"They may yet," Doc answered.

About two minutes later the birds came in
again, and this time Caliban turned off the
sound generator for a few seconds after they had
wheeled around to go in the other direction. The
dogs then had nothing to stop them except the
weapons of the party. While the others knocked

the dogs on the head as they struggled uphill to get at them, Doc Caliban pressed a button on the other box, which had been on the ground by him. He had rearranged its circuits so that the aggressive areas of the brains would be stimulated.

The others did not notice what he was doing, since they were concentrating on smashing in the dogs' skulls or backbones and doing a good job of it. He had not told them his plan, since he never confided to anyone unless he needed cooperation.

There were yells and screams to the right up the mountain, and then rifles and pistols banged away. Doc indulged himself with a broad smile. The others had their backs turned and would not be able to see him.

He switched off the aggression transmitter and turned on the sound generator. The two surviving dogs leaped backward down the hill as if they had stepped on a red-hot plate. One turned over and kept on sliding. The other regained his feet and fled.

"What's going on, Doc?" Pauncho said, jerking a thumb in the direction of the gunfire.

"As soon as the birds were deflected again, and presumably heading back toward the men who'd launched them, I switched off the noise generator and turned on the aggression stimulation on. The birds, of course, attacked the first living things they saw, which were our enemies."

"Fabulous!" Pauncho rumbled. "I wish I had one of those hemispheres stuck on Barney's head. Then I could keep him from making a monkey of himself."

"Since when does a monkey's uncle know any-thing about proper behavior?" Barney said.

"The conflict of noise generator versus aggression stimulation might have driven them mad, anyway," Doc said. He led the way toward the groanings and whimperings drifting ghostily through the bushes. Approaching cautiously, they found six men on the ground, all alive but three totally unconscious and the other semi-conscious. The birds were all dead, since they had not ceased to attack until killed. The onslaught had been so unexpected that none of the men had had time, or opportunity, to turn off the aggression stimulator. The birds had tried for the face and the throat and had blinded four. One man died of a ripped jugular vein while Doc was examining him.

After giving the survivors a shot to ensure that they would be unconscious for a long time, the party picked up some more magazines for their rifles and stuffed them in their capacious pockets. Pauncho and Barney threw the extra rifles down the mountain, and they continued climbing. They did not have far to go. Cobbs stopped suddenly, grunted, and said, "There it is."

In the blacklight of their projectors they could see the trenches that the two archeologists had dug.

"Where's the cave-in?" Pauncho said.

"It's not there any more," Barbara Villiers said.

Doc began to poke his alpenstock into the bottoms of the trenches but stopped. He had heard the far-off chutter of helicopter vanes. He resumed probing and then said, "It's been walled up."

"Where'd those men come from?" Villiers said.

Doc did not reply. He took from a side pocket of his vest a tiny instrument and, holding it in his hand, began to walk back and forth for twenty yards each way. He worked his way up the mountain while she wondered aloud what he was doing. Since neither of his colleagues were sure, they did not answer her.

Ten minutes later, Caliban reappeared so suddenly from behind a tree that Barbara jumped and Cobbs wheeled around swiftly, bringing his rifle up.

Doc stepped back behind the tree and said, "Don't shoot."

"Doc, you shouldn't do that," Cobbs said. "You're likely to get shot."

Caliban said, "Follow me."

He led them upward to the right for about twenty yards and stopped. They were facing a fairly smooth outcropping of rock. Doc Caliban walked forward on the apron of the rock extending from its base and pushed on a small boulder at one side. The boulder rocked; there was a grinding noise and a section of the outcropping slid to one side.

"How'd you find it, Doc?" Pauncho said.

Doc tapped at the pocket which now held the small device he had used when casting back and forth. "It indicates small changes in the local magnetic fields. It detected the hollow behind that rock, and so I looked for something that would be the entrance activator."

They went into the chamber which had been cut out of the solid granite. Doc pulled a lever sticking out of a box in a corner, and the ponderous section of rock slid back into place. Immediately after, electric light bulbs fixed to brackets about four feet from the floor, and about thirty feet from each other, lit up. These were connected to wires which, in turn, occasionally descended the wall to the generator on the floor. Doc recognized the foot-square metal boxes as his own invention. They stored electricity derived by amplification of the flux of the earth's magnetic lines of force. They could not provide much current for very long, but the bulbs probably did not get much use in these corridors. They became extinguished as soon as the last person passed them, and they lit up as soon as the first person got within ten feet of them.

Each one in the party held his rifle across his belly. Doc held his with one hand while the other was extended with the magnetic-field discriminator.

Whenever it was a question of going to left or right, Doc looked at the juncture of floor and wall. Cobbs had carefully made tiny markings with a pen the first time he had come here. These indicated their previous route so that they would be able to find their way out.

They went up steps cut out of stone to upper levels four times before Cobbs finally called a halt.

"We're getting close to the place where the dwarf captured us."

They were standing in a round chamber about

forty feet across. It contained a dozen large boxes of oak on which were carved hunting and battle scenes. The costumes of the dwarfs and the humans in the scenes were those worn circa 800-900 A.D.

"They look like coffins," Pauncho said to the woman.

"They are coffins," she said.

She tried to raise a lid but could not manage it. "It's so heavy," she said. "But you should see the mummified body and the jewelry and gold it's decorated with."

"Here, let me help you!" Barney and Pauncho said. They collided with each other in their eagerness to get to the coffin.

"Leave it alone!" Doc said. "They might be booby-trapped now!"

But Pauncho, grinning because he had shoved Barney out of the way, had started to raise the lid. Barney dived for the floor as if he expected the coffin to explode. Barbara gave a small scream. Pauncho had stepped back and dropped the lid, which was raised about eight inches. It did not drop. Instead, it continued to rise, and the figure in it sat up. He held an automatic pistol in one hand.

At the same time, the lids of the other coffins screeched upward, and other figures sat up aiming automatic pistols at them.

A voice behind them said, "Freeze!" A voice ahead of them said, "Not a move!"

"A beauty of a trap!" Pauncho whispered. He looked at Doc Caliban. The huge man was obeying instructions. He had no choice. The fire from three sides would have cut them all down within a few seconds.

Ten minutes later, their hands cuffed behind them, they went up stone steps onto another level. The twenty men who accompanied them kept pistols pressed against their backs. They marched down a long tunnel on the walls of which were hung many paintings done in a very primitive but forceful manner. It looked as if this were the place Iwaldi had chosen as his ancestral gallery. The paintings were mainly of long-bearded fierce-faced men with beetling brows, bushy eyebrows, round blobs of noses, and very broad shoulders.

Doc Caliban remembered, however, that Iwaldi had been born long before portrait painting of this sort was known. These dwarfs must be men who had inhabited this underground fortress; perhaps they were Iwaldi's descendants, not his grandsires.

Except for the paintings, the tunnel was bare rock.

They were marched into a square chamber and here all the prisoners were forced to undress. The inspection that followed was thorough and included probing for concealed objects. Doc's wig and facial pseudoskin was pulled off. Two false teeth containing explosives and a coil of very thin wire were removed from his mouth.

Barbara Villiers said nothing. She was as dignified as if she were wearing a formal at the opera. Out of regard for her, Barney and Pauncho repressed the ribald comments they would have made at each other's expense.

They were marched into a chamber about fifty feet square. Stone steps cut into the sides of the walls led up to three levels of runways carved out of the rock. A man led the way up on to the second level. Just past the nearest of many entrances was a room divided by two sections of thick iron bars. The man opened a door set in the first by inserting a thin metal rod into a hole and pressing a button on the rod. The door swung back, and the party was marched up to the next section of iron bars. This was opened in the same manner, and Caliban, van Veelar, and Banks were locked behind it. But Barbara Villiers and Carlos Cobbs were left outside. The men conducted them out onto the overhanging runway and around the corner. An iron door clanged. The men marched away. Presumably, the English couple had been locked in a cell facing the runway.

"I wonder why they separated us?" Pauncho said.

Doc did not answer.

Days passed. At least, it seemed that many days passed. They had no way of determining time except by the number of meals, and they got so hungry in between these that they were sure many were being skipped. They exercised and slept and talked much, though when they did not want to be understood they talked in the language of the People of the Blue.

The only person they saw was the man who brought their meals, and he never said a word.

Then, three or four or five days after they were captured, two men entered the outside cage.

Both were walking backward and holding a box with a short antenna directed at the beast which shambled around the corner. Two men came behind the animal, one of whom also held a box with an antenna directed at the beast.

This was a huge grizzly, the North American *Ursus horribilis*. Its head swung low, and its eyes were a bright red. Its open mouth dripped saliva.

The man with the box in front backed up to the wall, keeping his antenna pointed at the grizzly's head. Then he pressed a button, and the grizzly lay down and went to sleep.

The great head was only three feet from the prisoners, who could see the tiny hemisphere on top of it.

The two men got out of the cell quickly and closed the door with a loud clang. The grizzly quivered at the sound but continued sleeping.

One of the men holding a box pointed it at the beast, and, suddenly, the ponderous animal was on its feet and roaring. It reared upon its hind legs and advanced toward the prisoners as if it intended to go through the bars to get them. The man pressed another button, and the beast dropped to all fours. It no longer seemed angry; it was just curious as it prowled around the cell, sniffing here and there and stopping for some time to gaze at the prisoners.

Barney said, "Do you think Iwaldi intends to let that bear loose on us?"

Doc Caliban called loudly, "Mr. Cobbs! Miss Villiers! Can you hear me!"

Cobbs' voice was faint but distinct. "Yeah, I can hear you!"

"Just testing!" Doc Caliban said. "Can you see anything of note?"

"Just some of Iwaldi's men! Nothing of Iwaldi!"

A moment later, "Correction! Here comes Iwaldi!"

Doc Caliban looked through the double set of bars but did not see the old dwarf appear as he had expected. About ten minutes afterward, the long-bearded hunched figure appeared from the right. Evidently, he had come up steps to the right instead of taking the closer steps to the left.

The grizzly roared on seeing him and pressed against the bars as if it were trying to get its muzzle through and bite him.

Two boxes with antennas were pointed at the bear, which immediately backed away and stayed in a corner while Iwaldi and four men entered. Two kept their antennas directed at the grizzly, during the conversation that followed.

Iwaldi rolled forward like a sailor, his body hunched forward and his arms swinging at his sides. His long white hair fell to his shoulders and his white beard swung like bleached Spanish moss in a wind. The wrinkled face came close to the bars but not so close that Doc Caliban could reach through and grab him.

Iwaldi stood for two mintues staring at them while his thin lips slowly opened into a wide smile. The eyes were as red as the grizzly's.

Finally, the thin and cracked voice spoke.

"You'll not get out of this, Doctor Caliban!"

"And why not, ancient fossil?" Caliban replied evenly.

Iwaldi cackled. "Do you think that you, a baby, a born-just-yesterday, could anger me with your puerile words? So I'm a fossil? Well in a way, you're right, since fossils endure while flesh dies. And you'll die, Caliban, and soon! Very soon!"

Doc Caliban shrugged and said, "Maybe I will. Since you think I am going to die, it wouldn't hurt you to tell me what's going on. Are you and the Nine really at war? Or did I make a bad guess?"

Iwaldi fingered his beard with a deeply seamed and swollen-veined hand for a minute. Then he said, "It can't hurt to indulge an ephemera such as yourself. And the knowledge might make your end even less endurable to you.

"Yes, old Anana and her sycophants are at war with me! But it was I who declared war, not them! I almost got Anana and Shaumbim and Ing! We were to meet in Paris, and I arranged to have the walls of the house loaded with explosives! I was to arrive a few minutes late to the meeting, just after the smoke cleared away! But that Anana! She hasn't survived for over 30,000 years by being insensitive. She smelled death in that house! That's the only way I can account for it! She sniffed out the odor of coming death! And she left the house and took Shaumbim and Ing with her and was only a block away when the house blew up!

"She should have blamed you or Grandrith for that, since she knows you're capable of doing that! But the fact that I was late made her suspicious, and she sent me word to come to a house in London. She did not say why, but I knew. I was to be put on trial! Iwaldi! On trial!

"I sent her a letter impregnated with chemicals which would release a poison gas when the envelope was opened! But she had someone else open it, and that person died, of course! From then on, it has been a battle! I finally decided to hole up here in my ancient stronghold, this mountain that was the property of some of my ancestors, the kings of the southern branch of the Gbabuld family! But I'm getting out now—for the time being—and leaving you here to face whatever you must! And whatever you must will be a matter of choice! So thank me for giving you a choice of deaths, Caliban!"

"Why the war at all?" Caliban said, ignoring the reference to deaths.

"Because the others have opposed me! They have sided with Anana! I wanted to let the mortals poison themselves and so eliminate themselves in time! I wanted to permit pollution to continue, the air to be fouled, the waters to be fouled, the fish to die, the ocean plants to die, the trees to die! In a few years, most of mankind will be dying of starvation! You know that! You said so in your report to us in 1946. You extrapolated almost one hundred percent what would happen, what is happening now and what will happen! You stated that enough people would become alarmed that measures would be taken to combat pollution! But it would be too late! The politicians would take over the fight against pollution and use it for their own advancement!

And most measures would be band-aids whereas deep excisions and grafts were required! Those were your own words!

"So, in about twenty years from now, a flicker of an eyelid in my lifetime, mortal, the sea life will be dying and there will be the very good chance that the world's oxygen supply will be seriously reduced.

"I wanted the Nine to keep their hands off! Let the mortals kill themselves off! Not that all of them would die, which is a pity, though it would be nice to have servants. But so many would die that civilization would collapse, and then the planet could begin the process of cleansing itself. Once again, we'd have pure air and pure water and trees would cover the land and the animals would return in great numbers. And we could set ourselves up as gods, as we did in the old days, and this time ensure that the mortals stayed few in numbers and poor in science. We wouldn't make the same mistake all over again of letting them multiply and invent until suddenly the entire Earth was threatened!

"But Anana said no. She said that if we let them go, we might die, too. The whole Earth might die. Only the most primitive forms of life would survive.

"I said that we had the means to restore the proper balance when we wished. Your report said that your own researchers had come up with a means whereby the phytoplankton balance could be restored and the chief source of the world's oxygen would thrive again. We could use that after the mortals had become savages again

and the cities were being uprooted by the plants
and being buried under the good earth.

"But they overruled me. Anana said that we
could not afford to take a chance. We did not
want to die, too, though she admitted that the
prospect of a return to the good old days was
tempting. She is very very old, as you know,
Caliban, but she remembers when the great forests covered Europe and even the isles of Greece
were green with trees. She remembers when
North Africa was wet and verdant. She remembers when you could travel for days in what is
now France and not encounter a single human
being. She remembers the great and the small
beasts that lived in the forests.

"But she decided that we would not let things
take their course as determined by the mortals.
She said that we must start using our influence
on the governments to determine the effective
course in fighting pollution. Action had to be
taken now, and we would start planning our
campaign immediately. Not for the sake of you
ephemerae, you know that. But for the sake of
the blessed green Earth. And for our sake.

"So I appeared to agree, and I left. But Anana
found out that I was secretly preparing coun-
termeasures, and she summoned me to that
house in Paris. And I set the trap, and it failed.
But I will win. Old Iwaldi won't fail! Although
you won't be around to witness my victory!"

"And that is the only reason why you have
deserted the ancient table of the Nine?" Caliban
said.

Iwaldi stared for a moment and then said, "Is

that *all?* What do you mean?"

"There isn't some other reason you haven't told me?"

Iwaldi laughed so hard he had to bend over, and his beard almost touched the floor. When he managed to straighten up, he wiped the tears from his bloodshot eyes with the tip of his beard, and he said, "You're very clever, indeed, mortal! Very perceptive! It is too bad . . . if I could trust you . . . if only . . . but no, I can't! Yes, there is another reason, but even though you are to die, I won't tell you that! It'll give me some pleasure to know that you'll be wondering what that other reason is up to the moment that you start suffering so much you'll have no thought for anything but the pain!"

"Does this other reason have something to do with the English couple?"

"Why do you ask that?"

"Because they must have some value to you, otherwise you would have killed them the first time you had them. It would be easy to find out if they were spies for Anana by injecting calibanite. And once you found out, you would kill them whether they were innocent or guilty."

Iwaldi made a smacking sound and said, "Very well reasoned out! You are indeed a worthy descendant of mine!"

It was Caliban's turn to be surprised, but he did not betray it with any change of expression. He said, "I know that XauXaz was my ancestor and I had suspected that his brothers were, too. But I did not suspect . . ."

"The Grandrith family tree has more than one

god in its branches," Iwaldi said. "Even Anana
was one of your ancestors, though she provided
a son a long time ago, about the time the
primitive Germanic speech was starting to split
up into its North, West, and East branches.
Which means that you have none of her genes, of
course. But her sons became heroes of their people. They were as strong as you or your half-
brother. But I was your great-grandfather, Doctor Caliban, though my genes seem to have been
most prominent in another branch of your family, not in your direct heritage. Didn't you know
that Simmons, your colleague, was my grandson? Haven't you thought about his extreme
shortness, his massive trunk, his abnormally
long arms and short legs? His Neanderthalish
supraorbital ridges? All of which characteristics,
except for his height, have been inherited by his
son, Mr. van Veelar, doomed to die with you
also. Then there is another illustrious descendant of mine, a second cousin of yours and of
Simmons, a scientist who brought back some
rather strange specimens from a high plateau in
South America in the early part of this century.
He also looked much like me."

"Cousin George Edward!" Caliban said.

"Grandpa!" Pauncho said, sinking to one
knee and spreading his arms out wide. "Grandpa!"

Iwaldi stared at him and then smiled thinly.
"Very well! Clown away to the last minute!
Very admirable! I wouldn't like to think that my
great-grandson was a coward, though it doesn't
really matter."

"And you'd kill your own flesh and blood?" Pauncho said, rising.

"Why not? It wouldn't be the first time. An ephemeral is an ephemeral."

A man appeared at the outside bars. The grizzly growled but did not move from the corner. The man said, "Pardon, sir, but the invaders are getting closer. They'll soon be on the third level."

Iwaldi said, "In a moment the servants of the Nine will find out they will have to keep on going down. A river of flame will appear behind them. Napalm is being forced by pumps into the tunnels. They'll try to take tunnels leading away but will find their route barred by big blocks of stone. They'll be herded, as it were, down to this level.

"In the meantime, I've opened a vein of water, and the tunnels below this are filling with water. They'll flood this level—unless the river of napalm gets here first. It'll be quite a race between the two, and if you prefer drowning to burning to death, you had better start praying."

He stopped. Caliban, van Veelar, and Banks returned his gaze. He said, "I like spirit in a man except when it's turned against me, and even then it affords me a challenge, however brief—a break from the boredom of mundane life. Do you see that?"

He pointed at a metal box protruding from the corner of the ceiling and the right wall.

"That's a movie camera. It will record your last moments, and then the front end will be automatically covered by a metal plate. When I re-

turn, I'll recover it and run off the film. It'll be a
pleasure to review your deaths."

He gestured at the two men with the boxes
directed at the grizzly. They stepped backward,
and the men with the rifles followed them.
Iwaldi walked backward for a few steps, too.

"I've made a little arrangement here. Possibly
even given you a chance to escape from this cell,
though I don't really think so. But if you shculd
get out, Caliban, you will then only have the
choice of throwing yourself into the flames or
into the water. You can't get past them."

He turned and walked through the outer door,
which a man clanged shut. The grizzly roared
and charged the men behind the bars. They
flinched, but Iwaldi did not move back, though
the grizzly's paw was slashing the air only a few
inches from his face. He said something, and the
men with the boxes turned the antennas toward
the bear again. He sat down and became quite
docile. Iwaldi spoke loudly.

"Caliban, at any time you wish, you can slide
your door aside and enter the cell with the bear!
But the moment you move that door, a mechanism will radiate a frequency which will cause
the bear to become insane with a desire to kill.
Nor can you all go through the door and then
shut it with the hopes that the grizzly won't attack you once the stimulus is removed. That frequency will keep operating even if the door is
shut again.

"This outer door can be opened by you, if you
can get to it. But it won't open immediately
when you pull on it. A delay mechanism will

keep it closed until five minutes have passed after pressure is applied. Which means that two of you can't keep the bear occupied while one opens the door and then all of you escape. The bear will be driven with the desire to kill every living thing in sight. He's nine and a half feet long and weighs one thousand one hundred and twenty pounds.

"You can stay in your cell and wait to be burned or drowned. Or you can fight your way out, and then be burned or drowned, but you'll have a choice. And this time, you'll have nothing but your bare hands and feet, Caliban! Use them well!"

He was silent for a moment as he stared at them and, doubtless, was hoping for a reaction of some sort. But the three were stony-faced.

"I'm going now," Iwaldi said. "It can't hurt to tell you that I'll be in Stonehenge for the winter solstice to attend XauXaz's funeral!"

Doc Caliban was surprised when he heard this, but he did not show it.

"Yes, XauXaz's funeral!" Iwaldi snarled. "You didn't know that, did you? His body has been kept in a big box in a London warehouse. It'll be shipped to Salisbury and then taken to the ruins of Stonehenge, where the Nine will hold the funeral ceremonies for him! And I'll be there, though uninvited! I'll kill all of them! Old Anana! Ing! All of them!

"And then I'll be free to release my biobomb! While the mortals are starving to death and also gasping for oxygen, I'll be in my mountain retreat, snug and safe, eating well, breathing a rich

air! After it's over for the mortals, then I and a
few of my servants, mostly female, and my stock
of beasts and plants, will come out!

"What do you think of that?"

The prisoners continued to stare without expression.

"You can pretend to be unconcerned!" he
shouted. "But you are naked, and I can see your
hearts thumping! A long goodnight to you, mortals!"

He spat and walked away, two men preceding
him, the others trailing.

Pauncho broke the long silence. "Maybe the
invaders will take pity on us."

"Yeah," Barney said. "They might shoot us.
At that, they'd be doing us a favor."

Pauncho looked at Doc and said, "I didn't
know we were related. That makes me several
cuts superior to this proletarian peasant, heh,
Doc? I got the blood of English nobility in my
veins, right? And the blood of ancient Viking sea
kings. And what's more, the blood of men and
women that were once gods and goddesses to the
common herd, lowly swine like Barney. Say,
Doc, what about that that hero stuff? Who do
you think were those ancient Germanic heroes
he was talking about?"

"I don't know. Maybe the men whose exploits
formed the basis of the *Volsunga* and
Nibelungenlied epics. Or maybe the man or men
who were the originals of the *Beowulf* stories. I'm
more concerned about his descendants, three in
particular."

Pauncho's small eyes widened. "Three?"

"Yes. That man's descendants have to include most of the present populace of north Europe or anybody descended from north Europeans and probably from south Europeans, and many Africans and Asiatics, too. Figure it out mathematically, if you ever get a chance."

Barney haw-hawed but quit when the grizzly, roaring, hurled himself against the bars.

Doc said, "Iwaldi didn't say whether or not pressure has to be maintained on that door. We can't afford to take a chance, so one man should keep pulling on it."

"If I had a pocket, I'd pull out a coin and we could flip it to see who's the lucky guy," Pauncho said. "But I'll be magnanimous, Barney. I'll handle the door while you help Doc with the bear."

Pauncho's voice was steady and he was grinning, but his reddish skin had turned pale.

"No," Caliban said firmly. "We'd be stupid to reduce our strength by one-third. We either put the grizzly out of commission and then open the door—provided Iwaldi wasn't lying to us—or we don't make it at all."

"Well, Barney, you always said you might be skinny but you could lick your weight in wild-cats," Pauncho said. "Here's your chance to prove it."

"I said cats not bears," Barney replied. "Anyway, the three of us total about seven hundred and seventy so that gives the grizzly an edge of three hundred and fifty pounds. And he's got teeth and claws a hell of a lot sharper than ours."

"Tell me something I don't know," Pauncho said. "Like how're we going to take him?"

He pressed his blobbish nose against a bar and stared at the grizzly. It was pacing back and forth, it's head low and swinging, the brownish silver-tipped fur beautiful but the beauty lost on the watcher. There was fat under that loose glossy hide but there were also giant bones and the strength of two gorillas.

"I want you two to hang back in here until I give the word to join me," Doc Caliban said. "I'm going to make him chase me until he gets tired."

Barney and Pauncho looked at the cell, forty feet square, and they said, at the same time, *"Chase* you?"

"It's worth a try," Caliban said. For him, that was equivalent to a long speech by Hector urging the discouraged Trojans to venture out against the Achaeans again.

He pulled back on the door and slipped through. The grizzly bellowed and whirled around, glared at Caliban, and then charged. It went so swiftly that it was a blur to Pauncho and Barney.

But the reddish-brown golden-tinted skin and dark auburn metallic-looking hair of Doc Caliban was a blur, too. He sprang to one side just before the grizzly was on him, ran at the wall, and bounced off it like a handball.

The grizzly rammed head-on into the bars with a crash that shook the bars and quivered the iron floor under the feet of the two men. But the enormous and clumsy-looking beast recovered swiftly, whirled, and was after Caliban, who had sped to the corner where the wall and the outside barred wall met. Again, he leaped to one side, and again the beast crashed with wall-quivering impact.

"If that grizzly's smart, and he doesn't look dumb," Barney said, "he'll be watching for Doc's sidewise maneuver."

"Yeah, but his thinking processes may be overwhelmed by the aggression stimulation," Pauncho said. "It may make him all fury and no brains at all."

The third time, Doc startled his aides by suddenly running at the bear just after it had started its charge. Events happened so swiftly that they looked as if they were being run by a speeded-up projector. The bronze blur and the brownish silver-tipped blur met. But Doc had leaped up and leveled out, and his legs shot out. His bare feet struck the grizzly on the nose and the sides of the head. The two bulks stopped. Doc fell backward but rolled and landed on his side and then was up and away. The bear, roaring, shook his head, while blood flowed from his nostrils, and launched himself at Caliban. The man did not quite succeed in escaping untouched. Claws, backed by a great paw swinging with strength enough to remove a man's head, barely nicked the back of his right leg. The skin came off in a wide band across the back of his calf, and blood ran down his leg.

Caliban spun and ran straight into the bear. The grizzly heaved himself up, coming up off of all fours like a killer whale bursting from the sea's surface, and opened his front legs to receive the foolhardy human.

Doc Caliban went on in as if he had lost his desire to live.

Pauncho and Barney cried out, "Doc!" and Pauncho yanked at the door to pull it back. He and Barney would go out there now; surely this was the time.

But Doc had planted a blow with his huge fist with all the power of his left arm and his back and legs. The arm sank into the fur of the animal's belly, into the fat, and into the muscle.

The grizzly went, *"Oof,"* and it fell backwards.

Doc Caliban leaped back, then, but even as it fell the grizzly's left paw raked the top of Caliban's head, and blood gushed out from a torn scalp.

Doc was momentarily blinded. He turned and ran, judging the distance to the wall by memory, stopped there three paces away, and turned. He wiped away the blood from his eyes, but more flowed down.

The grizzly had gotten to all fours and stood for a minute while it sucked in air. Its belly heaved, and its tongue dangled far out.

Then it charged, more slowly than it had before but still fast enough to have kept pace with many Olympic dashers.

Doc waited until it was very close and then, putting his feet against the wall behind as a springboard, dived under the beast.

It was completely taken by surprise by this maneuver. It whirled around but Caliban had gone between its legs, come up behind it, and was on its back. He seized its ears as it reared up on its hind legs and whirled around and around as if it could catch the man clinging to its back.

Pauncho and Barney, knowing that it would roll over in a minute and crush Caliban, went through the door. Yelling, their hands waving, they charged the bear. It roared and batted at them as it kept on dancing with its partner in its strange position on his back. They danced, too, around the perimeter described by its long claws. Once, the tip of a claw caught the end of Barney's long slender nose, and blood squirted out. A second later, he slipped in the blood which had spilled on the floor from Caliban's wounds and the nose of the bear. The grizzly was so close that it could have dropped on all fours and covered him, but it whirled away.

Doc's hand stabbed out and plucked the hemisphere from its head.

Pauncho lifted up Barney, who was half-stunned when the back of his head had hit the metal floor. Then Pauncho, looking something like a bear with the mange, charged the grizzly. He came diving in just as the animal was half-turned away, and his three hundred and twenty pounds slammed into the side of the bear's right leg.

The grizzly toppled over on its side, which was just what Caliban did not want. But he hung on to the ears and then bent his body back, his muscles cracking with the effort, and tore the ears of the grizzly off with a sound like the ripping of a sail under an overwhelming wind.

The beast bellowed so loudly that it half-deafened the three men. It spun around, and its jaws clamped down on Caliban's leg as he was trying to crawl away through a pool of blood.

Doc, instead of continuing to try to get away, twisted around and brought both fists down hard on the grizzly's skull. And then he hammered the big wet bloody nose with his fists.

The twisting around resulted in great pain and more loss of blood. It was so painful, he felt faint. The grizzly, if it had been able to seize him then, might have finished him in a few seconds.

But Pauncho, roaring, landed up in the air and came down with both feet on the back of the grizzly's massive neck. The impact of those feet, driven by those two extremely powerful legs, stunned the creature, even if only for a very short time. Its jaws opened enough for Doc to pull his leg loose. He rolled away but without his customary speed. Barney, imitating Pauncho's example, leaped into the air and came down on the bear's back. He did not have the weight nor the strength of his partner, but he did the bear some damage.

It coughed and then got to its feet slowly. Blood was running from its nose, from the places where the ears had been, and its eyes were crossed. It stood for a minute, looking at Doc Caliban, who was now crawling away, leaving a red trail.

Pauncho came up from behind the grizzly and kicked him beneath the tail with his right foot. The bear was turned into a maniac again by the kick. It whirled so swiftly that it caught Pauncho

by surprise. He tried to run away, but it charged
and grabbed him with both its front paws.
Pauncho went down screaming under the bear.

Barney, yelling, leaped upon the huge shaggy
back and, his legs clamped around the body, dug
his thumbs into the eyes. The grizzly, bellowing,
released Pauncho and reared up on its hind legs
and then fell back, apparently by design, to
crush Barney.

Barney fell off and rolled away but not before
a paw, batting blindly, scraped his left leg from
the top of the thigh to the knee. His blood
mingled with Caliban's and the bear's on the
floor.

Barney was slight compared to Caliban or van
Veelar, but he had a wiry strength that had surprised many a large man who had tackled him.
His hands were slender, even delicate looking,
but he could double a steel poker. And his hands
were strong enough to have dug into the sockets
of the skull and popped out the bear's eyes.
These were now hanging from the nerve cables
on its cheeks.

It was blind, but it could smell, though not
efficiently because of the damage to its nose; and
it could hear, though no efficiently, because of
the pain from the tearing off of its ears. But it
located Caliban and went after him, ignoring the
others. Doc, hearing the warning cries, turned
and got to his feet, though not without difficulty
and not without gritting his teeth to suppress a
groan.

The bear charged straight into him. Doc
reached out and jerked the eyes loose and cast

them on the floor and then, as he went down
under the beast, rammed his arm all the way
into the bear's mouth. It choked, and its paws
tore at his back, and then it backed away swiftly.
Its jaws opened, to get rid of the object that was
strangling it, and Doc's hand came out, closed
on the huge wet tongue. The slipperiness almost
balked him, but he managed to keep his grip.
Only one other man in the world could have
done what he did.

When the tongue came out by the roots, the
grizzly shot blood all over Caliban and the wall
of the room. And then it turned and charged
blindly across the floor until it rammed its head
into the bars of the inner door. It collapsed there,
wailing until blood choked it and it died.

But Doc Caliban had lost much skin and his
back muscles were so torn up they were causing
him intense pain.

Doc sat up and waved Barney's helping hand
away. "Open the door!" he said. "We have to
get out of here!"

Pauncho was there before Barney. He pulled
the sliding door back and said, "No five minute
wait."

Doc Caliban tried to get to his feet, but he
slipped twice. Barney, standing by his side,
made no move to help him because he did not
think that Doc would like it. It was Doc who
always helped others; he never needed anybody
else.

Doc wiped the blood from his forehead, looked
at Barney with the yellow-flecked verdigris eyes,
and said, "You too weak to assist me?"

"Hell, no, Doc, glad to do it!"

Barney leaned down and let Doc put a massive arm around his shoulder and then he straightened up. Doc came up slowly but not with the full weight of his three hundred plus pounds on Barney's slim shoulder.

"Now I'm up, I can make it by myself," Doc said. Then he clamped his teeth and pressed his lips together.

"I think I hear something!" Pauncho said. "Yeah! And I smell something! Smoke! Hey, there's somebody down that way!"

He pointed to the left.

"The invaders," Doc said. "Anana's men. Driven here by the flowing napalm, I suppose. We'd better go the other way. Barney, check on Cobbs and Villiers. I don't think they're still here, but . . ."

When Barney returned he said, "Not there. And there's nothing we can use for a weapon. I didn't see our stuff either. You'd think Iwaldi wouldn't have bothered to hide it, since he didn't figure we'd even get out of the cell."

"He knew it wasn't impossible for us to get out," Caliban replied. "But he must have figured we'd never get out of the cave even if we somehow got past the bear."

They went down the runway to the nearest stone steps on the right and descended to the floor of the chamber. There were a number of exits. Doc picked the middle central one, and they went down a tunnel. Smoke was pouring out of several of the entrances behind them, and Doc could hear, faintly, coughing from one.

They went down the tunnel and came to a shaft
which contained no ladder. Caliban, looking
down it, saw ankle-deep water on the floor of the
tunnel under the shaft. It was rising swiftly.

"This is the tunnel we came up after being
captured," he said. "It should still hold Cobbs'
marks, unless Iwaldi rubbed them out. We'll
have to chance that; it's our only hope."

Slowly, because he felt weak and because the
movements pained him considerably, he let himself down the shaft and dropped. The impact
almost made him faint. His colleagues dropped
down, too, and they went toward the direction
which—he hoped—was the right way. The
lights along the tunnel were still on but might
soon go out. However, since this system was
based on one he had originated, it was possible
that the lights would operate long after the tunnel was flooded.

"Hold it a minute!" Pauncho said.

They stopped. Seemingly from faraway came
voices. But if they could be heard there, they
would not be too far distant.

"They've probably seen our blood by now and
are trailing us," Caliban said. "If only we could
ambush some of them. They have guns and they
may have first-aid kits; and they must have
blacklight projectors and just possibly under-
water breathing plugs."

"Wouldn't Iwaldi know that and take care of
that possibility?" Barney said.

"Yes. But we know the way, and we know
what kind of traps Iwaldi has sprung," Doc said.
He did not mention the probability that Iwaldi

had closed off all exits.

They went on, splashing. The water around their feet was tinged with red. Doc suddenly stopped at a corner where the tunnel ran into another. He bent over, peering, and said, "There's Cobbs' marks."

They went down the tunnel, turned right, walked ten yards, turned left, and were confronted with a stairway the top of which was a foot under water. The marking at the corner of the wall was still visible through the water. It indicated that the way led down the steps.

"There are three levels to go before we get to the exit," Pauncho said.

Doc held up his hand for silence. A splashing was coming from far around the corner.

"We can't make it unless we have breathing plugs," he said. "And there's only one source for them. Here's what we'll do."

Barney walked back to the far end of the tunnel and looked around the corner. Within a minute, he jerked his head back, turned, and waved at them. Then he trotted toward them. By the time he reached them, the water was up to his calves.

"Ten of them," he said. "Automatic rifles and pistols. Blacklight projectors on their caps but they're not using their goggles. It's impossible to tell if they have breathing plugs."

He added, "And I smelled smoke. The napalm can't be too far behind."

The invaders would not know about Cobb's markings, of course, so they would go on down the tunnel. They would be looking for a way out

which would not force them to submerge. Doc
had looked down the corridor and seen the hole
in the middle of the floor. There was a shaft
there which the ancient kobolds had made apparently for quick exits, as if they were human-
sized mouse holes. This was the pivotal point of
his attack.

He waded down the steps until the water was
up to his waist and then he swam along the wall.
The bulbs along the wall guided his path and enabled Barney to see him. When Doc was opposite the shaft, Barney signaled him. Doc dived,
was visible in the lights until he went under the
ceiling, and then popped up in the well in the
middle of the tunnel. Pauncho went down the
tunnel to the end and around the corner. Doc
Caliban submerged and came back up in the
other tunnel. He hung on to a light bulb while
Barney sat on the steps with his ear placed near
the juncture of wall and steps.

In a few seconds, Barney heard the loud
splashing of the ten men. He waited until he
judged that the lead man was just about to come
opposite the stairway, and he slid off the stairs
into the water and down alongside it. When he
reached the bottom, he flattened himself against
the side. Now all he could do was to hold his
breath and hope that the leader would take time
out for a glance into this tunnel before deciding
to go on. If anybody leaned out and looked down
the side of the steps, he would see Barney in the
light of the closest bulb.

Doc had submerged also and swam the few
feet necessary to get to the bottom of the well.

Here he placed one hand on the ceiling next to the lip of the shaft and waited. He hoped the bleeding would slow down enough so the men would not notice that the waters were reddened. And he hoped the enemy would not loiter in that corridor. Normally, he could hold his breath for fifteen minutes if he hyperventilated for thirty minutes (the official world's record was 13 minutes, 42.5 seconds). But he had no time to hyperventilate and he was too weakened to hold his breath for much more than two minutes.

Fortunately, the lighting was such that the men above cast their shadows over the well as they passed on its right. He counted ten and swam up with all his strength as the last shadow passed. He came out of the shaft without making any noise and pulled himself with one fluid motion onto the floor. The water was then a foot and a half high and the splashing made by the men drowned out any noise he made. He stood up and quickly approached the rear man whose eyes were straight ahead. He hit him in the back of the neck and caught the rifle as it fell. By then Barney was coming down the hall behind him, and he threw the rifle to him and then waded up and knocked out the next man.

He did not fire at once. He waited until the lead man got to the corner and he saw Pauncho's long thick arm reach out and grab the rifle and pluck it out of the man's hands. The stock of the rifle, reversed, caught the man under the chin, and he went down.

Doc called, "Freeze!"

Pauncho stuck the barrel of the rifle around

the corner and said, "Don't move!"

The shock held the others in its grip long enough for them to see that they could only die if they tried to resist. They dropped their rifles into the water and put their hands, slowly, behind their necks.

Pauncho stepped out from the corner and said, "You there!" indicating the man now at the head of the line. "Drop your belt! Slowly! Then get the nose plugs of this guy!" He tilted his head to indicate the man he had knocked out. This one lay face down on the floor, covered entirely by the water. He had drowned, but he would have drowned in any event, since Pauncho was taking his breathers away from him. Three men had to be sacrificed. The survivors could consider themselves lucky that they had had the right positions in the line.

While Barney kept the rifle on the men, Doc felt through the pockets of the two men he had knocked out, who had also drowned. He came up with the plugs and handed two to Barney. The enemy were dropping their belts, which held knives and pistols and bullets, into the water. At Pauncho's command, they completely undressed.

One of the men carried a medical kit. Doc opened this and popped hemenerogen tablets into his mouth. Barney swallowed some, and one man carried some to Pauncho and then returned to his place in line. There were also ointments and some pseudoprotein dressings which Doc and Pauncho applied while Barney held his rifle on the prisoners. Both immediately felt better though far from being in one hundred percent good health.

While they were doing this, the water had risen three inches.

Doc Caliban explained to the prisoners what they would have to do if they wanted to survive. They did not like the idea, but a gush of smoke and a steady rise in the air temperature convinced them that they had no other choice.

Caliban removed the ammunition from the rifles and gave one to each man. They went back to the entranceway and down the steps, shivering at the coldness of the water. The only clothing they wore were the blacklight projectors and the goggles around their necks in case they came to dark tunnels. Their captors wore only belts with sheathed knives, and they carried rifles.

The three stayed behind the seven men, who moved through the water, swimming with one hand while they held the rifles against their bellies and at right angle to the longitudinal axis of their bodies. This made for slow swimming, but it also made for safe swimming, as they found out. On the last level down, a section of the wall slid out, displacing much water as the first four men went by. Three of the rifles caught as they were supposed to do; the fourth was dropped as the man swam away in a panic. The movement of the block had been impeded by the water and the displacement of the water had warned the defenders.

There was no other incident. They reached the chamber where they had entered. By then, they were all so numb that they could hardly feel anything with their hands. Their strength was spurting out swiftly.

Doc Caliban had told his colleagues what to expect while they were getting ready to ambush the enemy. He gestured at them to make ready, and he swam to him and clung to the pipe protruding from the wall. He hoped that the massive wall of stone would slide back; the pressure of the water was immense against it. It was true that Iwaldi and his party had probably gone through this way. But they would have done so when the pressure was much less.

He turned the valve. The screaking of the stone against stone was shrill in the water. It hurt their ears. But the wall was moving slowly to the right, and then they felt the current as the water began to spurt out of the opening. The current became stronger as the opening widened. Doc clung to the valve until, seeing that the exit was now broad enough, he tapped the others on the shoulders. He let loose and was swept toward the opening, scraped against the edge of the still moving wall, and was shot out into the mountainside. Pauncho and Barney were close behind him.

The others had become momentarily jammed in the opening when it was only two feet wide. Then, as the wall withdrew, one went out and the others had followed. Since they had not come in this way, they did not know what to expect. They went out across the ledge and were carried over the edge and down the mountainside. This was not so steep that they were in a free fall, but the slope was rough with rocks where it was not muddy.

Caliban and his friends straightened themselves out, letting the current shoot them across the stone ledge and on down the incline. They became their own toboggans, though not without loss of more skin on their backs. The pseudoprotein that Doc had spread over his back was torn loose again, and the agony in his back would have been worse if he had not been so anesthetized by the icy water.

They managed to stop themselves by grabbing hold of bushes about forty feet down the slope. Though the water struck them hard, they held on, half-drowned and almost completely frozen. Then, frighteningly, they began to slide on down even though they kept their grips on the branches. The earth had become loosened under the pressure of the water and was now moving.

Below them came yells as their seven predecessors saw the large mass sludging above them. These men had managed to stand up, even though the water was up to their knees and threatening to knock them down and roll them for another bruising, banging slide. Now, seeing what looked like the beginning of an avalanche, they tried to run away. Their feet slid out, and they were carried away by the water and the loose mud under them.

They did not, however, go far. About forty feet further, a ledge stopped them, and they managed to grab bushes. A moment later, they screamed as the cliff of mud and rocks and bushes bearing Caliban and his aides flowed around them and then began to cover them up.

Suddenly, the flow of water became a trickle. The wall of stone had shut, and the water was penned up in the mountain again.

The seven, half-buried, struggled to pull themselves free. Caliban and his colleagues, shivering with the cold and with repugnance, took out their knives and did what had to be done. They could not afford to let the Nine know that they were here and that they had gotten free.

Just before dawn three men, covered with dried mud and nothing else, walked into the side door. Nobody saw them, which was fortunate, because the police would have been called. The three found themselves locked out, but the big-gest rammed the heel of his bare foot against the door, and it flew inward with a crash. They entered, showered, shaved, ordered food sent up, dressed, and the apish-looking man went down to pay the bill. The clerk was surprised that his ugly guest no longer wore a moustache, and he noted several other lost characteristics. But he said nothing except the customary pleasantries.

The three drove off with Barney, in the back seat, operating the shortwave set.

"Trish says that Lady Grandrith has disappeared," Barney said. "She tried to phone her, didn't get an answer, and went over to see for herself if anything was wrong. She saw two suspicious-looking characters hanging around and went in the back way. A guy tried to knife her on the second floor; she broke his arm and stuck his own knife in his ribs; but he got away.

Clio wasn't in her room. She hadn't packed; so if she took off it was in a hurry. Trish'll keep trying to get into contact with her."

Doc Caliban took the microphone and said, "Trish! We'll let you know, in the usual way, when we've arrived. But you send a message to Grandrith. Tell him to come to Salisbury by way of Bournemouth. Make the arrangements; we'll have somebody meet him if he can make it. Tell him the Nine will be at Stonehenge. If he can get there, he should do so by all means. The end of the world may come if Iwaldi isn't stopped."

Trish had a husky voice that sent delicious chills up a man's spine. "O.K., Doc. I gave my love to Barney. Tell that big ape Pauncho I love him—like a sister. Please hurry. It's so lonely, especially since Clio disappeared. We didn't see each other, but we did have phone conversations now and then."

"We'll be there soon. So long," Doc said, and handed the microphone back to Barney.

"That's the first time I ever heard Trish complain," Barney said. "The tension is really getting her down. But then she's been through so much for so long. Ever since that nut that thought he was Tarzan kidnapped her. Things have been coming one after the other, like bad news was an endless snake, a Midgard serpent."

Barney put on a fake beard and thick glasses and took over the driving while Pauncho and Caliban crouched down on the floor after covering themselves with blankets. Barney drove through Karlskopf slowly. If there were any agents of the Nine here, they would see only a hairy-faced old man who looked as if he taught philosophy at the University of Heidelberg. Moreover, the license plates on the Benz had been changed, so that if the agents knew the old number, they would see at a glance that this could not be Caliban's car.

Once out of Karlskopf, the two got up off the floor. Barney kept on driving, headed toward Kieselsfuss, a small town which had an airstrip nearby.

The following day, three men met near Charing Cross station. Each had come in on a separate airliner, twenty minutes apart. Each was disguised. They took the taxi to Marylebone Borough, went past the building where Clio Cloamby, Lady Grandrith, had a room, and stopped outside another building six blocks away. They were confident that they had not been tailed. They removed their suitcases and went into the building. After the taxi had left, they came out, walked two blocks, flagged down another taxi, and drove off to an apartment on Portobello Road. They were admitted by the doorman, who had been told to expect them, went up the elevator to the third floor, and knocked on Trish's door. She opened it and was in Doc's arms and kissing him, though complaining about the bristly salt-and-pepper moustache he was wearing.

"I don't have one," Pauncho said. "Here, give us a kiss."

"Both of you?" Trish said, turning and grabbing Pauncho around the neck.

"Yeah, I'm man enough to make two," Pauncho said.

"Two gorillas, maybe," Barney said. "Kiss me first, Trish. I come in second to no *Pan satyrus*. And speaking of pans, did you ever see an uglier one?"

"You two remind me so much of your fathers!" Trish said. She hugged and kissed them both and a few tears ran down her cheeks. "It's almost like having them back again!"

Barney and Pauncho did not look too pleased, though they knew that Trish meant nothing derogatory. Also, it was still difficult for them to realize that Patricia Wilde, though she looked a fresh twenty-five, had been born in 1911 and that their fathers had courted her.

Doc and the others began to remove their disguises. In a short time, they would put on others, and Trish would become a blue-eyed ash blonde, concealing her bronzish yellow-flecked eyes and deep metallic auburn hair, so much like her cousin's.

"Well, at least you don't have to conceal that superb build!" Pauncho said, as she put on a Kelly green miniskirt. "And them legs! Whoo! Whoo!" He blew her a kiss. "I'm sure glad you didn't inherit the Grandrith muscles!"

"I did," she said. "But their quality, not their quantity, as you well know, you big orangutang. Just don't ever get fresh with me again, unless I tell you you can."

Barney grinned when Pauncho blushed. Pauncho had been high on something—vodka, which he loved on the rocks or rum-soaked pot, which he also loved, or maybe both—when he had lost his inhibitions about Trish and tried to make love to her. Trish had been in a bad mood

that night—she and Doc had had an argument
—and she had thrown Pauncho's three hundred
and twenty pounds over her back and halfway
across the room. Pauncho had acted as Krazy
Kat does when Ignatz Mouse brains her with a
brick, that is, as if violence and pain expressed
deepest love. He had come back for more and
gotten it, this time knocking plaster off the wall
with his head as he sailed through the air for a
short distance.

"Don't look so sheepish," Trish said. "You
know I love you," and she slapped him on the
back. Pauncho leaped into the air, bellowing
with pain. Barney laughed so hard he fell on the
floor. Doc had taken off his shirt and undershirt,
revealing the patches of pseudoprotein on his
back and chest. He smiled slightly and said,
"Take it easy when you touch us, Trish."

An hour later, the first one left the building.
No one who had seen any of them enter would
have recognized them, though the simian body
and features of Pauncho and the giant body of
Caliban were difficult to disguise. Doc, however,
was a bent-over old man with the palsy, and
Pauncho looked like a fat middle-aged man with
definitely feminine characteristics. Barney wore
a waxed handlebar moustache and very long
sideburns. His eyes bulged out as if he had goiter
disease. Trish was a blonde with a big nose and
big ears.

None of their disguises were designed to make
them merge into the woodwork. They did not
care if they were noticed as long as they were not
recognized. They left at intervals of ten minutes

apart and took taxis to Charing Cross station.
They went into the restrooms and when they
emerged they had shed their former disguises.
Now Doc was a big American mulatto tourist
with a camera hung from his neck. Pauncho was
a rather brutal-looking turbaned Sikh. Barney
was a racetrack toff. It hurt him to dress so
flashily, since he had inherited his father's delight in sartorial elegance. Trish was a bulky-
bodied, wattle-chinned, dowdily dressed,
middle-aged woman with messy gray hair.

As she passed Doc, she said, "Called Clio. No
answer."

Doc Caliban took a taxi to a rental car agency
and, using the forged papers and credit cards,
rented an automobile under the name of Mr.
Joshua King. He drove away, picked up the others one by one at different places and then drove
into a large warehouse. A man wheeled several
large boxes on a cart out of an office. Doc gave
him some money after the boxes were loaded
into the trunk of the big Cadillac.

Mr. Sargent was a tall, thin, heavily
moustached, middle-aged man. He had once
been one of the best safecrackers in the world,
operating in the States and England. Doc had
caught him one night when he was trying to
open a safe in Doc's laboratory in the Empire
State Building. Doc had taken him to the Lake
George sanatorium after finding out who had
hired him. He had performed the usual operation, implanting a microcircuit in his brain and
then putting him through a series of hypnotic
treatments. The man was unable thereafter to

crack safes, even under legitimate circumstances. He got a job as a salesman for burglar
alarm systems and seemed well on the way to
being a completely honest citizen. But, as had
happened more than once before, the ex-crimi-
nal backslid. Not into his former profession.
That was forever barred to him. Sargent became
a dope addict and a pusher. To raise money for
his habit, he became a lowly stickup man.

Doc Caliban heard about him and again sent
him to his sanatorium. He cured him of his dope
habit and gave him more hypnotic treatments.
Sargent went to England to work as manager of
a warehouse which Caliban owned in London.
(Caliban owned businesses all over the world.)
He was one of Doc's most trusted agents. He had
done much for Caliban when Caliban was in the
Nine but the Nine did not know of his existence
(as far as Doc knew).

Sargent was also the last man on whom Doc
had ever operated to change his criminal ways.
It was just too discouraging to implant a re-
pulsion against one form of criminality only to
have the man take up another. Or, sometimes, to
go insane from, apparently, a subconscious conflict.

Sargent pulled an envelope from his coat
pocket and handed it to Caliban. "Gilligan not
only saw them getting off an airliner, he took
their photos," he said.

Doc opened the envelope. Pauncho, looking
over his broad shoulder, said, "Cobbs! And
Barbara!"

Trish looked over Doc's shoulder, too. "No

wonder you said she was so beautiful! Makes me jealous just to look at her!"

"She looks a lot like you," Pauncho said. "That's why I flipped over her."

"I heard him say he'd leave anybody, even you, for her," Barney said.

"You should've been a lawyer like your father," Pauncho snarled. "The truth is not in you."

Doc turned the photo over. On the back was the address of a Carlton House Terrace mansion.

"They left yesterday, late last night," Sargent said. "Crothers didn't know where. He asked around but the servants were mum."

"Salisbury," Caliban said.

A minute later, the four drove out with Caliban at the wheel. The trip was mainly occupied with telling Trish what had happened at Gramzdorf and with Doc going over their plans for Stonehenge. Pauncho kept coming back to Barbara Villiers as if he could not believe that she could be guilty of collaboration with Iwaldi.

"That Cobbs cat, yeah, he's pretty oily. I could believe it of him. But that Barbara, she's just too beautiful to be anything other than an angel. Besides, Doc, you haven't got any real proof! Maybe Iwaldi is forcing them to help him. They know what he's capable of; they don't want to be tortured."

"They could go to the police," Trish said.

"A man with Iwaldi's connections and organization could get them, police protection or not," Barney said.

"I had Sargent check them out at the university," Caliban said. "A Villiers and a Cobbs are on leave from the archeology department. Their photos resemble those of the Cobbs and Villiers we know. But they're not the same. And the university said they're supposed to be digging in Austria, not Germany."

"What do you make of that?" Pauncho said. He did not ask Caliban if he was sure. Caliban never made a statement unless he was sure or he had defined it as speculation.

An hour later, they pulled into a farm off the highway and drove the Cadillac into the barn. Leaving by the back door, they went down a tree-covered path to a small hangar on the edge of a meadow. The two men here assured Caliban that the plane was ready.

On the way, they disguised themselves again. Doc was an English businessman with brown hair and eyes, a crooked nose, and a walrus moustache. Trish became a housewife with a more conservative miniskirt. Barney and Pauncho became informally dressed Americans.

Forty miles from the southern coast, the gray day suddenly became gray night. The plane flew into a dense fog, and from then on it was on instruments. They circled a while above the airport at Salisbury and then made a perfect landing.

"How long has this fog been here, Doc?" Trish said.

"Since two days ago. It's extraordinary for it to go so far inland for so long. The papers have been full of stories of letters from cranks who insist that a coven of witches near Amesbury are responsible for it. Or so the radio says. I wouldn't be surprised if old Anana had something to do with it. Not with the coven. With the fog. She's the most ancient and most powerful of witches."

They were tramping down the sidewalk to report in at the office before driving away. Trish could not see his face, so she did not know if he was kidding or not. Her cousin was not the least bit superstitious, but he admitted that some superstitions might turn out not to be such.

"Whatever is responsible for the fog," Doc said, "it'll suit the purpose of the Nine fine. They can hold the funeral of XauXaz without being observed. Of course, the Nine can bring enough pressure so they could get Stonehenge to themselves even during the winter solstice tomorrow. But this way nobody will be spying on them with binoculars. The good thing about it is, we'll have a better chance to get close to them."

"And Iwaldi'll have a better chance to sneak in a bomb," Pauncho said.

"Everything has its checks and balances," Barney said. "Except maybe you, Pauncho. Aren't you overdrawn at the bank?"

"My patience is overdrawn!"

While at the airport, Doc showed an official a photo of Cobbs and Villiers and asked if they had landed there that day. The official said no, not while he was on duty. Doc was satisfied that they had probably motored down, unless the official had been bribed to deny that they had flown in, or unless the two had been disguised.

Caliban did not plan to send his people around to hotels in Salisbury and Amesbury to find out if any of the Nine were staying there. It would arouse suspicion, since it could be assumed that the servants of the Nine would be looking for too-nosy strangers. Also, it was doubtful that any of the Nine would trust themselves to a hotel. With their immense wealth, they probably owned houses all over England. These would be left unoccupied most of the time, waiting for whenever the owners needed them.

They got two hotel rooms under their aliases, Mr. and Mrs. Clark and John Booth and William Dunlap. A half hour later, a man phoned in a message for Mr. Clark. It was from a Mr. T. Lord (the T. was for Tree) and said he and party would be arriving at Bournemouth at the stipulated time. The landing would be made at the agreed-upon spot.

Caliban called the two men in. "We'll go up to Stonehenge late tonight after we get some sleep," he said. "You'll go with us, Pauncho, but you'll leave as soon as you know how to get back to us. Then you'll go to Bournemouth. Crothers will handle the first meeting with Grandrith; you'll pick him up and bring him to us. Barney, Trish, and I and six of my men will be waiting for you to join us."

When they awoke—having put themselves to sleep with the hypnotic techniques taught them by Caliban—they were refreshed. They ate and dressed and then left the hotel. Their equipment had remained in a rented Rolls Royce. Two more cars, filled with men and equipment, joined them. They drove away swiftly in the fog

with Doc at the wheel of the first car, watching
the big radar screen he had affixed to the instrument panel. They drove on A360 out of
Salisbury and in fifteen minutes had slowed
down for a right turn onto A303(T). They could
see the signposts quite clearly when they were
close because they were wearing the blacklight
projectors and the goggles. Doc drove onto the
side of the road near a fence a few yards past the
junction and stopped. The goggles enabled them
to see the ancient burial mounds, the long barrows beyond the fence.

Doc advanced cautiously, a mass detector
held out before him. Pauncho held a small box
with several other instruments before him, and
others carried shovels and pickaxes and weapons. They went over the fence on a folding stile
brought from the car and walked about twenty
yards past the barrow. Here two men started
digging.

Others made several trips back to the cars,
each time bringing parts of a device switch that,
put together by Doc, made a metal box two feet
high, four feet broad, and six feet long. Two
short antennas stuck out of the top of the box.
The device went into a hole and was covered
with dirt with the antenna tips barely sticking
up.

"No doubt the Nine have already buried
theirs or will soon," Doc said. "And if Iwaldi
shows, he'll bury his somewhere around here.
Which one of us activates his first is anybody's
guess. But you can bet it'll be some hours before
the ceremony starts."

He stuck a device in his pocket. When the time

came for it to be used, it would activate the buried equipment, which was an atomic-powered generator of an extremely powerful inductive field. In its field of influence, a cone-shaped beam with a range of a mile and a half, metal objects turned hot. Copper wires and aluminum wires would eventually melt. Gasoline was ignited and explosives were detonated because of their metal containers. Radar and heat-detectors would be unusable in its field because the circuits would melt and then the cases, if they were thin.

Doc had already ascertained that no one in the party had any metal fillings in his teeth or metal plates in his skull.

Tomorrow, when the ceremony begins, the only weapons would be the baseball bats, plastic knives, crossbows, and the gas grenades that Doc had brought along. They were wearing plastic helmets and chain mail under their clothes. The crossbows were of wood and plastic and gut, a small type with a pistollike butt held in one hand. They fired wooden bolts with sharp plastic tips.

If the fog held, the battle would be conducted by almost blind soldiers.

Doc looked at his watch and then removed it. A man was putting everything metal in a bag which would be taken away in a car.

Pauncho shook Barney's and Doc's hands and kissed Trish before he left. He hated to go, but he did not complain. If Doc wanted him to carry out his mission, so be it.

"We won't be staying here," Doc said, "since

the Nine will undoubtedly send men through here ahead of them. We'll be hiding out across the road north of Stonehenge. But I'll be back by the long barrow by the time you return with Grandrith's party, unless something prevents me. In which case you and Grandrith just come on up to the ruins. That'll be where it's at."

Pauncho drove off. The other cars were driven away to a point half a mile away along A303(T) to the west. Doc figured that they would be outside the range of all three of the inductors he expected to be operating by morning. The men would bicycle back on the plastic collapsible vehicles they had brought along in the trunks of the cars. The others had been unloaded.

They waited. Presently, they heard footsteps and issued soft challenges, ready to fire if they proved to be the enemy. But the proper codeword—Pongo—was returned, and the men joined them. Then they went across the field, blindly, the wet grayness allowing them to see only a few inches. They carried their weapons in their hands and packs on their backs. These contained pup tents, which could be folded into the space of a large box of kitchen matches, and cans of self-heating food and water and medical kits.

After a walk of about four-fifths of a mile, they came to the fence along A344. They crossed it and the road and went over another fence into a field near the Fargo Plantation and The Cursus, that strange roadway that the builders of Stonehenge had made. There they bedded down for the night.

"The servants of the Nine will be poking

around," Doc said, "but they'll probably confine their scouting to the triangle formed by the three main roads. Then the old ones will be coming in their plastic steam-driven cars—my invention, ironically enough, and made for just such occasions—and they'll start the ceremony, fog or no fog. They won't be able to bury XauXaz in the circle of Stonehenge. Not even the Nine could do that without causing embarrassing questions. So they'll probably bury him someplace close by."

"Why hold the ceremony here?" Trish said. "I thought XauXaz was at least 10,000 years old when Stonehenge was built. What's his association with it?"

"I don't know. Stonehenge was built in three phases from about 1900 B.C. to about 1600 B.C. by the Wessex People (so named by the archeologists). It may have been built as a temple to some deity. No one knows except the Nine. It does seem that, whatever else the *rude enormous monoliths* were, they did form a sort of calendar to predict seasons, and they could be used to predict lunar and solar eclipses. Those circles of monoliths and trilithons made a prehistoric computer.

"XauXaz may have been a living god of the Wessex People. He may have supervised the building of Stonehenge. His name would not then have been XauXaz, since this was a primitive Germanic name meaning *High*. In fact, our English word *high* is directly evolved from XauXaz. But primitive Germanic did not even exist then. It hadn't developed out of Indo-Hittite yet."

After a system of guards were arranged, they got into their sleeping bags. At five A.M., Doc was awakened to stand his watch, the length of which was determined by the time it took sand to fill the bottom of an hourglass. He squatted on top of his sleeping bag by the fence for a while, then got up and walked slowly back and forth. The fog showed no sign of thinning out; he was in a cold and wet world without light. Though his party was only a few feet away, he could not see them. He could see nothing. He could hear the snores of a few men and, once, far off, muffled by the fog, the barking of a farm dog. This was the world after death, and he was a soul floating around in the mists of eternity, cut off from the sight and touch of other beings but tortured by being able to hear them in the distance.

When would the struggle stop? When would the killing cease? When would he be able to live as he wished; peacefully, studying, researching, inventing devices to help mankind?

Probably never. The only long-lasting peace was in death.

His sense of time was almost perfect. When he lit a match and held it by the hourglass, he saw that only a few grains remained in the upper part. The match went out, and suddenly the activator in his pants pocket began to get warm. He knew then that either the Nine or Iwaldi were in the area and had turned on an inductor. He removed the activator from his pocket with his bare hand, since it was not yet too hot to hold. He pressed its button and then threw it into the fog. It had done its work and its circuits would, in a few minutes, be melting.

He awoke everybody and told them what was happening. They bundled up their bags and ate a light breakfast from their cans. About fifteen minutes after Doc had noticed the activator's warmth, they heard shouts down the road.

They went over the fence, which was becoming hot, and ran across the road to the fence on the other side. After climbing over this, which was by then red-hot, they proceeded slowly along it. It was the only guide to the east. If it were out of sight, they could just as easily have turned around and gone westward or southward within a few steps.

Doc suddenly stopped and held up his gloved hand, though those behind him could not see it until they had bumped into him. More shouts and a few screams had come from ahead. He estimated that their sources were about a hundred yards away, but it was difficult to be accurate because of the distortions caused by the heavy fog. Underneath the cries was a strange note, a heavy grinding noise.

He moved on, and within a few yards he thought he could identify the strange noise. It was the growling of many dogs.

It would be a good thing to use dogs in this fog. They could not see, but they could smell, and this would lead them quickly to the enemy.

But the hemispherical devices could not be used because of the inductive fields. The metal in the circuits of the hemispheres and the controlling boxes and the wires inserted into the brains would get too hot. The dogs were being used without cerebral regulators.

His guess was confirmed a moment later when a dog yelped sharply. He went on, and then two more dogs cried out in agony. The crack of clubs against bone and flesh pierced the fog. And then a loud boom made them stop.

"They must be out of their minds, using grenades!" Trish said. "They have to be throwing blindly!"

Doc Caliban did not think that they were so insane. As long as a group stayed closely together, so that its members knew that the others were in an area near him, they could throw the grenades anywhere else. They could hope that the little bombs would strike by chance among the enemy.

He pulled from the bulging pocket of his jacket one of the tennis-ball-sized plastic gas grenades. He twisted the pin in its north pole to the left and then yanked it out and heaved the grenade into the fog. Six seconds later, a roar and a faint orange flash came through the fog.

He removed another grenade and pulled the pin, but he never had a chance to throw it. Dark figures suddenly appeared ahead of him. And something struck him in the shoulder and spun him around.

He staggered backward then. His shoulder and arm felt as if they had been cut off. But he knew even in the shock that a bolt from a small crossbow had hit him. The plastic chain mail beneath its covering of shirt and jacket had kept the plastic point from piercing him. The shock of the impact from the bolt, fired at above five feet or so, had paralyzed his side for a moment.

He had dropped the grenade, and it had rolled
to one side out of his sight. He staggered back
away from where he thought it was, shouting to
the others to run. They did not hear him because
they were struggling with the people who had
run into them.

The grenade had bounced and rolled further
away than he had expected. It split the fog in a
blaze of light and a wave that half-deafened
Caliban. He saw the body of a man flying, turning as it arced toward him, its legs and arms
spread out as if it were sky diving. The body
struck near him, but the light was gone, and he
could not see it.

A large man, striking out with a baseball bat,
sprang at him. Doc jumped to one side, lost the
man, jumped back in as the man was turning
around to locate him or perhaps to make sure
that no one was sneaking up on him. Doc still
could not use his right arm, but his left drove in
with the plastic dagger he had pulled from its
sheath on his belt, and the sharp point went over
the man's raised right arm and into his jugular
vein. Doc stepped back, pulling the knife out,
whirled in case anybody was behind him,
crouched, and caught another man in the throat
as this man flew out of the fog. The man dropped
his crossbow. Doc picked it up—he suddenly remembered having dropped his when the bolt hit
him—and he waited. Because he was still partly
deafened, the sounds of battle came dimly from
all around him: shouts, snarls, shrieks, bats hit-
ting helmets and flesh or other bats, the twang of

a released crossbow string, the grunt of a man hit with something.

Then a woman came running through the fog, and Doc, instead of shooting, threw himself in a football player's block at her legs and knocked her over. Then he was sitting on Barbara Villier's chest and twisting her wrist with his left hand to force her to drop her dagger.

Another figure shot out of the fog. Doc knocked Barbara out with a left to the jaw and sprang up and rammed his head into that man's stomach.

The man went, *"Oof!"* and staggered back. A released crossbow gut twanged and the bolt touched his ear, burning it. The crossbow fell to the ground, and then the man was on the ground. Doc's left hand gripped the man's throat and squeezed just as the point of a plastic dagger drove through his shirt into the chain mail undershirt. The dagger fell, and the man choked and then became still. However, he was not dead. Even in the gray wetness, Doc Caliban had recognized the man was Carlos Cobbs. His hair was short and yellowish, and his nose was long and his chin too jutting. But the gait had been Cobbs'. Even though he had had only a second to see his manner of carrying himself, he had identified it.

Trish loomed out of the pearly mists. She put her mouth close to his ear, and said, "You deaf, Doc?"

"Partly. But my hearing is coming back. I'm taping these two up. Get her before she comes to, will you?"

Carlos Cobbs, sitting on the ground and bending over, his wrists bound behind him, coughed and choked for a minute. Finally he gasped, "So it's you, Caliban! I thought . . . !"

"Thought what?" Caliban said. He was squatting so he could see Cobbs' expressions better.

He had to keep twisting his neck to look around because the struggle around him, though much diminished, was still going on. From the shouts he could hear, as the victors identified themselves to others, his men seemed to be winning. Then Barney Banks appeared with the announcement that the group they'd run into had either been killed or had run off into the fog. As far as he could tell, they had three men left who could fight, not counting Trish, and Caliban and himself, of course.

"You started to say that you thought that . . . ?" Doc Caliban said to Cobbs.

"Never mind that!" Cobbs said. "Let me go! And you get out of here! Fast! If you don't, we'll all get killed! I'm telling you this because I have to! Get out of here!"

"Why?" Caliban said. Cobbs did not seem to be acting; his voice shook with urgency and with dread.

Barbara suddenly sat up. She said, "You fool! He's left a bomb back there that'll go off in fifteen minutes, in less now, and blow everybody for a half a mile around to kingdom come!"

"That right!" Cobbs said. "It'll take the Nine with it! They'll not get away this time! Anana and Ing and Yeshua and Shaumbim and Jiizfan and Tilatoc, they'll all go out in a blaze of glory!

And I, I will have done it! Listen, Caliban, we don't have time to talk about this here! We have to get going! Now! I've got plastic bicycles waiting on the road and we can get away on them to my steam cars only a quarter mile down the road and get out of here before the bomb goes off! Don't delay, man! I cut it close as it was, too close! But I didn't want them to get suspicious and take off! You know how Anana is! She's got a nose for anything that smells of death!"

A grenade cracked about forty yards behind him. More screams and yells.

Brightness dispelled some of the fog high up in the mists. (The flare was nonmetallic, of course.) Doc could see for at least a hundred feet. Shadowy figures struggled at the edge of his vision, and then, when he turned his head, the flare died.

"We could all take off and talk at my leisure," Doc Caliban said. "But friends of mine are out there fighting, and if we ran they'd die with the Nine. They might say that the sacrifice would be worth it. But I can't ask them, and if I could, I wouldn't. You tell me what kind of bomb it is and where we can find it. Now! Either I stop it from going off or we all die!"

"You stupid mortal!" Cobbs screamed. "What do you care what happens to your friends if you can live forever? Listen, I can get you the elixir! I'll give you the formula! I know you've been cut off, and that the aging has started! And you'll die in a few years because you'll never have the elixir unless one of . . . The Nine gives it to you!"

"One of . . . us?" Caliban said. "What's your

part in this, Cobbs? It's obvious you're hand in hand with Iwaldi. You were just pretending to be prisoners of Iwaldi, for some reason I can't comprehend, unless it was to infiltrate into my organization and catch us all when you had us cold."

"Time's running out!" Cobbs said, his voice cracking. "Would you throw away eternity, man?"

Caliban reached out and pulled Cobbs' large nose loose. It came off with a slight tearing sound, and the rest of the pseudoskin over his face followed. When the wig came off, the Cobbs he knew looked out of the fog.

Barbara Villiers said, "For God's sake, Caliban! We don't have time to play around! Get us out of here and then we'll give you whatever you want! The elixir! The map of the caves of the Nine and the traps set in it! Even some of the addresses of the Nine, though they won't go near there anymore, of course, unless they think we're all dead!"

"For two who are just candidates, or maybe just servants, you know a great deal," Caliban said. "Old Iwaldi must have taken you into his deepest confidences. By the way, where is Iwaldi? He wouldn't have let you go running off while he fought a rearguard action. Not old Iwaldi. He may be a mad goblin, but he's not that mad. Unless he thinks you double-crossed him figuring to blow him up with the rest of the Nine and then you two would take over. Did you plan on carrying out his ideas, releasing the phytoplankton bomb? Or did you plan to kill him so you cold stop that but still get the elixir and his wealth?"

Cobbs bent over so he could get his face closer to Caliban's. His features were twisted with agony, and the moisture on his face seemed to be even heavier than the fog droplets could account for.

"Get us out of here, and I'll tell you where you can lay your hands on Iwaldi!"

"You'd betray him?"

"Why not? He'd betray anyone if it meant saving his life!"

"Where is he?"

Barbara Villiers' voice cracked, too. "We can't tell you at this moment. He sent us in to do his dirty work for him. But we'll show you where you can ambush him. Just get us out of here!"

"What kind of bomb?" Caliban said.

"It's a heavy irradiated plastic box containing the explosive in liquid form! The dial and the time mechanism are all plastic or hard wood, too! I set it to go off in fifteen minutes! The mechanism pulls a pin out of a vial of plastic containing the gas that'll mix with the liquid and set it off! There won't be anybody living left within a half a mile radius and it'll kill many outside that area! The stone monuments of Stonehenge will be knocked down and maybe shattered! Old XauXaz's body and his coffin and the stones he set up as a temple for the sun god—himself—will be gone! Along with the rest of the Nine! Even old Anana, who said she was going to defeat death!"

"Who's fighting the Nine out there?" Caliban

said. "Or are they blundering around fighting among themselves? Grandrith can't be responsible for all that!"

"I left most of my men there to hold them, keep them occupied!"

"Doublecrossing your own men, too? Well, that's to be expected, *Iwaldi!*"

Trish and Barney said, "What?"

Villiers gasped. Cobbs' jaw dropped.

"He can do what I can do," Caliban said. "He has enough control of his muscles to pull his spine and add or subtract inches to his height. I've done it plenty of times myself. It takes much practice and knowledge. But what I can do in my short lifetime, Iwaldi has had many lifetimes to learn."

He pulled on Cobbs' nose and when that would not come pulled on the skin of the face and then on the dark hair.

"That won't do any good, you fool!" Barbara Villiers said. "That is his own skin and hair! The old goblin you knew was the false one! The wrinkled skin and the redshot eyes and the long white hair and beard, those were the fakes! They were true enough once, but when he regained his youth—"

"Shut up!" Iwaldi yelled.

"We haven't got time to carry this deception out!" Villiers said. "Besides, there's no sense in not telling him that we can have the rejuvenation elixir. He won't leave us here to die if he knows that he has to take us away to get the elixir! You should have known that, you greedy old man! It was our main card, and you've wasted too much

time holding out! It may be too late because of
your stupidity!"

"You can't talk to me that way, my dear
Countess Cleveland!"

Caliban's eyebrows went up. He said, "Then
Barney was telling the truth, not kidding you as
he thought he was, when he said you must be the
Lady Castlemaine whose petticoats hanging out
to dry made Pepys flip? Charles the Second's
mistress, mother of his three sons? You did not
die as history said, but you used makeup to look
as if you were getting older and then you pre-
tended to die and some woman died so that you
could be buried, and you—"

"Yes!" Barbara Villiers snarled. "Yes! How
many candidates have done that? Hundreds,
thousands? You and Grandrith are my own de-
scendents! My grandson had a child by a
Grandrith woman; so I'm your many times
great-grandmother! For the sake of us all, for the
sake of eternal life for you and your friends, and
for me, your ancestress, get us out of here! You
will not only have eternal life but eternal
youth!"

"I appropriated your notes, after you turned
against us," Iwaldi said. "I knew you'd been
working on rejuvenation and I hired the best scientists in the world to develop the elixir from the
information in your notes. One did develop it,
and I got rid of him in an 'accident.' In two
years' time, I became a young man again! The
wrinkles and the white hair and the ropy veins
disappeared! But I used makeup so that the others would not know! But . . . *must* I talk away our

lives! Let's get out of here! Plenty of time for talk later!''

The old man—now turned young man—knew that even if he was taken out of the explosion area, he was in grave danger from Caliban. But he was wily, and he had survived so many millennia by being more tricky than his contemporaries. He must have something up his sleeve besides sheer desperation.

"It's too late!" Barbara Villiers wailed. "We can't get away in time now!"

"Then give me the combination!" Caliban said.

"Why not *make* him do it?" Trish said.

There was the sound of running feet nearby, a twang, a cry, and a man slid across the cold wet winter grass on his face. He stopped so close to Caliban that he could see the crossbow bolt sticking out of the back of his neck.

"We might not even be able to find the bomb!" Caliban said. "Quickly, Iwaldi! The combination! It does have a combination to turn it off, I hope?"

"If I tell you, you'll kill me!" Iwaldi said. The voice of Cobbs had become the familiar deep growling voice of Iwaldi. The panic and the cracking were gone.

"I promise to release you and Villiers," Caliban said. "After you give me the formulae, of course. But my word is not to be given lightly and will not be broken. I will let you two go free, give you twelve hours' headstart, after which I will try to kill you, Iwaldi. Villiers can go with you if she chooses, in which case I'll try to kill her, too. But if she wants to work with me, and

I decide I can trust her, well, I don't like the idea of breaking the neck of my own grandmother several times removed, even if she's so distant I couldn't possibly have any of her genes."

"Talk our lives away!" Villiers said. "Iwaldi, tell him the combination! Now! There isn't much time left! He doesn't even know where the bomb is! He may not even be able to get to it in time!"

"Hey, Doc! Trish! Barney!" a deep grunting voice said somewhere in the fog. "Pongo! Pongo!"

"Pongo! Pongo! You hairy ape!" Barney called out joyfully. "This way!"

The squat and monstrous form of Pauncho van Veelar appeared. He rolled toward them and then stopped. "What the hell's going on? Cobbs! Barbara!"

Barney capsuled what had happened, but Doc listened to Iwaldi.

"There are ten numbers on the dial," Iwaldi said. "You set the dial on each number from 1 to 10. Then go right to 3. Then back to 9. If you do that in time, you can make the mechanism push the pin back into the gas vial container. *But* you'll have to *push in* on the dial while you're working the combination. Push in hard! If you don't, the mechanism not only won't reinsert the pin, it'll pull the pin immediately. And you'll have to keep the pressure applied for five minutes after you have worked the combination."

"Why all those provisions?" Caliban said.

"You never know when they can be used to your advantage. Now, if I could have gotten away in time, you would have set off the explosion trying to stop it. But it didn't work out that way. Also—"

"Never mind. Later." Doc stood up, then said, "Pauncho, where's Grandrith?"

"Out there. I left him to find you. Why weren't you at the long barrow?"

"I sent Rickson to meet you."

"He must've been killed before he got there."

"Watch these two," Doc Caliban said. "I'm going after the bomb. Watch for Grandrith."

He picked up a crossbow, fitted a bolt to the string and pulled it back to the third notch and locked it. Then he walked off into the fog while Trish said, "Doc! I want to go with you!"

He did not answer. He did not want to be hampered. He ran back and forth, bent over, looking at the ground between glances on all sides. No grenades had burst for several minutes, but the crack of bats and yells were still filtering through the wooly dampness. And then, as the dim figure of a trilithon—two upright stones with a third laid across them—solidified out of the grayness, he saw a body with a plastic shovel beside it. There were other bodies near it, but this one was the one that Iwaldi had told him to look for. It was that of the man who had dug the hole into which the bomb had been put. A bolt from out of the fog had caught him in the right eye as he straightened up, and he had fallen across the heap of dirt.

Caliban rolled him over and then began digging. The box was buried under a few inches of dirt, so it did not take him long to unearth it from its chalky cavity. While he was working, the grayness became luminous, as if the sun had appeared and was striving to burn the fog away. At the same time, a grenade boomed about thirty yards away, and he dived for the ground. He was up at once but heard cries from near the ruins. He faced toward the trilithon but kept on digging. Then he got down on his knees and pried out the box. It was about eleven inches square and was smooth except for the dial and the numbers around it on its top.

He had to bend close to distinguish the numbers, which was lucky for him. A bolt whizzed over his head. Two figures, interlocked, whirled by him and were swallowed up in the grayness. One of them cried out a minute later, and then Doc heard footsteps on the wet earth. He wanted to start working the combination, because he had no idea of how much time was left before the pin would be entirely pulled out of the detonating gas container. But he could not start turning the dial unless he knew that he would not be disturbed. If he had to release the pressure, he and everybody here were done for.

The man suddenly came out of the fog. Doc said, "Pongo?" and the man cursed and jumped back. Doc could not afford to wait any longer; he fired at where the man had been, aiming so the bolt would hit the belly, if it hit at all.

The gut twanged; the bolt leaped out; a thud came; a man groaned. And immediately after, Doc heard the slight squishing of feet in wet earth and the rustle of weeds. He turned, and a giant was on him, striking out at him with a baseball bat.

Doc hurled the box at him. The man ducked
but not quickly enough. He staggered as the impact sent him back, and then Doc was at him
with his plastic knife in his left hand. His right
arm had recovered enough for him to use it, but
it was still far from having regained all its
strength. The giant stepped up to him and swung
with both hands on the bat, bringing it around
so that it caught Doc against the side of his
helmet even though he had almost ducked entirely under it. Doc saw phosphene streaks but
kept on lunging, and his knife drove up. The
man had dropped the club after it glanced off
Doc's helmet and had put out his hands. The
knife went through one; the giant roared. Doc
jerked the knife out. The man brought his knee
up and caught Doc in the chest. If it had hit him
in the chin, it would have shattered even his
massive bones. The man was wearing irradiated
plastic knee guards.

The knee hurt Doc's chest and knocked the
wind out of him. But his right arm closed around
the leg, and he brought the knife up between the
man's legs. It tore the man's pocket and slid off
the plastic groinguard and then off the plastic
chain mail around his leg. The man brought
both fists down against the top of Doc's helmet,
half-stunning him. The man howled, because
the blow had hurt his fist hand. But Doc fell
backward, not knowing exactly what was going
on. The dagger did not fall from his hand; many
years of fighting had built in a conditioned reflex
so that he would have had to be entirely unconscious or dead before his hand would have re-

laxed. And his wind quickly came back.

The giant charged in, roaring. Doc Caliban rolled over, not realizing consciously what he was doing, and he was out of sight of the man. But a few seconds later, the giant thrust out of the fog, and, seeing Doc starting to get onto his feet, cried, "No, you don't!" and rushed him, his huge hands clasped to bring them down on top of Caliban's helmet again.

Doc bent his legs and leaped outward as if he had been shot from a cannon in a circus. His head drove into the man's big paunch with an impact that did not help Doc regain his senses. But the breath went out of the man—who must have weighed three hundred and thirty—and he went backward. Stunned, Doc did not act as quickly as he should have, and the man, though struggling for breath, knocked the dagger from Caliban's hand with a blow of his arm against Caliban's wrist.

Their faces were close enough that Doc could distinguish his features in the milky grayness.

"Krotonides!" Doc said.

He was one of the candidates, a bodyguard for old Ing. Doc had seen him a number of times at the caves during the annual ceremonies. He had endured the boastings of Krotonides that he was the strongest and fastest human in the world when it came to hand-to-hand combat and that Caliban's reputation was overrated.

"Caliban!" Krotonides said. His dark, big-nosed, bushy-eyebrowed face hung in the fog. "I always said I could take you!"

Caliban's hand with fingers stiffly extended

stabbed him in the eye, and Krotonides bellowed with agony. He rolled away, but as Caliban got to his feet the giant leaped out of the fog, his hands in the classical position to deliver a karate chop.

Doc snatched off his helmet and threw it with all the force of his left arm and the body behind it. There was a thud, and Krotonides staggered, slowly rotating around and around, while dark blood gushed from his nose, which had been almost severed by the sharp edge of the helmet. Caliban moved in swiftly though not incautiously, since Krotonides was still a very dangerous man. Before he could reach him, three figures advanced through the mists, and he felt it discreet to withdraw. Besides, he had to get to the box as quickly as possible.

Suddenly, he heard steps behind him. He whirled and then a rumbling voice said, "Pongo! Pongo!"

"Pongo! It's me, Doc!" Caliban said. "Help me find that bomb before it's too late!"

The three men had been engulfed in the fog, but they were still in the immediate neighborhood, so Doc and Pauncho had to keep an eye out for them. Doc hoped that none of them would toss out a grenade in their general direction.

Pauncho suddenly cursed, and then he said, "I fell over it, Doc! Hey, Doc! Quick! Over here!"

Caliban found him squatting by the box with his crossbow ready. Caliban got down on his knees and put his face close to the face of the dial. "I'm starting now," he said. "Once I get going, I can't stop. I have to hang on to this for five minutes at least. So you'll have to handle anybody that shows up. But as soon as I get the combination worked, we'll run away from here. I can hang on to the box. We'll worry about killing the old geezers some other time."

He started to turn the dials, stopping them briefly on each number, starting with 1, advancing to 2 when the mechanism clicked at 1. He kept pressure on the dial, which had sunk within a recess about one-tenth of an inch deep when he had first pushed. He clicked the dial through each of the numbers, and at 10 reversed the dial quickly to 3 and then turned it back again to 9. On reaching this, he breathed deeply and then started to count. "One thousand and one. One thousand and two. One thousand and three."

When he got to "One thousand and three hundred," he would have counted out five minutes, but he would go to one thousand and four hundred just to make sure before he let the dial push back to its level with the box.

He stood up, holding one corner of the box with his giant hand and pressing in on the dial with the other.

"Run, Doc!" Pauncho said. "Here comes a whole army!"

Caliban twisted his head. A number of dark figures were emerging from the fog. He said, "Follow me! Don't stand and fight!" and he trotted away. He dared not run at full speed because he might stumble over a body or slip on the half-frozen mud. Behind him feet slapped as Pauncho kept on his heels. Somebody shouted and then about forty feet ahead of them, the fog opened up with an orange-bordered roar. Doc's feet slipped from under him as the blast hit, and he fell on his back. But he kept hold of the box and his pressure on the dial.

Pauncho was bellowing in his ear, "Hey, Doc! Can you hear me? You all right? I'm half-deaf, Doc!"

"Quiet!" Doc shouted back.

He put his mouth close to Pauncho's ear. "Get rid of all your grenades, and mine, too, fast as you can. Maybe you can get those guys before—"

The second grenade from the enemy was about three feet closer, and it was followed by a third which landed almost on the same spot. Since they were on level ground, the impact of the blasts was not softened. They were rolled over, and their heads sang and their ears were dead. But the plastic bombs depended almost entirely on concussion for effect, since the explosion reduced the plastic shell to dust. And they were not within the killing range of the blasts.

They would be if the enemy continued to lob grenades at random. They got to their feet and ran on. Pauncho stopped to toss grenades behind him, and Doc lost sight of him. Suddenly, he saw a body ahead of him. He tried to dodge to one side, slipped, and fell on his side. He came down heavily because his primary concern was keeping pressure on the dial. He called, "Pongo!" and then rolled away, holding the box up, hoping that if it was the enemy it would fire at where he had been. He wasn't worried about the person tossing a grenade, since he'd be committing suicide if he threw one that close to himself.

"Pongo!" Trish said. She looked as if she were shouting, yet he could barely hear her.

He got up and approached her cautiously, since it was possible the situation had changed and she was being forced to lure him in. He preferred to believe that she would die before doing that, but she might be depending on him to get her out of the situation, no matter how bad it looked. She tended to think of him as a superman, despite his lectures to her that he might be a superior man but he was also flesh and blood and one little .22 bullet or a slip on a piece of soap in the shower could make him just as dead as anybody else.

He peered through the fog. "Talk loudly. I'm almost deaf. Pauncho may be coming along, so don't shoot without giving the codeword. Where's Barney?"

"He went after you," she said, shouting in his ear. "Well, not exactly *after* you. He said he was going to make contact with the enemy and explain the situation. He thought that if they knew about the bomb, and that you were trying to keep it from going off, they'd quit fighting. They might even take off and leave us alone."

"Doesn't sound like it," Caliban said. The crump of grenades going off in the distance— somewhere around the Stonehenge circle—was still continuing. But there were no blasts nearer, where Pauncho and the three men should have been.

Suddenly, there was a silence. From far off, as

if behind piles of wood, a voice cried. It was saying something. And then another voice cried. And then he heard, very faintly—dimmed by distance or by his injured hearing, or both—a rushing sound.

"Tires," his cousin said. "It could be the Nine taking off in their steam cars.

"Maybe Barney got to them," Caliban said. "He disobeyed orders, but he was doing something I should have thought of. Pauncho disobeyed, too, luckily for me."

A form like a truncated monolith from Stonehenge stepped out of the fog. Trish shouted the codeword back at him. Pauncho walked up to them and said, "Where's Barney?"

Trish told him. Doc had resumed his interrupted counting. He stared at Iwaldi and Villiers, who were standing up now. One of the three men, Elmus, was holding a loaded crossbow on them.

"It's ironic that I came here to kill the Nine and now I have to let them go, even Iwaldi," he thought, managing to count at the same time.

Trish stopped talking to Pauncho. They had heard the squeal of tires as they suddenly accelerated and then the screams of men and the thump of a massive swiftly moving object striking flesh and bone. Then a grenade boomed, and immediately thereafter was another screech as of tires sliding on pavement. Then there was a crash, and a series of bangs. More screeches as a vehicle accelerated again and sped away. Another boom of a grenade. Then, silence.

Doc continued to count. Barney came like a

ghost out of the ectoplasmic pearliness. "I thought I'd lost you," he said. "I've been wandering around, afraid to go too fast or to yell out. Even though I think most of the enemy has gone. They didn't know whether or not to believe me, but they must've decided they couldn't take a chance. Besides, as one said, it'd be just the thing the crazy old dwarf would do. They think he's insane; no doubt of that."

Doc Caliban did not ask him if he had seen anything of the Grandrith party. If Barney had, he would have said something about it.

Doc kept on counting. Undoubtedly, five minutes were passed, at least seven minutes had gone by, but he preferred not to take a chance. The blasts had hurt his head, so that his sense of timing might have been disturbed. But he could put it off for only so long, and he finally decided to take his hand off the dial. He cold see Cobbs —no, Iwaldi—and Barbara Villiers watching him. When they saw his hand drop away, and nothing happened, they sighed. At least, they looked as if they had. He could not hear them. He still could hear only loud sounds.

Trish put a hand on his shoulder, causing him to jump. She put her mouth close to his ear and said, "There's something still going on out there. In the ruins, I think. I heard a woman scream."

They waited. There was no more evidence that a fight was still occuring among the stones, but they had a feeling that something important was taking place under the monoliths and the trilithons standing like the ghosts of ghosts in the mists.

A faraway hoarse bellow, the cry of something not quite human, reached him. Silence again.

"You said we could go free," Barbara Villiers said.

"Leave. Or stay here," Doc Caliban said. "Do whatever you wish. You have a twelve-hour headstart."

"Untie us," she said. Iwaldi merely glared.

"I said you could go free," Caliban replied. "I wouldn't feel easy with you in this fog and your hands free to pick up some weapons. Come on, the rest of you. We'll find the bicycles and then the steam car."

"I'll come with you as far as the car," Villiers said. "Iwaldi told me he'd kill me because I betrayed him, though I don't know how he figures that."

"You want to throw in with us?" Doc said. He was not inclined to trust her one bit, but she undoubtedly had very valuable information about Iwaldi's organization.

She hesitated, then said, "Why not? I know a winner when I see one."

"Thank you, Benedictine Arnold," Trish said.

Iwaldi strode off into the fog. The others started to walk away, staying close to each other so they would not lose sight of each other. But they had not gone more than five steps when Doc stopped. Trish had put a hand on his shoulder. She said in his ear, "There was a low cry! I think Iwaldi—"

They walked in the direction Iwaldi had taken. Suddenly, he was on the ground at their feet. His throat was still pumping blood through the broad wound.

Something came through the fog, and only Caliban would have been quick enough to see it and to react with the swiftness of a leopard. He batted at the round object as if he were playing handball; his hand struck it and sent it back into the fog with terrific force. There was a roar. The blast knocked them all down, and his ears hurt even more, and his head felt as if it had been squeezed in a vise.

They got to their feet with Doc assisting Villiers, whose hands were still taped behind her. They went ahead slowly, and then they felt the breeze, and before they had gone thirty feet, the fog began to fall apart. The sun dropped through in pale golden threads and then the threads coalesced into a blazing ball.

A wisp of fog, like a snake, moved across the face of a man on the ground, seeming to disappear into his open mouth. Doc approached him cautiously, though the fellow looked dead. His clothes were half-ripped off by the explosion, and blood ran down from his nose, ears, and mouth. A bloody plastic knife lay near his outflung hand. His helmet had been blown off, revealing an extraordinarily high forehead. He was bald, and his jaws thrust outward, giving the lower part of his face an apish appearance. His body was tall and skinny.

"I think I know him," Caliban murmured. "I've seen him at one or more of the annual ceremonies in the caves."

The name would come, though it would not matter to the man, who was dead. He had come across Iwaldi and cut his throat, though he could not have recognized him as Iwaldi. But he did not know him, and that meant that he was an enemy. Then he had heard the others and tossed the grenade and it had come back so swiftly he must have thought for a horrified moment that he had bounced it off a nearby wall.

"Hey, Doc!" Pauncho bellowed. "I think that's Grandrith inside the ruins! He's waving at us!"

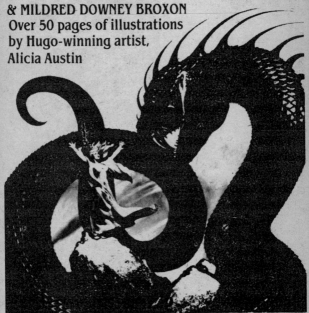

Ace Science Fiction
Purchase Order

NAME _____

STREET _____

CITY OR TOWN _____

STATE & ZIP _____

Please send me the following:

COVER PRICE

TITLE _____

AUTHOR _____   _____

TITLE _____

AUTHOR _____   _____

TITLE _____

AUTHOR _____   _____

TITLE _____

AUTHOR _____   _____

TITLE _____

AUTHOR _____   _____

POSTAGE & HANDLING   _____

TOTAL   _____

Please enclose a check or money order made out to
BOOK MAILING SERVICE for the total of the cover
prices of the books ordered plus 50¢ per book for postage
and handling. (Maximum $1.50) No postage and han-
dling required if order is accompanied by <u>DESTINIES</u>
subscription.

The Book Mailing Service policy is to fill an order for any
title currently in stock upon receipt. However, delivery is
usually from one to four weeks since postal transit time
must be taken into account. Payments for titles not in stock
will be promptly refunded.